The Two Sides of the Shield

by

Charlotte M. Yonge

Double 9
BOOKS

The Two Sides of the Shield
by Charlotte M. Yonge

ISBN: 978-93-67146-21-7

Published by

DOUBLE 9 BOOKS

2/13-B, Ansari Road
Daryaganj, New Delhi – 110002
info@double9books.com
www.double9books.com
Tel. 011-40042856

ABOUT THE AUTHOR

Charlotte M. Yonge was an English novelist and historian, born on August 11, 1823, in Otterbourne, Hampshire, England. She is best known for her prolific writing career, which spanned over 60 years and produced more than 160 works, including novels, children's books, and historical studies. Yonge's writing was strongly influenced by her deep religious beliefs and her interest in history and education. Many of her novels, such as "The Heir of Redclyffe" and "Heartsease," explore moral and religious themes and are known for their wholesome and uplifting tone. She also wrote numerous works for children, including the popular "Book of Golden Deeds," which features stories of heroism and selflessness. In addition to her writing, Yonge was a prominent figure in the Church of England and was involved in various philanthropic and educational endeavours. She founded a school for girls in her hometown and was a supporter of the National Society for Promoting Religious Education. Yonge died on May 24, 1901, in Otterbourne, Hampshire, England. Her legacy as a writer and educator continues to be celebrated, and her works remain popular with readers today.

CONTENTS

PREFACE

It is sometimes treated as an impertinence to revive the personages of one story in another, even though it is after the example of Shakespeare, who revived Falstaff, after his death, at the behest of Queen Elizabeth. This precedent is, however, a true impertinence in calling on the very great to justify the very small!

Yet many a letter in youthful handwriting has begged for further information on the fate of the beings that had become favourites of the school-room; and this has induced me to believe that the following out of my own notions as to the careers of former heroes and heroines might not be unwelcome; while I have tried to make the story stand independently for new readers, unacquainted with the tale in which Lady Merrifield and her brothers and sisters first appeared.

'Scenes and Characters' was, however, published so long ago, that the young readers of this generation certainly will only know it if it has had the good fortune to have been preserved by their mothers. It was only my second book, and in looking back at it so as to preserve consistency, I have been astonished at its crudeness.

It will explain a few illusions to state that it is the story of the motherless family of Mohuns of Beechcroft, with a kindly deaf father at the head, Mr. Mohun, whose pet name was the Baron of Beechcroft, owing to a romantic notion of his daughters made fun of by his sons. The eldest sister, a stiff, sensible, dry woman, had just married and gone to India, leaving her post to the next in age, Emily, who was much too indolent for the charge. Lilies, the third in age, with her head full of the kind of high romance and sentiment more prevalent thirty or forty years ago than now, imagined that whereas the household had formerly been ruled by duty, it now might be so by love. Of course, confusion dire was the consequence, chiefly with the younger boys, the scientific, cross-grained Maurice, and the high-spirited, turbulent Reginald, all the mischief being fomented by Jane's pertness and curiosity, and only mitigated by the honest simplicity and dutifulness of eight years old Phyllis. The remedy was found at last in the marriage of the eldest son William with Alethea Weston, already Lilias's favourite friend and model.

That in a youthful composition there should be a cavalier ancestry, a family much given to dying of consumption, and a young marquess cousin is, perhaps, inevitable. Lord Rotherwood was Mr. Mohun's ward, and having a dull home of his own, found his chief happiness as well as all the best influences of his life, in the merry, highly-principled, though easy-going life at his uncle's, whom he revered like a father, while his eager, somewhat shatter-brained nature often made him a butt to his cousins. All this may account for the tone of camaraderie with which the scattered members of the family meet again, especially around Lilias, who had, with her cleverness and enthusiasm, always been the leading member of the group.

It should, perhaps, also be mentioned that Lord Rotherwood's greatest friend was also Lilias's favourite brother, Claude, who had become a clergyman and died early. Aunt Adeline had been the spoilt child and beauty of the family, the youngest of all.

C. M. YONGE.

March 8th, 1885.

CHAPTER I
WHAT WILL BECOME OF ME?

A London dining-room was lighted with gas, which showed a table of small dimensions, with a vase of somewhat dirty and dilapidated grasses in the centre, and at one end a soup tureen, from which a gentleman had helped himself and a young girl of about thirteen, without much apparent consciousness of what he was about, being absorbed in a pile of papers, pamphlets, and letters, while she on her side kept a book pinned open by a gravy spoon. The elderly maid-servant, who set the dishes before them, handed the vegetables and changed the plates, really came as near to feeding the pair as was possible with people above three years old.

The one was a dark, thin man, with a good deal of white in his thick beard and scanty hair, the absence of which made the breadth of his forehead the more remarkable. The girl would have shown an equally remarkable brow, but that her dark hair was cut square over it, so as to take off from its height, and give a heavy over-hanging look to the upper part of the face, which below was tin and sallow, well-featured, but with a want of glow and colour. The thick masses of dark hair were plaited into a very long thick tail behind, hanging down over a black evening frock, whose white trimmings were, like everything else about the place, rather dingy. She was far less absorbed than her father, and raised a quick, wistful brown eye whenever he made the least sound, or shuffled his papers. Indeed, it seemed that she was reading in order to distract her anxiety rather than for the sake of occupation.

It was not till after the last pieces of cheese had been offered and refused, and the maid had retired, leaving some dull crackers and veteran biscuits, with two decanters and a claret-jug, that he spoke.

'Dolores!'

'Yes, father.'

But he only cleared his throat, and looked at his letter again, while she fixed her eager eyes upon him so earnestly that he let his fall again, and looked once more over his letters before he spoke again.

'Dolores,' and the tone was dry, as if all feeling were driven from it.

'Yes, father.'

'You know that I have accepted this appointment?'

'Yes, father.'

'And that I shall be absent three years at the least?'

'Yes.'

'Then comes the question, how you are to be disposed of in the meantime?'

'Could not I go with you?' she said, under her breath.

'No, my dear.' And somehow the tone had more tenderness in it, though it was so explicit. 'I shall have no fixed residence, no one with whom to leave you; and the climate is not fit for you. Your Aunt Lilias has kindly offered to take charge of you.'

'Oh, father!'

'Well?'

'If you would only let me stay here with Caroline and Fraulein. I like it so much better.'

'That cannot be, Dolly. I have this morning promised to let the house as it is to Mr. Smithson.'

'And Caroline?'

'If Caroline takes my advice, she will remain here as his housekeeper, and I think she will. Well, what is it? You do not mean that you would prefer going to your Aunts Jane and Ada?'

'Oh no, no; only if I might go to school.'

'This is nonsense, Dolores. It will be much better for you on all accounts to be with your aunt at Silverfold. I have no fear that she and her girls will not do their best to make you happy and good, and to give you what you have sadly wanted, my poor child. I have always wished you could have seen more of her.'

There could be no doubt from the tone, in the mind of any one who knew Mr. Maurine Mohun, that the decision was final; but perhaps Dolores would have asked more if the door-bell had not rung at the moment and Mr. Smithson had not been announced. Fate was closing in on her. She retired into her book, and remained as long as she possibly could, for the sake of seeing her father and hearing his voice; but after a time she was desired to call Caroline, and to go to bed herself, for it was a good deal past nine o'clock.

She had been aware, she could hardly tell how, that her father had been offered a government appointment connected with the Fiji Islands, and then that, glad to escape from the dreariness which had settled down on the house since his wife's death, about eighteen months previously, he had accepted it, and she had speculated much on her probable fate; but had never before been officially informed of his designs for himself or for her.

He was a barrister, who spent all his leisure time on scientific studies, and his wife had been equally devoted to the same pursuits. Dolores had been her constant companion; but after the mother's death, from an accident on a glacier, a strange barrier of throwing himself into the ways of a girl past the charms of infancy. It was as if they had lost their interpreter.

The German governess, chosen by Mrs. Mohun, was very German indeed, and greatly occupied in her own studies. When she found that the armes-liebes Madchen shrank from being wept over and caressed on the mournful return, she decided that the English had no feeling, and acquiesced in the routine of lessons and expeditions to classes. She was never unkind, but she did not try to be a companion; and old Caroline was excellent in the attention she paid to the comforts of her master and his daughter, but had no love of children, and would not have encouraged familiarities, even if Dolores had not been too entirely a drawing-room child to offer them.

The morning came, and everything went on as usual; Dolores poured out the coffee, Mr. Mohun read his Times, Fraulein ate as usual, but afterwards he asked for a few minutes' conversation with Fraulein. All that Dolores heard of the result of it was 'So,' and then lessons went on until twelve o'clock, when it was the custom that the girl should have an hour's recreation, which was, in any tolerable weather, spent in the gardens of the far west Crescent, where she lived. There she was nearly certain of meeting her one great friend, Maude Sefton, who was always sent out for her airing at the same time.

They spied each other issuing from their doors, met, linked their arms, and entered together. Maude was a tall, rosy girl, with a great yellow bush down her back, half a year older than Dolores, and a great deal bigger.

'My dearest Doll!'

'Oh yes, it is come.'

'Then he is really going? I heard the pater and mater talking about it yesterday, and they said it would be an excellent thing for him.'

'Oh, Maude! Then they did not say anything about what we hoped?'

'What, the mater's offering for you to come and live with us, darling? Oh no; and I's afraid it is of no use to ask her, for she said of herself, that she knew Mr. Mohun had sisters, and—'

'And what? Tell me, Maude. You must!'

'Well, then, you know you made me, and I think it is a shame. She said she was glad she wasn't one of them, for you were such a peculiar child.'

'Dear me, Maude, you needn't mind telling me that! I'm sure I don't want to be like everybody else.'

'And are you going to one of your aunts?'

'Yes, to Aunt Lilias. Oh, Maude, he would not hear a word against it, and I know it will be so horrid! Aunts are always nasty!'

'Kate is very fond of her aunt,' said Maude, who did not happen to have any personal experiences to oppose to this sweeping assertion.

'Oh, I don't mean proper aunts, but aunts that have orphans left to them.'

'But you are not an orphan, darling.'

'I dare say I shall be. 'Tis a horrible climate, and there are no end of cannibals there, so that he would not take me out for anything,—and sharks, and volcanoes, and hurricanes.'

'I don't think they eat people there now.'

'It's bad enough if they don't! And you know those aunts begin pretty well, while they are in fear of the father, but then they get worse.'

'There was Ada Morton,' said Maude, in a tone of conviction, 'and Anna Ross.'

'Oh yes, and another book, 'Rose Turquand.' It was a grown-up book, that I read once—long ago,' said Dolores, who had in her mother's time been allowed a pretty free range of 'book-box.'

"And there's 'Under the Shield,' but that was a boy."

'There are lots and lots,' said Dolores. 'They are ever so much worse than the stepmothers! Not that there is any fear of that!' she added quickly.

'But isn't this Aunt Lilias nice? It's a pretty name. Which is she? You have one aunt a Lady Something, haven't you?'

'Yes, it is this one, Lady Merrifield. Her husband is a general, Sir Jasper Merrifield, and he is gone out to command in some place in India; but she cannot stand the climate, and is living at home at a place called Silverfold, with a whole lot of children. I think two are gone out with their father, but there are a great many more.'

'Don't you know them at all?'

'No, and don't want to! I think my aunts were unkind to mother!'

'Oh!' exclaimed Maude.

'I am sure of it. They were horrid, stuck-up, fine ladies, and looked down on her, though she was ever so much nicer, and cleverer, and more intellectual than they; and she looked down on them.'

'Are you sure?' asked Maude, to whom it was as good as a story.

'Yes, indeed. She was civil, of course, because they were father's sisters, but I know she couldn't bear them. If any of them came to London, there was a calling, but all very stupid, and a dining at Lord Rotherwood's; but she never would, except once, when I can hardly remember, go to stay at their slow places in the country. I've heard father try to persuade her when they didn't think I understood. You know we always went abroad, or to the sea or something, except last year, when we were at Beechcroft. That wasn't so bad, for there were lots of books, and Uncle Reginald was there, and he is jolly.'

'Can't you get Mr. Mohun to send you there?'

'No, I don't think they would have me, for every body there is grown up, and father seems to have a wish for me to be with this Aunt Lilias, because she has a schoolroom.'

'I wonder he should wish it, if she was unkind to Mrs. Mohun.'

'Well, she was out of the way most of the time. They have lived at Malta and Gibraltar, and Belfast, and all sorts of places, so they will all have regular garrison frivolous manner, and think of nothing but officers and balls. I know she was a beauty, and wants to be one still.'

'Maude, whose father was a professor, looked quite appalled and said—

'You will be the one to infuse better things.' She felt quite proud of the word.

'Perhaps,' returned Dolores; 'they always do that in time, but not till they've been awfully bullied. All the cousins are jealous, and the aunt spites them because they are nicer and prettier than her own.'

'Yes,' said Maude, 'but then there's always some tremendously nice boy-cousin, or uncle, or something, that makes up for it all. Will Sir Jasper Merrifield's eldest son be a Sir?'

'Oh no; he's not a baronet, but a G.C.B., Knight Grand Cross of the Bath, that is. Besides, I don't care for love, and titles, and all that nonsense, though father is first cousin to Lord Rotherwood.'

'And you never saw any of them?'

'Yes, Aunt Lilias was at the Charing Cross Hotel with Uncle Jasper and the two eldest daughters, Alethea and Phyllis, and some more of them, just before they sailed; and father took me there on Sunday to luncheon; but there were so many people, and such a talk, and such a bustle, that I hardly knew which was which. Aunt Jane and Aunt Ada were a talking that it made my head turn round; but I saw how affected Aunt Lilias is, and I knew that whenever they looked at me they said 'poor child,' and I always hate any one who does that! All I was afraid of then was that father would let Aunt Jane and Aunt Ada come and live with us; but this is ever so much worse.'

'You have such a lot of aunts and uncles!' said Maude, 'and I have not got anything but one old uncle.'

'Uncles are all very well,' said Dolores, said Maude. 'There are the two Miss Mohuns—'

'Oh, that's beginning at the wrong end. Aunt Ada is the youngest of them all, and she thinks she is a young lady still, and wears little curls on her forehead, and a tennis pinafore, and makes her waist just like a wasp. She and Aunt Jane live together at Rockquay, because she has bad health—at least she has whenever she likes; and Aunt Jane does all sorts of charities and worries, and sets everybody to rights,' said Dolly, in a very grown-up voice, speaking partly from her own observation, and partly repeating what she had caught from her elders.

'Oh yes, I know her,' said Maude. 'She asked me questions about all I did, and she did bother mamma so about a maid she recommended that we are never going to take another from her.'

'Aunt Phyllis comes between them, I believe; but she has married a sailor captain and gone to settle in New Zealand, and I have not seen her since I was a very little girl. Then there's Aunt Emily, who is a very great swell indeed. Her husband was a canon, Lord Henry Grey; but he is dead, and she lives at Brighton, a regular fat, comfortable down-pillow of a woman, who isn't bad to lunch with, only she sends one out to the Parade with her maid, as if one was a baby. Mother used to laugh at her. And I think there was an older one who went to India and died long ago.'

'I have seen your two uncles. There's Major Mohun. Oh! he is fun!'

'Yes, dear old Uncle Regie! I wish he was not in Ireland. He will be so sorry to miss seeing father off, but he can't get leave. And there was a clergyman who is dead, and father grieved for very much. I think he did something to make them all nicer to mother, for it was just after that we went to stay at Beechcroft with Uncle William. You know him, and how mother used to call him the very model of a country squire; and I like his wife, Aunt Alethea. Only it is very pokey and slow down there, and they are always after flannel petticoats and soup kitchens, and all the old fads that are exploded. I should get awfully tired of it before a year was out, only I should not be teased with strange children, and there would be no one to be jealous of me.'

'Can't you get your father to change and send you there?'

'Not a chance. You see Aunt Lilias had offered, and they haven't, and I must go on with my education. I hope, though I shall have no advantages, I shall still be able to go up for the Cambridge examination, if Aunt Lilias has not prejudices, as I dare say she has, since of course none of her own will be able to try.'

'You'll come up to us for the examination, Dolly dear, and we shall do it together, and that will be nice!'

'If they will let me; but I don't expect to be allowed to do anything that I wish. Only perhaps father may be come home by that time.'

'Is it three years?'

'Yes. It is a terrible time, isn't it? However, when I'm seventeen perhaps he will talk to me, and I can really keep house.'

'And then you'll come back here?'

'Do you know, Maudie—listen—I've another uncle, belonging to mother.'

'Oh, Dolly! I thought she had no one!'

'He told me he was my Uncle Alfred once when he met me in the park with Fraulein, and gave me a note for mother. He is called Mr. Flinders.'

'But I thought your mother was daughter to Professor Hay?'

'But this is a half-brother; my grandmother was married before. Uncle Alfrey has an immense light beard, and I think he is very poor. He came once or twice to see mother, and they always sent me out of the room; but I am sure she gave him money—not father's housekeeping money, but what she got for herself by writing. Once I heard father go out of the house, saying, 'Well, it's your own to do as you please with.' And then mother went to her room, and I know she cried. It was the only time that ever mother cried!' And as Maude listened, much impressed—'Once when she had got eleven pounds, and we were going to have bought father such a binocular for a secret as a birthday present, Mr. Flinders came, and she gave him ten of it, and we could only buy just a few slides for father. And she told me she was grieved, but she could not help it, and it would be time for me to understand when I was older.'

'I don't think this Uncle Alfrey can be nice,' said Maude.

''Tis quite disgusting if he kisses me,' said Dolly; 'but you see he is poor, and all the Mohuns are stuck up, except father, and they wanted mother to despise him, and not help him. And you see, she stuck to him. I don't like him much; but you see nobody ever was like her! Oh, Maude, if she wasn't dead!'

And poor Dolores cried as she had not done even at the time of the accident, or in the terrible week that followed, or at the desolate home coming.

CHAPTER II
THE MERRIFIELDS

The cool twilight of a long sunny summer's day was freshening the pleasant garden of a country house, and three people were walking slowly along a garden path enjoying the contrast with the heat, glare, and noise of the day. The central one was a tall, slender lady, with a light shawl hung round her shoulders. On one side was a youth who had begun to overtop her, on the other a girl of shorter and sturdier mould, who only reached up to her shoulder.

'So she is coming!' the girl said.

'Yes, Uncle Maurice has answered my letter very kindly.'

'I should think he would be very much obliged,' observed the boy.

'Please, mamma, do tell us all about it,' said the girl. 'You know I stopped directly when you made me a sign not to go on asking questions before the little ones. And you said you should have to make us your friends while papa and the grown-ups are away.'

'Well, Gillian, I know you can be discreet when you are warned, and perhaps it is best that you should know how things stand. Do you remember anything about it, Hal?'

'Only a general perception that there were tempests in the higher regions, but I think that was more from hearing Alley and Phyl talk than from my native sagacity.'

'So I should suppose, since you were only six years old, at the utmost.'

'But Uncle Maurice always was under a cloud, wasn't he, especially at Beechcroft, where I never saw him or his wife in the holidays except once, when I believe she was not at all liked, and was thought to be very proud, and stuck-up, and pretentious.'

'But was she just nobody? not a lady?' cried Gillian. 'Aunt Emily always called her, '"Poor thing."'

'Perhaps she did the same by Aunt Emily,' returned Hal.

'And I am sure I have heard Aunt Ada say that she wasn't a lady; and Aunt Jane that she had all sorts of discreditable connections.'

'Come now, Gill, if you chatter so, how is mamma to get a word in between?'

'I'm afraid we have all been hard on her, poor thing!'

'There now, mamma has done it, just like Aunt Emily!'

'Anybody would be poor who got killed in a glacier!'

'No, but one doesn't say poor when people are—nice.'

'When I said poor,' now put in Lady Merrifield, 'it was not so much that I was thinking of her death as of her having come into a family where nobody welcomed her, and I really do not suppose it was her fault.'

'Moreover, she seemed to do very well without a welcome,' added Hal.

'Who is interrupting now?' cried Gillian, 'but was she a lady?'

'I never saw her, you know,' said the mother; 'but from all I ever heard of her, I should think she was, and cleverer and more highly educated than any of us.'

'Yes,' said Hal, 'that was the kind of pretension that exasperated them all at Beechcroft, especially Uncle William.'

'I wonder if Dolores will have it!' said Gillian. 'I suppose she will know much more than we do.'

'Probably, being the only child of such parents, and with every advantage London can give. Maurice was always much the cleverest of us all, and with a very strong mechanical and scientific turn, so that I now think it might have been better to have let him follow his bent. But when we were young there was a good deal of mistrust of anything outside the beaten tracks of gentlemanlike professions, and my dear old father did not like what he heard of the course of study for those lines. Things were not as they are now. So Maurice went to Cambridge, and was fifth wrangler of his year, and then had to go to the bar. It somehow always gave him a thwarted, injured feeling of working against the grain, and he cultivated all these scientific pursuits to the utmost, getting more and more into opinions and society that distressed grandpapa and Uncle William. So he fell in with Mr. Hay, a professor at a German university. I can hear William's tone of utter contempt and disgust. I believe this poor man was exceedingly learned, and had made some remarkable discoveries, but he was very poor, and lived in lodgings at Bonn with his daughter in the small way people are content to do in Germany. As to his opinions, we all took it for granted that he was a freethinker; but I can't tell how that might be. Maurice lodged in the same house one year when he went to learn German and attend lectures, and he went back again every long vacation. At last came your dear grandfather's death. Maurice hurried away from Beechcroft immediately after the funeral, and the next thing that was heard of him was that he had married Miss Hay. It was no wonder that your Uncle William was bitterly hurt and offended at the apparent disrespect to our father, and would make no move towards Maurice.'

'It was when we were at the Cape, wasn't it?' asked Hal.

'Yes, the year Gillian was born. Well, your dear Uncle Claude went to see Maurice in London, and found there was much excuse. Maurice had learnt that the old professor was dying, and his daughter had nothing, and would have had to be a governess, so that Maurice had married her in haste in order to be able to help them.'

'Then it really was very kind and noble in him!' exclaimed Gillian.

'And I believe every one would have felt it so; but for his unfortunately reserved way of concealing the extent of the acquaintance, and showing that he would not be interfered with. Claude did his best to close the breach, but there had been something to forgive on both sides, and perhaps SHE was prouder than the Mohuns themselves. Oh! my dears, I hope you will never have a family quarrel among you! It is so sad to look back upon a change after the happy years when we were all together, and were laughing and making fun of one another!'

'But you were quite out of it, mamma.'

'So I was in a way, but I knew nothing of the justification till too late for any advances from us to take much effect. I am four years older than Maurice, we had never been a pair, and had never corresponded. And when I wrote to him and to his wife, I only received stiff, formal answers. They were abroad when we were in London on coming home, and they would not come to see us at Belfast, so that I could never make acquaintance with her; but I believe she was an excellent wife, suiting him admirably in every way, and I expect to find this little daughter of theirs very well brought up, and much forwarder than honest old Mysie.'

'Mysie is in perfect raptures at the notion of having a cousin here exactly of her own age,' said Gillian. 'What she would wish is that the two should be so much alike as to be taken for twins. I have been trying to remember Dolores on that dreadful Sunday at the hotel, when Uncle Maurice came to see us, just when papa was setting off for Bombay, but it all seems confusion. I can think of nothing but a little black, shy figure. I remember Phyllis telling me that she thought I ought to do something to entertain her, but I could not think of a word to say to her.'

'For which perhaps she was thankful,' said her brother.

'I am not sure. You are all too apt, when you are shy, to console yourself with fancying that you are doing as you would be done by. It might have worried her then perhaps, but it would have made it easier for her to begin among us now! I am very glad her father consents to my having her! I do hope we may make her happy.'

'Happy!' said Gillian. 'Anybody must be happy with such a number to play with, and with you to mother her, mamma.'

'I am afraid she will not feel me much like her own mother, poor child! But it will not be for want of the will. When I look back now I feel sorry for myself for the early loss of my mother, for though we were all merry enough as children and young people, there always seems to have been a lack of something fostering and repressing. There was a kind of desolateness in our life, though we did not understand it at the time. I am thankful you have not known it, my dears.' There was a strange rush of tears nearly choking her voice, and she shook them away with a sort of laugh. 'That I should cry for that at this time of day!'

Gillian raised her face for a kiss, and even Harry did the same. Their hearts were very full, as the perception swept over them in one flash what their lives would have been without mamma. It seemed like the solid earth giving way under their feet!

'I am very sorry for poor Dolores,' said Gillian presently. 'It seems as if we could never be kind enough to her.'

'Yes. Indeed I hope we may do something towards supplying her with a real home, wandering sprites as we have been,' said Lady Merrifield.

'What a name it is! Dolores! It is as bad as Peter Grievous! How did she get it?' grumbled Harry.

'That I cannot tell, but I think we must call her Dora or Dolly, as I fancy your Aunt Jane told me she was called at home. I hope Wilfred will not get hold of it and tease her about it. You must defend her from that.'

'If we can,' said Gillian; 'but Wilfred is rather an imp.'

'Yes,' said Harry. 'I found Primrose reduced to the verge of distraction yesterday because 'Willie would call her Leg of Mutton.''

'I hope you boxed his ears!' cried Gillian.

'I did give it to him well,' said Hal, laughing.

'Thank you,' said his mother. 'A big brother is more effective in such cases than any one else can be. Wilfred is the only one of you all who ever seemed to take pleasure in causing pain—and I hardly know how to meet the propensity.'

'He is the only one who is not quite certain to be nice with Dolores,' said Gillian.

'And I really don't quite see how to manage,' said the mother. 'If we show him our anxiety to shield her, it is very likely to direct his attention that way.'

'She must take her chance,' said Hal, 'and if she is any way rational, she can soon put a stop to it.'

'But, oh dear! I wish he could go to school,' said Gillian.

'So do I, my dear,' returned her mother; 'but you know the doctors say we must not risk it for another year, and I can only hope that as he grows stronger, he may become more manly. Meantime we must be patient with him, and Hal can help more than any one else. There—what's that striking?'

'Three quarters.'

'Then we must make haste in, or we shall not have finished supper before ten.'

Lilias Mohun had married a soldier, and after many wanderings through military stations, the health and education of a large proportion of her family had necessitated her remaining at home with them, while her husband held a command in India, taking out with him the two grown-up daughters and the second son, who was on his staff. She was established in a large house not far from a country town, for the convenience of daily governess, tutor, and masters. She herself had grown up on the old system which made education depend more on the family than on the governess, and she preferred honestly the company and training of her children to going into society in her husband's absence. Therefore she arranged her habits with a view to being constantly with them, and though exchanging calls, and occasionally accepting invitations in the neighbourhood, it was an understood thing that she went out very little. The chief exceptions were when her eldest son, Harry, was at home from Oxford. He was devotedly fond of her, and all the more pleased and proud to take her about with him because it had not always been possible that his holidays in his school life should be spent at home, and thus the privilege was doubly prized.

The two sisters above and one brother below him were in India with their father, and Gillian was not yet out of the schoolroom, though this did not cut her off from being her mother's prime companion. Then followed a schoolboy at Wellington, named Jasper, two more girls, a brace of boys, and the five-year-old baby of the establishment—sufficient reasons to detain Lady Merrifield in England after more than twenty years of travels as a soldier's wife, so that scarcely three of her children had the same birthplace. She had been able to see very little of her English relations, being much tied by the number of her children while all were very young, and the expense of journeys; but she was now within easy reach of her two unmarried sisters, and after the Cape, Gibraltar, Malta, and Dublin, the homes of her eldest sister, and of her eldest brother did not seem very far off.

Indeed Beechcroft, the home of her childhood, had always been the headquarters of herself and her children on their rare visits to England. Her elder boys had been sure of a welcome there in the holidays, and loved it scarcely less than she did herself; and when looking for her present abode, the whole family had stayed there for three months. Her brother Maurice, however, she had scarcely seen, and she had been much pained at being included in his persistent avoidance of the whole family, who felt that he resented their displeasure at his marriage even more since his wife's death than he had done during her lifetime, as if he felt doubly bound, for her sake, not to forgive and forget. At least so said some of the family, while others hoped that his distaste to all intercourse with them only arose from the apathy succeeding a great blow.

CHAPTER III
GOOD-BYE

A passage was offered to Mr. Mohun in a Queen's ship, and this hurried the preparations so much that to Dolores it appeared that there was nothing but bustle and confusion, from the day of her conversation with Maude, until she found herself in the railway carriage returning from Plymouth with her eldest uncle. Her father had intended to take her himself to Silverfold; but detentions at the office in London, and then a telegram from Plymouth, had disconcerted his plans, and when he found that his eldest brother would come and meet him at the last, he was glad to yield to his little daughter's earnest desire to be with him as long as possible.

Shy and reserved as both were, and almost incapable of finding expression for their feelings, they still clung closely together, though the only tears the girl was seen to shed came in church on the last Sunday evening, blinding and choking, and she could barely restrain her sobs. Her father would have taken her out, but she resisted, and leant against him, while he put his arm round her. After this, whenever it was possible, she crept up to him, and he held her close.

There had been no further discussion on her home. Lady Merrifield had written kindly to her, as well as to her father, but that was small consolation to one so well instructed by story books in the hypocrisy of aunts until fathers were at a distance. And her father was so manifestly gratified by the letter, that it would be of no use to say a word to him now. Her fate was determined, and, as she heroically told Maude in their last interview, she was determined to make the best of it. She would endure the unjust aunt, and jealous, silly cousins, and be so clever, and wise, and superior, that she would force them to admire and respect her, and by-and-by follow her example, and be good and sensible, so that when father came home, he would find them acknowledging that they owed everything to her; she had saved two or three of their lives, nursed half of them when the other half were helpless, fainting, and hysterical, and, in short, been the Providence of the household. Then father would look at her, and say, 'My Mary again!' and he would take her home, and talk to her with the free confidence he had shown her mother, and would be comforted.

This was the hope that had carried her through the last parting, when she went on board with her uncle and saw her father's cabin, and looked with a dull kind of entertainment at all the curious arrangements of the big ship. It seemed more like sight-seeing than good-bye, when at last they were sent on shore, and hurried up to the station just in time for the train.

Uncle William was a very unapproachable person. He did not profess to understand little girls. He looked at Dolores rather anxiously, afraid, perhaps, that she was crying, and put her into the carriage, then rushed out and brought back a handful of newspapers, giving her the Graphic, and hiding himself in the Times.

She felt too dull and stunned to read, or to look at the pictures, though she held the paper in her hands, and she gazed out dreamily at the Ton's and rocks and woody ravines of Dartmoor as they flew past her, the leaves and ferns all golden brown with autumn colouring. She had had little sleep that night; her little legs had all the morning been keeping up with the two men's hasty steps, and though an excellent meal had been set before her in the ship, she had not been able to swallow much, and she was a good deal worn out. So when at last they reached Exeter, and finding there would be two hours to wait, her uncle asked whether she would come down into the town with him and see the Cathedral, she much preferred to stay where she was. He put her under the care of the woman in the waiting-room, who gave her some tea, took off her hat, and made her lie down on a couch, where she slept quite sound for more than an hour, until she was roused by some ladies coming in with a crying baby.

It was, she thought, nearly time to go on, for the gas was being lighted. She put on her hat, and went out to look for her uncle on the platform, so as to get into a better light to see the face of her mother's little Swiss watch, which her father had just made over to her. She had just made out that there was not more than a quarter of an hour to spare, when she heard an exclamation.

'By Jove! if that ain't Mary's little girl!' and, looking up she saw Mr. Flinders' huge, bushy, light-coloured beard. 'Is your father here?' he asked.

'No; he sailed this afternoon.'

'Always my luck! Ticket wasted! Sailed—really?'

'Oh yes. We did not come back till the ship was out of harbour.'

He muttered some exclamation, and asked—

'Whom are you with?'

'Uncle William. Mr. Mohun—my eldest uncle. He will be back directly.'

Mr. Flinders whistled a note of discontent.

'Going to rusticate with him, poor little mite?' he asked.

'No. I'm to live with my Aunt Lilias—Lady Merrifield.'

'Where?'

'At Silverfold Grange, near Silverfold.'

'Well, you'll get among the swells. They'll make you cut all your poor mother's connections. So there's an end of it. She was a good creature—she was!'

'I'll never forget any one that belongs to her,' said Dolores. 'Oh, there's Uncle William!' as on the top of the stairs she spied the welcome sight of his grey locks and burly figure. Before he had descended, her other uncle had vanished, and she fancied she had heard something about, 'Mum about our meeting. Ta ta!'

Uncle William's eyes being less sharp than hers, he was on his way to the waiting-room before she joined him, and as he had not seen her encounter, she would not tell him. They were settled in the carriage again, and she was tolerably refreshed. Mr. Mohun fell asleep, and she, after reading by the lamp-light as long as she could find anything to read, gazed at the odd reflections in the windows till she, too, nodded and dozed, half waking at every station.

At last, she was aware of a stop in earnest, voices, and being called. There was her uncle saying, 'Well, Hal, here we are!' and she was lifted out and set on the platform, with gas all round. Her uncle was saying, 'We didn't get away in time for the express,' and a young man was answering, 'We'd better put Dolly into the waggonette at once. Then I'll see to the luggage.'

Very like a parcel, so stiff were her legs, she was bundled into the dark cavern of a closed waggonette, and, after a little lumbering, her uncle and the young man got in after her, saying something about eleven o'clock.

She was more awake now, and knew that they were driving through lighted streets, and then, after an interval, turned into darkness, upon gravel, and stopped at last before a door full of light, with figures standing up dark in it. She heard a 'Well, William!' 'Well Lily, here we are at last!' Then there were arms embracing her, and a kiss on each cheek, as a soft voice said, 'My poor little girl! They wanted to sit up for you, but it was too late, and I dare say you had rather be quiet.'

She was led into a lamp-lit room, which dazzled her. It was spread with food, but she was too much tired to eat, and her aunt saw how it was, and telling Harry to take care of his uncle, she took the hand—though it did not close on hers — and, climbing up what seemed to Dolores an endless number of stairs, she said —

'You are up high, my dear; but I thought you would like a room to yourself.'

'Poked away in an attic,' was Dolores's dreamy thought; while her aunt added, to a tall, thin woman, who came out with a lamp in her hand —

'She is so tired that she had better go to bed directly, Mrs. Halfpenny. You will make her comfortable, and don't let her be disturbed in the morning till she has had her sleep out.'

Dolly found herself undressed, without many words, till it came to — 'Your prayers, Miss Dora. I am sure you've need not to miss them.'

She did not like to be told, besides, poor child, prayers were not much more than a form to her. She did not contest the point, but knelt down and muttered something, then laid her weary head on the pillow, was tucked up by Mrs. Halfpenny, and left in the dark. It was a dreary half sleep into which she fell. The noise of the train seemed to be still in her ears, and at the same time she was always being driven up — up — up endless stairs, by tall, cruel aunts; or they were shutting her up to do all their children's work, and keeping away father's letters from her. Then she awoke and told herself it was a dream, but she missed the noises of the street, and the patch of light on the wall from the gas lamps, and recollected that father was gone, and she was really in the power of one of these cruel aunts; and she felt like screaming, only then she might have been heard; and a great horrid clock went on making a noise like a church bell, and striking so many odd quarters that there was no guessing when morning was coming. And after all, why should she wish it to come? Oh, if she could but sleep the three years while father was away!

At last, however, she fell into a really calm sleep, and when she awoke, the room was full of light, but her watch had stopped; she had been too much tired to remember to wind it; and she lay a little while hearing sounds that made it clear that the world was astir, and she could see that preparations had been made for her getting up.

'They shan't begin by scolding me for being late,' she thought, and she began her toilette.

Just as she came to her hair, the old nurse knocked and asked whether she wanted help.

'Thank you, I've been used to dress myself,' said Dolores, rather proudly.

'I'll help you now, missy, for prayers are over, and they are all gone to breakfast, only my lady said you were not to be disturbed, and Miss Mysie will be up presently again to bring you down.'

She spoke low, and in an accent that Dolores afterwards learnt was Scotch; and she was a tall, thin, bony woman, with sandy hair, who looked as if she had never been young. She brushed and plaited the dark hair in a manner that seemed to the owner more wearisome and less tender than Caroline's fashion; and did not talk more than to inquire into the fashion of wearing it, and to say that Miss Mohun's boxes had been sent from London, demanding the keys that they might be unpacked.

'I can do that myself,' said Dolores, who did not like any stranger to meddle with her things.

'Ye could tak them oot, nae doubt, but I must sort them. It's my lady's orders,' said Mrs. Halfpenny, with all the determination of the sergeant, her husband, and Dolores, with a sense of despair, and a sort of expectation that she should be deprived of all her treasures on one plea or another, gave up the keys.

Mrs. Halfpenny then observed that the frock which had been worn for the last two days on the railway, and evening and morning, needed a better brushing and setting to rights than she had had time to give it. She had better take out another. Which box were her frocks in?

Dolores expected her heartless relations to insist on her leaving off her mourning, and she knew she ought to struggle and shed tears over it; but, to tell the truth, she was a good deal tired of her hot and fusty black; and when she had followed Mrs. Halfpenny into a passage where the boxes stood uncorded; and the first dress that came to light was a pretty fresh-looking holland that had been sent home just before the accident, she exclaimed —

'Oh, let me put that on.'

'Bless me, miss, it has blue braid, and you in mourning for your poor mamma!'

Dolores stood abashed, but a grey alpaca, which she had always much disliked, came out next, and Mrs. Halfpenny decided that with her black ribbons that would do, though it turned out to be rather shockingly short, and to show a great display of black legs; but as the box containing the clothes in present wear had not come to hand, this must stand for the present — and besides, a voice was heard, saying, 'Is Dora ready?' and a young person darted up, put her arms round her neck, and kissed her before she knew what she was about. 'Mamma said I should come because I am just your age, thirteen and a half,' she said. 'I'm Mysie, though my proper name is Maria Millicent.'

Dolores looked her over. She was a good deal taller than herself, and had rich-looking shining brown hair, dark brown eyes full of merriment, and a bright rosy colour, and she danced on her active feet as if she were full of perpetual life. 'All happy and not caring,' thought Dolores.

'Now don't fash Miss Mohun with your tricks. She has stood like a lamb,' said Mrs. Halfpenny reprovingly. 'There, we'll not keep her to find an apron.'

'I don't wear pinafores,' said Mysie, 'but I don't mind pretty aprons like this. 'Why, my sisters had them for tennis, before they went out to India. Come along, Dora,' grasping her hand.

'My name isn't Dora,' said the new-comer, as they went down the passage.

'No,' said Mysie, in a low voice; 'but mamma told Gill—that's Gillian, and me, that we had better not tell anybody, because if the boys heard they might tease you so about it; for Wilfred is a tease, and there's no stopping him when mamma isn't there. So she said she would call you Dora, or Dolly, whichever you liked, and you are not a bit like a Dolly.'

'They always called me Dolly,' said Dolores; 'and if I am not to have my name, I like that best; but I had rather have my proper name.'

'Oh, very well,' said Mysie; 'it is more out of the way, only it is very long.'

By this time they had descended a long narrow flight of uncarpeted stairs, 'the back ones,' as Mysie explained, and had reached a slippery oak hall with high-backed chairs, and all the odds and ends of a family-garden hats, waterproofs, galoshes, bats, rackets, umbrellas, etc., ranged round, and a great white cockatoo upon a stand, who observed—'Mysie, Cockie wants his breakfast,' as they went by towards the door, whence proceeded a hubbub of voices and a clatter of knives and jingle of teaspoons and cups, a room that as Mysie threw open the door seemed a blaze of sunshine, pouring in at the large window, and reflected in the glass and silver. Yes, and in the bright eyes and glossy hair of the party who sat round the breakfast-table, further brightened by the fire, pleasant in the early autumn.

Eyes, as it seemed to Dolores, eyes without number were levelled on her, as Mysie led her in, saying—

'Here's a place by mamma; she kept it for you, between her and Uncle William.'

'No, don't all jump up at once and rush at her,' said Lady Merrifield. 'Give her a little time. Here, my dear;' and she held out her hand and drew in the stranger to her, kissing her kindly, and placing her in a chair close to herself, as she presided over the teacups—not at the end, but at the middle of the table—while all that could be desired to eat and drink found its way at once to Dolores, who had arrived at being hungry now, and was glad to have the employment for hands and eyes, instead of feeling herself gazed at. She was not so much occupied, however, as not to perceive that Uncle William's voice had a free, merry ring in it, such as she had never heard in his visits to her father, and that there was a great deal of fun and laughter going on over the thin sheets of an Indian letter, which Aunt Lily was reading aloud.

No one seemed to be attending to anything else, when Dolores ventured to cast a glance around and endeavour to count heads as she sat between her uncle and aunt. Two boys and a girl were opposite. Harry, who had come to meet them last night, was at one end of the table, a tall girl, but still a schoolroom girl, was at the other, and Mysie had been lost sights of on her own side of the table; also there was a very tiny girl on a high chair on the other side of her mamma. 'Seven,' thought Dolores with sinking heart. 'Eight oppressors!'

They were mostly brown-eyed, well-grown creatures. One boy, at the further corner, had a cast in his eye, and was thin and wizen-looking, and when he saw her eyes on him, he made up an ugly face, which he got rid of like a flash of lightning before any one else could see it, but her heart sank all the more for it. He must be Wilfred, the teaser.

Aunt Lilias was a tall, slender woman, dressed in some kind of soft grey, with a little carnation colour at her throat, and a pretty lace cap on her still rich, abundant, dark brown hair, where diligent search could only detect a very few white threads. Her complexion was always of a soft, paly, brunette tint, and though her cheeks showed signs that she was not young, her dark, soft, long-lashed eyes and sweet-looking lips made her face full of life and freshness; and the figure and long slender hands had the kind of grace that some people call willowy, but which is perhaps more like the general air of a young birch tree, or, as Hal had once said, 'Early pointed architecture reminded him of his mother.'

The little one was getting restless, and two of the boys began filliping crumbs at one another.

'Wilfred! Fergus!' said the mother quite low and gently; but they stopped directly. 'We will say grace,' she said, lifting the little one down. 'Now, Primrose.'

Every one stood up, to Dolores' surprise, a pair of little fat hands were put together, a little clear voice said a few words of thanksgiving perfectly pronounced.

'You may go, if you like,' she said. 'Hal, take care of Prim.'

Up jumped the two boys and a sprite of a girl, who took the hand of little Primrose, a beautiful little maiden with rich chestnut wavy curls. They all paused at the door, the boys making a salute, the girls a little curtsey. Primrose's was as pretty a little 'bob' as ever was seen.

'I am glad you keep that custom up,' said Mr. Mohun.

'Jasper had been brought up to it, and wished it to be the habit among us; and I find it a great protection against bouncing and rudeness.'

But Dolly's blood boiled at such stupid, antiquated, military nonsense. She would never give in to it, if they made her live on bread and water!

The uncle and aunt, who perhaps had lengthened out their breakfast from politeness to her, had finished when she had, and the pony-chaise came to the door, in which Hal was to drive Uncle William to the station. Everybody flocked to the door to bid him good-bye, and then Aunt Lilias stooped down to ask Dolores if she were quite rested and felt quite well, Mysie standing anxiously by as if she felt her a great charge.

'Quite well, quite rested, thank you,' the girl answered in her stiff, shy way.

'There is half an hour to spare before Miss Vincent comes. The children generally spend it in feeding the creatures. I am not going to give a holiday, because I think people get more pleasantly acquainted over something, than over nothing, to do, but you need not begin lessons to-day if you had rather settle your thoughts and write your letters.'

'I had rather begin at once,' said Dolores, who thought she would now establish her pre-eminence at the cost of any amount of jealousy.

'Very well, then, when you hear the gong—'

'Mamma,' said Mysie solemnly, after long waiting, 'she says she had rather not be called out of her name.'

'I thought you had been called Dolly, my dear.'

'Yes, at home,' with a strong emphasis.

'Well, my dear, I dare say it may be better to keep to your proper name at once. We won't take liberties with it, till you feel as if you could call this home,' said Lady Merrifield, looking as if she would have kissed her niece on the slightest encouragement, but no one ever looked less kissable than Dolores Mohun at that moment. Was it not cruel and hypocritical to talk of this tiresome multitude as ever making home?

CHAPTER IV
TURNED IN AMONG THEM

'Do you like pets?' asked Mysie eagerly, as her mother left the two girls together.

'I never had any,' said Dolores.

'Oh how dreadful! Why, old Cockie, and Aga and Begum, the two oldest pussies, have been everywhere with us. And, besides, there's Basto, the big Pyrenean dog, and,—oh, here comes little Quiz, mamma's little Maltese— Quiz, Quiz.'

Dolores started, she did not like either dogs or cats; and the little spun-glass looking dog smelt about her.

'I must go and feed my guinea-pig,' said Mysie; 'won't you come? Here are some over shoes and Poncho.'

Dolores was afraid Poncho was another beast, but it turned out to be a sort of cape, and she discovered that all the cloaks and most of the sticks had names of their own. She was afraid to be left standing on the steps alone lest any amount of animals or boys should fall on her there, so she consented to accompany Mysie, who shuffled along in a pair of overshoes vastly too big for her, since she had put her cousin into the well-fitting ones. She chattered all the way.

'We do like this place so. It is the nicest we have ever been in. All that is wanting is that papa will buy it, and then we shall never go away again.'

It was a pleasant place, though not grand; a homely-looking, roomy, red-brick house, covered with creepers—the Virginian one with its leaves just beginning to be painted. There was a bright sunny garden full of flowers in front, and then a paddock, with cows belonging to a farmer, Mysie said. It was her ambition to have them of their own 'when papa came home,' when all good things were to happen. Behind there were large stable-yards and offices, too large for Lady Merrifield's one horse and one pony, and thus available for the children's menagerie of rabbits, guinea-pigs, magpie, and the like. On the way Mysie was only too happy to explain the family as she called it, when she had recovered from her astonishment that Dolores, always living in England, could not 'count up her cousins.' 'Why they always had been shown their photographs on a Sunday evening after the Bible pictures, and even little Primrose knew all the likeness, even of those she had never seen.'

The catalogue of names and ages followed.

Dolores heard it with a feeling of bewilderment, and a sense that one Maude was worth all the eight put together with whom she was called on to be familiar. She found herself standing in a court, rather grass-grown, where Gillian, with little Primrose by her side, was flinging peas to a number of pigeons, grey, white, and brown, who fluttered round her. Valetta and Fergus were on the granary steps, throwing meal and sop mixed together to a host of cackling, struggling fowls, who tried to leap over each other's backs. Wilfred seemed busy at some hutches where some rabbits twitched their noses at cabbage leaves. Mysie proceeded to minister to some black and rust-coloured guinea-pigs, which Dolores thought very ugly, uninteresting, and odorous.

Then there were dogs jumping about everywhere, and cats and kittens parading before people's feet, so that Dolores felt as if she had been turned into a den of wild beasts, and resolved against ever again venturing into the court at 'feeding-time.' A big bell gathered all the children up together into a race to the house. There was another scurry to change shoes and wash hands, and then Mysie conducted her cousin into a large, cheerful, wainscoted room on the ground floor, with deep windows, and numerous little, solid-looking deal tables. There were Lady Merrifield and a young lady in spectacles, to whom Dolores was presented as 'your new pupil,' and every one sat down at one of the little tables, on which there were Bibles and Prayer-books.

Lady Merrifield took the two youngest on each side of her. Dolores found a table ready for her with the books. A passage in the New Testament was given out and read verse by verse, to the end of the subject, which was the Parable of the Tares, and then Lady Merrifield gave a short lesson on it, asking questions, and causing references to be found, according to a book of notes, she had ready at hand.

'Just like a charity school,' thought Dolores, when she was able to glance at the time-table, and saw that two days in the week there was Old Testament, two days New, one day Catechism, one day Prayer-book. Only half an hour was thus appropriated, but to her mind it was an old-fashioned waste of time, and very tiresome.

Then came a ring at the door-bell. 'Mr. Poulter,' she heard, and to her amazement, she found that Gillian and Mysie, as well as their brothers, had Latin lessons in the dining-room with the curate. The two girls and Fergus only went to him every other day, Wilfred every day, as Gillian was learning Greek and mathematics. What was Dolores to do?

'Have you done any Latin, my dear?' asked her aunt.

'Not yet. Father wished to be quite convinced that the professor was a good scholar,' said Dolores.

'Very well. We will wait a little,' said Aunt Lilias, and Dolores indignantly thought that she was amused.

Mysie was sent off to her music in the drawing-room, whither her mother followed with Primrose's little lessons, leaving the schoolroom piano to Valetta, and Fergus to write copies and to do sums, while Miss Vincent examined the new-comer, which she did by giving her some questions to answer in writing, and some French and German to translate and parse also in writing.

The music was inconvenient to a girl who had always prepared her work alone. She could do the language work easily, but the questions teased her. They seemed to her of no use, and quite out of her beat. No dates, none of the subject she had specially got up. Why, if Miss Vincent did not know that people were not to be expected to answer stupid questions about history quite out of their own line, that was her fault.

She did what she knew, and then sat biting the top of her pen till her aunt came back, and there was a change in occupations all round, resulting in her having to read French aloud, which she knew she did well; but it was provoking to find that Gillian read quite as well, and knew a word at which she had made a shot, and a wrong one.

She heard the observation pass between her aunt and the governess, 'Languages fair, but she seems to have very little general information.'

General information, indeed! Just as if she who had lived in London, gone to lectures, and travelled on the Continent, must not know more than these children cast up and down in a soldier's life; and as if her Fraulein, with all her diplomas, must not be far superior to a mere little daily governess, and a mother! It was all for the sake of depreciating her.

At twelve o'clock, to her further indignation, she found there was to be an hour of reading aloud and of needlework-actual plain needlework. The three girls were making under-garments for themselves; and on Dolores proving to have no work of any sort, her aunt sent Gillian to the drawer, and produced a child's pinafore, which she was desired to hem. Each, however, had a quarter of an hour's reading aloud of history to do in turn, all from one big book, a history of Rome, and there was a map hung up over the black board, where they were in turn to point to the places mentioned. Before Gillian began reading, the date, and something about the former lesson was required to be told by the children, and it came quite readily, Valetta especially declaring that she did love Pyrrhus, which the others seemed to think very bad taste.

Dolores knew nothing about ancient history, and thought it foolish to study anything that did not tell in a Cambridge examination; but she supposed they knew no better down there; and when it came to her turn to read, she mangled the names so, that Val burst out laughing when she spoke of A-pious-Claudius. Lady Merrifield hushed this at once, and the girl read in a bewildered manner, and as one affronted. She saw he aunt looking at her piece of hemming, which, to say the truth, would not have done credit to Primrose, and the recollection came across her of all the oppressed orphans who had been made household drudges, so that her reading did not become more intelligible. As the clock struck one, a warning gong was heard; everybody jumped up, the work was folded away, and with the obeisance at the door, Gillian and Val ran away.

Mysie stayed a little longer, it being her turn to tidy the room; and Lady Merrifield said to Dolores—

'I must teach you how to hold your needle tomorrow, my dear.'

'I hate work,' responded Dolores.

'Val does not like it,' said her aunt; 'nor indeed did I at your age; but one cannot be an independent woman without being able to take care of one's own clothes, so I resolved that these children should learn better than I did. Do you like a take a run with Mysie before dinner? Or there is the amusing shelf. Books may be taken out after one o'clock, and they must be put back at eight, or they are confiscated for the ensuing day,' she added, pointing to a paper below where this sentence was written.

Dolores was still rather tired, and more inclined to make friends with the books than with the cousins. There were fewer than she expected, and nothing like so many absolute stories as she was used to reading with Maude Sefton.

'Those are such grown-up books,' she said to Mysie, who came to assist her choice, and pointed to the upper shelves.

'Oh, but grown-up books are nicest!' returned Mysie; 'at least, when they don't begin being stupid and marrying too soon. They must do it at last to get out of the story, and it's nicer than dying, but they can have lots of nice adventures first. But here are the 'Feats on the Fiords' and the 'Crofton Boys' and 'Water Babies,' and all the volumes of 'Aunt Judy,' if you like the younger sort. Or the dear, dear 'Thorn Fortress;' that's good for young and old.'

'Haven't you any books of your own?'

'Oh yes; this 'Thorn Fortress' is Val's, and 'A York and a Lancaster Rose' is mine, but whenever any one gives us a book, if it is not a weeny little gem like Gill's 'Christian Year,' or my 'Little Pillow,' or Val's 'Children in the Wood,' we bring it to mother, and if it is nice, we keep it here, for every one to read. If it is just rather silly, and stupid, we may read it once, and then she keeps it; and if it is very silly indeed, she puts it out of the way.'

Mysie said it as if it had been killing an animal.

'Have you got many books?'

'Yes; but I don't mean to have them knocked about by all the boys, nor put out of the way neither.'

'Mamma said we were to be all like sisters,' said Mysie, with rather a craving for the new books; but Dolores tossed up her head and said—

'We can't be. It's nonsense to say so.'

To her surprise, Mysie turned round to Lady Merrifield, who was looking at some exercises that Miss Vincent had laid before her.

'Mamma,' she said, 'is it fair that Dolores should read our books, if she won't give you up hers to look over, and be like ours?'

'Mysie,' said Lady Merrifield, 'you can't expect Dolores to like all our home plans till she is used to them. No, my dear, you need not be afraid; you shall keep your books in your own room, and nobody shall meddle with them. I am sure your cousins would not wish to be so unkind as to deprive you of the use of theirs.'

By the time Dolores had made up her mind to take 'Tom Brown,' it was time for the general flight to prepare for dinner, and she found her room made to look very pleasant, and almost homelike, for her books and little knickknacks had been put out, not quite as she preferred, but still so as to make the place seem like her own. She was pleased enough to be quite gracious to Mysie and Val who came to visit her, and to offer to let them read any of her books; when they both thanked her and said—

'If mamma lets us.'

'Oh, then you won't have them,' said Dolores; 'I'm not going to let her have my books to take away.'

'You don't think she would take them away, when she said she wouldn't?' said Mysie, hotly.

'Why, what would she do if she didn't happen to approve of them?'

'Only tell us not to read them.'

'And wouldn't you?'

'Why, Dolores!' in such a tone as made her ashamed of her question; and she said, 'Well, father never makes any fuss about what I read. He has other things to think of.'

'How do you get books, then?'

'I buy them. And Maude Sefton, she's my great friend, has lots given to her, but nobody bothers about reading them. They aren't grown-up books, you know.'

'How stupid,' said Val. 'You had better read the 'Talisman,' and then you'll see how nice a grown-up book is.'

'The 'Talisman!' Why, Maude Sefton's brother had to get it up for his holiday task, and he said it was all rot and bosh.'

'What a horridly stupid boy he must be,' returned Mysie. 'Why, I remember when Jasper once had the 'Talisman' to do, and the big ones were so delighted. Mamma read it out, and I was just old enough to listen. I remembered all about Sir Kenneth and Roswal.'

'Tom Sefton's not stupid!' said Dolores, in wrath; 'but—but the book is stupid and out of date! I heard father and the professor say it was gone by.'

Mysie and Valetta looked perfectly astounded, and Dolores pursued her advantage.

'Of course it is all very well for you that have never lived in London, nor had any advantages.'

'But we have advantages!' cried Val.

'You don't know what advantages are,' said Dolores.

'There's the gong,' cried Mysie, and down they all plunged into the dining-room, where the family were again collected, with Hal at one end and his mother at the other.

Dolores was amazed when, at the first pause, after every one was help, Valetta's voice arose.

'Mamma, what are advantages?'

'Don't you know, Val?'

'Dolores says we haven't any. And I said we have. And she says I don't know what advantages are.'

Hal and Gillian were both laughing with all their might. Their mother kept her countenance, and said—

'I suppose every one has advantages of some sort, and perhaps without knowing them.'

'I'm sure I know,' cried Fergus.

'Well, what are they?' asked Harry.

'Having mamma!' cried the little boy.

'Hear, hear! That's right, Fergy man! Couldn't be better!' cried Harry, and there was a general acclamation, which inspired gentle Mysie with the fear that her motherless cousin might feel the contrast, and, though against rules, she whispered—

'She will make you like one of us.'

'That wasn't what I meant,' returned Dolores, a little contemptuously.

'What did you mean?' said Mysie.

'Why, you've no classes, nor lectures, nor master, and only just a mere daily governess.'

Dolores did not mean this to be heard beyond her neighbour, but Mysie demanded—

'What, do you want to be doing lessons all day long?'

'No, but good governesses never are daily!'

'That's a pity,' said Gillian, turning round on her. 'Perhaps you don't know that Miss Vincent has a First Class Cambridge Certificate in everything, and is daily, because she likes to live with her mother.'

'I think,' added Lady Merrifield, with a smile, 'that Dolores has been in the way of seeing more clever people, and getting superior teaching of some kind, but we will do the best we can for her, and try not to let her miss many advantages.'

Dolores felt a little abashed, and decidedly angry at being put in the wrong.

The elders kindly turned away the general attention from her. There was a great deal of merry family fun going on, which was quite like a new language to her. Fergus and Primrose wanted to go out in search of blackberries. Gillian undertook to drive them in the cart, but as the donkey had once or twice refused to cross a little stream of water that traversed the road, the brothers foretold that she would ignominiously come back again.

'Gill and water are perilous!' observed Hal.

'Jack's not here,' said Gillian; 'besides, it is down, not up the hill, and I'm sure I don't want to draw a pail of water.'

'No—Sancho will do that.'

'The gong will sound and sound, buzz and roar,' said Wilfred. 'No Gill! no little ones! We shall send out and find them stuck fast in the lane, Sancho with his feet spread out wide, Gill with three or four sticks lying broken on the road round her, the kids reduced to eating blackberries like the children in the wood.'

'Don't Fred,' said Gillian. 'You'll frighten them.'

'Little donkeys!' said Wilfred.

'If they were, we shouldn't want Sancho,' said Val.

It was not a very sublime bit of wit, but there was a great laugh at it all round the table. Val and Fergus declared they would go too, till they heard that Nurse Halfpenny said she would not let the little ones go out without her to tear their clothes to pieces.

Every one unanimously declared that would be no fun at all, and turned to mamma to beg her to forbid nurse to come out and spoil everything.

'That's just her view,' said mamma, laughing; 'she thinks you spoil everything.'

'Oh, that's clothes! Spoiling fun is worse.'

'But were you really going with the old Halfpenny, Gill?' said Mysie, turning to her.

'Yes,' said Gillian. 'You know I can manage her pretty well when it is only the little ones and they wouldn't have any pleasure otherwise.'

'Oh come, Gill,' intreated Fergus, 'or nurse will make us sit in the donkey-cart all the time while Lois picks the blackberries!'

'Mamma, do tell her not to come,' intreated Valetta, and more of them joined in with her.

'No, my dears, I don't like to vex her when she thinks she is doing her duty.'

'She wouldn't come if you did, mamma,' and there was a general outcry of intreaty that mamma would come with them, and defend them from Mrs. Halfpenny, as Fergus, who was rather a formal little fellow, expressed it, and mamma, after a little consideration, consented to drive the pony-carriage in that direction, and to announce to Nurse Halfpenny that she herself would take charge of the children. Whereupon there was a whoop and a war-dance of jubilee, quite overwhelming to Dolores, who could not but privately ask Mysie if Nurse Halfpenny was so very cross.

'Awfully,' said Mysie, and Wilfred added—

'As savage as a bear with a sore head.'

'Like Mrs. Crabtree?' asked Dolores.

'Exactly. Jasper called her so when he wanted to lash her up, till at lash she got hold of his 'Holiday House' and threw it into the sea, and it was in Malta and we couldn't get another,' said Mysie.

'And haven't you one?'

'Yes, Gill and I save for it; but mamma only let us have it on condition we made a solemn promise never to tease nurse about it.'

'And does she go at you with that dreadful thing—what's it name—the tawse?'

'Ah! you'll soon know,' said Wilfred.

'No, no; nonsense, Fred,' said Mysie, as Dolores' face worked with consternation. 'She never hits us, not if we are ever so tiresome. Papa and mamma would not let her.'

'But why do they let her be so dreadful? Maude's nurse used to be horrid and slap her, and when her mother found it out the woman was sent away directly.'

Nurse Halfpenny isn't that sort,' said Mysie. 'Her husband was papa's colour-sergeant, and he got a sun-stroke and died, and then she came when Gillian was just born, and so weak and tiny that she would never have lived if nurse hadn't watched her day and night, and so Gillian's her favourite, except the youngest, and she is ever so good, you know. I've heard the ladies, when we were with the dear old 111th, telling mamma how they envied her her trustworthy treasure.'

'I'm sure they might have had her at half-price,' said Wilfred. 'She's be dear at a farthing!'

At that moment Mrs. Halfpenny's voice was heard demanding if it were really her ladyship's pleasure to go out, fatiguing herself to the very death with all the children rampaging about her and tearing themselves to pieces, if not poisoning themselves with all sorts of nasty berries.

'Indeed I'll take care of them and bring them back safe to you,' responded her ladyship, very much in the tone of one of her own children making promises. 'Put them on their brown hollands and they can't come to much harm.'

'Well, if it's your wish, ma'am, my leddy; what must be, must, but I know how it will be—you'll come back tired out, fit to drop, and Miss Val and Miss Primrose won't have a rag fit to be seen on them. But if it's your will, what must be must, for you're no better than a bairn yourself, general's lady though you be, and G.C.B.'

'No, nurse, you'll be G.C.B.—Grand Commander of the Bath—when we come home,' called out Hall, who was leaning on the banister at the bottom, and there was a general laugh, during which Dolly tardily climbed the stairs, so tardily that her aunt, meeting her, asked whether she was still tired, and if she would rather have the afternoon to arrange her room.

She said 'yes,' but not 'thank you,' and went on, relieved that Mysie did not offer to stay and help her, and yet rather offended at being left alone, while all the others went their own way. She heard them pattering and clattering, shouting and calling up and down the passages, and then came a great silence, while they could be seen going down the drive, some on foot, some in the pony-chaise or donkey-cart.

Her things had all been unpacked and put in order, and her room had a very cheerful window. It was prettily furnished with fresh pink and white dimity, and choice-looking earthenware, but to London eyes like those of Dolores it seemed very old-fashioned and what she called 'poked up.' The paper was ugly, the chimney-piece was a narrow, painting thing, of the same dull, stone-colour as the door and the window-frame. And then the clear air, the perfect stillness, the absence of anything moving in the view from the window gave the citybred child a sense of dreadful loneliness and dreariness as she sat on the side of her bed, with one foot under her, gazing dolefully round her, and in he head composing her own memoirs.

'Fully occupied with their own plans and amusements, the lonely orphan was left in solitude. Her aunt knew not how her heart ached after the home she had left, but the machine of the family went its own way and trod her under its wheels.'

This was such a fine sentence that it was almost a comfort, and she thought of writing it to Maude Sefton, but as she got up to fetch her writing-case from the schoolroom, she saw that her books were standing just in the way she did not like, and with all the volumes mixed up together. So she tumbled them all out of the shelves on the floor, and at that moment Mrs. Halfpenny looked into the room.

'Well, to be sure!' she exclaimed, 'when me and Lois have been working at them books all the morning.'

'They were all nohow—as I don't like them,' said Dolores.

'Oh, very well, please yourself then, miss, if that's all the thanks you have in your pocket, you may put them up your own way, for all I care. Only my lady will have the young ladies' rooms kept neat and orderly, or they lose marks for it.'

'I don't want any help,' said Dolores, crossly, and Mrs. Halfpenny shut the door with a bang. 'The menials are insulting me,' said Dolores to herself, and a tear came to her eye, while all the time there was a certain mournful satisfaction in being so entirely the heroine of a book.

She went to work upon her books, at first hotly and sharply, and very carefully putting the tallest in the centre so as to form a gradual ascent with the tops and not for the world letting a second volume stand before its elder brother, but she soon got tired, took to peeping at one or two parting gifts which she had not yet been able to read, and at last got quite absorbed in the sorrows of a certain Clare, whose golden hair was cut short by her wicked aunt, because it outshone her cousin's sandy locks. There was reason to think that a tress of this same golden hair would lead to her recognition by some grandfather of unknown magnificence, as exactly like that of his long-lost Claribel, and this might result in her assuming splendours that would annihilate the aunt. Things seemed tending to a fracture of the ice under the cruellest cousin of all, and her rescue by Clare, when they would be carried senseless into the great house, and the recognition of Clare and the discomfiture of her foes would take place. How could Dolores shut the book at such a critical moment!

So there she was sitting in the midst of her scattered books, when the galloping and scampering began again, and Mysie knocked at the door to tell her there were pears, apples, biscuits, and milk in the dining-room, and that after consuming them, lessons had to be learnt for the next day, and then would follow amusements, evening toilette, seven o'clock tea, and either games or reading aloud till bedtime. As to the books, Mysie stood aghast.

'I thought nurse and Lois had done them all for you.'

'They did them all wrong, so I took them down.'

Oh, dear! We must put them in, or there'll be a report.'

'A report!'

'Yes, Nurse Halfpenny reports us whenever she doesn't find our rooms tidy, and then we get a bad mark. Perhaps mamma wouldn't give you one this first day, but it is best to make sure. Shall I help you, or you won't have time to eat any pears?'

Dolores was thankful for help, and the books were scrambled in anyhow on the shelves; for Mysie's good nature was endangering her share of the afternoon's gouter, though perhaps it consoled her that her curiosity was gratified by a hasty glance at the backs of her cousin's story-books.

By the time the two girls got down to the dining-table, every one had left the room, and there only remained one doubtful pear, and three baked apples, besides the loaf and the jug of milk. Mysie explained that not being a regular meal, no one was obliged to come punctually to it, or to come at all, but these who came tardily might fare the worse. As to the blackberries, for which Dolores inquired, the girls were going to make jam of them themselves the next day; but Mysie added, with an effort, she would fetch some, as her cousin had had none in the gathering.

'Oh no, thank you; I hate blackberries,' said Dolores, helping herself to an apple.

'Do you?' said Mysie, blankly. 'We don't. They are such fun. You can't think how delicious the great overhanging clusters are in the lane. Some was up so high that Hal had to stand up in the cart to reach them, and to take Fergus up on his shoulder. We never had such a blackberrying as with mamma and Hal to help us. And only think, a great carriage came by, with some very grand people in it; we think it was the Dean; and they looked down the lane and stared, so surprised to see what great mind to call out, 'Fee, faw, fum.' You know nothing makes such a good giant as Fergus standing on Hal's shoulders, and a curtain over them to hide Hal's face. Oh dear, I wish I hadn't told you! You would have been a new person to show it to.'

Dolores made very little answer, finished her apple, and followed to the schoolroom, where an irregular verb, some geography, and some dates awaited her.

Then followed another rush of the populace for the evening meal of the live stock, but in this Dolores was too wary to share. She made her way up to her retreat again, and tried to lose the sense of her trouble and loneliness in a book. Then came the warning bell, and a prodigious scuffling, racing and chasing, accompanied by yells as of terror and roars as of victory, all cut short by the growls of Mrs. Halfpenny. Everything then subsided. The world was dressing; Dolores dressed too, feeling hurt and forlorn at no one's coming to help her, and yet worried when Mysie arrived with orders from Mrs. Halfpenny to come to her to have her sash tied.

'I think a servant ought to come to me. Caroline always does,' said the only daughter with dignity.

'She can't, for she is putting Primrose to bed. Oh, it's so delicious to see Prim in her bath,' said Mysie, with a little skip. 'Make haste, or we shall miss her, the darling.'

Dolores did not feel pressed to behold the spectacle, and not being in the habit of dressing without assistance, she was tardy, and Mysie fidgeted about and nearly distracted her. Thus, when she reached the nursery, Primrose was already in her little white bed-gown, and was being incited by Valetta to caper about on her cot, like a little acrobat, as her sisters said, while Mrs. Halfpenny declared that 'they were making the child that rampageous, she should not get her to sleep till midnight.'

They would have been turned out much sooner, and Primrose hushed into silence, if nurse's soul had not been horrified by the state of Dolores' hair and the general set of her garments.

'My certie!' she exclaimed—a dreadful exclamation in the eyes of the family, who knew it implied that in all her experience Mrs. Halfpenny had never known the like! And taking Dolores by the hand, she led the wrathful and indignant girl back into her bedroom, untied and tied, unbuttoned and buttoned, brushed and combed in spite of the second bell ringing, the general scamper, and the sudden apparition of Mysie and Val, whom she bade run away and tell her leddyship that 'Miss Mohoone should come as soon as she was sorted, but she ought to come up early to have her hair looked to, for 'twas shame to see how thae fine London servants sorted a motherless bairn.'

Dolores felt herself insulted; she turned red all over, with feelings the old Scotchwoman could not understand. She expected to hear the message roared out to the whole assembly round the tea-table, but Mysie had discretion enough to withhold her sister from making it public.

The tea itself, though partaken of by Lady Merrifield, seemed an indignity to the young lady accustomed to late dinners. After it, the whole family played at 'dumb crambo.' Dolores was invited to join, and instructed to 'do the thing you think it is;' but she was entirely unused to social games, and thought it only ridiculous and stupid when the word being a rhyme to ite, Fergus gave rather too real a blow to Wilfred, and Gillian answered,

"Tis not smite;' Wilfred held out a hand, and was told, "Tis not right;' Val flourished in the air as if holding a string, and was informed that 'kite' was wrong; when Hal ran away as if pursued by Fergus by way of flight; and Mysie performed antics which she was finally obliged to explain were those of a sprite. Dolores could not recollect anything, and only felt annoyed at being made to feel stupid by such nonsense, when Mysie tried to make her a present of a suggestion by pointing to the back of a letter. Neither write nor white would come into her head, though little Fergus signalized himself, just before he was swept off to bed, by seizing a pen and making strokes!

After his departure, Lady Merrifield read aloud 'The Old oak Staircase,' which had been kept to begin when Dolores came, Hal taking the book in turn with his mother. And so ended Dolores' first day of banishment.

CHAPTER V
THE FIRST WALK

'What a lot of letters for you, mamma!' cried Mysie.

'Papa!' exclaimed Fergus and Primrose.

'No, it is not the right day, my dears. But here is a letter from Aunt Ada.'

'Oh!' in a different tone.

'She writes for Aunt Jane. They will come down here next Monday because Aunt Jane is wanted to address the girls at the G.F.S. festival on Tuesday.'

'Aunt Jane seems to have taken to public speaking,' said Harry. 'It would be rather a lark to hear her.'

'You may have a chance,' said Lady Merrifield, 'for here is a note from Mrs. Blackburn to ask if I will be so very kind as to let them have the festival here. They had reckoned upon Tillington Park, where they have always had it before, but they hear that all the little Tillingtons have the measles, and they don't think it safe to venture there.'

'It will be great fun!' said Gillian. 'We will have all sorts of games, only I'm afraid they will be much stupider than the Irish girls.'

'And ever so much stupider than the dear 111th children,' sighed Mysie.

'Aren't they all great big girls?' asked Valetta, disconsolately.

'I believe twelve years old is the limit,' said her mother. 'Twelve-year-old girls have plenty of play in them, Vals, haven't they, Mysie? Let me see—two hundred and thirty of them.'

'For you to feast?' asked Harry.

'Oh, no—that cost comes out of their own funds, Mrs. Blackburn takes care to tell me, and Miss Hacket will find some one in Siverfold who will provide tables and forms and crockery. I must go down and talk to Miss Hacket as soon as lessons are over. Or perhaps it would save time and trouble if I wrote and asked her to come up to luncheon and see the capabilities of the place. Why, what's the matter?' pausing at the blank looks.

'The jam, mamma—the blackberry jam!' cried Valetta.

'Well?'

'We can't do it without Gill, and she will have to be after that Miss Constance,' explained Val.

'Oh! never mind. She won't stay all the afternoon,' said Gillian, cheerfully. 'Luncheon people don't.'

'Yes, but then there will be lessons to be learnt.'

'Look here, Val,' said Gillian, 'if you and Mysie will learn your lessons for tomorrow while I'm bound to Miss Con., I'll do mine some time in the evening, and be free for the jam when she is gone.'

'The dear delicious jam!' cried Val, springing about upon her chair; and Lady Merrifield further said—

'I wonder whether Mysie and Dolores would like to take the note down. They could bring back a message by word of mouth.'

'Oh, thank you, mamma!' cried Mysie.

'Then I will write the note as soon as we have done breakfast. Don't dawdle, Fergus boy.'

'Mayn't I go?' demanded Wilfred.

'No, my dear. It is your morning with Mr. Poulter. And you must take care not to come back later than eleven, Mysie dear; I cannot have him kept waiting. Dolores, do you like to go?'

'Yes, please,' said Dolores, partly because it was at any rate gain to escape from that charity-school lesson in the morning, and partly because Valetta was looking at her in the ardent hope that she would refuse the privilege of the walk, and it therefore became valuable; but there was so little alacrity in her voice that her aunt asked her whether she were quite rested and really liked the walk, which would be only half a mile to the outskirts of the town.

Dolores hated personal inquiries beyond everything, and replied that she was quite well, and didn't mind.

So soon as she and Mysie had finished, they were sent off to get ready, while Aunt Lilias wrote her note in pencil at the corner of the table, which she never left, while Fergus and Primrose were finishing their meal; but she had to silence a storm at the 'didn't mind'—Gillian even venturing to ask how she could send one to whom it was evidently no pleasure to go. 'I think she likes it more than she shows,' said the mother, 'and she wants air, and will settle to her lessons the better for it. What's that, Val?'

'It was my turn, mamma,' said Valetta, in an injured voice.

'It will be your turn next, Val,' said her mother, cheerfully. 'Dolores comes between you and Mysie, so she must take her place accordingly. And today we grant her the privilege of the new-comer.'

Dolores would have esteemed the privilege more, if, while she was going upstairs to put on her hat, the recollection had not occurred to her of one of the victim's of an aunt's cruelty who was always made to run on errands while her favoured cousins were at their studies. Was this the beginning? Somehow, though her better sense knew this was a foolish fancy, she had a secret pleasure in pitying herself, and posing to herself as a persecuted heroine. And then she was greatly fretted to find the housemaid in her room, looking as if no one else had any business there. What was worse, she could not find her jacket. She pulled out all her drawers with fierce, noisy jerks, and then turned round on the maid, sharply demanding—

'Who has taken my jacket?'

'I'm sure I don't know, Miss Dollars. You'd best ask Mrs. Halfpenny.'

'If—' but at that moment Mysie ran in, holding the jacket in her hand. 'I saw it in the nursery,' she said, triumphantly. 'Nurse had taken it to mend! Come along. Where's your hat?'

But there was pursuit; Mrs. Halfpenny was at the door. 'Young ladies, you are not going out of the policy in that fashion.'

'Mamma sent us. Mamma wants us to take a note in a hurry. Only to Miss Hacket,' pleaded Mysie, as Mrs. Halfpenny laid violent hands on her brown Holland jacket, observing—

'My leddy never bade ye run off mair like a wild worricow than a general officer's daughter, Miss Mysie. What's that? Only Miss Hacket, do you say? You should respect yourself and them you come of mair than to show yourself to a blind beetle in an unbecoming way. 'Tis well that there's one in the house that knows what is befitting. Miss Dollars, you stand still; I must sort your necktie before you go. 'Tis all of a wisp. Miss Mysie, you tell your mamma that I should be fain to know her pleasure about Miss Dollars' frocks. She've scarce got one—coloured or mourning—that don't want altering.'

Mrs. Halfpenny always caused Dolores such extreme astonishment and awe that she obeyed her instantly, but to be turned about and tidied by an authoritative hand was extremely disagreeable to the independent young lady. Caroline had never treated her thus, being more willing to permit untidiness than to endure her temper. She only durst, after the pair were released, remonstrate with Mysie on being termed Miss Dollars.

'They can't make out your name,' said Mysie. 'I tried to teach Lois, but nurse said she had no notion of new-fangled nonsense names.'

'I'm sure Valetta and Primrose are worse.'

'Ah! but Val was born at Malta, and mamma had always loved the Grand Master La Valetta so much, and had written verses about him when she was only sixteen. And Primrose was named after the first primrose mamma had seen for twelve years—the first one Val and I had ever seen.'

'They called me Miss Mohun at home.'

'Yes, but we can't here, because of Aunt Jane.'

All this was chattered forth on the stairs before the two girls reached the dining-room, where Mysie committed the feeding of her pets to Val, and received the note, with fresh injunctions to come home by eleven, and bring word whether Miss Hacket and Miss Constance would both come to luncheon.

'Oh dear!' sighed Gillian, and there was a general groan round the table.

'It can't be helped, my dear.'

'Oh no, I know it can't,' said Gillian, resignedly.

'You see,' said Mysie. 'Yes, come along, Basto dear. You see Gill has to be—down, Basto, I say!—a young lady when.... Never mind him, Dolores, he won't hurt. When Miss Constance Hacket and—leave her alone, Basto, I say!—and she is such a goose. Not you, Dolores, but Miss Constance.'

'Oh that dog! I wish you would not take him.'

'Not take dear old Basto! Why 'tis such a treat for him to get a walk in the morning—the delight of his jolly old black heart. Isn't he a dear old fellow? and he never hurt anybody in his life! It's only setting off! He will quiet down in a minute; but I couldn't disappoint him. Could I, my old man?'

Never having lived with animals nor entered into their feelings, Dolores could not understand how a dog's pleasure could be preferred to her comfort, and felt a good deal hurt, though Basto's antics subsided as soon as they were past the inner gate shutting in the garden from the paddock, which was let out to a farmer. Mysie, however, ran on as usual with her stream of information—

'The Miss Hacket were sister or daughters or something to some old man who used to be clergyman here, and they are all married up but these two, and they've got the dearest little house you ever saw. They had a nephew in the 111th, and so they came and called on us at once. Miss Hacket is a regular old dear, but we none of us can bear Miss Constance, except that mamma says we ought to be sorry for her because she leads such a confined life. Miss Hacket and Aunt Jane always do go on so about the G.F.S. They both are branch secretaries, you know.'

'I know! Aunt Jane did bother Mrs. Sefton so that she says she will never have another of those G.F.S. girls. She says it is a society for interference.'

'Mamma likes it,' said Mysie.

'Oh! but she is only just come.'

'Yes; but she always looked after the school children at Beechcroft before she married, and she and Alethea and Phyllis had the soldiers' children up on Sunday. Alethea taught the little drummer boys, and they were so funny. I wonder who teaches them now! Gill always goes down to help Miss Hacket with her G.F.S. classes. She has one on Sunday afternoon, and one on Tuesday for sewing, and she is the only young lady in the place who can do plain needlework properly.'

'Sewing-machines can work. What the use of fussing about it!'

'They can't mend,' said Mysie. 'Besides, do you know, in the American war, all the sewing-machines in the Southern States got out of order, and as all the machinery people were in the north, the poor ladies didn't know what to do, and couldn't work without them.'

'Sewing-machines are a recent invention,' said Dolores.

'Oh! you didn't think I meant the great old War of Independence. No, I meant the war about the slaves—secession they called it.'

'That is not in the history of England,' said Dolores, as if Mysie had no business to look beyond.

'Why! of course not, when it happened in America. Papa told us about it. He read it in some paper, I think. Don't you like learning things in that way?'

'No. I don't approve of irregular unsystematic knowledge.'

Dolores has heard her mother say something of this kind, and it came into her head most opportunely as a defence of her father—for she would not for the world have confessed that he did not talk to her as Sir Jasper Merrifield seemed to have done to his children. In fact she rather despised the General for so doing.

'Oh! but it is such fun picking up things out of lesson time!' said Mysie.

'That is the Edge—,' Dolores was not sure of the word Edgeworthian, so she went on to 'system. Professor Sefton says he does not approve of harassing children with cramming them with irregular information at all sorts of times. Let play be play and lessons be lessons, he says, not mixed up together, and so Rex and Maude never learnt anything—not a letter—till they were seven years old.'

'How stupid!' cried Mysie.

'Maude's not stupid!' cried Dolores, 'nor the professor either! She's my great friend.'

'I didn't say she was stupid,' said Mysie, apologetically, 'only that it must be very stupid not to be able to read till one was seven. Could you?'

'Oh, yes. I can't remember when I couldn't read. But Maude used to play with a little girl who could read and talk French at five years old, and she died of water upon her brain.'

'Dear me! Primrose can read quite well,' said Mysie, somewhat alarmed; 'but then,' she went on in a reassured voice, 'so could all of us except Jasper and Gillian, and they felt the heat so much at Gibraltar that they were quite stupid while they were there.'

This discussion brought the two girls across the paddock out into a road with a broad, neat footpath, where numerous little children were being exercised with nurses and perambulators. At first it was bordered by fields on either side, but villas soon began to spring up, and presently the girls reached what looked like a long, low 'cottage residence,' but was really two, with a verandah along the front, and a garden divided in the middle by a paling covered with canary nasturtium shrubs. The verandah on one side was hung with a rich purple pall of the dark clematis, on the other by a Gloire de Dijon rose. There were bright flower beds, and the dormer windows over the verandah looked like smiling eyes under their deep brows of creeper-trimmed verge-board. What London-bred Dolores saw was a sight that shocked her—a lady standing unbonnetted just beyond the verandah, talking to a girl whose black hat and jacket looked what Mysie called 'very G.F.S.-y.'

The lady did not turn out to be young or beautiful. She was near middle age, and looked as if she were far too busy to be ever plump; she had a very considerable amount of nose and rather thin, dark hair, done in a fashion which, like that of her navy blue linen dress, looked perfectly antiquated to Dolores. As she saw the two girls at the gate she came down the path eagerly to welcome them.

'Ah! my dear Mysie! so kind of your dear mother! I thought I should hear from her.' And as she kissed Mysie, she added, 'And this is the new cousin. My dear, I am glad to see you here.'

Dolores thought her own dignified manner had kept off a kiss, not knowing that Miss Hacket was far too ladylike to be over-familiar, and that there was no need to put on such a forbidding look.

Mysie gave her message and note, but Miss Hacket could not give the verbal answer at once till she had consulted her sister. She was not sure whether Constance had not made an engagement to play lawn-tennis, so they must come in.

There sounded 'coo-roo-oo coo-roo-oo' in the verandah, and Mysie cried—

'Oh, the dear doves!'

Miss Hacket said she had been just feeding them when the G.F.S. girl arrived, and as Mysie came to a halt in delight at the aspect of a young one that had just crept out into public life, the sister was called to the window. She was a great deal younger and more of the present day in style than her sister, and had pensive-looking grey eyes, with a somewhat bored languid manner as she shook hands with the early visitors.

The sisters had a little consultation over the note, during which Dolores studied them, and Mysie studied the doves, longing to see the curious process of feeding the young ones.

When Miss Hacket turned back to her with the acceptance of the invitation, she thought she might wait just to help Miss Hacket to put in the corn and the sop. Meantime Miss Constance talked to Dolores.

'Did you arrive yesterday?'

'No, the day before.'

'Ah! it must be a great change to you.'

'Indeed it is.'

'This must be the dullest place in England, I think,' said Miss Constance. 'No variety, no advantages of any kind! And have not you lived in London?'

'Yes.'

'That is my ambition! I once spent six weeks in London, and it was an absolute revelation—the opening of another world. And I understand that Mr. Maurice Mohun is such a clever man, and that you saw a great deal of his friends.'

'I used,' said Dolores, thinking of those days of her mother when she was the pet and plaything of the guests, incited to say clever and pert things, which then were passed round and embellished till she neither knew them nor comprehended them.

'That is what I pine for!' exclaimed Miss Constance. 'Nobody here has any ideas. You can't conceive how borne and prejudiced every one her who is used to something better! Don't you love art needlework?'

'Maude Sefton has been working Goosey Goosey Gander on a toilet-cover.'

'Oh! how sweet! We never get any new patterns here! Do come in and see, I don't know which to take; I brought three beginnings home to choose from, and I am quite undecided.'

'Mrs. Sefton draws her own patterns,' said Dolores. 'Something she gets ideas from Lorenzo Dellman—he's an artist, you know, and a regular aesthete! He made her do a dado all sunflowers last year, but they are a little gone out now, and are very staring besides, and I think she will have some nymphs dancing among almond-trees in blue vases instead, as soon as she has designed it.'

'Isn't that lovely! Oh! what would I not give for such opportunities? Do let me have your opinion.'

So Dolores went in with her, and looked at three patterns, one of tall daisies; another of odd-looking doves, one on each side of a red Etruscan vase, where the water must have been as much out of their reach as that in the pitcher was beyond the crow's; and a third, of Little Bo Peep. Having given her opinion in favour of Bo Peep, she was taken upstairs to inspect the young lady's store of crewels, and choose the colours.

Dolores neither knew nor cared anything about fancy work, but to be treated as an authority was quite soothing, and she fully believed that the mere glimpses she had had of Mrs. Sefton's work and the shop windows, enabled her to give great enlightenment to this poor country mouse; so she gladly went to the bedroom, with a muslin-worked toilet-cover, embroidered curtains, plates fastened against the wall, and table all over knick-knacks, which Miss Constance called her little den, where she could study beauty after her own bent, while her sister Mary was wholly engrossed with the useful, and could endure nothing but the prose of the last century.

Meantime Mysie had forgotten how time flew in her belief that in one minute more the young doves would want to be fed, and then in amusement at seeing them pursue their parents with low squeaks and flutterings, watching, too, the airs and graces, bowing, cooing, and laughing of the old ones. When at last she was startled by hearing eleven struck, there had to be a great hunt for Dolores in the drawing-room and garden, and when at last Miss Hacket's calls for her sister brought the tow downstairs more than ten minutes had passed! Mysie was too much dismayed, and in too great a hurry to do anything but cry, 'Come along, Dolores,' and set off at such a gallop as to scandalize the Londoner, even when Mysie recollected that it was too public a place for running, and slackened her pace. Dolores was soon gasping, and with a stitch in her side. Mysie would have exclaimed, 'What were you doing with Miss Constance?' but breathlessness happily prevented it. The way across the paddock seemed endless, and Mysie was chafed at having to hold back for her companion, who panted in distress, leant against a tree, declared she could not go on, she did not care, and then when, Mysie set off running, was seized with fright at being left alone in this vast unknown space, cried after her and made a rush, soon ending in sobbing breath.

At last they were at the door, and Wilfred just coming out of the dining-room greeted them with, 'A quarter to twelve. Won't you catch it? Oh my!'

'Are they come?' said Lady Merrifield, looking out of the schoolroom. 'My dear children! Did Miss Hacket keep you?'

'No, mamma,' gasped Mysie. 'At least it was my fault for watching the doves.'

'Ah! Mysie, I must not send you on a message next time. Mr. Poulter has been waiting these twenty minutes, and I am afraid you are not fit to take a lesson now. Dolores looks quite done up! I shall send you both to lie down on your beds and learn your poetry for an hour. And you must write an apology to Mr. Poulter this afternoon. No, don't go in now. Go up at once, Gillian shall bring your books. Does Miss Hacket come?'

'Yes, mamma,' said Mysie humbly, looking at Dolores all the time. She was too generous to say that part of the delay had been caused by looking for her cousin, and having to adapt her pace to the slower one, but she decidedly expected the avowal from Dolores, and thought it mean not to make it. 'And, oh, the jam!' she mourned as she went upstairs. While, on the other hand, Dolores considered what she called 'being sent to bed' an unmerited and unjust sentence given without a hearing; when their tardiness had been all Mysie's fault, not hers. She had no notion that her aunt only sent them to lie down, because they looked heated, tired, and spent, and was really letting them off their morning's lessons. It was a pity that she felt too forlorn and sullen even to complain when Gillian brought up Macaulay's 'Armada' for her to learn the first twelve lines, or she might have come to an understanding, but all that was elicited from her was a glum 'No,' when asked if she knew it already. Gillian told her not to keep her dusty boots on the bed, and she vouchsafed no answer, for she did not consider Gillian her mistress, though, after she was left to herself, she found them so tight and hot that she took them off. Then she looked over the verses rather contemptuously—she who always learnt German poetry; and she had a great mind to assert her independence by getting off the bed, and writing a letter to Maude Sefton, describing the narrow stupidity of the whole family, and how her aunt, without hearing her, had send her to be for Mysie's fault. However she felt so shaky and tired that she thought she had better rest a little first, and somehow she fell fast asleep, and was only awakened by the gong. She jumped up in haste, recollecting that the delightful sympathizing Miss Constance was coming to luncheon, and set her hair and dress to rights eagerly, observing, however, to herself, that her horrid aunt was quite capable of imprisoning her all the time for not having learnt that stupid poetry.

She hesitated a little where to go when she reached the hall, but the schoolroom door was open, and she heard a mournful voice concluding with a gasp—

'Our glorious semper eadem, the banner of our pride.'

And Miss Vincent saying, 'Now, my dear, go and wash your face, and try not to be such a dismal spectacle.'

And then Mysie came out, with heavy eyes and a mottled face, showing that she had been crying all the time she had been learning, over her own fault certainly, but likewise over mamma's displeasure and Dolly's shabbiness.

'Well, Dora,' said Miss Vincent, 'have you come to repeat your poetry?'

'No,' said Dolores. 'I went to sleep instead.'

'Oh! I'm glad of that. I wish poor Mysie had done the same. I believe it was what Lady Merrifield intended, you both looked so knocked up.'

Dolores cleared up a little at this, especially as Miss Vincent was no relation, and she thought it a good time to make her protest against mere English.

'Oh!' she said. 'I supposed that was the reason she gave me such a stupid, childish, sing-song nursery rhyme to learn. I can say lots of Schiller and some Goethe.'

'I advise you not to let any one hear you call Lord Macaulay's poem a nursery rhyme, or it might never be forgotten,' said Miss Vincent gaily. Then seeing the cloud return to Dolores's face, she added, 'You have been brought forward in German, I see. We must try to bring your knowledge of English literature up to be even with it.'

Dolores liked this better than anything she had yet heard, chiefly because she had learnt from her books that governesses were not uniformly so cruel as aunts. And besides, she felt that she had been spared a public humiliation.

By this time the guests were ringing at the door, and Miss Vincent, with her had on, only waiting till their entrance was made to depart. Dolores asked whether to go into the drawing-room, and was told that Lady Merrifield preferred that the children should only appear in the dining-room on the sound of the gong, which was not long in being heard.

The Merrifields were trained not to chatter when there was company at table, besides Mysie and Val were in low spirits about the chance of the blackberry cookery. Miss Hacket sat on one side of Lady Merrifield, and talked about what associates had answered her letters, and what villages would send contingents of girls, and it sounded very dull to the young people. Miss Constance was next to Hal. She looked amiable and sympathetic at Dolores on the opposite side of the table, but discussed lawn-tennis tournaments with her neighbour, which was quite as little interesting to the general public as was the G.F.S. However, as soon as Primrose had said grace, Lady Merrifield proposed to take Miss Hacket down to the stable-yard; and the whole train followed excepting the two girls, who trusted Hal to see whether their pets would suffer inconvenience. However it soon was made evident to Gillian that she was not wanted, and that Dolores and Constance had no notion of wandering about the paved courts and bare coach-houses, among the dogs and cats, guinea-pigs, and fowls. Indeed, Constance, who was at least seven years older than Gillian, and a full-blown young lady, dismissed her by saying 'that she was going to see Miss Mohun's books.'

'Oh, certainly,' said Gillian, in a voice as though she were rather surprised, though much relieved.

So off the friends went together—for of course they were to be friends. The Miss Mohun had been uttered in a tone that clearly meant to be asked to drop it, so they were to be Dolores and Constance henceforth, if not Dolly and Cons. Dolores was such a lovely name that Constance could not mangle it, and was sure there was some reason for it. The girl had, in fact, been named after a Spanish lady, whom her mother had known and admired in early girlhood, and to whom she had made a promise of naming her first daughter after her. No doubt Dolores did not know that Mrs. Mohun had regretted the childish promise which she had felt bound to keep in spite of her husband's dislike to the name, which he declared would be a misfortune to the child.

Dolores was really proud of its peculiarity, and delighted to have any one to sympathize with her, in that and a great deal besides, which she communicated to her new friend in the window-seat of her room. When the two ladies went home, Constance told her sister that 'dear little Dolores was a remarkable character, sadly misunderstood among those common-place people, the Merrifields, and unjustly used, too, and she should do her best for her!'

Meantime Gillian, finding herself not wanted, had repaired to the schoolroom.

'Oh, it is of no use,' sighed Mysie, disconsolately. 'I've ever so much morning's work to make up, too. And I never shall! I've muzzled my head!'

By which remarkable expression Mysie signified that fatigue, crying, and dinner had made her brains dull and heavy; but Gillian was a sensible elder sister.

'Don't try your sum yet, then,' she said. 'Practise your scales for half an hour, while I do my algebra, and then we'll go over your German verbs together. I'll tell Miss Vincent, and she wont' mind, and I think mamma will be pleased if you try.'

Gillian was too much used to noises not to be able to work an equation, and prepare her Virgil, to the sound of scales, and Mysie was a good deal restored by them and by hope.

So when at length Constance had been summoned by her sister, who tore herself away from the arrangements, being bound to five-o'clock tea elsewhere, Mysie was discovered with a face still rather woe-begone, but hopeful and persevering, and though there still was a 'bill of parcels' where 11 and 3/4 lbs. of mutton at 13 and 1/2d. per lb. refused to come right, Lady Merrifield kissed her, said she had been a diligent child, and sent her off prancing in bliss to the old 'still-room' stove, where they were allowed a fire, basins, spoons, and strainers, and where the sugar lay in a snowy heap, and the blackberries in a sanguine pile.

'There's partiality!' thought Dolores, and scowled, as she stood at the front door still gazing after Constance.

'Won't you come, Dolly?' said Mysie. 'Or haven't you learnt your lessons?'

'No,' said Dolly, making one answer serve for both questions.

'Oh! then you can't. Shall I ask mamma to let you off?'

'No, I don't care. I don't like messes! And what's the use if you haven't a cookery class?'

'It's such fun,' said Val.

'And our sisters did go to a cookery class at Dublin and taught Gill,' added Mysie.

'But if you haven't done your lessons, you can't go,' said Valetta decidedly.

Off they went, and Lady Merrifield presently crossed the hall, and saw Dolores' attitude.

'My dear, are you waiting to say those verses?' she said kindly.

'I hadn't time to learn them, I went to sleep,' said Dolores.

'A very good thing too, my dear. Suppose we go over them together.'

Aunt Lilias took the unwilling hand, led Dolores into the schoolroom, and for half an hour she went over the verses with her, explaining what was new to the girl, and vividly describing the agitation of Plymouth, and the flocks of people thronging in. 'I must show her that I will be minded, but I will make it pleasant to her, poor child,' she thought.

And it could not have been otherwise than pleasant to her, but that she was reflecting all this time that she was being punished while Mysie was enjoying herself. Therefore she put the lid on her intellect, and was inconceivably stupid.

CHAPTER VI
PERSECUTION

On Monday afternoon Dolores was sitting at the end of the long garden walk, upon a green garden-bench, with a crocodile's head and tail roughly carved. The shouts of the others were audible in the distance beyond the belt of trees. Aunt Lily had driven into the town to meet her sisters, taking Fergus with her, whereas Dolores had never been out in the carriage. There was partiality! Though, to be sure, Fergus was to have a tooth out! Harry and Gillian were playing with the rest, and she had been invited to join, but she had made answer that she hated romping, and on being assured that no romping was necessary, she replied that she only wanted to read in peace. She had refused the "Thorn Fortress," which she was told would explain the game, and had hunted out "Clare, or No Home," to compare her lot with that of the homeless one.

Certainly, she had not yet been sent to bed with a box on the ear because a countess had shown symptoms of noticing her more than her ugly, over-dressed cousin. But then Aunt Lily would not allow her to walk down alone to the Casement Villas to see dear Constance, and would let that farmer keep all those dreadful cows in the paddock, so that even going escorted was a terror to her.

Nor had her handsome mourning been taken from her and old clothes of her cousin substituted for it. No, but she had been cruelly pulled about between Mrs. Halfpenny and the Silverton dressmaker with a mouthful of pins; and Aunt Lily had insisted on her dress being trimmed with velvet, instead of the jingling jet she preferred.

Did they intercept her letters? She had had one from her father, sent from Falmouth, but only one from Maude Sefton in ten days! Moreover, she had one from Constance in her apron pocket, arrived that very afternoon, asking her to come down with Gillian on the Sundays, that the friends might enjoy themselves together while the classes were going on; but she made sure that all were so jealous of her friendship with Constance that no consent would be given.

She did not hear or notice the whisperings in the laurels behind her—

'Do you see that sulky old Croat, smoking his pipe under the tree?'

'No, he is a Black Brunswicker.'

'Nonsense, Willie; the Black Brunswickers weren't till Bonaparte's time.'

'I don't care, he is anything black and nasty; here goes!'

'Oh stop; don't shoot. I believe he is only a vivandiere. Besides, it's treacherous—'

'I tell you he is laying a train to blow up the tower. There!'

An arrow struck the bench beside Dolores, who, more angry than she had ever been in her life, snatched it up, unheeding that it had no point to speak of, rushed headlong in pursuit, while, with a tremendous shout, Valetta and Wilfred flew before her to a waste overgrown place at the end of the kitchen garden.

'We've shot a Croat!'

'No, a Black Brunswicker.'

'Oh ah! They are coming—the enemy! Into the fortress! Bar the wolf's passage!'

And as Dolores struggled through the bushes, she saw the whole family dashing into an outhouse, and the door slammed. She pushed against it, but an unearthly compound of howls, yells, shouts and bangs replied.

'Gillian! Harry, I say,' she cried in great anger; 'come out, I want to speak to you.'

But her voice was lost in the war-whoops within, and the louder she knocked, the louder grew the din, till she walked off, swelling with grief and indignation. Mysie, after all her professions of friendship, to use her in this way! And Harry and Gillian, who should have kept the others within bounds!

Slowly she crossed the lawn, just as Lady Merrifield, the other two aunts, and Fergus, all came out from the glass door of the drawing-room. Aunt Jane, a trim little dark-eyed woman, looking at two and forty much the same as she might have done at five and twenty; and Aunt Adeline, pretty and delicately fair, with somewhat of the same grace as Lady Merrifield, but more languor, and an air as if everything about her were for effect. Though not specially fond of theses aunts, Dolores was glad to have them as witnesses of her ill-usage.

'There stands Dolly, like a statue of Diana, dart in hand,' exclaimed Aunt Adeline.

'Yes,' said Dolores; 'I wish to know, Aunt Lilias, if Wilfred and Valetta are to call me names, and shoot arrows at me?'

'What do you mean, my dear?'

'They came at me while I was sitting quietly reading—there—and shot at me, and called me such horrid names I can't repeat them, and ran away. Then the others, Gillian and Harry and all, would not listen to me, but shut themselves up in an out-house and shouted at me.'

'I think there must be some mistake, Dolores,' said her aunt. 'Where are they?'

'Out beyond there,' said Dolores, pointing in the direction in which Fergus was running.

Lady Merrifield set off with her, and the other two ladies followed more slowly.

'I thought it would not do,' said Aunt Jane.

'Lily's children are so rough,' added Aunt Adeline.

'I am not so sure that the fault is theirs,' was the reply. 'She is a priggish little puss, who wants shaking up.'

'Ah! here come the hordes,' sighed Adeline, shrinking a little, as the entire population, summoned by Fergus, came pouring forth to meet the advancing mother.

'How is this, Wilfred? Have you been shooting arrows at your cousin?'

'Mama!' cried Valetta, indignantly, 'he did not shoot at her; he only pretended, and shot the old crocodile-bench. He never meant any more. It was only play.'

'Have you not been forbidden to shoot in the direction of any person?'

'Nor I didn't!' said Wilfred. 'I only shot the crocodile. I never tried to hit her. She is quite big enough to miss.'

'And she did look such a nice Croat, mamma,' added Valetta. 'We were scouts out of the Thorn Fortress, Willie and I, and it was such a jolly dodge to steal upon one of the enemy.'

'You should have warned her.'

Then it would not have been a surprise,' said Val, seriously.

'Was she not at play with you?'

'No, mamma,' said Mysie. 'We asked her, and she would not. I say,' pausing in consternation, 'Dolores, was it you that came and called at the door of the Wolf's passage?'

'Of course. I wanted to show Gillian how Wilfred behaved to me.'

I thought it was Fergus come home to be the enemy.'

'Didn't you know her voice?' asked the mother

'We were all making such a noise ourselves in the dark,' said Gillian, 'that there was no hearing any one; and Primrose was rather frightened, so that Hal was attending to her. Indeed, Dolores, I am very sorry. If we had guessed that it was you, we would have opened the door at once, and then you would have known that it was all fun and play, and not have troubled mamma about it.'

'Wilfred and Valetta knew,' said Dolores, rather sullenly.

'Oh! but it was such fun,' said Val.

'It was fun that became unkindness on your part,' said her mother. 'You ought not to have kept it up without warning to her. And what do I hear about names? I hope that was also misunderstanding of the game. What did you call her?'

'Only a Croat,' said Valetta, indignantly, 'and a Black Brunswicker.'

'Was that it, Dolores?'

'Perhaps,' she muttered, disconcerted by a laugh from her Aunt Jane.

'I do not know what you took them for,' said Lady Merrifield, 'but you see some part of this trouble arose from a mistake on you part. Now, Wilfred and Valetta, remember that is not right to force a person into play against her will. And as to the shooting near, but not at her, you both know perfectly well that it is forbidden. So give me your bow, Wilfred. I shall keep it for a week, that you may remember obedience.'

Wilfred looked sullen, but obeyed. Dolores could not call her aunt unjust, but as she look round, she met glances that made her think it prudent to shelter herself among the elders. Aunt Jane asked what the game was.

'The Thorn Fortress,' said Gillian. 'It comes out of that delightful S.P.C.K. book so called, where, in the 'Thirty Years' War,' all the people of a village took refuge from the soldiers in a field in the middle of a forest guarded by a tremendous hedge of thorns. Val had it for a birthday present, and the children have been acting it ever since.'

'It has quite put out the Desert Island passion, which used to be a regular stage in these children's lives. Every voyage we have taken, somebody has come to ask whether there was any hope of being wrecked on one.'

'Fergus even asked when we crossed from Dublin,' said Gillian.

'He was put up to that, to keep up the tradition,' observed Harry.

On reaching the house, the elders proceeded to five o'clock tea in the drawing-room, the juniors to gouter in the dining-room. As Dolores entered, she beheld a row of all her five younger cousins drawn up looking at her as if she had committed high treason, and she was instantly addressed—

'Tell-take tit!' began Valetta.

'Sneak!' cried Wilfred.

'I will call her Croat!' added Fergus.

'Worse than Croat! Bashi Bazouk!' exclaimed Valetta.

'Worse than Crow!' chimed in Primrose.

'Oh, Dolores! How could you?' said Mysie.

'To get poor Willie punished!' said Val.

Dolores stood her ground. 'It was time to speak when it came to shooting arrows at me.'

'Hush! hush! Willie,' cried Mysie. 'I told you so. Now Dolores, listen. Nobody ever tells of anybody when it is only being tiresome and they don't mean it, or there never would be any peace at all. That's honour! Do you see? One may go to Gill sometimes.'

'One's a sneak if one does,' put in Wilfred; but Mysie, unheeding went on—

'And Gill can help without a fuss or going to mamma.'

'Mamma always knows,' said Val.

'Mamma knows all about everything,' said Mysie. 'I think it's nature; ad if she does not always take notice at the time, she will have it out sooner or later.' Then resuming the thread of her discourse: 'So you see, Dolly, we have made up our minds that we will forgive you this time, because you are an only child and don't know what's what, and that's some excuse. Only you mustn't go on telling tales whenever an evident happens.'

Dolores thought it was she who ought to forgive, but the force against her was overpowering, though still she hesitated. 'But if I promise not to tell,' she said, 'how do I know what may be done to me?'

'You might trust us,' cried Mysie, with flashing eyes.

'And I can tell you,' added Wilfred, 'that if you do tell, it will be ever so much the worse for you—girl that you are.'

'War to the knife! Cried Valetta, and everybody except Mysie joined in the outcry. 'War to the knife with traitors in the camp.'

Mysie managed to produce a pause, and again acted orator. 'You see, Dolores, if you did tell, it would not be possible for mamma or Gill to be always looking after you, and I couldn't do you much good—and if all these three are set against you, and are horrid to you, and I couldn't do you much good—horrid to you, you'll have no peace in your life; and, after all, we only ask of you to give and take in a good-natured sort of way, and not to be always making a fuss about everything you don't like. It is the only way, I assure you.'

Dolores saw the fates were against her, and said—

'Very well.'

'You promise?'

'Yes.'

'Then we forgive you, and here's the box of chocolate things Aunt Ada brought. We'll have a cigar all round and be friends. Smoke the pipe of peace.'

Dolores afterwards thought how grand it would have been to have replied, 'Dolores Mohun will never be intimidated;' but the fact was that her spirit did quail at the thought of the tortures which the two boys might inflict on her if Mysie abandoned her to their mercy, and she was relieved, as well as surprised to find that her offence was condoned, and she was treated as if nothing had happened.

Meantime Aunt Jane was asking in the drawing-room, 'How do you get on?'

'Fairly well,' was Lady Merrifield's answer. 'We shall work together in time.'

'What does Gill say?' asked the aunt, rather mischievously.

'Well,' said the young lady, 'I don't think we get on at all, not even poor Mysie, who works steadily on at her, gets snubbed a dozen times a day, and never seems to feel it.'

I hoped her father would have sent her to school,' said Aunt Adeline. 'I knew she would be troublesome. She has all her mother's pride.'

'The proudest people are those who have least to be proud of,' said Aunt Jane.

'School would have hardened the crust and kept up the alienation,' said Lady Merrifield.

'Perhaps not. It might teach her to value the holidays, and learn that blood is thicker than water,' said Miss Jane.

'It is always in reserve,' added Miss Adeline.

'Yes, Maurice told her to send her if I grew tired of her, as he said,' replied Lady Merrifield, 'but of course I should not think of that unless for very strong reasons.'

'Oh, mamma!' and Gillian remained with her mouth open.

'Well?' said Aunt Jane.

'I meant to have told you mamma, but Mr. Leadbitter came in about the G.F.S. and stopped me, and I have never seen you to speak to since. Yesterday you know, I stayed from evensong to look after the little ones, and you said Dolores might do as she pleased, so she stayed at home. The children were looking at the book of Bible Pictures, and it came out that Dolly knew nothing at all about Joshua and the walls of Jericho, nor Gideon and the lamps in the pitchers, nor anything else. Then, when I was surprised, she said that it was not the present system to perplex children with the myths of ancient Jewish history.'

Gillian was speaking rapidly, in the growing consciousness that her mother had rather have had this communication reserved for her private ear—and her answer was, 'Poor child!'

'Just what I should expect!' said Aunt Jane.

'Probably it was jargon half understood, and repeated in defence of her ignorance,' said Lady Merrifield. 'She is an odd mixture of defiant loyalty and self-defence.'

'What shall you do about this kind of talk?' asked her sister.

'One must hear it sooner or later,' said Harry.

'That is true,' returned his mother, 'but I suppose Fergus and Primrose did not hear or understand.'

'Oh no, mamma. I know they did not, for they were squabbling because Primrose wanted to turn over before Fergus had done with Gideon.'

'Then I don't think there is any harm done. If it comes before Mysie or Val I will talk to them, and I mean to take this poor child alone for a little while each day in the week and try to get at her.'

'There's another thing,' said Gillian. 'Is she to go down with me always to Casement Cottages on Sunday afternoons when I take the class?'

'To teach or to learn?' ironically exclaimed Aunt Jane.

'Neither,' said Gillian. 'To chatter to Constance Hacket. They both spoke to me about it yesterday before I went home, and I believe Constance has written a note to her to ask her today! Fancy, that goose told me my sweet cousin was a dear, and that we didn't appreciate her. Even Miss Hacket gave me quite a lecture on kindness and consideration to an orphan stranger.'

'Not uncalled for, perhaps,' said Aunt Jane. 'I hope you received it in an edifying manner.'

'Now, Aunt Jane! Well, I believe I said we were as kind as she would let us be, especially Mysie.'

Lady Merrifield here made the move to conduct her sisters to their rooms; Miss Mohun detained her when they had reached hers, and had left Adeline to rest on her sofa. The two, though very unlike, had still the habits of absolute confidential intimacy belonging to sisters next in age.

'Lily,' said Miss Mohun, 'Gillian spoke of a note. Did Maurice give you any directions about this child's correspondence?'

'You know I did not see him. I was so much disappointed. I would give anything to have talked her over with him.'

'I am not sure that you would have gained much. I doubt whether he knows much about her, poor fellow. But the letters?'

'He wrote that she had been a good deal with Professor Sefton's family, and he thought they might like to keep up their intercourse.'

'Nothing about Flinders? He ought to have warned you.'

'No. Who is he?'

'A half-brother—no, a step-brother to poor Mary. He was the son by a former marriage of her father's first wife, and has been always a thorn in their sides. He is a low, dissipated kind of creature; writes theatrical criticisms for third-rate papers, or something of that kind, when he is at his best. I believe Mary was really fond of him, and helped him more than Maurice could well bear, and since her death the man has perfectly pestered him with appeals to her memory. I really believe one reason he welcomed this post was to get out of his reach.'

'You always know everything Jenny. Now how did you know this?'

'I called once in the midst of an interview between him and Mary. And afterwards I came on poor Maurice when he was really very much provoked, and had it all out; ad since her death—well, I saw him get a begging letter from the man, and he spoke of it again. I wish I had advised him to warn you against the wretch.'

'I don't suppose he knows where the child is. He is no relation to her, you say?'

'None at all, happily. But on that occasion, when I was an uncomfortable third, Maurice was very angry that she should have been allowed to call him Uncle Alfred; and Mary screwed up her little mouth, and evidently rather liked the aggravation to Mohun pride.'

'Poor Maurice, so he had a skeleton! Well, I don't see how it can hurt us. The man probably knows nothing about us, and even if he could trace the girl, he must know that she can do nothing for him.'

'You had better keep an eye on her letters. He is quite capable of asking for the poor child's half sovereigns. I wish Maurice had given you authority.'

'Perhaps he spoke to her about it. At any rate, what he said of the Seftons is quite sufficient to imply that there is no sanction to any other correspondence.'

'That is true. Really, Lily, I believe you are the most likely person to do some good with her, though I don't think you know what you are in for. But Gillian does!'

'I believe it is very good for the children to have to exercise a little forbearance. In spite of all our knocking about the world, our family exclusiveness is pretty much what ours was in the old Beechcroft days—'

'When Rotherwood and Robert Mohun were out only outsiders and the Westons came on us like new revelations!'

'It is curious to look back on,' said Lady Merrifield. 'It seems to me that the system, or no system, on which we were brought up was rather passing away even then.'

'Specks we growed,' said Jane. 'What do you call the system?'

'Just that people thought it their own business to bring up their children themselves, and let the actual technical teaching depend upon opportunities, whereas now they get them taught, but let the bringing up take it chance.'

'People lived with their children then—yes, I see what you mean, Lily. Poor Eleanor, intending with all her might to be a mother to us, brought us up, as you call it, with all her powers; but public opinion would never have suffered us to get merely the odd sort of teaching that she could give us. It was regular, or course; but oh! do you remember the old atlas, with Germany divided into circles, and everything as it was before the Congress of Vienna?'

'You liked geography; I hated it.'

'Yes, I was young enough to come in for the elder boys' old school atlases, which had some sense in them. It seems to me that we had more the spirit of working for ourselves according to our individual tastes than people have now. We learnt, they are taught.'

'Well! and what did we learn?'

'As much as we could carry,' said Aunt Jane, laughing. 'Assimilate, if you like it better; and I doubt if people will turn out to have done more now. What becomes of all the German that is crammed down girl's throats, whether they have a turn for languages or not? Do they ever read a German book? Now you learnt it for love of Fouque and Max Piccolomini, and you have kept it up ever since.'

'Yes, by cramming it down my children's throats. But what I complain of, Jane, in the young folk that come across me is not over-knowledge, but want of knowledge—want of general culture. This Dolores, for instance, can do what she has been taught better than Mysie, some tings better than Gillian, but she has absolutely no interest in general knowledge, not even in the glaciers which she has seen; she does not know whether Homer wrote in Greek or Latin, considers "Marmion" a lesson, cannot tell a planet from a star, and neither knows nor cares anything about the two Napoleons. Now we seem to have breathed in such things. Why! I remember being made into Astyanax for a very unwilling Andromache (poor Eleanor) for caress, and being told to shudder at the bright copper coal-scuttle, before Harry went to school.'

'Of course poor Maurice could not cultivate his child. Yet, after all, we grew up without a mother; but then the dear old Baron lived among us, and knew what we were doing, instead of shutting us up in a schoolroom with some one, with only knowledge, not culture. Those very late dinners have quite upset all the intelligent intercourse between fathers and children not come out.'

'Yes, Jasper and I have felt that difficulty. But after all, Jenny, when I look back, I cannot say I think ours was a model bringing up. What a strange year that was after Eleanor's marriage!'

'Ah! you felt responsible and were too young for it, but to me it was a very jolly time, though I suppose I was an ingredient in your troubles. Yes, we brought ourselves up; but I maintain that it was better alternative than being drilled so hard as never to think of anything but arrant idling out of lesson-time.'

'Lessons should be lessons, and play, play, is one of the professor's maxims to which that poor child has treated us.'

'Ah! on that system, where would have been all your grand heraldic pedigrees? I've got them still.'

'Oh! Jenny, you good old Brownie, have you? How I should like to look at them again and show them the Gillian and Mysie. Do you remember the little scalloped line we drew round all the true knights?'

'Ay! and where would have been all your romancing about Sir Maurice de Mohun, the pride of his name? For my part, I much prefer a cavalier dead two hundred years ago as the object of a girl's enthusiasm—if enthusiasm she must have—to the existing lieutenant, or even curate.'

'Certainly; I should be sorry to have been bred up to history with individual interest and romance squeezed out of it. You see when Jasper came home from the Crimea he exactly continued mine.'

'You have fulfilled your ideal better than falls to the lot of most people, even to the item of knighthood.'

'Ah! you should have heard us grumble over the expense of it. And, after all, I dare say Sir Maurice found his knight's fee quite as inconvenient! Oh!' with a start, 'there's the first bell, and here have I been dawdling here instead of minding my business! But it is so nice to have you! I day, Jenny, we will have one of our good old games at threadpaper verses and all the rest tonight. I want you to show the children how we used to play at them.'

And the party played at paper games for nearly two hours that evening, to the extreme delight of Gillian, Mysie, and Harry, to say nothing of their mother and aunts, who played with all their might, even Aunt Adeline lighting up into droll, quiet humour. Only Dolores was first bewildered, then believed herself affronted, and soon gave up altogether, wondering that grown-up people could be so foolish.

CHAPTER VII
G.F.S.

The first thought of Dolores was that she should see Constance Hacket, when she heard 'Hurrah for a holiday!' resounding over the house.

As she came out of her room Mysie met her. 'Hurrah! Aunt Jane has got us a holiday that we may help get ready for the G.F.S.! Mamma has sent down notes to Miss Vincent and Mr. Pollock. Oh! jolly, jolly!'

And, obvious of past offences, Mysie caught her cousin's arms, and whirled her round and round in an exulting dance, extremely unpleasant to so quiet a personage. 'Don't!' she cried. 'You hurt! You make me dizzy!'

'My certie, Miss Mysie!' exclaimed Mrs. Halfpenny at the same time, 'ye're daft! Gae doon canny, and keep your apron on, for if I see a stain on that clean dress—'

Mysie hopped downstairs without waiting to hear the terrible consequences.'

Aunt Adeline did not come down to breakfast, but Aunt Jane appeared, fresh and glowing, just in time for prayers, having been with Gillian and Harry to survey the scene of operations, and to judge of the day, which threatened showers, the grass being dank and sparkling with something more than September dews.

'The tables must be in the coach-house,' said Lady Merrifield. 'Happily, our equipages are not on a large scale, and we must not get the poor girls' best things drenched.'

'No; and it is rather disheartening to have to address double ranks of umbrellas,' said Aunt Jane. 'Is the post come?'

'It is always infamously late here,' said Harry. 'We complained, as the appointed hour is eight, but we were told 'all the other ladies were satisfied.' I do believe they think no one not in business has a right to wish for letters before nine.'

'Here it comes, though,' said Gillian; and in due time the locked letter-bag was delivered to Lady Merrifield, and Primrose waited eagerly to act as postman.

It was not the day for the Indian mail, but Aunt Jane expected some last directions, and Lady Merrifield the final intelligence as to the numbers of each contingent of girls. Dolores was on the qui vive for a letter from Maude Sefton, and devoured her aunt and the bag with her eyes. She was quite sure that among the bundle of post-cards that were taken out there was a letter. Also she saw her aunt give a little start, and put it aside, and when she demanded. 'Is there no letter for me?' Lady Merrifield's answer was,' None, my dear, from Miss Sefton.'

Hot indignation glowed in Dolores's cheeks and eyes, more especially as she perceived a look pass between the two aunts. She sat swelling while talk about the chances of rain was passing round her, the forecasts in the paper, the cats washing their faces, the swallows flying low, the upshot being that it might be fine, but that emergencies were to be prepared for. All the time that Lady Merrifield was giving orders to children and servants for the preparations, Dolores kept her station, and the instant there was a vacant moment, she said fiercely —

'Aunt Lilias, I know there is a letter for me. Let me have it.'

'Your father told me you might have letter from Miss Sefton, and there is none from her,' said Lady Merrifield, with a somewhat perplexed air.

'I may have letters from whom I choose.'

'My dear, that is not the custom in general with girls of your age, and I know your father would not wish it. Tell me, is there any one you have reason to expect to hear from?'

Dolores had an instinct that all the Mohuns were set against the person she was thinking of, but she had an answer ready, true, but which would serve her purpose.

'There was a person, Herr Muhlwausser, that father ordered some scientific plates from — of microscopic zoophytes. He said he did not know whether anything would come of it, but, in case it should, he gave my address, and left me a cheque to pay him with. I have it in my desk upstairs.'

'Very well, my dear,' said Lady Merrifield, 'you shall have the letter when it comes.'

'The men are come, my lady, to put up the tables. Miss Mohun says will you come down?' came the information at that moment, sweeping away Aunt Lilias and everybody else into the whirl of preparation; while Dolores remained, feeling absolutely certain that a letter was being withheld from her, and she stood on the garden steps burning with hot indignation, when

Mysie, armed with the key of the linen-press, flashed past her breathlessly, exclaiming—

'Aren't you coming down, Dolly? 'Tis such fun! I'm come for some table-cloths.'

This didn't stir Dolores, but presently Mysie returned again, followed by Mrs. Halfpenny, grumbling that 'A' the bonnie napery that she had packed and carried sae mony miles by sea and land should be waured on a wheen silly feckless taupies that 'tis the leddies' wull to cocker up till not a lass of 'em will do a stroke of wark, nor gie a ceevil answer to her elders.'

Mysie, with a bundle of damask cloths under her arm, paused to repeat, 'Are you not coming Dolly? Your dear Miss Constance is there looking for you?'

This did move Dolores, and she followed to the coach-house, where everybody was buzzing about like bees, the tables and forms being arranged, and upon them dishes with piles of fruit and cakes, contributions from other associates. All the vases, great and small, were brought out, and raids were made on the flower garden to fill them. Little scarlet flags, with the name of each parish in white, were placed to direct the parties of guests to their places, and Harry, Macrae, and the little groom were adorning the beams with festoons. The men from the coffee-tavern supplied the essentials, but the ladies undertook the decoration, and Aunt Adeline, in a basket-chair, with her feet on a box, directed the ornamentation with great taste and ability. Constance Hacket had been told off to make up a little bouquet to lay beside each plate, and Dolores volunteered to help her.

'Well, dearest, will you come to me on Sunday?'

'I don't know. I have not been able to ask Aunt Lilias yet, and Gillian was very cross about it.'

'What did she say?'

'She said she did not think Aunt Lilias approved of visiting and gossiping on Sunday.'

'Oh! now. What does Gillian do herself?' said Constance in a hurt voice. 'She does come and teach, certainly, but she stays ever so long talking after the class is over. Why should we gossip more than she does?'

'Yes; but people's own children can do no wrong.'

There Constance became inattentive. Mr. Poulter had come up, and wanted to be useful, so she jumped up with a handful of nosegays to instruct him in laying them by each plate, leaving Dolores to herself, which she found dull. The other two, however, came back again, and the work continued, but the talk was entirely between the gentleman and lady, chiefly about music for the choral society, and the voices of the singers, about which Dolores neither knew nor cared.

By one o'clock the long tables were a pretty sight, covered with piles of fruit and cakes, vases of flowers and little flags, establishments of teacups at intervals, and a bouquet and pretty card at every one of the plates.

Then came early dinner at the house, and such rest as could be had after it, till the pony-chaise, waggonette, and Mrs. Blackburne's carriage came to the door to convey to church all whom they could carry, the rest walking.

The church was a sea of neat round hats, mostly black, with a considerable proportion of feathers, tufts, and flowers. On their dark dresses were pinned rosettes of different-coloured ribbon, to show to which parish they belonged. There was a bright, short service, in which the clear, high voices of the multitudinous maidens quite overcame those of the choir boys, and then an address, respecting which Constance pronounced that 'Canon Fremont was always so sweet,' and Dolores assented, without in the least knowing what it had been about.

Constance, who had driven down, was to have kept guard, in the walk from church, over the white-rosed Silverton detachment; but another shower was impending, and Miss Hacket, declaring that Conny must not get wet, rushed up and packed her into the waggonette, where Dolores was climbing after, when at a touch from Gillian, Lady Merrifield looked round.

'Dolores,' she said, 'you forget that Miss Hacket walked to church.'

Dolores turned on the step, her face looking as black as thunder, and Miss Hacket protested that she was not tired, and could not leave her girls.

'Never mind the girls, I will look after them; I meant to walk. Don't stand on the step. Come down,' she added sharply, but not in time, for the horses gave a jerk, and, with a scream from Constance, down tumbled Dolores, or would have tumbled, but that she was caught between her aunt and Miss Hacket, who with one voice admonished her never to do that again, for there was nothing more dangerous. Indeed, there was more anger in Lady Merrifield's tone than her niece had yet heard, and as there was no making out that there was the least injury to the girl, she was forced to walk home, in spite of all Miss Hacket's protestations and refusals, which had nearly ended in her exposing herself to the same peril as Dolores, only that Lady Merrifield fairly pushed her in and shut the door on her. Nothing would have compensated to Dolores but that her Constance should have jumped out to accompany her and bewail her aunt's cruelty, but devotion did not reach to such an extent. Her aunt, however, said in a tone that might be either apology or reproof—

'My dear, I could not let poor Miss Hacket walk after all she has done and with all she has to do today.'

Dolores vouchsafed no answer, but Aunt Jane said—

'All which applies doubly to you, Lily.'

'Not a bit; I am not run about like all of you,' she answered, brightly. 'Besides, it is such fun! I feel like Whit Monday at Beechcroft! Don't you remember the pink and blue glazed calico banners crowned with summer snowballs? And the big drum? What a nice-looking set of girls! How pleasant to see rosy, English faces tidily got up! They were rosy enough in Ireland, but a great deal too picturesque. Now these are a sort of flower of maidenhood—'

'You are getting quite poetical, Lily.'

'It's the effect of walking in procession—there's something quite exhilarating in it; ay, and of having a bit of old Beechcroft about me. Do tell me who that lady is; I ought to know her, I'm sure! Oh, Miss Smith, good morning. How many girls have you brought? Oh! the crimson rosettes, are they? York and Lancaster?—indeed. I'm glad we have some shelter for them; I'm afraid there is another shower. Have you no umbrella, my dear? Come under mine.'

It was a fierce scud of hail, hitting rather than wetting, but Dolores had the satisfaction of declaring the edges of her dress to be damp and going off to change it, though Aunt Jane pinched the kilting and said the damp was imperceptible, and Wilfred muttered, 'Made of sugar, only not so sweet.'

In fact, she hoped that Constance, who had told of her hatred to these great functions and willingness to do anything to avoid them, would avail herself of the excuse; but though the young lady must have seen her go, she never attempted to follow; and Dolores, feeling her own room dull, came down again to find the drawing-room empty, and on the next gleam of sunshine, she decided on going to seek her friend.

What a hum and buzz pervaded the stable-yard! There was a coach-house with all its great doors open, and the rows of girls awakening from their first shy and hungry silence into laughter and talking. There were big urns and fountains steaming, active hands filling cups, all the cousins, all their congeners, and four or five clergymen acting as waiters, Aunt Adeline pouring out tea a the upper table for any associate who had time to swallow it, and Constance Hacket talking away to a sandy-haired curate, without so much as seeing her friend! Only Wilfred, at sight of his cousin again, getting up a violent mock cough, declaring that he thought she had gone to bed with congealed lungs or else Brown Titus, as the old women called it. His mother, however, heard the cough—which, indeed, was too remarkable a sound not to attract any one—and with a short, sharp word to him to take care, she put Dolores down under Aunt Ada's wing, and provided her with a lovely peach and a delicious Bath bun. Constance just looked up and nodded, saying, 'You dear little thing, I couldn't think what was become of you,' and then went on with her sandy curate, about—what was it?—Dolores know not, only that it seemed very interesting, and she was left out of it.

Down came the rain, a hopeless downpour, and there was a consultation among the elders, some laughing, some doubtful looks, and at last Harry, with Macrae and one of the curates, disappeared. Then grace was sung, and speeches followed—one by the rector, Mr. Leadbitter, fatherly and prosy;—a paper read by the Branch Secretary, about affairs in general; and a very amusing speech by Miss Mohun, full of anecdotes of example and warning. 'You know,' she said, 'all the school story-books end—when the grown up books marry their people—with the good girl going out to service under her young lady, and there she lives happy ever after! But some of us know better! We don't know how far the marrying ones always do live very happy ever after—'

'For shame, Jenny!' muttered Lady Merrifield.

'But,' went on Miss Mohun, 'even you that have been lucky enough to get under your own young ladies know that life here is all new beginnings at the bottom, just as when you were very proud of yourselves for getting out of the infant school, you found it was only being at the bottom of the upper one; and I can tell the twelve-year-olds—I see some of them—that it is often a finer thing to be at the head of the school than the last in the house. Ay, you've got to work up there again, and it is a long business and a steady business, but it is to be done. I knew a girl, thirty-five years ago, that my sister-in-law took from school, and she was not a genius either, and I am quite sure she could not do rule-of-three, nor tell what is the capital of Dahomey, as I dare say every one here can do, but I'll tell you what she did, and that was, her best, and there she has been ever since; and the last time I saw her was sitting up in her housekeeper's room, in her silk gown, with her master's grandchildren hanging about her, respected and loved by us all. And I knew another, a much clever girl at school, with prettier ways to begin with, but—I'm sorry to say, her finger were too clever, and it was not very happy ever after, though she did right herself.' And then Aunt Jane went on to the difficulties of having to deal with such quantities of pots and pans, and knives and forks, and cloths and brushes, each with a use of its very own, just as if she had been a scullery-maid herself; telling how sense and memory must be brought to bear on these things just as much as in analyzing a sentence, and how even those would not do without the higher motive of faithfulness to Him whose servants we all are. Her finish was a picture of the roving servant girl, always saying, 'I don't like it,' and always seeking novelty, illustrated by her experience of a little maid who left one place because she could not sleep alone, and another because the little girl slept with her, a third because it was so lonesome, and a fourth because it was so noisy, and quitted her fifth within a half year because she could not eat twice cooked meat.

Aunt Jane varied her voice in the most comical way, and the girls, as well as all her audience, laughed heartily.

'Bravo, Jenny!' said a voice close to her, and a gentleman with a rather bald head, a fluffy, light beard touched with white, dancing eyes, and a slim, youthful figure, was seen standing in the group.

Lady Merrifield and her sisters cried with one glad voice, 'Oh! Rotherwood!' holding out their hands.

'Yes. I found I'd a few hours between the trains, so I ran down to look you up. I met Harry at the house, and he told me I should find Jane qualifying for the female parliament.'

'It's such a pity you should fall on all this turmoil,' said Aunt Ada.

'Pity! I wouldn't have missed Jenny's wisdom for the world. What is it, Lily? Temperance, or have you set up a Salvation Army?

'G.F.S., of course, you Rotherwood of old! And now you are come, you shall save me from what has been my bugbear for the last week. You shall give the premiums.'

'Come, it's no use making faces and pretending you know nothing about it,' added Miss Mohun. 'I know very well that Florence is deep in it!'

'Ay, they'll have you over to repeat that splendid harangue about pots and pans!' said he, bowing at Lady Merrifield's introductions of him to the bystanders, and obediently accepting the sheaf of envelopes, while Mr. Leadbitter made it known that the premiums would be given by the Marquess of Rotherwood. Certainly it was a much more lively business than if Lady Merrifield had performed it, for he had something droll to observe to each girl. One he pretended to envy, telling her he had worked hard for may a year, and never got such a card as that for it—far less five shillings. Another he was sure kept her pans bright, and always knew which was which; a very little one was asked if she had gone from her cradle, and so on, always sending them away with a broad smile, and professing great respect for the three seven-year-card maidens who came up last. Then in a concluding speech he demanded—where were the premiums for the mistresses, who, he was quite sure, deserved them quite as much or more than the maids!

While everybody was still laughing, Lady Merrifield asked Mr. Leadbitter to explain that as it was still raining hard, she must ask all to adjourn to the great loft over the stable, where they could enjoy themselves. Each associate was to gather her own flock and bring them in order. Lady Merrifield said she would lead the way, Lord Rotherwood coming with her, picking up little Primrose in his arms to carry her upstairs to the loft.

Every one was moving. Dolores was among a crowd of strangers. She heard them saying how delightful Lord Rotherwood was, and charming and handsome and graceful Lady Merrifield, with her beautiful eyes. It worried Dolores, who thought it rather foolish to be pretty, except in the case of persecuted orphan, and, moreover, admiration of her aunt always seemed to her disparagement of her mother. And where was Constance?

She followed the stream, and, climbing some stairs, came out into a large, long, empty hay-loft, over what had once been hunting stables—the children's wet-day play-place. The deputation dispatched to the house had managed to get up there the schoolroom piano, and one of the curates sat down to it, and began playing dance music, while Miss Mohun, Miss Hacket, and the other ladies began arranging couples for a country dance—all girls, of course, except that Lord Rotherwood danced with the tiny premium girl, and Harry with Primrose. Wilfred and Fergus could not be incited to make the attempt; Mysie offered herself to Dolores, but in vain. 'I hate dancing,' was all the answer she got, and she went off to persuade Lois, the nursery girl. Constance Hacket arranged herself on a chair, and looked out from between two curates; there was no getting at her.

Then there came a pause; Lord Rotherwood spoke to Gillian, and must have asked her to point Dolores out, for presently he made his way to the little dark figure in the window, and, kindly laying his hand on her shoulder, asked whether she had heard from her father yet.

'No, I suppose you can't,' he added. 'It is a great break-up for you; but you are a lucky girl to be taken in here! It reminds me of what Beechcroft used to be to me when I was a stray fish, though not quite so lonely as you are. Make the most of it, for there aren't many in these days like Aunt Lily there!'

'He little knows,' thought Dolores, as a waltz began to be played.

'They want an example,' he said. 'Come along. You know how, I'm sure—a Londoner like you!'

Pairs were whirling about the floor in full career in a short time, to the astonishment of other maidens who had never seen dancing in their lives. Dolores, afraid to refuse, and certainly flattered, really was wonderfully exhilarated and brightened by her career wither good-natured cousin.

'I do believe Cousin Rotherwood has shaken her out of the dumps,' observed Gillian to Aunt Jane, who returned—

'He can do it if any one can.'

The funny thing was the effect upon Constance, who, in the next pause, shook off her curates, advanced to Dolores, who was recovering her breath under the window, called her a dear thing whom she had not been able to get to all this time, sat rather forward with an arm round her waist for the next half-hour, and, when Sir Roger de Coverley was getting up, proposed that they should be partners, but not till she had seen Lord Rotherwood pair himself off with Mysie.

'I must,' said he to Lady Merrifield, 'it's so like dancing with honest Phyl.'

'The greatest compliment you could have, Mysie,' said her mother, looking very much pleased.

The last yellow patches of evening sunshine on the sloping roof faded; watches were looked at, the music turned to the National Anthem, everybody stood up, or stood still, and sung it. Then at the close, Mr. Leadbitter stood by the piano and said—

'One word more, my young friends. Some of you may have been surprised at this evening's amusement, but we want you to understand that there is no harm in dancing itself, provided that the place, the manner, and the companions are fit. I hope that you will all prove the truth of my words, by not taking this pleasant evening as an excuse for running into places of temptation. Now, good night, with many thanks to Lady Merrifield for the happy day she has given us.'

A voice added, 'Three cheers for Lady Merrifield!' and the G.F.S. showed itself by no means backward in the matter of cheering. There was a hunting up of ulsters and umbrellas; one associate after another got her flock together, and clattered downstairs, either to get into vans, to walk to the station, or to disperse to their homes in the town.

Meantime Lord Rotherwood had time to explain that he was on his way to fetch his wife home from some German baths, where she had gone to recruit after the season; and, as he meant to cross at night, had come to spend a few hours with his cousin. There was still an hour to spare, during which Lady Merrifield insisted that he must have more solid food than G.F.S. provided.

'Lily,' said Miss Mohun, as the elders walked to the house together, 'it strikes me that Rotherwood could satisfy your mind about that letter. He would know the handwriting. You remember a certain brother—very much in law—of Maurice's?'

'I have reason to do so,' said Lord Rotherwood. 'You don't mean that he has been troubling Lily?'

'No; but from the nature of the animal it is much to be apprehended that he will,' said Miss Mohun, 'if he knows that the child is here.'

'In fact,' said Lady Merrifield, 'Jane has made me suppress, till examination, a letter to her, in case it should be from him. It is a horrid thing to do. What do you think, Rotherwood?'

'There should be no correspondence. Did not Maurice warn you? Then he ought. Look here, Lily. His wife—under strong compulsion from the fellow, I should think—begged me to find some employment for him. I got him a secretaryship to our Board of—what d'ye call it? I'll do Maurice the justice to say that he was considerably cool about it; but the end of it was that there was an unaccountable deficit, and my lady said it served me right. I was a fool, as I always am, and gave way to the poor woman about not bringing it home to him. And she insisted on making it up to me by degrees—out of her literary work, I fancy—for I don't think Maurice knew the extent of the peculation. Ever since I've been getting begging letters from the fellow at intervals. If he had the impertinence to molest you, Lily, simply refer him to me.'

'And if he writes to the child?'

'Return him the letter. Say she can have no such thing without her father's consent.'

'Is this a case in point?' said Lady Merrifield, producing the letter.

'No,' said he, holding it up in the waning light. 'I know the fellow's fist too well! This is a gentleman's hand.'

'What a relief!' said Lady Merrifield.

'Nay, don't be in a hurry,' said Miss Mohun. 'Don't give it to her unopened. Your only safety is in maintaining your right to see all the child's letters, except what her father specified.'

'Don't you wish it was you, Brownie?' asked her cousin.

'I hate it!' said Lady Merrifield; 'but I suppose I ought! However, there's no harm in this, that's a comfort; it is simply that the gentleman that the house is let to has found this note to her somewhere about, and thinks she would wish to have it. I think it is her mother's hand. How nice of him!'

'Now, Lily, don't go and be too apologetic,' said Jane. 'Assert your right, or you'll have it all over again.'

'Without Jenny to do prudence,' said Lord Rotherwood, while Lady Merrifield, hardly hearing either of them, hurried on in search of her niece, but they would have been satisfied if they could have heard her.

'My dear, here's your letter. I am so sorry to have been too much hindered to look at it before. You must not mind, Dolly. I know it is very disagreeable; but every one who has the care of precious articles like young ladies is bound to look after them.'

Dolores took the letter with a kind of acknowledgement, but no more, for its detention offended her, and she was aggrieved at the prospect of future inspection, as another cruel stroke inflicted upon her.

Aunt Adeline was found in the drawing-room, where she had entertained such ladies as were afraid of the damp, or who did not approve of the dancing, and would not look on at it. Thence all went off to a merry meal, where the elders plunged into old stories, and went on capping each others' recollections and making fun, to the extreme delight of the young folk, who had often been entertained with tales of Beechcroft. Aunt Ada declared that she had not laughed so much for ten years, and Aunt Jane declared that it was too bad to lower their dignity and be so absurd before all these young things.

'It's having four of the old set together!' said Lord Rotherwood; 'a chance one doesn't get every day. I wonder how soon Maurice and Phyllis will meet.'

'It depends on whether the Zenobia touches at Auckland before going to the Fijis,' said Lady Merrifield.

'There is at least a sort of neighbourhood between them,' said Miss Mohun, 'though it may be about as close as between us and Sicily.'

'She is looking out for Maurice,' said Aunt Ada. 'She wrote, only it was too late, to propose his bringing Dolores to be at least nearer to him.'

'Just like Phyllis!' ejaculated the marquess. 'You have one of your flock with something of her countenance, Lily.'

'I am so glad you see it, Rotherwood. It is what I am always trying to believe in, and I hope the likeness is a little within as well as without—but we poor creatures who have been tumbled about the world get sophisticated, and can't attain to the sweet, blundering freshness of "Honest Simplicity."'

'It is a plant that must be spontaneous—can't be grown to order.'

'His lordship's carriage at the door,' announced Macrae.

'Ah, well! Trains must be caught, I suppose. I'm glad you're settled here, Lilias. I feel as if a sort of reflex of old Beechcroft were attainable now.'

'I hope it won't be a G.F.S. day next time you come!'

'Oh, it was very jolly. I shall bring my child next time, if I can get her out of the clutches of the governesses for a day, but it is a hard matter. They look daggers at me if I put my head into the schoolroom.'

'You always were a dangerous element there, you know.'

'Poor dear Eleanor! What did I not make her go through! But she never went the length of one of my lady's governesses, who declared that she had as much call to interfere in my stable, as I had with her schoolroom.'

'What mischief were you doing there?'

'Well, if you must know, I was enlivening a very dry and Cromwellian abridgement with some of Lily's old cavalier anecdotes, so Lily was at the bottom of it, you see.'

'But did she fall on you then and there?'

'No, no. I trust my beard is too grey for that. But she looked at me with impressive dignity such as neither poor little Fly nor I could stand, and afterwards betook herself to Victoria, who, I am happy to say, sent her to the right about.'

'As I am about to do,' said Lady Merrifield; 'for if you don't miss your train, it will be by cruelty to animals. No, you've not got time to shake hands with all that rabble. Be off with you.'

'Ah! I shall tell Victoria that if she sees me tomorrow it's all owing to your unpitying punctuality,' said he, shaking himself into his overcoat.

'Dear old fellow!' said Lady Merrifield, as she turned from the front door, while he drove off. 'He is like a gust of old Beechcroft air! But I should think Victoria had a handful.'

'She knew what she was doing,' said Aunt Ada. 'I always thought she married him for the sake of breaking him in.'

'And very well she has done it, too,' returned Aunt Jane. 'Only now and then he gets a holiday, and then the real creature breaks out again. But it is much better so. He would not have been of half so much good otherwise.'

Lady Merrifield looked from one to the other, but said no more, for all the young folks were round her; but every one was so much tired, children, servants, and all, that prayers were read early, and all went to their rooms. Yet, tired as she was, Lady Merrifield sat on in her sister Jane's room, in her dressing-gown, talking according to another revival of olden time.

'What did Ada mean about Rotherwood? Isn't he happy?'

'Oh yes, very happy; and it is much the best thing that could have happened. It is only another of the proofs that life is very long, especially for men.'

'Come, now, tell me all about it. You don't know how often I feel as if I had been buried and dug up again.'

'There are things one can't write about. Poor fellow! he never really wanted to marry anybody but Phyllis.'

'No! you don't mean it! I never knew it.'

'No, for you were in the utmost parts of the earth; and he was very good, so that I don't believe honest Phyl herself, or any one without eyes, guessed it; but he had it all out with our father, who begged him, almost on that allegiance he had always shown, to abstain from beginning about it. You see, not only are they first cousins, but our mother and his father both were consumptive, and there was dear Claude even then regularly breaking down every winter, and Ada needing to be looked after like a hothouse plan. I'm sure, when I think of the last generation of Devereuxes, I wonder so many of us have been tough enough to weather the dangerous age; and there had been an alarm or two about Rotherwood himself. Well, he was very good, half from obedience, half from being convinced that it would be a selfish thing, and especially from being wholly convinced that Phyl's feelings were not stirred. That was the way I came to know about it, for papa took me out for a drive in the old gig to ask what I thought about her heart, and I could truly and honestly say she had never found it, cared for Rotherwood just as she did for Reggie, and was not the sort to think whether a man was attentive to her. Besides, she was eighteen, and he thirty-one, and she thought him venerable. I believe, if he had asked her then, she might have taken him (because Cousin Rotherwood wished it), but she would have had to fall in love in the second place instead of the first. Well, he was very good, poor old fellow, except that by way of taking himself off, and diverting his mind, he went dear-stalking with such unnecessary vehemence that a Scotch mist was very nearly the death of him, and he discovered that he had as many lungs as other people. If you could only have seen our dear old father then, how distressed and how guilty he felt, and how he used to watch Phyllis, and examine Alethea and me as to whether she seemed more than reasonably concerned for Rotherwood had come and hit the right nail on the head he might have carried her off.'

'But he didn't.'

'No; for, you see, he was ill enough to convince himself, as well as other people, that he was a consumptive Devereux after all.'

'Oh yes! I remember the shock with which I heard like a doom that he was going the way of the others; and hen he and the dear Claude came out in his yacht to us at Gibraltar, and were so bright! We had a wonderful little journey into Spain together, and how Jasper enjoyed it! Little did I think I was never to see Claude here again. But it was true, was it not, that all Rotherwood's care gave the dear fellow much more comfort—perhaps kept him longer?'

'I am sure it was so. Rotherwood soon got over his own attachment—the missing an English winter was all he needed; but he would hear of nothing but devoting himself to Claude. Papa and Claude were both uneasy at his going off from all his cares and duties, but I believe—and Claude knew it—that he actually could not settle down quietly while Phyllis remained unmarried, and that having Claude to nurse and carry about from climate was the comfort of his life. Or, I believe, dear Claude would have been glad to have been left in peace to do what he could. Well, then Phyllis and Ada went to stay in the Close with Emily, and Ada wrote conscious letters and came home bridling and blushing about Captain May, so that we were quite prepared for his turning up at Beechcroft, but not at all for what I saw before he had been ten minutes in the house, that it was Phyllis that he meant, and had meant all along! Dear Harry! it almost made up for its not being Rotherwood. Well, poor Ada! It hadn't gone too deep, happily, and I opened her eyes in time to hinder any demonstration that could have left pain and shame—at least, I think so; but poor Ada has had too many little fits for one to have told much more than another. I believe Phyl did tell Harry that he meant Ada, but she let herself be convinced to the contrary; and the only objection I have to it is his having taken that appointment at Auckland, and carried her out of reach of any of us. However, it was better for Rotherwood, and when she was gone, and his occupation over with our dear Claude, his mother was always at him to let her see him married before she died. And so he let her have her way. No, don't look concerned. Lady Rotherwood is an excellent, good woman, just the wife for him, and he knows it, and does as she tells him most faithfully and gratefully. They are pattern-folk from top to toe, and so is the boy. But the girl! He would have his way, and named her Phyllis—Fly he calls her. She is a little skittish elf—Rotherwood himself all over; and doesn't he worship her! and doesn't he think it a holiday to carry her off to play pranks with! and isn't he happy to get amongst a good lot of us, and be his old self again!'

CHAPTER VIII
MY PERSECUTED UNCLE

Dolores was allowed to go to Casement Cottage on Sunday. It was always rather an awful thing to her to get through the paddock when the farmer's cattle turned out there. She did not mind it so much in the broad road and in the midst of a large party, with Hal among them, and no dogs; but alone with only one companion, and in the easy path which was the shortest way to the cottage, she winced and trembled at the little black, shaggy Scotch oxen, with white horns and faces that looked to her very wild and fierce.

'Oh, Gillian, those creatures! Can't we go the other way?'

'No; it is a great deal further round, and there's no time. They won't hurt. The farmer engaged not to turn out anything vicious here.'

'But how can he be sure?'

'Well, don't come if you don't like it,' said Gillian, impatiently. 'It is your own concern. I must go.'

Dolores did not like the notion of Constance being told that she would not come because she was afraid of the oxen. She thought it very unkind of Gillian, but she came, and kept carefully on the side furthest from the formidable animals. And Gillian really was forbearing. She did make allowances for the London-bred girl's fears; and the only thing she did was, that when one of the animals lifted up its head and looked, and Dolores made a spring as if to run away, she caught the girl's arm, crying, 'Don't! That's the very way to make him run after you.'

They got safe out of the paddock at last, and rang at the door. They were both kissed, Dolores with especial affectionateness, because the good ladies pitied her so much; and then while Miss Hacket and Gillian went off to their class, Constance took Dolores up into her own room, and began to tell her how disappointed she was not to have seen more of her at the Festival.

'But those curates would not let me alone. I was obliged to attend to them.'

And then she was very eager to know all about Lord Rotherwood, which rather amazed Dolores, who had been in the habit of hearing her father mention him as 'that mad fellow Rotherwood,' while her mother always spoke with contempt of people who ran after lords and ladies, and had been heard to say that Lord Rotherwood himself was well enough, but his wife was a mere fine lady.

But Dolores had a matter on which she was very anxious.

'Connie, do they always read one's letters first? I mean the old people, like Aunt Lily.'

'What! has she been reading your letters?'

'She says she always shall, except father's and Maude Sefton's, because papa spoke to her about that. She took a letter of mine the other day, and never let me have it till the evening, and I am sure Aunt Jane put her up to it.'

'You poor darling!' exclaimed Constance. 'Was it anything you cared about?'

'Oh no—not that—but there might be. And I want to know whether she has the right.'

'I should not have thought Lady Merrifield would have been so like an old schoolmistress. Miss Dormer always did, the old cat! where I went to school,' said Constance. 'We did hate it so! She looked over every one's letters, except parents', so that we never could have anything nice, except by a chance or so.'

'It is tyranny,' said Dolores, solemnly. 'I do not see why one should submit to it.'

'We had dodges,' continued Constance, warming with the history of her school-days, and far too eager to talk to think of the harm she might be doing to the younger girl. 'Sometimes, when a lot of us went to a shop with one of the governesses, one would slip out and post a letter. Fraulein was so short-sighted, she never guessed. We used to call her the jolly old Kafer. But Mademoiselle was very sharp. She once caught Alice Bell, so that she had to make an excuse and say she had dropped something. You see, she really had—the letter into the slit.'

'But that was an equivocation.'

'Oh, you darling scrupulous, long-worded child! You aren't like the girls at Miss Dormer's, only she drove us to it, you know. You'll be horribly shocked, but I'll tell you what Louie Preston did. There was a young man in the town whom she had met at a picnic in the holidays—a clerk, he was, at

So she awaited anxiously the next Sunday when Dolores's letter was to be written in her room. To tell the truth, Dolores could quite as easily have written in her own, and brought down the letter in her pocket, if she had been eager about the matter; but she was not, except under the influence of making a grievance. She had never written to Uncle Alfred in her life, nor he to her; and his visits to her mother had always led to something uncomfortable. Nor would she have thought about the subject at all if it had not been for the sore sense that she was cut off from him, as she fancied, because he belonged to her mother.

Nothing particular had happened that week. There had been no very striking offences one way or the other; she was working better with her lessons and understanding more of Miss Vincent's methods. She perceived that they were thorough, and respected them accordingly, and she had had the great satisfaction of getting more good marks for French and German than Mysie. She had become interested in 'The Old Oak Staircase,' and began to look forward to Aunt Lily's readings as the best part of the day. But she had not drawn in the least nearer to any of the family. She absolutely disliked, almost hated, the quarter of an hour which Aunt Lily devoted to her religious teaching every morning, though nobody was present, not even Primrose. She nearly refused to learn, and said as badly as possible the very small portions she was bidden to learn by heart, and she closed her mind up against taking in the sense of the very short readings and her aunt's comments on them. It seemed to her to be treating her like a Sunday-school child, and insulting her mother, who had never troubled her in this manner. Her aunt said no word of reproach, except to insist on attention and accuracy of repetition; but there came to be an unusual gravity and gentleness about her in these lessons, as if she were keeping a guard over herself, and often a greatly disappointed look, which exasperated Dolores much more than a scolding.

Mysie had left off courting her cousin, finding that it only brought her rebuffs, and went her own way as before, pleased and honoured when Gillian would consort with her, but generally paring with her younger sister.

Dolores, though hitherto ungracious, missed her attentions, and decided that they were 'all falseness.' Wilfred absolutely did tease and annoy her whenever he could, Fergus imitated him, and Valetta enjoyed and abetted him. These three had all been against her ever since the affair of the arrow; but Wilfred had not many opportunities of tormenting her, for in the house there was a perpetual quiet supervision and influence. Mrs. Halfpenny was sure to detect traps in the passage, or bounces at the door. Miss Vincent looked daggers if other people's lesson books were interfered with. Mamma had eyes all round, and nobody dared to tease or play tricks in her presence.

Hal, Gillian, and even Mysie always thwarted such amiable acts as putting a dead wasp into a shoe, or snapping a book in the reader's face; while, as to venturing into the general family active games, Dolores would have felt it like rushing into a corobboree of savages!

There was one wet afternoon when they could not even get as far as to the loft over the stables; at least the little ones could not have done so, and it was decided that it would be very cruel to them for all the others to run off, and leave them to Mrs. Halfpenny; so the plan was given up.

Partly because Lady Merrifield thought it very amiable in Mysie and Valetta to make the sacrifice, and partly to disperse the thundercloud she saw gathering on Wilfred's brow, she not only consented to a magnificent and extraordinary game at wolves and bears all over the house, but even devoted herself to keeping Mrs. Halfpenny quiet by shutting herself into the nursery to look over all the wardrobes, and decide what was to 'go down' in the family, and what was to be given away, and what must be absolutely renewed. It was an operation that Mrs. Halfpenny enjoyed so much, that it warranted her to be deaf to shrieks and trampling, and almost to forget the chances of gathers and kilting being torn out, and trap-doors appearing in skirts and pinafores.

All that time Dolores sat hunched up in her own room, reading 'Clare, or No Home,' and realizing the persecutions suffered by that afflicted child, who had just been nearly drowned in rescuing her wickedest cousin, and was being carried into her noble grandfather's house, there to be recognized by her golden hair being exactly the colour it was when she was a baby.

There were horrible growlings at times outside her door, and she bolted it by way of precaution. Once there was a bounce against it, but Gillian's voice might be heard in the distance calling off the wolves.

Then came a lull. The wolves and bears had rushed up and down stairs till they were quite exhausted and out of breath, especially as Primrose had always been a cub, and gone in the arms of Hal or Gillian; Fergus at last had rolled down three steps, and been caught by Wilfred, who, in his character of bear, hugged and mauled him till his screams grew violent. Harry had come to the rescue, and it was decided that there had been enough of this, and that there should be a grand exhibition of tableaux from the history of England in the dining-room, which of course mamma was to guess, with the assistance of any one who was not required to act.

Mama, ever obliging, hastily condemned two or three sunburnt hats and ancient pairs of shoes, to be added to the bundle for Miss Hacket's distribution, and let herself be hauled off to act audience.

'But where's Dolly?' she asked, as she looked at the assemblage on the stairs.

'Bolted into her room, like a donkey,' said Wilfred, the last clause under his breath.

'Indeed, mamma, we did ask her, and gave her the choice between wolves and bears,' said Mysie.

'Unfortunately she is bear without choosing,' said Gill.

'A sucking of her paws in a hollow tree,' chimed in Hal.

'Hush! hush!' said Lady Merrifield, looking pained; 'perhaps the choice seemed very terrible to a poor only child like that. We, who had the luck to be one of many, don't know what wild cats you may all seem to her.'

'She never will play at anything,' said Val.

'She doesn't know how to,' said Mysie.

'And won't be taught,' added Wilfred.

'But that's very dreadful,' exclaimed Lady Merrifield. 'Fancy a poor child of thirteen not knowing how to play. I shall go and dig her out!'

So there came a gentle tap at the closed door, to which Dolores answered—

'Can't you let me alone? Go away,' thinking it a treacherous ruse of the enemy to effect an entrance; but when her aunt said—

'Is there anything the matter, my dear? Won't you let me in?' she was obliged to open it.

'No, there's nothing the matter,' she allowed. 'Only I wanted them to let me alone.'

'They have not been rude to you, I hope.'

Dolores was too much afraid of Wilfred to mention the bouncing, so she allowed that no one had been rude to her, but she hated romping, which she managed to say in the tone of a rebuke to her aunt for suffering it.

However, Aunt Lily only smiled and said—

'Ah! you have not been used to wholesome exercise in large families. I dare say it seems formidable; but, my dear, you are looking quite pale. I can't allow you to stay stuffed up there, poking over a book all the afternoon. It is very bad for you. We are going to have some historical tableaux. They are to have one set, and I thought perhaps you and I would get up some for them to guess in turn.'

Dolores was not in a mood to be pleased, but she did not quite dare to say she did not choose to make herself ridiculous, and she knew there was authority in the tone, so she followed and endured.

So they beheld Alfred watching the cakes before the bright grate in the dining-room, and having his ears beautifully boxed. Also Knut and the waves, which were graphically represented by letting the wind in under the drugget, and pulling it up gradually over his feet, but these, Mysie explained, were only for the little ones. Rollo and his substitute doing homage to Charles the Simple, were much more effective; as Gillian in that old military cloak of her father's, which had seen as much service in the play-room as in the field, stood and scowled at Wilfred in the crown and mamma's ermine mantle, being overthrown by Harry at his full height.

The excitement was immense when it was announced that mamma had a tableau to represent with the help of Dolores, who was really warming a little to the interest of the thing, and did not at all dislike being dressed up with one of the boy's caps with three ostrich feathers, to accompany her aunt in hood and cloak, and be challenged by Hal, who had, together with the bow and papa's old regimental sword, been borrowed to personate the robber of Hexham. Everybody screamed with ecstasy except Fergus, who thought it very hard that he should not have been Prince Edward instead of a stupid girl.

So, to content all parties, mama undertook to bring in as many as possible, and a series from the life of Elizabeth Woodville was accordingly arranged.

She stood under the oak, represented by the hall chandelier, with Fergus and Primrose as her infant sons, and fascinated King Edward on the rocking-horse, which was much too vivant, for it reared as perpendicularly as it could, and then nearly descended on its nose, to mark the rider's feelings.

Then, with her hair let down, which was stipulated for, though, as she observed, nothing would make it the right colour, she sat desolate on the hearth, surrounded by as many daughters as could be spared from being spectators, as her youngest son was born off from her maternal arms by a being as like a cardinal as a Galway cloak, disposed tippet fashion, could make him.

She could not be spared to put up her hair again before she had to forget her maternal feelings and be mere audience, while her two sons were smothered by Mysie and Dolores, converted into murderers one and two by slouched hats. Fergus, a little afraid of being actually suffocated, began to struggle, setting off Wilfred, and the adventure was having a conclusion, which would have accounted for the authentic existence of Perkin Warbeck, when—oh horror! there was a peal at the door-bell, and before there was a moment for the general scurry, Herbert the button-boy popped out of the pantry passage and admitted Mr. Leadbitter, to whom, as a late sixth standard boy, he had a special allegiance, and, having spied him coming, hurried to let him in out of the rain instantly.

At least, such was the charitable interpretation. Harry strongly suspected that the imp had been a concealed spectator all the time, and had particularly relished the mischief of the discomfiture, which, after all, was much greater on the part of the Vicar than any one else, as he was a rather stiff, old-fashioned gentleman. Lady Merrifield only laughed, said she had been beguiled into wet day sports with the children, begged him to excuse her for a moment or two, and tripped away, followed by Gillian to help her, quickly reappearing in her lace cap as the graceful matron, even before Mr. Leadbitter had quite done blushing and quoting to Harry 'desipere in loco,' as he was assisted off with his dripping, shiny waterproof.

After all no harm would have been done if—Harry and Gillian being both off guard—Valetta had not exclaimed most unreasonably in her disappointment—

'I knew the fun would be spoilt the instant Dolores came in for it.'

'Yes, Mr. Murderer, you squashed my little finger and all but smothered me,' cried Fergus, throwing himself on Dolores and dropping her down.

'Don't! don't! you know you mustn't,' screamed valiant Mysie, flying to the rescue.

'Murderers! Murderers must be done for,' shouted Wilfred, falling upon Mysie.

'You shan't hurt my Mysie,' bellowed Valetta, hurling herself upon Wilfred.

And there they were all in a heap, when Gillian, summoned by the shrieks, came down from helping her mother, pulled Valetta off Wilfred, Wilfred off Mysie, Mysie off Fergus, and Fergus off Dolores, who was discovered at the bottom with an angry, frightened face, and all her hair standing on end.

'Are you hurt, Dolores? I am very sorry,' said Gillian. 'It was very naughty. Go up to the nursery, Fergus and Val, and be made fit to be seen.'

They obeyed, crestfallen. Dolores felt herself all over. It would have been gratifying to have had some injury to complain of, but she had fallen on the prince's cushions, and there really was none. So she only said, 'No, I'm not hurt, though it is a wonder;' and off she walked to bolt herself into her own room again, there to brood on Valetta's speech.

It worked up into a very telling and pathetic history for Constance's sympathizing ears on Sunday, especially as it turned out to be one of the things not reported to mamma.

And on that day, Dolores, being reminded of it by her friend, sent a letter to Mr. Flinders to the office of the paper for which he worked in London, to tell him that if he wished to write to her as he had promised he must address under cover to Miss Constance Hacket, Casement Cottage, as otherwise Aunt Lilias would certainly read all his letters.

CHAPTER IX
LETTERS

Constance Hacket was very much excited about the address to Dolores's letter to her uncle. She had not noticed it at the moment that it was written, but she did when she posted it; and the next time she could get her young friend alone, she eagerly demanded what Mr. Flinders had to do with the Many Tongues, and why her niece wrote to him at the office.

'He writes the criticisms,' said Dolores, magnificently; for though she despised pluming herself on any connection with a marquess, she did greatly esteem that with the world of letters. 'You know we are all literary.'

'Oh yes, I know! But what kind of criticisms do you mean? I suppose it is a very clever paper?'

'Of course it it,' said Dolores, 'but I don't think I ever saw it. Father never takes in society papers. I believe he does criticisms on plays and novels. I know he always has tickets for all the theatres and exhibitions.

She did not say how she did know it, for a pang smote her as she remembered dimly a scene, when her father had forbidden her mother to avail herself of escort thus obtained. Nor was she sure that the word all was accurately the fact; but it was delightful to impress Constance, who cried, 'How perfectly delicious! I suppose he can get any article into his paper!'

'Oh yes, of course,' said Dolores.

'Did your dear mother write in it?'

'No; it was not her line. She used to write metaphysical and scientific articles in the first-class reviews and magazines, and the Many Tongues is what they call a society paper, you know.'

'Oh yes, I know. There are charming things about the Upper Ten Thousand. They tell all that is going on, but I hardly ever can see one. Mary won't take in anything about Church Bells, and we get the Guardian when it is a week old, and my brother James has done with it.'

'Dear me! How dreadful!' said Dolores, who had been used to see all manner of papers come in as regularly as hot rolls. 'Why, you never can know anything! We didn't take in society papers, because father does not care for gossip or grandees. He has other pursuits. I can show you some of dear mother's articles. There's one called 'Unconscious Volition,' and another on the 'Progress of Species.' I'll bring them down next time I come.'

'Have you read them?'

'No; they are too difficult. Mother was so very clever, you know.'

'She must have been,' said Constance, with a sigh; 'but how did she get them published?'

'Sent them to the editor, of course,' said Dolores. 'They all knew her, and were glad to get anything that she wrote.'

'Ah! that is what it is to have an introduction,' sighed Constance.

'What! have you written anything?' cried Dolores.

'Only a few little trifles,' said Constance, modestly. 'It is a great secret, you know, a dead secret.'

'Oh! I'll keep it. I told you my secret, you know, so you might tell me yours.'

And so to Dolores were confided sundry verses and tales on which Constance had been wont to spend a good deal of her time in that pretty sitting-room. She had actually sent her manuscripts to magazines, but she had heard no more of one, and the other had been returned declined with thanks—all for want of an introduction. Dolores was delighted to promise that as soon as she heard from Uncle Alfred, she would get him to patronize them, and the reading occupied several Sunday afternoons. Dolores suggested, however, that a goody-goody story about a choir-boy lost in the snow would never do for the Many Tongues, and a far more exciting one was taken up, called 'The Waif of the Moorland,' being the story of a maiden, whom a wicked step-mother was suspected of murdering, but who walked from time to time like the 'Woman in White.' There was only too much time for the romance; for weeks passed and there was no answer from Mr. Flinders. It was possible that he might have broken off his connection with the paper, only then the letter would probably have been returned; and the other alternative was less agreeable, that it was not worth his while to write to his niece. While as to Maude Sefton, nothing was heard of her. Were her letters intercepted? And so the winter side of autumn set in. Hal was gone to Oxford, and there had been time for letters to come from Mr. Mohun, posted from Auckland, New Zealand, where he had made a halt with his sister, Mrs. Harry May, otherwise Aunt Phyllis. Dolores was very much pleased to receive her letter, and to have it all to herself; but, after all, she was somewhat disappointed in it, for there was really nothing in it that might not have been proclaimed round the breakfast-table, like the public letters from that quarter of the family who were at Rawul Pindee. It told of deep-sea soundings and investigations into the creatures at the bottom of the sea, of Portuguese men-of-war, and albatrosses; and there were some orders to scientific-instrument makers for her to send to them—a very improving letter, but a good deal like a book of travels. Only at the end did the writer say, 'I hope my little daughter is happy among her cousins, and takes care to give her aunt no trouble, and to profit by her kind care. Your three cousins here, Mary, Lily, and Maggie, are exceedingly nice girls, and much interested about you; indeed, they wish I had brought you with me.'

Dolores read her letter over and over and over, for the pleasure of having something all to herself, and never communicated a word about the miscroscopic monsters her father had described, but she drew her head back and reflected, 'He little knows,' when he spoke of her being happy among her cousins.

Lady Merrifield likewise received a letter, about which she did not say much to her children, but Miss Mohun, who had had a much longer one, came over for the day to read this to her sister. In point of fact, she had paired in childhood with her brother Maurice. She had been his correspondent in school and college days, and being a person never easily rebuffed, she had kept up more intercourse with him and his wife than any others of the family had done, and he had preserved the habit of writing to her much more freely and unreservedly than to any one else. So the day after the New Zealand letters came, just as the historical reading and needlework were in full force, the schoolroom door was opened, and a brisk little figure stood there in sealskin coat and hat.

Up jumped mamma. 'Oh! Jenny! Brownie indeed! How did you come? You didn't walk from the station?'

'Yes, why not? Otherwise I should have been too soon, and have disturbed the lessons,' said Aunt Jane, in the intervals of the greeting kisses. 'All well with the Indian folks?'

'Oh yes; they've come back from the emerald valleys of Cashmere, and Alethea has actually sent me a primrose—just like an English one—that they found growing there. They did enjoy it so. Have you heard from Maurice?'

'Yes, I thought you would like to hear about Phyllis, so, having enjoyed it with Ada, I brought it over for further enjoyment with you.'

'That's a dear old Brownie! We've a good hour before dinner. Shall we read it to the general public, or shall we adjourn to the drawing-room?'

"Oh! I assure you it is very instructive. Quite as much so as Miss Sewell's 'Rome.'"

And Aunt Jane, whom Gillian had aided in disrobing herself of her outdoor garments, was installed by the fire, and unfolded a whole volume of thin, mauve sheets in Mr. Mohun's tiny Greek-looking handwriting.

It was a sort of journal of his voyage. There were all the same accounts of the minute creatures that are incipient chalk, and their exquisite cells, made, some of coral, some of silex spicule from sponges; the some descriptions of phosphorescent animals, meduse, and the like, that Dolores had thought her own special treasure and privilege, only a great deal fuller, and with the scientific terms untranslated—indeed, Aunt Jane had now and then to stop and explain, since she had always kept up with the course of modern discovery. There was also much more about his shipmates, with one or two of whom Mr. Mohun had evidently made great friends. He told his sister a great deal about them, and his conversations with them, whereas he had only told Dolores abut one little midshipman getting into a scrape. Perhaps nothing else was to be expected, but it made her feel the contrast between being treated with real confidence and as a mere child, and it seemed to put her father further away from her than ever.

Then came the conclusion, written on shore—

'Harry May came on board to take me home with him. He is a fine, genial fellow and his welcome did one's heart good. I never did him justice before; but I see his good sense and superiority called into play out here. Depend upon it, there's nothing like going to the other end of the world to teach the value of home ties.'

'Well done, Maurice,' exclaimed Lady Merrifield; but she glanced at Dolores and checked herself.

Miss Mohun went on, 'Phyllis met me at the door of a pleasant, English-looking house, with all her tribe about her. She has the true 'honest Phyl' face still, carrying me back over some thirty or forty years of life, and as you would imagine, she is a capital mother, with all her flock well in hand, and making themselves thoroughly useful in the scarcity of servants; though the other matters do not seem neglected. The eldest can talk like a well informed girl, and shows reasonable interest in things in general; but Phyllis wants to put finishing touches to their education, and her husband talks of throwing up his appointment before long, as he is anxious to go home while his father lives. I wish I had gone to Stoneborough before coming out here, now that I see what a gratification it would have been if I could have brought a fresh report of old Dr. May. (Somehow, I think there has been a numbness or obtuseness about me all these last two years which hindered me from perceiving or doing much that I now regret, since either the change or the wholesome atmosphere of this house has wakened me as it were. Among these ungracious omissions is what I now am much concerned to think of, that I never went to see Lilias when I committed my child to her charge; nor talked over her disposition. Not that I really understand it as I ought to have done when the poor child was left to me. I take shame to myself when Phyllis questions me about her), but as I watch these children with their parents I am quite convinced that the being taken under Lily's motherly wing is by far the best thing that could have befallen Dolores, and that my absence is for her real benefit as well as mine.'

The part between brackets was omitted by Miss Mohun in the public reading, but the last sentence she did read, thinking it good for both parties to hear it. However, Dolores both disliked the conclusion to which her father had come, and still more that her aunt and cousins should hear it, though, after all, it was only Gillian and Mysie who remained to listen by the time the end of the letter was reached. The long words had frightened away Valetta as soon as her appointed task of work was finished.

Aunt Lily did not see the omitted sentence till the two sisters were alone together later in the afternoon. It filled her eyes with tears. 'Poor Maurice,' she said; 'he wrote something of the same kind to me.'

'I expect we shall see him wonderfully shaken up and brightened when he comes home. The numbness he talks of was half of it Mary's dislike to us all, only I never would let her keep me aloof from him.'

'I almost wish he had taken Dolores out to Phyllis. I am not in the least fulfilling his ideal towards her.'

'Nor would Phyllis, unless the voyage had had as much effect on her as it seems to have had upon Maurice. So you don't get on any better?'

'Not a bit. It is a case of parallel lines. We don't often have collisions— unless Wilfred gets an opportunity of provoking her.'

'Why don't you send that boy to school?'

'I shall after Christmas. He is quite well now, and to have him at home is bad both for himself and the others. He needs licking into shape as only boys can do to one another, and he is not a model for Fergus, especially since Harry has been away.'

'What does he do?'

'Nothing very brilliant, nor of the kind one half forgives for the drollery of it. Putting mustard into the custard was the worst, I think; inciting the dogs to bring the cattle down on the girls when they cross the paddock; shutting up their books when the places are found—those are the sort of things; putting that very life-like wild cat chauffe-pied with glaring eyes in Dolly's bed. I believe he does such things to all, but his sisters would let him torture them rather than complain, whereas Dolores does her best to bring them under my notice without actually laying an information, which she is evidently afraid to do. It is very unlucky that her coming should have been just when we had such an element about—for it really gives her some just cause of complaint.'

'But you say he is impartial?'

'Teasing is unfortunately his delight. He will even frighten Primrose, but I am afraid there is active dislike making Dolores his favourite victim; and then Val and Fergus, who don't tease actively on their own account, have come to enjoy her discomfiture.'

"And you go on the principle of 'tolerer beaucoup?'"

'I do; hoping that it is not laziness and weakness that makes me abstain from nagging about what is not brought before my eyes by the children or the police—I mean Gill, Halfpenny, and Miss Vincent. Then I scold, or I punish, and that I think maintains the principle, without danger to truth or forbearance. At least, I hope it does. I am pretty sure that if I punished Wilfred for every teasing trick I know, or guess at, he would—in his present mood—only become deceitful, and esprit de corps might make Val and Fergus the same, though I don't think Mysie's truth could be shaken any more than honest Phyl's.'

'Besides, mutual discipline is not a thing to upset. Lily, I revere you! I never thought you were going to turn out such a sensible mother.'

'Well, you see, the difficulty is, that what may work for one's own children may not work for other people's. And I confess I don't understand her persistent repulse of Mysie.'

'Nor of you, the nasty little cat!' said Aunt Jane, with a little fierce shake of the head.

'I do understand that a little. I am too unlike Mary for her to stand being mothered by me.'

'There must be some other influence at work for this perverseness to keep on so long. Tell me, did she take up with that very goosey girl, that Miss Hacket?'

'Oh yes; she goes there every Sunday afternoon. It is the only thing the poor child seem much to care about, and I don't think there can be any harm in it.'

'Humph! the folly of girl is unfathomable! Oh! you may say what you like—you who have thrown yourself into your daughters and kept them one with you. You little know in your innocence the product of an ill-managed boarding-school!'

'Nay,' said Lady Merrifield, a little hotly, 'I do know that Miss Hacket is one of the most excellent people in the world, a little tiresome and borne, perhaps, but thoroughly good, and every inch a lady.'

'Granted, but that's not the other one—Constance is her name? My dear, I saw her goings on at the G.F.S. affair—If she had only been a member, wouldn't I have been at her.'

'My dear Jenny, you always had more eyes to your share than other people.'

'And you think that being an old maid has not lessened their sharpness, eh! Lily? Well, I can't help it, but my notion is that the sweet Constance— whatever her sister may be—is the boarding-school miss a little further developed into sentiment and flirtation.'

'Nay, but that would be so utterly uncongenial to a grave, reserved, intellectual girl, brought up as Dolores has been.'

'Don't trust to that! Dolores is an interesting orphan, and the notice of a grown-up young lady is so flattering that it carries off a great deal of folly.'

'Well, Jenny, I must think about it. I hope I have done no harm by allowing the friendship—the only indulgence she has seemed to wish for; and I am afraid checking it would only alienate he still more! Poor Maurice, when he is trusting and hoping in vain!'

'Three year is a long time, Lily; and you have no had three months of her yet—'

The door opened at that moment for the afternoon tea, which was earlier than usual, to follow of Miss Mohun's reaching the station in time for her train. Lady Merrifield was to drive her, and it was the turn of Dolores to go out, so that she shared the refection instead of waiting for gouter. In the midst the Miss Hackets were announced, and there were exclamations of great joy at the sight of Miss Mohun; as she and Miss Hacket flew upon each other, and to the very last moment, discussed the all-engrossing subject of G.F.S. politics.

Nevertheless, while Miss Mohun was hurrying on her sealskin in her sister's room, she found an opportunity of saying, 'Take care, Lily, I saw a note pass between those two.'

'My dear Jenny, how could you? You were going on the whole time about cards and premiums and associates. Oh! yes, I know a peacock or a lynx is nothing to you, but how was it possible? Why, I was making talk to Constance all along, and trying to make Dolly speak of her father's letter.'

'I might retort by talking of moles and bats! Did you never hear of the London clergyman whose silver cream-jug, full of cream too, was abstracted by the penitent Sunday school boy whom he was exhorting over his breakfast-table?'

'I don't believe London curates have silver jugs or cream either!'

'A relic of past wealth, like St. Gregory's one silver dish, and perhaps it was milk. Well, to descend to particulars. It was done with a meaning glance, as Dolores was helping her on with her cloud, and was instantly disposed of in the pocket.'

'I wonder what I ought to do about it,' sighed Lady Merrifield, 'If I had seen it myself I should have no doubts. Oh! if Jasper were but here! And yet it is hardly a thing to worry him about. It is most likely to be quite innocent.'

'Well, then you can speak of the appearance of secrecy as bad manners. You will have her all to yourself as you go home.'

But when the aunts came downstairs, Dolores was not there. On being called, she sent a voice down, over the balusters, that she was not going.

Aunt Jane shrugged her shoulders. There was barely time to reach the train, so that it was impossible to do anything at the moment; but in the Merrifield family bad manners and disrespect were never passed over, Sir Jasper having made his wife very particular in that respect; and as soon as she came home in the twilight, she looked into the school-room, but Dolores was not there, and then into the drawing-room, where she was found learning her lessons by firelight.

'My dear, why did you not go with your Aunt Jane and me?'

'I did not want to go. It was so cold,' said Dolores in a glum tone.

'Would it not have been kinder to have found that out sooner? If I had not met the others in the paddock, and picked up Valetta, the chance would have been missed, and you knew she wanted to go.'

Dolores knew it well enough. The reason she was in this room was that all the returning party had fallen upon her; Wilfred had called her a dog in the manger, and Gillian herself had not gainsayed him—but the general indignation had only made her feel, 'what a fuss about the darling.'

'Another time, too,' added Lady Merrifield, 'remember that it would be proper to come down and speak to me instead of shouting over the balusters in that unmannerly way; without so much as taking leave of your Aunt Jane. If she had not been almost late for her train, I should have insisted.'

'You might, and I should not have come if you had dragged me,' thought, but did not say, Dolores. She only stood looking dogged, and not attempting the 'I beg your pardon,' for which her aunt was waiting.

'I think,' said Lady Merrifield, gently, 'that when you consider it a little, you will see that it would be well to be more considerate and gracious. And one thing more, my dear, I can have no passing of private notes between you and Constance Hacket. You see a good deal of each other openly, and such doings are very silly and missish, and have an underhand appearance such as I am sure your father would not like.'

Dolores burst out with, 'I didn't,' and as Primrose at this instant ran in to help mamma take off her things, she turned on her heel and went away, leaving Lady Merrifield trusting to a word never hitherto in that house proved to be false, rather than to those glances of Aunt Jane, which had been always held in the Mohun family to be a little too discerning and ubiquitous to be always relied on; and it was a satisfactory recollection that at the farewell moment when Miss Jane professed to have observed the transaction, she had been heard saying, 'Yes, it will never do to be too slack in inquiring into antecedents, or the whole character of the society will be given up,' and with her black eyes fixed full upon Miss Hacket's face.

CHAPTER X
THE EVENING STAR

'Oh, Connie dear, I had such a fright! Do you know you must never venture to give me anything when any one is there—especially Aunt Jane. I am sure it was her, she is always spying about?'

'Well, but dearest Dolly, I couldn't tell that she would be there, and when I got your letter I could not keep it back, you know, so I made Mary come up and call on Lady Merrifield for the chance of being able to give it to you—and I thought it was so lucky Miss Mohun was there, for she and Mary were quite swallowed up in their dear G.F.S.'

'You don't know Aunt Jane! And the worst of it is she always makes Aunt Lilias twice as cross! I did get into such a row only because I didn't want to go driving with the two old aunts in the dark and cold, and be scolded all the way there and back.'

'When you had a letter to read too!'

'And then Aunt Lily said all manner of cross things about giving notes between us. I was so glad I could say I didn't, for you know I didn't give it to you, and it wasn't between us.'

'You cunning child!' laughed Constance, rather amused at the sophistry.

'Besides,' argued Dolores, 'what right has she to interfere between my uncle and my friends and me?

'You dear! Yes, it is all jealousy!'

'I have heard—or I have read,' said Dolores, 'that when people ask questions they have no right to put, it is quite fair to give them a denial, or at least to go as near the wind as one can.'

'To be sure,' assented Constance, 'or one would not get on at all! But you have no told me a word about your letters.'

'Father's letter? Oh, he tells me a great deal about his voyage, and all the funny creatures they get up with the dredge. I think he will be sure to write a book about them, and make great discoveries. And now he is staying with

Aunt Phyllis in New Zealand, and he is thinking, poor father, how well off I must be with Aunt Lilias. He little knows!'

'Oh, but you could write to him, dearest!'

'He wouldn't get the letter for so long. Besides, I don't think I could say anything he would care about. Gentlemen don't, you know.'

'No! gentlemen can't enter into our feelings, or know what it is to be rubbed against and never appreciated. But your uncle! Was the letter from him?'

'Oh yes! And where do you think he is? At Darminster—editing a paper there. It is called the Darminster Politician. He said he sent a copy here.'

"Oh yes, I know; Mary and I could not think where it came from. It had a piece of a story in it, and some poetry. I wonder if he would put in my 'Evening Star.'"

'You may read his letter if you like; you see he says he would run over to see me if it were not for the dragons.'

'I wish he could come and meet you here. It would be so romantic, but you see Mary is half a dragon herself, and would be afraid of Lady Merrifield'—then, reading the letter,—'How droll! How clever! What a delightful man he must be! How very strange that all your family should be so prejudiced against him! I'll tell you what, Dolores, I will write and subscribe for the Darminster Politician my own self—I must see the rest of that story—and then Mary can't make any objection; I can't stand never seeing anything but Church Bells, and then you can read it too, darling.'

'Oh, thank you, Connie. Then I shall have got him one subscriber, as he asks me to do. I am afraid I shan't get any more, for I thought Aunt Lily was in a good humour yesterday, and I put one of the little advertisement papers he sent out on the table, and she found it, and only said something about wondering who had sent the advertisement of that paper that Mr. Leadbitter didn't approve of. She is so dreadfully fussy and particular. She won't let even Gillian read anything she hasn't looked over, and she doesn't like anything that isn't goody goody.'

'My poor darling! But couldn't you write and get your uncle to look at some of my poor little verses that have never seen the light?'

'I dare say I could,' said Dolores, pleased to be able to patronize. 'Oh, but you must not write on both sides of the paper, I know, for father and mother were always writing for the press.'

'Oh, I'll copy them out fresh! Here's the 'Evening Star.' It was suggested by the sound of the guns firing at the autumn manoevres; here's the 'Bereaved Mother's Address to her Infant:'

> 'Sweet little bud of stainless white,
> Thou'lt blossom in the garden of light.'

'Mary thought that so sweet she asked Miss Mohun to send it to Friendly Leaves, but she wouldn't—Miss Mohun I mean; she said she didn't think they would accept it, and that the lines didn't scan. Now I'm sure its only Latin and Greek that scan! English rhymes, and doesn't scan! That's the difference!'

'To be sure!' said Dolores, 'but Aunt Jane always does look out for what nobody else cares about. Still I wouldn't send the baby-verses to Uncle Alfred, for they do sound a little bit goody, and the 'Evening Star' would be better.'

The verses were turned over and discussed until the summons came to tea, poured out by kind old Miss Hacket, who had delighted in providing her young guests with buttered toast and tea cakes.

Dolores went home quite exhilarated and unusually amiable.

Her letter to her father was finished the next day. It contained the following information.

'Uncle Alfred is at Darminster. He is sub-editor to the Politician, the Liberal county paper. I do not suppose Aunt Lilias will let me see him, for she does not like anything that dear mother did. There is a childish obsolete tone of mind here; I suppose it is because they have never lived in London, and the children are all so young of their age, and so rude, Wilfred most especially. Even Gillian, who is sixteen, likes quite childish games, and Mysie, who is my age, is a mere child in tastes, and no companion. I do wish I could have gone with you.'

Lady Merrifield wrote by the same mail, 'Your Dolores is quite well, and shows herself both clever and well taught. Miss Vincent thinks highly of her abilities, and gets on with her better than any one else, except the daughter of our late Vicar, for whom she has set up a strong girlish friendship. She plainly has very deep affections, which are not readily transferred to new claimants, but I feel sure that we shall get on in time.'

Miss Mohun wrote, 'Lily and I enjoyed your letter together. Dolly looks all the better for country life, though I am afraid she has not learnt to relish it, nor to assimilate with the Merrifield children as I expected. I don't think Lily has quite fathomed her as yet, but 'cela viendra' with patience, only mayhap not without a previous explosion. I fancy it takes a long time for an only child to settle in among a large family. It was a great pity you could not see Lily yourself. To my dismay I encountered Flinders in the street at Darminster last week. I believe he is on the staff of a paper there, happily Dolly does not know it, nor do I think he knows where she is.'

In another three weeks, Constance was in the utmost elation, for 'On hearing the cannonade of the Autumn Manoeuvres' was in print, and Miss Hacket was so much delighted that justice should be done to her sister's abilities, that she forgot Mr. Leadbitter's disapproval, and ordered half a dozen copies of the Politician for the present, and one for the future.

Dolores, walking home in the twilight, could not help showing Gillian, in confidence, the precious slip, though it was almost too dark to read the small type.

'Newspaper poetry, I thought that always was trumpery,' said Gillian, making a youthfully sweeping assertion.

'Many great poets have begun with a periodical press,' said Dolores, picking up a sentence which she had somewhere read.

'I thought you hated English poetry, Dolly! You always grumble at having to learn it.'

'Oh, that is lessons.'

"'Il Penseroso,' for instance."

'This is a very different thing.'

'That it certainly is,' said Gillian, beginning to read—

> 'How lovely mounts the evening star
> Climbing the sunset skies afar.'

'What a wonderful evening! Why, the evening star was going up backward!'

'You only want to make nonsense of it.'

'It is not I that make nonsense!' said Gillian, 'why, don't you see, Dolly, which way the sun and everything moves?'

'This is the evening star,' said Dolores, sulkily. 'It was just rising.'

'I do believe you think it rises in the west.'

'You always see it there. You showed it to me only last Sunday.'

'Do you think it had just risen?'

'Of course the stars rise when the sun sets.'

Gillian could hardly move for laughing. 'My dear Dolores, you to be daughter to a scientific man! Don't you know that the stars are in the sky, going on all the time, only we can't see them till the sunlight is gone?'

But Dolores was too much offended to attend, and only grunted. She wanted to get the cutting away from Gillian, but there was no doing so.

'The mist is rising o'er the mead,
With silver hiding grass and reed;
'Tis silent all, on hill and heath,
The evening winds, they hardly breathe;
What sudden breaks the silent charm,
The echo wakes with wild alarm.
With rapid, loud, and furious rattle,
Sure 'tis the voice of deadly battle,
Bidding the rustic swain to fly
Before his country's enemy.'

'Did anybody ever hear of a sham fight in the evening?' cried the soldier's daughter indignantly. 'There, I can't see any more of it.'

'Give it to me, then.'

'You are welcome! Where did it come from? Let me look. C.H. Oh, did Constance Hacket write it? Nobody else could be so delicious, or so far superior to Milton.'

'You knew it all the time, and that was the reason you made game of it.'

'No, indeed it was not, Dolores. I did not guess. You should have told me at first.'

'You would have gone on about it all the same.'

'No, indeed, I hope not. I did not mean to vex you; but how was I to know it was so near your heart?'

'I ought to have known better than to have shown it to you! You are always laughing at her and me all over the house—and now—'

'Come, Dolly. I never meant to hurt your feelings. I will promise not to tell the others about it.'

No answer. There was something hard and swelling in Dolores's throat.

'Won't that do?' said Gillian. 'You know I can't say that I admire it, but I'm sorry I hurt you, and I'll take care the others don't tease you about it.'

Dolores made hardly any answer, but it was a sort of pacification, and Gillian said not a word to the younger ones. Still she thought it no breach of her promise, when they were all gone to bed, and she the sole survivor, to tell her mother how inadvertently she had affronted Dolores by cutting up the verses, before she knew whose they were.

'I am sorry,' said Lady Merrifield. 'Anything that tends to keep Dolores aloof from us is a pity.'

'But, mama, I had no notion whose they were.'

'You saw that she was pleased with them.'

'Yes, but that was the more ridiculous. Fancy the evening star climbing up—up—you know in the sunset!'

'Portentous, certainly! Yet still I wish you could have found it in your heart to take advantage of any feeler towards sympathy.'

'How could I pretend to admire such stuff?'

'You need not pretend; but there are two ways of taking hold of a thing without being untrue. If you had been a little wiser and more forbearing you need not have given Dolores such a shock as would drive her in upon herself. Depend upon it, the older you grow, the more dangerous you will find it to begin by hitting the blots.'

Gillian looked on in some curiosity when the next day good Miss Hacket, enchanted with her dear Connie's success, trotted up to display the lines to Lady Merrifield, who on her side felt bound to set an example alike of tenderness and sincerity, and was glad to be able to observe, 'The lines run very smoothly. This must be a great pleasure to her.'

'Indeed it is! Connie is so clever. I always say I can't think where she got it from; but we always tried to give her very advantage, and she was quite a favourite pupil at Miss Dormer's. Is not it a sweet idea, the stillness of the evening broken by the sounds of battle, and then it proving to be only our brave defenders?'

'Yes,' was the answer. 'I have often thought of that, and of what it might be to hear those volleys of musketry in earnest. It has made me very thankful.'

So Miss Hacket went away gratified, and Gillian owned that it would have been useless to wound the good lady's feelings by criticism, though her mother made her understand that if her opinion had been asked, or Connie herself had shown the verses, it would have been desirable to point out the faults, in a kindly spirit. The wonder was, how they could have found their way into the paper, and they were followed by more with the like signature.

Indeed, the great sensational tale, 'The Waif of the Moorland,' was being copied out of the books where it had been first written. Dolores had sounded Mr. Flinders on the subject, and he had replied that he could ensure its consideration by a publisher, but that her fair friend must be aware that an untried author must be prepared for some risk.

Constance could hardly abstain from communicating her hopes to her sister; but Mr. Leadbitter—to whom the poetry was duly shown—had given such a character of the Darminster Politician that Miss Hacket besought Constance to have no more to do with it. Besides, she was so entirely a lady, and so conscientious, that all her tender blindness would not have prevented her from being shocked at encouraging, or profiting by, a surreptitious correspondence.

Constance declared that Mr. Leadbitter's objection to the paper was merely political, and her sister was too willing that she should be gratified to protest any further. The copying had to be done in secret, since it was impossible to confess the hopes founded on Mr. Flinders, and it therefore lasted several weeks, each fresh portion being communicated to Dolores on Sunday afternoons. There were at first a few scruples on Constance's part whether this were exactly a Sunday occupation; but Dolores pronounced that 'the Sabbatarian system was gone out,' and after Constance had introduced the ghostly double of her vanished waif walking in a surpliced procession, she persuaded herself that there was a sufficient aroma of religion about the story to bring it within the pale of Sunday books.

The days were shortening so that Lady Merrifield had doubts as to the fitness of letting the girls return in the dark, but Gillian would have been grieved to relinquish her class, and the matter was adjusted by the two remaining till evensong, when there was sure to be sufficient escort for them to come home with.

Therewith arrived the holidays and Jasper, whose age came between those of Gillian and Mysie. Dolores had looked forward to his coming, for, by all the laws of fiction, he was bound to be the champion of the orphan niece, and finally to develop into her lover and hero. In 'No Home,' when Clare's aunt locked her up and fed her on bread and water for playing the piano better than her spiteful cousin Augusta, Eric, the boy of the family, had solaced her with cold pie and ice-creams drawn up in a basket by a cord from the window. He had likewise forced from his cruel mother the locket which proved Clare's identity with the mourning countess's golden-haired grandchild and heiress, and he had finally been rewarded with her hand, becoming in some mysterious manner Lord Eric.

Jasper, however, or Japs, as his family preferred to call him, proved to be a big, shy boy, not at all delighted with the introduction of a stranger among his sisters, neither golden-haired nor all-accomplished, only making him feel his home invaded, and looking at him with her great eyes.

'Is that girl here for good?' he asked, when he found himself with Harry and Gillian.

'Yes, of course,' said the cousin, 'while her father is away, and that is for three years.'

Jasper whistled.

'Aunt Ada said,' added Gillian, 'that if she got too tiresome, mamma had Uncle Maurice's leave to send her to school.'

'That would be no good to me,' said Jasper, 'for she would still be here in the holidays.'

'Has she been getting worse?' asked Harry.

'No, I don't know that she has,' said Gillian, 'except that she runs after that Constance more than ever. But, I say, Jasper, mamma says she is particularly anxious that there should be no teasing of her; and you can hinder Wilfred better than anybody can. She wants her to be really at home, and one—'

But though Jasper was very fond both of mother and sister, he would not stand a second-hand lecture, and broke in with an inquiry about chances of rabbit-shooting.

Among his juniors he heard more opinions and more undisguised, when the whole party had rushed out together to the stable-yard to inspect the rabbits and other live-stock.

'And Dolly says you are a fright,' sighed Mysie, condoling with a very awkward-looking puppy which she was nursing.

'She! she thinks everything a fright!' said Valetta.

'Except Constance,' added Wilfred.

'Who is ugliest of all!' politely chimed in Fergus.

'Oh, Japs, she is such a nasty girl—Dolly, I mean!' cried Valetta.

"You know you ought not to say 'nasty,'" exclaimed Mysie.

'Well, but she is!' insisted Val. 'She squashed a dear little ladybird, and said it would sting!'

'She really thought it would,' said Mysie.

At which the young barbarians shouted aloud with contempt, and Valetta added. 'She is afraid of everything—cows and dogs and frogs.'

'I got a whole match-box full of grasshoppers to shut up in her desk and make her squall,' said Wilfred, 'only the girls went and turned them out.'

'It was so cruel to the poor grasshoppers,' said Mysie. 'One had his horn broken, and dragged his leg.'

'What does she do?' asked Jasper.

'She's always cross,' said Fergus.

'And she won't play,' added Valetta. 'And never will lend us anything of hers.'

'And she's a regular sneak,' said Wilfred. 'She wants to tell of everything—only we stopped that and she doesn't dare now.'

'You see,' said Mysie, gravely, 'she has always lived alone and in London, and that makes her horribly stupid about everything sensible. We thought we should soon teach her to be nice; and mamma says we shall if we are patient.'

'We'll teach her, won't we, Japs!' said Wilfred, aside, in an ominous voice.

'She is only thirteen,' added Valetta, 'and she pretends to be grown up, and only to care for a grown-up young lady—that Constance Hacket.'

'Yes,' added Mysie, 'only think—they write poetry!'

'What rot it must be!' said Jasper. 'There's a man in my house that writes poetry, and don't they chaff him! And this must be ever so much worse.'

'Oh, that it is,' said Valetta. 'I heard Mr. Poulter and Miss Vincent laughing about it like anything.'

'But they get it put into print,' said Mysie, still impressed. 'Miss Hacket brought it up to give to mamma, and there's ever so much of it shut up in the drawing-room blotting-book with the malachite knobs. I can't think why they laugh—I think it is very pretty. Old Miss Hacket read me the one about "My Lost Dove."'

'Mysie always will stick up for Dolores,' said Valetta in a grumbling voice.

'I always meant her to be my friend,' said Mysie, disconsolately.

'Well, I'm glad she's not,' said Jasper. 'What a sell it would have been for me to find you chummy with a stupid, poetry-writing, good-for-nothing girl like that, instead of my jolly old Mice!'

And at that minute all Dolly's slights were fully compensated for!

There was a lurking purpose in the boys' minds that if Dolores would not join in fun, yet still fun should be extracted from her. Jasper had brought home a box of Japanese fireworks, and Wilfred, who was superintending his unpacking, proposed to light the serpent and place it in Dolores's path as she was going up to bed; but Jasper was old enough to reply that he would have no concern with anything so low and snobbish as such a trick. In fact, there was in Jasper's mind a decided line between bullying and teasing, which did not exist as yet in Wilfred's conscience. And, altogether, Dolores was in a state of mind that made her stiff letters to her father betray low spirits and discontent.

On Sunday, while waiting for the early dinner, Jasper and Mysie happened to be together in the drawing-room, and Mysie took the opportunity of showing her brother the different cuttings of poetry. The lines were smooth, and some had a certain swing in them such as Mysie, with an unformed taste, a love for Miss Hacket, and amazement that the words of a familiar acquaintance of her own should appear in print, genuinely admired. But the eyes of a youth exercised in 'chaffing' the productions of one of his fellow 'men' were infinitely more critical. Besides, what could be more shocking to the General's son than the confusion between the evening gun and the sham fight? And Mysie had been reduced to confusion for not detecting the faults, and then pardoned in consideration of being only a girl, by the time the gong summoned them to the Sunday roast beef.

The dinner over, the female part of the family, scampered headlong upstairs, while Harry repaired with his mother to her room to talk over a letter from his father respecting his plans on leaving Oxford. The other boys hung about the hall, until Gillian and Dolores came down equipped for walking. 'Hollo, Gill! All right! Where's Mysie? We'll be off! Mysie! Mice! Mouse! Val!'

'You must wait for them, Japs,' said Gillian. 'They are having their dresses changed; and, don't you remember, I always go to Miss Hacket's.'

'Botheration! What for?'

'You know very well.'

'Oh yes. To help her to write touching verses about the sweet dead dove, with voice and plumage soft as love, eh? Only, Gill, I'm afraid your memory is failing, if you don't know the evening gun from rifle practice.'

'Nonsense! that's no concern of mine,' said Gillian, opening the front door, very anxious to get Dolores away from hearing anything worse.

'Oh, that's your modesty. Only such a conjunction could have produced such a scene that the evening star came up backwards to look at it!'

'For shame, Jasper! How in the world did you get hold of that?'

'Too sweet a thing not to meet with universal fame,' said Jasper, to whom it was exquisite fun to assume that Gillian devoted her Sunday afternoons to the concoction of such poetry with Constance Hacket, and thus to revenge himself for his disgust and jealousy at having his favourite companion and slave engrossed. Wilfred hopped about like an imp in ecstasy, grinning in the face of Dolores, whom Gillian longed to free from her tormentors. The shout was welcome, as Mysie and Valetta came tearing down the drive after them.

'Japs! Japs! Oh, we couldn't come before because nurse would make us take off our Sunday serges. Come and let out the dogs. Mamma says we may see if there are any nice fir cones in the plantation to gild for the Christmas-tree.'

'And you won't come?' said Jasper. 'The Muses must meet. What a poem you will produce!
>   'Hear I a cannon or a rifle,
>   That is an unessential trifle!'

'What nonsense boys do talk!' said Gillian, turning her back on them with regret; for much as she loved her class, she better loved a walk with Jasper, and here was Dolores on her hands in a state of exasperation, believing her to have broken her promise, and muttering,

'You set him on.'

'No, indeed I never did! You know I promised.'

'There are plenty of ways of getting out of a promise.'

'Speak for yourself, Dolores.'

There were ten minutes of offended silence, and then Gillian said, 'This is nonsense! You may believe me, I was sorry I laughed at the first verses you showed me, and mamma said I ought not. We never spoke of it, but Miss Hacket has been giving mamma all the poems, and Jasper must have got at them. Don't you see?'

'Oh yes, you say so,' said Dolores, sulkily.

'You don't believe me!'

'You promised that your brothers should never hear of it.'

'I promised for myself. I couldn't promise for what was put into a newspaper and trumpeted all over the place,' said Gillian, really angry now.

Dolores could not deny this, but she was hurt by the word trumpeted; and besides, her own slippery behaviour was weakening her trust in other people's sincerity, and she only gave a kind of grunt; but Gillian, recovering herself a little, and remembering her mother's words, proceeded to argue. 'Besides, it was me whom Jasper meant to tease, not you.'

'I don't care which it was. He is as bad as the rest of them!'

Gillian attempted no more conciliation, and they arrived in silence at the Casement Cottages, where Constance was awaiting her friend in the greatest excitement; for she had despatched 'The Waif of the Moorland' to Mr. Flinders in the course of the week, and had received a letter from him in return, saying that a personal interview with the gifted authoress would be desirable.

'And I do long to see him; don't you, darling?

'It is very hard that he should be kept away from me,' said Dolores, trying to stir up some tender feelings.

'That it is, my poor sweet! I thought whether he could come to me for a merely literary consultation without Mary's knowing anything further about it, and then we could contrive for you to come down and meet him; but there are so many horrid prejudices that I suppose it would not be safe.'

'I don't see how I could come down here without the others. Aunt Lily won't let me come alone, and though it is holiday time, that is no good, for those horrid boys are always about, and I see that Jasper is going to be worse even than Wilfred.

Various ways and means were discussed, but no excuse seemed available for either Constance's going to Darminster, or for Mr. Flinders coming to Silverton, without exciting suspicion.

CHAPTER XI
SECRET EXPEDITION

'The Christmas-tree! Oh, mamma, do let it be the Christmas-tree. It is quite well. We've been to look at it.'

'Christmas-trees have got so stale, Val,' said Gillian.

'Rot!' put in Jasper.

'Oh, please, please, mamma,' implored Valetta, 'please let it be the dear old Christmas-tree! You said I should choose because it will be my birthday.'

'There is no need to whine, Val; you shall have your tree.'

'I'm so glad!' cried Mysie. 'The dear old tree is best of all. I could never get tired of it if I lived to be a hundred years old.'

'Such are institutions,' said their mother. 'I never heard of a Christmas-tree till I was twice your age.'

'Oh, mamma! How dreadful! What did you do?'

'I suppose it is all very well for you kids,' said Jasper, loftily, putting his hands in his pockets.

'Perhaps something may be found interesting eve: to the high and mighty elders,' observed Lady Merrifield.

'Oh! What, mamma?'

Mamma, of course, only looked mysterious.

'And,' added Val, 'mayn't we all go on a secret expedition and buy things for it?'

'We've all been saving up,' added Mysie; 'and everybody knows every single thing in all the shop at Silverton.'

'Besides,' added Gillian, 'the sconces will none of them hold, and almost all the golden globes got smashed in coming from Dublin, and one of the birds has its head off, and another has lost its spun-glass tail, and another its legs.'

'A bird of Paradise,' said Lady Merrifield, laughing; 'but wasn't there a tree at Malta decked with no apparatus at all?'

'Yes, but Alley and Phyl can do anything!'

'I think we must ask Aunt Jane—-'

There was a howl. 'Oh, please, mamma, don't let Aunt Jane get all the things! We do so want to choose.'

'You impatient monsters! You haven't heard me out, and you don't deserve it.'

'Oh, mamma, I beg your pardon!' 'Oh, mamma, please!' 'Oh, mamma, pray!' cried the most impatient howlers, dancing round her.

'What I was about to observe, before the interruption by the honourable members, was, that we might perhaps ask Aunt Jane and Aunt Ada to receive at luncheon a party of caterers for this same tree.'

'Oh! oh! oh!' 'How delicious!' 'Hooray!' 'That's what I call jolly fun!'

'And, mamma,' added Gillian, 'perhaps we might let Miss Hacket join. I know she wants to get up something for a G.F.S. class; but mamma was attending to Primrose, and the brothers burst in.

'There goes Gill, spoiling it all!' exclaimed Wilfred.

'That's always the way,' said Jasper. 'Girls must puzzle everything up with some philanthropic Great Fuss Society dodge.'

'I am sure, Jasper,' said Gillian, 'I don't see why it should spoil anything to make other people happy. I thought we were told to make feasts not only for our own friends—'

'Gill's getting just like old Miss Hacket,' said Wilfred.

'Or sweet Constance,' put in Jasper. 'She'll be writing poems next.'

'Hush! hush! boys,' said Lady Merrifield. 'I do not mean to interfere with your pleasure, 'but I had rather our discussions were not entirely selfish. Suppose, Gillian, we walked down to Casement Cottages, and consulted Miss Hacket.'

This was done, in the company of all the little girls, for Miss Hacket's cats, doves, and gingerbread were highly popular; moreover, Dolores was glad of a chance sight of Constance.

'My dear,' said Lady Merrifield, as Gillian walked beside her, 'you must be satisfied with giving Miss Hacket the reversion of our tree, and you and Mysie can go and help her. It will not do to make these kind of works a nuisance to your brothers.'

'I did not think Jasper would have been so selfish as to object,' said Gillian, almost tearfully.

'Remember that boys have a very short time at home, and cannot be expected to care for these things like those who work in them,' said Lady Merrifield. 'It will not make them do so, to bore them, and take away their sense of home and liberty. At the same time, they must not expect to have everything sacrificed to them, and so I shall make Jasper understand.'

'You won't scold him, mamma?'

'Can't you, any of you, trust me, Gill?'

'Oh! mamma! Only I didn't want him to think. I wouldn't do everything he liked, except that I don't want him to be unkind about those poor girls.'

Miss Hacket was perfectly enraptured at the offer of the reversion of the Christmas-tree and its trapping. Valetta's birthday was on the 28th of December and the tree was to be lighted on the ensuing evening for G.F.S. Moreover, the party would go to Rockstone as soon as an appointment could be made with Miss Mohun, to make selections at a great German fancy shop, recently opened there, and in full glory; and the Hacket sisters were invited to join the party, starting at a quarter to eight, and returning at a few minutes after seven, the element of darkness at each end only adding to the charm in the eyes of the children, and Valetta, with a little leap, repeated that it would be a real secret expedition.

'Very secret indeed,' said her mother, 'considering how many it is known to—'

'Yes, but it is, mamma, for everybody has a secret from everybody.'

The words made Constance and Dolores look round with a start from their colloquy under the shade of the window-curtains, but no one was thinking of them. Just as the plans were settled, Constance came forward, saying, 'Lady Merrifield, may I have dear Dolores to spend the day with me? We neither of us wish to join your kind party to Rockstone, and we should so enjoy being together.'

'I had much rather stay,' added Dolores.

'Very well,' said Lady Merrifield, reflecting that her sisters would be grateful for the diminution of the party, and that it would be easier to keep the peace without Dolores.

The defection was hailed with joy by her cousins, though they were struck dumb at her extraordinary taste in not liking shopping.

Jasper did look rather small when his mother assured him in private he might have trusted her to see that he was not to be incommoded with Gillian's girls, and he only observed, in excuse for his murmurs, that it made a man mad to see his sisters always off after some charity fad or other.

"'Always' being a few hours once a week," she said.

'Just when one wants her.'

'Look here, my boy,' she said, 'you don't want your sisters to be selfish, useless, fine ladies—never doing any one any good. If they take up good works, they can't drop them entirely to wait on you. Gillian does give up a great deal, and it would be kinder to forbear a little, and not treat all she does as an injury to yourself.'

'I only meant to get a rise out of her.'

'You are quite welcome to do that, provided it is done in good nature. Gill is quite sound stuff enough to be laughed at! But, I say, my Japs, I should prefer your letting Dolores alone; she has not learned to be laughed at yet, and has not come even to the stage for being taught to bear it.'

'She looks fit to turn the cream sour,' observed Jasper. 'I say, mamma, you don't want me to go on this shopping business, do you?'

'Not by any means, sir.'

Happily, the chance of a day's rabbit shooting presented itself at a warren some miles off, and Harry undertook the care of Wilfred, who gave his word of honour to obey implicitly and take no liberties with the guns. Fergus would gladly have gone with them, but he was still young enough to be sensible of the attractions of toy-shops. Only Primrose had to be left to the nursery, and there was no need to waste pity on her, for on such an occasion Mrs. Halfpenny would relax her mood, and lay herself out to be agreeable, when she had exhausted her forebodings about her leddyship making herself ill for a week gaun rampaging about with all the bairns, as if she was no better than one herself.

'I shall let Miss Mohun do most of the rampaging, nurse; but, if it is fine, will you take Miss Primrose into the town and let her choose her own cards. I have given her a florin, and if you make the most of that for her, she will be as happy as going with us.'

'That I will, my leddy. Bairns is easy content when ye ken how to sort 'em.'

'And, nurse, I believe there will be a box from Sir Jasper at the station. It may come home in the waggonette that takes us. Will you and Macrae get it safe into the store-room, for I don't want the children to see it too soon?'

There was nothing but satisfaction in the house on the morning of the expedition. The untimely candle-light breakfast was only a fresh element of delight, and so was the paling gas at the station, the round, red sun peeping out through a yellow break between grey sky and greyer woods; the meeting Miss Hacket in her fur cloak, the taking of the tickets, the coughing of the train, the tumbling into one of the many empty carriages, the triumphant start,—all seemed as fresh and delicious as if the young people had never taken a journey before in all their lives. The fog in the valleys, the sleepy villages, the half-roused stations, all gave rise to exclamations, and nothing was regretted but that the windows would get clouded over.

Even the waiting at the junction had its charms, for it was enlivened by a supplementary breakfast on rolls and milk! and at a few minutes past eleven the train was drawing up at Rockstone, and Aunt Jane, sealskins and all, was beckoning from the platform, hurrying after the carriage as it swept past, and holding out a hand to jump the party from the door.

There she was, ready to take them to the most charming and cheapest shops, where the coins burning in those five pockets would go the furthest. Go in a cab? No, I thank you, it is far more delightful to walk. So mamma and Miss Hacket were stowed away in the despised vehicle, to make the purchases that nobody cared about, or which were to be unseen and unknown till the great day; while Aunt Jane undertook to guide the young people through the town, for her house was at the other end of it securing the Christmas-cards on the way, if nothin' else. For, though all the cards and gifts to mamma, and a good many besides, were of domestic manufacture, some had to be purchased, and she knew, this wonderful woman, where to get cards of former seasons at reduced prices to suit their youthful finances.

Considerable patience was requisite before all the choices were made, and the balance cast between cards and presents, and Miss Mohun got her quartette past all the shop windows, to the seaside villa, shut in by tamarisks, which Aunt Adeline believed to be the only place that suited her health. Mamma and Miss Hacket had already arrived, and filled the little vestibule with parcels and boxes.

Then the early dinner! The aunts had anticipated their Christmas turkey for that goodly company to help them eat it, but afterwards there was only time for a mince pie all round; for more than half the work remained to be done by all except mamma, who would stay and rest with Aunt Ada, having finished all that could not be deputed.

However, first she had a conference in private with Aunt Jane, who undertook therein to come to Silverton for Valetta's birthday, and add astonishment and mystery sufficient to satisfy such of the public as were weary of Christmas-trees. She added, however, 'You will think I am always at you. Lily, but did you know that Flinders is living at Darminster?'

'No; but it is five and twenty miles off, and he has never troubled us.'

'Don't be too secure. He is in connection with that low paper—the Politician—which methinks, is the place where those remarkable poems of Miss Constance's have appeared.'

'Is it not the way of poetry of that calibre to see the light in county papers?'

'This seems to me of a lower calibre than is likely to get in without private interest.'

'But to my certain knowledge the child has neither written to, nor heard of the man all this time.'

'You don't know what goes on with her bosom friend.'

'I am certain Miss Hacket would connive at nothing underhand. Besides, I have never seen any thing sly or deceitful in poor Dolores. She will not make friends with us, that is all, and that may be our fault.'

'I only say, look out, you unsuspicious dame!'

'Now, Jenny, satisfy my curiosity as to how you know all this. I am sure I never showed you those effusions. We have had trouble enough about them, for the children cut them up in a way Dolores has never forgiven.'

'Oh! Miss Hacket sent them to me, to ask if 'Mollsey to her Babe' and 'The Canary' might not be passed on to Friendly Leaves. And as to Flinders, when I went to the G.F.S. Conference at Darminster I met the man full in the street, and, of course, I inquired afterwards how he came there. So there's nothing preternatural about it.'

'It is well you did not live two hundred years ago, or you would certainly have been burnt for a witch.'

'See what a witch I shall make on the 28th! But I hear those unfortunate children dancing and prancing with impatience on the stairs. I must go, before they have driven Ada distracted.'

What would the two aunts have said, could they have seen Dolores and Constance, at that moment partaking of the most elaborate meal the Darminster refreshment-room could supply, at a little round marble table, in company with Mr. Flinders! They had not been obliged to start nearly so early as the other party, as the journey was much shorter, and with no change of line, so they had quietly walked to the station by ten o'clock, arrived at Darminster at half-past eleven, and have been met by the personage whom Dolores recognized as Uncle Alfred. Constance was a little disappointed not to see something more distinguished, and less flashy in style, but he was so polite and complimentary, and made such touching allusions to his misfortunes and his dear sister, that she soon began to think him exceedingly interesting, and pitied him greatly when he said he could not take them to his lodgings—they were not fit for his niece or her friend, who had done him a kindness for which he could never be sufficiently grateful, in affording him a glimpse of his dear sister's child. It made Dolores wince, for she never could bear the mention of her mother, it was like touching a wound, and the old sensation of discomfort and dislike to her uncle's company began to grow over her again, now that she was not struggling against Mohun opposition to her meeting him. He lionized them about the town, but it was a foggy, drizzly day, one of those when the fringe of sea-coast often enjoys finer weather than inland places; the streets were very sloppy, and Dolores and Constance did not do much beyond purchasing a few cards and some presents at a fancy shop, as they had agreed to do, to serve as an excuse for their expedition in case it could not be kept a secret, and most of the visit was made in the waiting-room at the station, or walking up and down the platform. As to the grand point, Mr. Flinders told Constance that her tale was talented and striking, full of great excellence; she might hope for success equal to Ouida's—but that he had found it quite impossible to induce a publisher to accept a work by an unknown author, unless she advanced something. He could guarantee the return, but she must entrust him with thirty pounds. Poor Constance! it was a fatal blow; she had not thirty pounds in the world; she doubted if she could raise the sum, even by her sister's help. Then Mr. Flinders sighed, and thought that if he represented the circumstances, the firm might be content with twenty—nay, even fifteen. Constance cheered up a little. She did think she could make up fifteen, after the 21st, when certain moneys became due, which she shared with her sister. She would be left very bare all the spring—but what was that to the return she was promised? Only Mr. Flinders impressed on her the necessity of secrecy—even from her sister— since, he said, if he were once known to have obtained such terms for a young authoress, he should be besieged for ever!

'But, Uncle Alfred,' said Dolores, 'surely my father and mother, and all the other people I have known, did not pay to get their things published.'

'My dear niece, you speak as one who has been with persons of high and established fame—the literary aristocracy, in fact. The doors once opened, Miss Hacket will, like them, make her own terms; but such doors, like many others, are only to be opened by a silver key.'

There were other particulars which he talked over with the authoress in a promenade on the platform while Dolores was left in the waiting-room; but afterwards he indulged his niece with a tete-a-tete, asking her father's address, and mourning over the length of time it would take to obtain an answer from Fiji. Mr. Mohun had promised to help him, solemnly and kindly promised, for the sake of her whom they had both loved so much, and here he was, cut off and quite in extremity. Unfortunate as usual, through his determined enemies, a company in which he had shares had collapsed, he was penniless till his salary from the Politician became due in March. Meanwhile, he should be expelled from his lodging and brought to ruin if he could not raise a few pounds—even one.

Dolores had nearly two pounds in her purse. Her father had left her amply provided, and she had not much opportunity of spending. She knew he had seen the gold when she was shopping, and when she had paid for the refreshments, which of course she had found she had to do. With some hesitation she said, 'If thirty shillings would be of any good to you—'

'My dear, generous child, your dear mother's own daughter! It will be the saving of me temporarily! But among all your wealthy relatives, surely, considering your father's promise, you could obtain some advance until he can be communicated with!'

'If he is still in New Zealand, we could telegraph, and hear directly. He did not know how long he should be there, for the ship had something to be done to it.'

This did not suit Mr. Flinders. Such telegrams were very expensive, and it was too uncertain whether Mr. Mohun would be at Auckland. Surely, Lady Merrifield, whose husband was shaking the pagoda tree, would make an advance if she knew the circumstances.

'I don't think she would,' said Dolores, 'I don't think they are very rich. There is only one horse and one little pony, and my cousins have such very tiny allowances.'

'Haughty and poor! Stuck up and skimping. Yes, I understand. But I am not asking from her, only an advance, on your father's promise, which he would be certain to repay. Yes, quite certain! It is only a matter of time. It would save me at the present moment from utter ruin and destruction that would have broken your dear mother's heart. Oh! Mary, what I lost in you.' Then, as perhaps he saw reflection on Dolores's face, he added, 'She is gone, the only person who took an interest in me, so it matters the less, and when you hear again of your unhappy uncle you will know what drove him—'

'If it was only an advance—I have a cheque,' began Dolores. 'If seven pounds would do you any good—'

'It would be salvation!' he exclaimed.

'Father left it with me,' pursued Dolores, considering, 'in case Professor Muhlwasser went on with his great book of coloured plates of microscopic marine zoophytes, and sent it in. I was to keep this and pay with it—'

'Oh! Muhlwasser! you need not trouble about him. I saw his death in the paper a month ago.'

'Then I really think I might send you the cheque, and write to my father why I did so.'

'Ah! Dolly, I knew that your mother's daughter could never desert me.'

More followed of the same kind, tending to make Dolores feel that she was doing a heroically generous thing, and stifling the lurking sense in her mind that she had no right to dispose of her father's money without his consent. The December day began to close in, the gas was lighted, Constance was seen disconsolately peeping out at the waiting-room door to see whether the private conference were over. They joined her again, and Mr. Flinders discoursed about the envy and jealousy of critics, and success being only attained by getting into a certain clique, till she began to look rather frightened; but reassured by the voluble list of names and papers to which he assured her of recommendations. Then he began to be complimentary, and she, to put on the silly tituppy kind of face and tone wherewith she had talked to the curates at the festival. Dolores began to find this very dull, and to feel neglected, perhaps also cross, and doubts came across her whether she might not get into a dreadful scrape about the money, which she certainly had no right to dispose of. She at last broke in with, 'Uncle Alfred, are you quite sure Professor Muhlwasser is dead?'

'Bless your heart, child, he's as dead as Harry the Eighth,' said Mr. Flinders in haste;' died at Berlin, of fatty degeneration of the heart! Well, as I was saying, Miss Constance—'

'But, uncle, I was thinking—'

'Hush!' as a couple of ladies and a whole train of nurses and children invaded the waiting-room, 'it won't do to talk of such little matters in public places, you know. Would you not like a cup of tea, Miss Constance. Will you allow me to be your cavalier?'

People were beginning to arrive in expectation of the coming train, and talk was not possible in the throng; at least, Mr. Flinders did not make it so. At last the train swept up, and he was hurrying to find places for the ladies, when there was a moment's glimpse of a handsome moustached face at a smoking-carriage window. Dolores started, and had almost exclaimed, 'Uncle Reginald;' but before the words were out of her mouth, Mr. Flinders had drawn her on swiftly, among all the numbers of people getting out and getting in, hurled her into a distant carriage, handed Constance in after her, and muttering something about forgetting an appointment, he vanished, without any of the arrangements about foot-warmers that he had promised.

'Uncle Reginald!' again exclaimed Dolores, 'I am sure it was he!'

'Oh dear! What an escape!' answered Constance, breathless with surprise, and settling herself with disgust and difficulty next to a fat old farmer, as three or four more people entered and jammed them close together.

'Who is he?' she presently whispered.

'Colonel Mohun. His regiment is at Galway. I know he talked of getting over this winter if he possibly could; but Aunt Lily went away before the post was come in.'

'We shall have to take great care when we get out.'

Here the train started, and conversation in undertones became impossible, more especially as two of the farmers in the carriage were coming back from the Smithfield Cattle Show, and were discussing the prize oxen with all their might. It was very stuffy and close. Constance looked ineffably fastidious and uncomfortable, and Dolores gazed at the clouded window, and dull little lamp overhead, put in to enliven the deepening twilight. This avoiding of Uncle Reginald brought more before her mind a sense of wrong-doing than anything that had gone before. She was fond of this uncle, who always made her father's house his headquarters when in London, and used to play with her when she was a small child, and always to take her to the Zoological Gardens, till she declared she was too old to care for such a childish show, and then he and her father both laughed at her so much that she would never have forgiven anybody else; and she found he enjoyed it for his own sake far more than she did. However, he always did take her out for walks and sights that were sure to be amusing with him. Father, too, was quite bright and alive when he was in the house, and thus Dolores had nothing but pleasant associations connected with this uncle, and had heard of the chances of his coming like a ray of light, though without much hope, since the state of Ireland had prevented him from being able even to run over to take leave of her father. And now he was come, she must hide from him like a guilty thing! There was no spirit of opposition against him in her mind, and thus she could feel that she was doing something sad and strange. Moreover, she began to feel that her promise about the cheque had been a rash one, and the echo of her father's voice came back on her, saying, 'Surely, Mary, you know better than to believe a word out of Flinders's mouth.'

But then she thought of her mother's rare tears glistening in her eyes, and the answer, 'Poor Alfred! I cannot give him up. Everything has been against him.'

It was quite dark before Silverton was reached, at half-past five, with three quarters of an hour to spare before the other travellers were expected. Most of their fellow passengers had got out at previous stations, so that Constance was able to open the door and jump out so perilously before the train had quite stopped, that a porter caught her with a sharp word of reproof. She grasped Dolores's hand and scudded across the platform, giving the return tickets almost before the collector was ready. A cautious guard even exclaimed, 'What's those two young women up to?' but was answered at once, 'They're all right! That's nought but one of the old parson's daughters, as have been out with a return to Darminster.'

'A sweetheartin'?' demanded one of the bystanders, and there was a laugh.

Constance heard the tones and vulgar laugh, though not the words, and she was in such a panic as she hurried down the steps that she did not stop to look out for a cab. The place was small, and they were not very plentiful at any time, and she was mortally afraid, though she hardly knew why, of being over-taken and questioned by Colonel Mohun, who might know his niece, though he would not know her; but Dolores was tired, and had a headache, and did not at all like the walk in the dirt, and fog, and dark, after turning from the gas lit station.

'We were to have a cab, Constance.'

'We can't,' was the answer, still hurrying on. 'He would come out upon us.'

'He is much more likely to overtake us this way!' said Dolores, thinking of her uncle's long strides.

'Well, we can't turn back now!' said Constance, getting almost into a run, which lasted till they were past the paddock gate. Dolores, panting to keep up with her, had half a mind to turn up there and go straight home; but there might be any number of oxen in the way, and almost worse, she might meet Jasper and Wilfred, or if Uncle Reginald overtook her, what would he think?

The pair slackened their pace a little when they had satisfied themselves that the break in the dark hedge beside them was the gate. They heard wheels, and presently saw the lamps of a cab, bearing down, halt at the gate they had left behind, and turn in.

'We should have been off first,' said Dolores.

'If we could have got a cab in time?'

'One can always get cabs.'

'Oh! no, not at all for certain.'

'This is a nasty, stupid, out-of-the-way place,' said Dolores, wanting to say something cross.

'It isn't a vulgar place, full of traffic,' returned Constance, equally cross.

'Well, I never meant to walk home in this way! I'm sure my feet are wet. I wish I had waited and gone with Uncle Regie.'

'Now, Dolly, what do you mean? You would not have it all betrayed?'

'I've a great mind to tell Uncle Regie all about it.'

'Now, Dolly! When you said so much about the Mohun pride and scorn of your poor, dear uncle.'

'Uncle Regie is not proud. And he would know what to do.'

'But,' cried Constance, in a fright, 'you would never tell him! You promised that it should be a secret, and I should be in such a dreadful scrape with Lady Merrifield and Mary.'

'Well! it was your doing, and you had all the pleasure of it, flourishing about the platform with him.'

'How can you be so disagreeable, Dolores, when you know it was all on business. Though I do think he is the most interesting man I ever did see.'

'Just because he flattered you.'

However, there is no need to tell how many cross and quarrelsome things the two tired friends said to each other. They were sitting on opposite sides of the fire, one very gloomy, and the other very pettish, when the waggonette stopped at the gate, to put out Miss Hacket and take up Dolores. Hands pulled her up the step, and a hubbub of merry voices received her in the dark.

'Good girl, not to keep us waiting.'

'Oh, Dolly, Dolly, Macrae says Uncle Regie's come!'

'Oh, Dolly, it has been such fun!'

'Take care of my parcel!'

'Ah, ha! you don't know what is in there.'

'Here's something under my feet!'

'Oh! take care! 'Tisn't my—'

'Hush, hush, Val—'

And so it went on till on the steps was seen in full light among the boys, Uncle Reginald, ready to lift every one out with a kiss.'

'Ha! Dolly, is that you?' he said, as they came into the hall. 'I saw such a likeness of you at one station that I was as near as possible jumping out to speak to her. She had on just that fur tippet!'

'That comes of living in Ireland, Regie,' said Aunt Lily. 'Once in a shop at Belfast, a lady darted up to me with "And it's I that am glad to see you, me dear. And how's me sweet little god-daughter? Oh! and it isn't yourself. And aren't you Mrs. Phelim O'Shaugnessy?"' And under cover of this, Dolores retreated to her own room. She took off her things, and then looked at the cheque.

Professor Muhlwasser was a clever German, always at work on science, counting, in the most minute and accurate manner, such details as the rays in a sea anemone's tentacles, or the eggs in a shrimp's roe. He was engaged on a huge book, in numbers, of which Mr. Maurice Mohun had promised to take two copies—but whereas extravagances upon peculiar hobbies were apt not to be tolerated in the family, and it was really uncertain whether the work would ever be completed, Mr. Mohun had preferred leaving a cheque for the payment in his little daughter's hand, rather than entrust it to one of the brothers, who would have howled and growled at such a waste of good money on such a subject. Thus he had told Dolores to back the draft, get it changed, and send the amount by a postal order to Germany, if the books and account should come, which he thought very doubtful.

And now the professor was dead, Dolores looked at the cheque, and supposed she could do as she pleased with it. Mother helped Uncle Alfred. Yes, but mother earned all she sent him herself! Perhaps he would not ask again. How much more he had talked to Constance than to herself. Dolly wished she had not seen him to get into this difficulty. She was tired, cold, and damp. Oh! if she had never gone, and not been half caught by Uncle Regie!

CHAPTER XII
A HUNT

Dolores was glad to recollect, when she awoke, that Uncle Reginald was in the house. It was as if she had a friend of her own there who might enter into all the ill-usage she suffered, and whom she could even consult about Uncle Alfred, so far as she could do so without disclosing all the underhand correspondence. She called doing so betraying Constance, but, in truth, she shrank more from shocking him with what he might think very wrong— since, after all, he belonged to that hard-hearted generation of grown-up people who had no feeling nor understanding of one's troubles.

As she went downstairs she was aware of an increasing hubbub, and frequently looking over the balusters, perceived the top of Primrose's wavy head above the close-cropped one of Uncle Regie, as, with her mounted on his shoulder, he careered round the hall, with a pack of others vociferating behind him.

There was a lull, for Lady Merrifield came out of her room just as Dolores had paused; Primrose was put down, the morning salutations took place, and Dolores had her full share of them. She was even allowed to sit next her uncle at breakfast; but her rasher of bacon had not been half eaten, before she had perceived that, as to possessing him as she used to do at home, he was just as much everybody else's Uncle Regie as hers, for during the time of their being stationed at Belfast, he had been so often with them, that he was quite established as the prince of playfellows.

'Uncle Regie, will you have a crack at the rabbits tomorrow? Brown said we might have a day, and we have been keeping it for you.'

'Uncle Regie, the hounds meet at the Bugle this morning, won't you come and see them throw off?'

'Oh, let me come too!' 'And me!' 'And me!'

'My dear children,' exclaimed their mother, 'I can't have the whole tribe of little ones and girls going galloping after your uncle. You will only hinder him.'

'No, no, Lily! the more Merrifields, the merrier the field. I'll drill them well. How far off is this Bugle?'

'Not two miles over Furzy Common.'

'Oh! not so far, Hal!'

'That's nothing. Who is coming?'

A general outbreak of 'Me's' ensued, but mamma laid an embargo on Primrose, who must stay at home and 'help her,' while Gillian looked wistful and doubtful, knowing that more efficient help than the little one's might be desirable.

'You had better go, my dear,' said her mother, 'if you are not tired. I don't like to send Mysie and Val without some one to turn back with them if your uncle and the boys want to go further.'

But whereas it was not nearly time to start, Uncle Reginald was dragged down to inspect all the live stock in the stable-yard, at their feeding-time, and went off with Val and Primrose clinging to his hands, and the general rabble surrounding him.

Nothing could have been more alien to Dolores's taste than going out to a meet on foot through mud and mire — she who hated the being driven out to take a constitutional walk on the gravel road or the paved path! But she had some hope that while all the others ran off madly, as was their wont, she might secure a little rational conversation with Uncle Reginald. So she came down in hat and ulster, and was rewarded with 'That's right, Doll; I'm glad to see they have taught you to take country walks.'

'It is all compliment to you, Uncle Regie,' said Gillian. 'She hates them generally.'

'Are we all ready? Where are Japs and Will?'

'Gone to shut up the dogs; and Hal is not coming.'

'Beneath his dignity, eh?'

'I think he has some reading to do,' said Gillian.

'Now mind, Reginald,' said Aunt Lily, coming on the scene, 'you are not to let those imps drag you farther than you like. It is a very different thing, remember, children, from going out with the hounds like a gentleman.'

'Yes, mamma,' returned Fergus. 'If you would only let me have the pony!'

'And send home the girls as soon as you find them in the way,' she added.

'All right,' answered he, and off plunged the party; but Dolores soon found that she was not to be allowed much of Uncle Reginald's exclusive society. He did begin talking to her about her father's voyage, last letters, and intended departure from Auckland, but Valetta kept fast hold of his other hand, and the others were all round, every moment pointing out something—to them noticeable—and telling the story of some exploit, delighted when their uncle capped it with some boyish tales of Beechcroft, or with some droll, Irish story.

With such talk, the strong, healthy young folk little heeded the surface mud or the lanes. Even Dolores when she heard her father's name in the reminiscences,' was interested for a time, and was always hoping that the others would fly off and leave her to her uncle; but she was much less used to country mud and stout boots than the others, and she had been very much tired by her expedition on the previous day, so that she had begun to find the way very long before they came out on an open green, with a few cottages standing a good way back in their gardens, and as their centre, one of the great old coaching inns of past days, now chiefly farmhouse, though a sign, bearing a golden bugle-horn upon a blue ground, stood aloft in front of it, over the heads of the speckled mass of tan, black, and white, pervaded with curved tails, over which the scarlet-coated whips kept guard, while shining horses, bearing red coats and black coats, boys, and a few ladies, were moving about, and carriages drew up from time to time.

There was a long standing about, and Colonel Mohun, being a stranger there himself, kept his flock on the outskirts, only Jasper plunging in, at sight of a mounted schoolfellow, while Gillian and Mysie told the names of the few they recognized. At last there was a move, and Jasper came back to point out the wood they were going to draw, close at hand. Should they not all go on and see it?

'Oh! let us! do come, Uncle Regie,' cried Mysie and Val.

'Look here, Gill,' said the uncle, 'this child doesn't look fit to go any farther.'

'I'm very tired, and so cold,' said Dolores.

'Yes,' said Gillian, 'we ought to go home now.'

Not me! not me;' cried the other two girls; 'Uncle Regie will take care of us.'

'I think you must come,' said Gillian, 'mamma said you had better come home when I do.'

'Yes,' said Wilfred, 'we don't want a pack of girls to go and get tired.'

'We shall go into all sorts of places not fit for you,' said Jasper; 'you wouldn't come back with a whole petticoat among you.'

'And Val would be left stodged in a ditch for a month of Sundays,' added Wilfred.

'I am afraid we had better part company, Gill,' said the colonel. 'I would take you on a little further, but this poor little Londoner won't have a leg to stand upon by the time she gets home.'

'More shame for her to come out to spoil our fun,' muttered Valetta, too low for her uncle to hear.

'Mamma will think we have gone quite far enough, thank you, uncle,' said the sage Gillian, 'and I think Fergus had better come too.'

'That he had,' said Jasper. 'Fancy him over Peat Hill.'

'He'll be left behind to be picked up as we come back,' said Wilfred.

'No, no, no! I can keep up better than you can, Wil! Take me, Uncle Regie.' The little boy was so near a howl that good-natured Colonel Mohun's heart was touched, and he consented to let him come on, though Jasper argued, 'You'll have to carry him, uncle.'

'No, I'll make you, master! Tell your mother not to wait luncheon for us, Gillian; we'll pick up something somewhere.'

'Hurrah!' cried Wilfred and Fergus, to whom this was an immense additional pleasure.

The girls turned away into the lane, Valetta indulging in an outrageous grumble. 'Why should Dolores have come out to spoil everything?'

Dolores did not speak.

'Just our one chance,' sighed Mysie, 'and perhaps we should have seen the fox.'

'We may do that yet,' said Gillian; 'he may come this way.'

'I don't care if he does,' said Valetta. 'I wanted to see them draw the copse. I believe Dolores did it on purpose to spoil our pleasure.'

'Don't be so cross, Val,' said Mysie. 'She can't help being tired.'

'Why did she come, then, when nobody wanted her?'

'For shame, Val,' said Gillian, 'you know mamma would be very angry to hear you say anything so unkind.'

'It's quite true, though,' muttered Valetta.

'Never mind, Dolly, dear,' said Mysie, shocked. 'Val doesn't really mean it, you know.'

'Yes, she does,' said Dolores, shaking her comforter off; 'you all do! I wish I had never come here.'

Mysie tried in her own persevering way to argue again that Val was only put out, and disappointed at having to turn back, to which Valetta, in spite of Gillian's endeavour to silence her, added, 'So stupid of her to come out! What did she do it for?'

Dolores, who hardly ever cried, was tired into crying now. 'You grudge me everything; you wouldn't let me speak one single word to Uncle Regie, and kept bothering about! I'll never do anything with you again! I won't.'

'Did you want to speak to Uncle Regie?' asked Mysie.

'To be sure I did! He is my uncle, that I knew ever so long before you did, and you never let him speak to me.'

'Mrs. Halfpenny always put us on the high chair, with our faces to the wall when we were jealous,' remarked Valetta.

'But did you want to say anything to him in particular?' said Mysie, revolving means of contriving a private interview.

'That's no business of yours! I wish you would let me alone!' broke out Dolores, in a fretful fright lest any one should guess that she had anything on her mind.

'To make up stories of us, of course,' growled Valetta, but Gillian here interposed, declaring with authority that if she heard another word before they reached the paddock gate, she should certainly tell mother how disgracefully they had been behaving. When Gillian said such things she kept her word. Besides, by way of precaution, she marched down the muddy middle of the road, with Dolores limping along the footpath on one side, and Val as far off as possible on the border of the ditch, on the other; the more inoffensive Mysie keeping by her side. They were all weary, and Dolores was very footsore also, by the time they reached home, at the very moment that the two Misses Hacket appeared coming up the drive. Lady Merrifield, having the day before invited the elder, as the purchases needed to be looked over, and preparations set in hand, and she did not then know that her brother was coming.

Dolores scarcely knew whether she was glad to see Constance. She had many doubts and qualms about that cheque. And if she had spent any quiet time alone with her uncle, she might have laid enough of her trouble before him to get some advice or help; but to ask for an interview, especially when 'everybody' thought it was to make complaints, was too uncomfortable and alarming; and she was inclined to escape from thought of the whole subject altogether by taking action quickly.

Gillian gave her uncle's message about not waiting; the dirty boots were taken off in the hall, and Constance followed her friend up to her room to take off her things.

Dolores sat on the side of her bed, too much tired at first to be willing to move, Constance's pity elicited tears, and that they had all been so very unkind to her; they were angry at her getting tired, and they were jealous of her even speaking to Uncle Regie. Again this alarmed Constance, 'You weren't going to tell him about Mr. Flinders—you know you promised.'

'He knows about him already, and he would tell me what to do.'

'Oh! but that would never do, darling Dolly. You told me all the family were hard and unjust, and he would tell Lady Merrifield, and we should never be allowed to see each other again. And only think of my poor little secret! I didn't think you would have turned from your poor relation in misfortune for the sake of this grand Colonel.'

The end of it was, that just as the gong was sounding, Dolores handed over to Constance an envelope directed to Mr. Flinders, and containing Mr. Maurice Mohun's cheque. It was off her mind now, she thought, as she shuffled down to dinner, lookup so pale and uneasy that her aunt made her have a glass of wine and some gravy soup to begin with, and, when dinner was over, turned all the parcels off the school-room sofa, and made her lie upon it during the grand unpacking, which was almost as charming as the purchasing, perhaps more so, since there was no comparison with costlier articles.

There was not very much time. This was Friday and Christmas Day was on Monday, so there were only two more clear week-days before the birthday and Miss Hacket would be church-decorating on the morrow; but Lady Merrifield would not send her daughters to help, as there were plenty of hands without them, and they were too young to trust in a mixed set, who were not always sure to be reverent.

Dinner had rested and refreshed them; they rejoiced in the absence of the man-kind, and Primrose was sent out for her walk while the numerous boxes and packages were opened, and displayed sconces and tapers, gilt balls and glass birds, oranges and bon-bons, disguised in every imaginable fashion. There was a double set of the tapers, and two relays of devices in sweets, for the benefit of the party of the second night, a list of whom Miss Hacket had brought, that heads might be counted, and any deficiency supplied in time through Aunt Jane. For Lady Merrifield had commissioned Gillian to lay in—unknown to the good lady—a stock of such treasures as are valuable indeed to the little maid: shell pin-cushions, Cinderella slippers holding thimbles, cases of hair-pins, queer housewives, and the like things, wonderfully pretty for the price, and which filled the kind heart of Miss Hacket with rapture and gratitude at such brilliant additions to her own home-made contrivances in the way of cuffs, comforters, and illuminated workbags, all beautifully neat; I though it was hard to persuade her of what Lady Merrifield averred, that such things ought to be far more precious than brilliant, shop-bought, ready-made ware, 'with no love-seed in it.'

'It is very hard,' she said; 'how fancy shops try to spoil all one used to be able to do for one's friends. The purses, and the penwipers, and the needle-cases that were one's choicest presents in my youth, are all turned out now smart and tight and fashioned, but without a scrap of the honest old labour and love that went into them.'

'But papa and mamma do care still,' cried Gillian; 'papa never will have any purse but the long ones mamma nets for him.'

'And mamma always will have the old brown and blue carriage-bag that Aunt Phyllis worked,' chimed in Mysie, 'though Claude did say he would throw it into the sea when we crossed from Dublin for it looked like an old housekeeper's.'

'Claude was in a superfine condition then—in awe of an old Sandhurst comrade. He would be gild enough to see the old brown bag now, poor fellow,' said Lady Merrifield, tenderly.

So it went on, with merry chat and a good deal of real preparation, till the early darkness came on, and a great noise in the haul announced the return of 'the boys,' among whom Lady Merrifield still classed her colonel brother. They were muddy up to the eyes, but they had seen a great deal more than was easy to understand in their incoherent accounts. Wilfed had rolled into a wet ditch, and been picked out by his uncle and hung up to dry at a little village inn, where—this seemed to have been the supreme glory—they had made a meal on pigs'-liver and bread-and-cheese before plodding home again—losing their way under Wilfred's confident pilotage—finding themselves five miles from home—getting a cast in a cart for the two little boys just as Fergus was almost ready to cry—Colonel Mohun and Jasper walking alongside of the carter for two miles, and conversing in a friendly manner, though the man said he knew the soldier by his step, and thought it was a pool-trade. Finally, he directed them by a short cut, which proved to be through a lane of clay and pools of such an adhesive nature that Fergus had to be pulled out step by step by main force by his uncle, who deposited him on some stones at the other end, and then came back to assist the struggles of Wilfred, who was slowly proceeding with Jasper's help.

'And that's the way we make you spend your Christmas holiday, Regie,' said Lady Merrifield.

'Never mind. Lily; mud was a congenial element to us both in old times, you know, so no wonder your brood take to it like ducks or hippopotamuses. I say, we ought to have come in by the rear. Couldn't that imp of a buttons of yours come and scrape us before we go upstairs?'

'You are certainly grown older, Regie. You never would have thought of that once.'

'No more would you, Lily—so do yourself justice.'

However, when five o'clock tea was spread in the drawing-room, and the Hacket ladies came in, Constance beheld such a splendid vision of a fine, fair, though sunburnt face, long, light moustaches, and tall figure, that she instantly assumed her most affected graces, and did not wonder the less that the Mohuns were all so very high.

Dolores's strong desire for a private interview with her uncle died away when Constance carried off the cheque. She knew he would tell her she had no right to give it, and she did not want to be told so, nor to have any special inquiries made. She was not sorry that an invitation from a neighbour kept him and Hal out shooting all Saturday, and, on the other hand, she so far shrank from Constance's talk about Mr. Flinders as not to be vexed that it was too wet on Sunday afternoon for any going down to Casement Cottages.

It was on that wet afternoon, however, that Uncle Reginald, crossing the hall for once without his tail of followers, saw her slowly dragging downstairs with a book in her hand.

'Well, Miss Doll,' he said; 'you don't look very jolly! What's the matter?'

'Nothing, Uncle Regie.'

'I don't believe in nothing. Here,' sitting down on the stairs, with an arm round her, 'tell me all about it, Dolly, we are old chums, you know. Have you got into a row?'

'Oh no!'

'Is there anything I can put straight?'

'No, thank you, Uncle Regie.'

'There's something amiss!' said the good-natured, puzzled uncle. 'What is it? I should have thought you would have got on with these young folks like—like a house on fire.'

'That's all you know about it,' thought Dolly. What she said was, 'One never does.'

'I don't understand that generalization,' answered her uncle; then, as she did not answer, he added, 'I am sure your Aunt Lily is very anxious to make you happy. Have you anything to complain of?'

'No,' said Dolores, 'I don't complain of anything.'

She was thinking of Valetta's notion that she wanted to 'make up stories of them,' and therefore she said it in a manner which conveyed that she had a good deal to complain of, if she would, though really she would have been a good deal puzzled to produce a grievance that a man like Uncle Reginald would understand, though she had plenty for sympathy like Constance's.

However, it was not to be expected that a private conference should last long in that house, and Mysie appeared at that moment, looking for her cousin, to say that 'Mamma was ready for her.' Dolores went off with more alacrity than usual, and Uncle Reginald beckoned up his other niece, and observed: 'I say, Mysie, what's the matter with Dolly?'

'She is always like that, uncle,' answered Mysie.

'Don't you hit it off with her, then?'

'I can't, uncle,' said Mysie, looking up, with a sudden wink now and then to stop her tears. 'I thought we should have been such friends; but she won't let me. I didn't mean to be stupid and disagreeable, like the girls in 'Ashenden Schoolroom,' but she doesn't care for anybody but Miss Constance and Maude Sefton.'

'I hope you are all very kind to her,' said Uncle Reginald, rather wistfully.

'We try,' said Mysie, who was not going to betray Wilfred and Valetta, and could honestly say so of herself and Gillian.

And there again came an interruption, in the shape of Gillian. 'Mysie, mamma says we may finish up our sacred illuminated cards, for it will be Sunday work.'

'Oh, jolly!' cried Mysie, jumping up. 'And will you give me one rub of your real good carmine Gilly-flower, dear.'

'And of my ultramarine, too,' responded Gillian, wherewith the two sisters disappeared, radiant with goodwill and gratitude; while poor Uncle Reginald, who had intended to devote this wet Sunday afternoon to writing to his brother that Dolores was perfectly happy and thriving in Lily's care, and like a sister to his other favourite, Mysie, remained disappointed and perplexed, wondering whether the poor little maiden were homesick, or whether no children could be depended on for kindness when out of sight, and deciding that he should defer his letter till he had seen a little more, and talked to his sister Jane, who could see through a milestone any day.

It was understood that mamma preferred home-made cards to bought ones, so there was always a great manufacture of them in the weeks previous to Christmas, the comparative failures being exchanged among the younger members.

The presents were always reserved for Valetta's birthday and the tree, and this rendered the circulation of the cards doubly interesting. In the immediate family alone, there were thirteen times thirteen, besides those coming from, and going to outsiders, so that it was as well that a good many should be of domestic manufacture, either with pencil and brush, or of tiny leaves carefully dried and gummed. And mamma had kept an album, with names and dates, into which all these home efforts were inserted, and nothing else! This year's series began with a little chestnut curl of Primrose's hair, fastened down on a card by Gillian, and rose to a beautiful drawing of a blue Indian Lotus lily, with a gorgeous dragon-fly on it, sent by Alethea. The Indian party had sent a card for every one—the girls, beautiful drawings of birds, insects, and scenery; the brother, a bundle of rice-paper figured with costumes, and papa, some clever pen-and-ink outlines of odd figures, which his daughters beguiled from him in his leisure moments!

As to the home circle, it is enough to say that their performances were highly satisfactory to the makers, and were rewarded by mamma's kisses, and the text or verse she had secretly illuminated for each. She had no time to do more, and the series were infinitely prized and laid up as treasures. There were plenty of ornamental cards from without to be admired: the Brighton and Beechcroft aunts; the Stokesley cousins, and whole multitudes of friends pouring them in as usual; so that the entire review seemed to occupy all those free moments of the Christmas Day, when the young folks were neither at church, nor at meals, nor singing carols themselves, nor hearing the choir sing in the hall, nor looking over photograph books and hearing old family stories. This last occupation was received in the family as the regular evening pleasure, ending in all singing, 'When shepherds watch their flocks by night.'

Dolores had a card from her aunt and each of her cousins, besides one of the parcel Uncle Reginald had brought. She did not think enough of the very bad drawing and smeared painting of the ambitious attempts she received, to feel at all disconcerted at having no reciprocity to offer. The only cards she had sent were to Constance Hacket, to Fraulein, and to Maude Sefton—the last with a sore sense of the long interval since she had heard.

However, there was a card from Maude, but it was a very poor one, looking very much like a last year's possession, and the letter was not much better, being chiefly an apology for having been too busy to write. Maude was going to lectures with Nona Styles—Nona was such a darling girl—and breaking off because she was wanted to rehearse Cinderella with this same darling Nona.

It made Dolores's heart go down farther, though there was a beautiful and unexpected card from Mrs. Sefton, one from her former servant, Caroline, also from Fraulein, and three or four from old friends of her mother, who had remembered the solitary girl. In truth, she had more beautiful ones than anybody else, but she kept these in their envelopes, and showed herself so much averse to free fingering and admiration of them that Lady Merrifield had to call off Valetta, remind her that her cousin had a right to her own cards, and hear in return that Dolores was so cross.

'Dolly,' said Uncle Reginald, in a low voice, since he was permitted to look over the cards with her, 'I think I have found out part of your troubles.'

She looked at him in alarm.

He put his finger on a card bearing the words, 'Goodwill to men.'

'Umph,' said she. 'I don't want everything of mine messed and spoilt.'

And as his eye fell on Fergus's cards, he felt there was reason in what she said.

Aunt Lily had taken her for a quarter of an hour that morning, trying to infuse the real thought underlying the joy that makes it Christmas, not only yule-tide. But it all fell flat—it was all lessons to her—imposed on her on a day that she had not been used to see made what she called 'goody.' Last year her father had shut himself up after church, and she had spent the evening in noisy mirth with the Seftons.

CHAPTER XIII
AN EGYPTIAN SPHYNX

Aunt Adeline was afraid of winter journeys as well as of the tumultuous festivities of Silverton; so at twelve o'clock. Colonel Mohun drove the pony-carriage to meet the little trim Brownie who stepped out of the station, the porter carrying behind her a huge thing, long, and swathed in brown paper. 'It is quite light; it won't hurt,' she said, 'It must go with us. Put your legs across it, Regie. That's right.'

'Then what becomes of yours?'

'Mine can go anywhere,' said Miss Mohun, crumpling herself up in some mysterious manner under the fur rug, while they drove off, her luggage sticking far off on either side of the splashboard.

'What, in the name of wonder, are you smuggling in there?'

'If you must know, it is the body of a mummy over whose dissection you will have to assist.'

'Ah! Rotherwood is coming.'

'Rotherwood!'

'And his little girl. Just like him. Lily gets a note this morning from London, telling her to telegraph if she can't have them by the 5.20 train. I've just been ordering a fly. It seems that Lady Rotherwood, going to meet Ivinghoe at the station, coming from school, found he had measles coming out! So they packed off his sister to Beechcroft without having seen him, and thence Rotherwood took her to London.'

'And is having a fine frolic with her, no doubt; but he might as well have given Lily more notice, considering that a marquess or two makes more difference to her household than it does to his.'

'Oh! she is glad enough, only in some trepidation as to how Mrs. Halfpenny may receive the unspecified maid that the child may bring.'

'How jolly we shall be! I wish Ada had come.'

'I tried to drag her out, but it gets harder and harder to shake her up. You must come back with me and see her.'

'I say, Jane, have you seen Maurice's child lately?'

'Not very. She wouldn't come with the others last week.'

'What do you think about her? I thought leaving her with Lily would have been the making of her. Indeed, I told Maurice there could not be a better brought up set anywhere than the Merrifields, and that Lily would mother her like one of her own; and now I find her moping about, looking regularly down in the mouth. I got hold of her one day and tried to find out what was the matter, but she only said she would not complain. Can they bully her?'

'I'll tell you what, Maurice, Lily is a great deal too kind to her. She has a kind of temper that won't let them make friends with her.'

'Come now! She was a nice jolly little girl at home. She and I have had no end of larks together, and it is hard to blame her for fretting after her home, poor child—Aye! I know you never liked her, or she might have done better with you and Ada than turned in among a lot of imps.'

'I'm thankful it was otherwise!'

'Now do, Jane, set your mind to it. Don't be prejudiced, but make those sharp eyes of some use. I really feel bound to give Maurice an account of Dolly, and tell him what is best for her.'

'I believe,' said Jane, 'that there is some counter-influence at work, and I am trying to find it out; but, after all, I believe patience is the only thing, and that Lily will conquer her if nobody meddles.'

''Tis not Lily I am afraid of, but her children.'

'Nonsense, Regie; one would think you had never been turned loose into school to be licked into shape.'

'She is a girl, not a cub like me.'

'A worse cub, for she has not your temper, sir, and, moreover, you had had the wholesome discipline of a large family. Besides, nobody teases but Wilfred. Gillian and Mysie behave like angels to the tiresome puss.'

'Well, I'm bound to believe you, Jenny, but I don't like the looks of it.'

Aunt Jane's mysterious parcel was greeted rapturously, and conveyed into the dining-room, which had a semi-circular end, filled with glass, and capable of being shut off with heavy curtains when the season made snugness desirable. This bay had been set apart from the first for her operations, the tree, whose second season it was, having been taken up and already erected in the centre of the room, not much the worse for last year's excursion, for, if rather stunted, that was all the better. No one was excluded from the decoration thereof, since that was the best part of the sport to those too old for the mystery—and yet young enough to fasten sconces where their candles would infallibly set fire to the twigs above them. The only defaulters were Jasper, who had preferred going down to the meadows with his gun; and Dolores, who had retired to the drawing-room with a book, on having a paper star removed from immediate risk of conflagration. 'They were determined not to let her help,' she said.

So she only emerged when the workers halted for a merry, hurried meal in the schoolroom, where Jasper appeared, very late, very cross at having had to make himself fit to be seen, and, likewise, at having brought home no spoil, the snipes having been so malicious as to escape him. Having sallied forth before the post came in, it was only now that it broke on him that visitors were expected, and he did not like it at all.

'I thought we had got rid of all the enemy!' he growled, at his end of the table.

'That's what he calls Constance.' thought Dolores.

'Polite,' observed Gillian.

'This will be worse still, being lord and ladies grumbled on Jasper, 'I hate swells.'

'Oh! but these aren't like horrid, common, fine lords and ladies,' cried Mysie; 'why, you know all mamma's old stories about the fun they had with cousin Rotherwood.

'What's the good of that! That's a hundred years ago. He'll just make mamma and Uncle Regie of no good at all! And then there's a girl too—' (in a tone of inconceivable disgust) 'I don't want strange girls—an awful stuck-up swell of a Londoner, not able to do anything! I wish I had gone to spend Christmas with Bruce! I would if I had known it was to be like this.'

The speech brought Mysie to the verge of tears. Aunt Jane's sharp ears heard it, and she looked at the head of the table, expecting to hear a rebuke; but Lady Merrifield turned a deaf ear on that side. Only after the meal, she called her son, 'Jasper,' she said, 'I want to send a note to Redford, if you like to ride over with it. You need not come home till eight o'clock, if it is moonlight, it the boys are disengaged, and if you do really wish to keep out of the way.'

Jasper's eyes fell under hers.

'Mamma, I don't want that.'

'Only you said more than you meant, Japs. If it relieves your mind, it hurts other people. But I do want the note taken, so go and come back in time for the sports; which I don't think you will find much damaged.'

Meantime, Aunt Jane had ensconced herself behind the curtains; where she admitted no one but Miss Vincent and Uncle Reginald, and in process of time, mamma and Macrae. The others were still fully employed in garnishing the tree, though it was only to bear lights, ornaments and sweets. All solid articles had been for some time past committed to a huge box, or ottoman, the veteran companion of the family travels, which stood in the centre of the bay. Into its capacious interior everybody had been dropping parcels of various sizes and shapes, with addresses in all sorts of hands, which were to find their destination on this great evening. This was part of the mystery that kept Mysie and Valetta in one continual dance and caper. It was all they could do not to peep between the curtains when the privileged mortals went in and out, bearing all sorts of mysterious loads well covered up from all eyes. Wilfred did make one attempt, but something extraordinary snapped at his nose, with a sharp crack, and drove him back with a start.

A lamp had been taken thither, and there really was nothing more to do to the tree, the scraps of packing had been picked up, and the hands, tingling from fir-needle pricks, had been washed, though not without protest from Valetta that it wasn't worth while, and from Wilfred that it was all along of these horrid swells—!

The sound of wheels summoned Lady Merrifield and her brother from the place of mystery, and they were in the hall when a fresh gust of keen air came in from the door, an ulstered figure hurried in, and something small and furred was put into the lady's embrace.

'Here's my Fly, Lily—! Look, Fly, here they all are—all the cousins. Off with the hat. Let us see your funny little face.'

It was a funny little smiling face, set in short, light, wavy hair, not exactly pretty, but with a bright, quaint, confiding look, as if used to be shown off by her father, and ready to make friends on the spot. 'And how is your boy?' as the round of greetings was completed, and the wraps thrown off.

'Going on capitally, better than he deserves, the young scamp, for suppressing all symptoms for fear he should be hindered from coming home. His mother was in a proper fright, she showed him to the doctor on the way, who told her to put him to bed at once, and send his sister out of the house. She never set eyes on him, or I would not have brought her here.'

'I am exceedingly glad you have,' said Lady Merrifield, bending for another kiss.

'And Lily, I've done another awful thing. Victoria kept old nurse to help with Ivinghoe, and we brought the Swiss bonne, Louise, away with us, but the poor thing found her sister very ill in London, and I hadn't the heart to bring her away, so Phyllis said she would do for herself, if your maid, or some of them, would have an eye to her.'

'There! I'm doubly glad, Rotherwood! If I had any fears it was not of you, or Phyllis; but that like Vich Ian Vhor, she should have her tail on. And, oh! Rotherwood, do you know what you are in for?'

'High jinks of some sort, I've no doubt. We picked up a couple of boxes at Gunter's and Miller's with a view thereto. Who is master of the revels?'

'Jane. She's too deep in preparations to come forth at present. Gillian, will you take Phyllis to the nursery, and take care of her. We are to have a very high tea at half-past six; but, Rotherwood, I promise that another day you shall have a respectable dinner in this house.'

'Return to the prose of life, eh, Lily? Well, Fly, what do you think of it?'

'Oh, daddy, aren't you glad we came?' she cried, dancing off, in Gillian's wake, arm-in-arm with Mysie and Valetta, while he called after her, 'Find the boxes, and make them over to the right quarter.'

This was enough to make the whole bevy of children rush away, and only the three elders remained. Lord Rotherwood said, 'This is short notice. Lily; but I did not know Reginald was here, and I thought you might want help. Don't be frightened, only a queer thing has happened. I went to W.'s bank yesterday. I thought they looked at me as if something was up, and by-and-by one of the partners came and took me into his private room. There he showed me a cheque, and asked my opinion whether the writing was Maurice's. And I should say it decidedly was, but it was actually for seventy pounds, payable to order of Miss Dolores M. Mohun.'

'Seventy!'

'Yes, and dated the 19th of August.'

'Just before Maurice went.'

There was a sudden silence, for the door opened; but it was to admit Miss Mohun, who began, 'Oh! Rotherwood, you are too munificent. Why, what's the matter?' Lady Merrifield hastily explained, as far as she yet understood, what had brought him.

'How did they get the cheque?' she asked.

'Sent up from the country bank where it had been cashed—Darminster.'

'Ah!' came from both the aunts.

Lord Rotherwood went on. 'They asked me who Miss Dolores Mohun was, and I could do no otherwise than tell them, and likewise where to find her, but I explained that she is a mere child; and I told them I would come down here, so I hope you will have as little annoyance as possible.'

'It is very good of you, Rotherwood, but I can't understand it at all. Was her name on the back?'

'Certainly; I told them I thought the whole thing must be a well got up forgery, and a confidential clerk was to go down today to Darminster to try to find out who gave it in there.'

'Darminster! Flinders!' ejaculated Miss Mohun.

'Regie,' exclaimed Lady Merrifield; 'what did you say about having seen some one like Dolores at Darminster station?'

'I was nearly jumping out after her. I should have said it was herself, if it had not been impossible. Why she was with you at Rockstone, and it was a pouring, dripping day,' said the colonel.

'No, she was not. She begged to spend the day with Constance Hacket, and we picked her up as we came home. Poor child, what has she been doing? I have not looked after her properly.'

'But need she have had anything to do with it?' said Colonel Mohun. 'How should a cheque of Maurice's come into her possession?'

'She did tell me,' said Lady Merrifield,' that her father had left one with her to pay for some German scientific book that might be sent for him.'

'I see, then!' cried Miss Mohun. 'That wretch Flinders must have got into communication with her, and induced her to fill up her father's cheque for him.'

'But why should it be Flinders?' said Lord Rotherwood.

'Jane found out that he is living at Darminster, and has been trying to put me on my guard,' returned Lady Merrifield.

'It is all that fellow Flinders, depend upon it,' said Colonel Mohun. 'He is quite capable of it, and you'll find poor Dolly has nothing to do with it. Quite preposterous. And look here, Lily, let the poor child alone to enjoy herself tonight. Most likely Rotherwood's clerk, or detective, or whatever he may be, will have ferreted out the rights of the matter at Darminster. I sincerely hope he will, and have Flinders in custody, and then you would have upset her and accused her all for nothing.'

'I am glad you think so, Regie,' said Lady Merrifield. 'I am thankful enough to wait, and hope it will be explained without spoiling the children's evening.'

'All right,' said the visitor; 'I only hope I have not spoilt yours.'

'Oh! one learns to throw things off. I shall believe it is all Flinders, and none of it the child's,' said Lady Merrifield, carefully avoiding a glance that could show her any gesture of dissent on the part of her sister, and only looking up for her brother's nod of approval. 'Besides, how foolish it would be to worry myself when I have two such protectors! It was very good in you, Rotherwood, I only hope we shall take good care of your Fly, and that her mother will be satisfied about her.'

'She knew the little woman and I should have a lark together,' said he. 'The governess was safe out of reach, holiday-making, so I could have her all to myself. Victoria suggested her brother's, and we must go there before we have done, but business and the pantomime by good luck took us to London first. So when I wrote to you from the bank, I also let her know that I was obliged to take the little woman down here first. I couldn't take her to High Court till Louise is available again.'

'So much the better, I'm sure.'

'And what I was going to say is, that Rotherwood has been startlingly munificent and splendid,' said Aunt Jane. 'We shall have a set of new surprises.'

'I don't in the least know what I brought. I only told each of them to put up such a box as they sent out for Christmas concerns. Do precisely what you please with them.'

'Come and see, Lily, for I think there will be enough to reserve a fresh lot of things for Miss Hacket's affair. By-the-by, Regie, did you say it rained at Darminster?'

'Poured all the way down.'

'Well, we had it quite fine.'

'Was it fine here?'

'Yes, certainly,' said Lady Merrifield,' or Primrose would not have gone out. Take care of Rotherwood, Regie. You know his room.'

And the two sisters crossed the hall, where the 'very high tea' was being laid; hearing from the regions above sounds of exquisite glee and merriment, as perfect and almost as inexpressive of anything else as the singing of birds, so that they themselves could not help answering with a laugh, before they vanished into the chamber of mystery.

Indeed, Phyllis's conversation was like a fairy tale. Her brother's illness, which was not enough to damp any one's spirits, had prevented or hindered a grand children's party as the Butterfly's Ball, where she was to have been the Butterfly, and Lord Ivinghoe the Grasshopper, and all the children were to appear as one of the characters in Roscoe's pretty poem. Never was anything more delightful to the imagination of the little cousins, and they could not marvel enough at her seeming so little uneasy about anything so charming, and quite ready and eager to throw herself headlong into all their present enjoyments, making wonderful surmises as to the mystery in preparation.

Dolores heard the laughing, and it did not suit with her vaguely uneasy and injured frame of mind; feeling dreadfully lonely too, as she came downstairs, dressed for the evening, but not knowing where to go, for the dining-room was engrossed, the schoolroom was dark and the fire out, the drawing-room occupied by the two gentlemen. She crouched down in one of the big arm-chairs on either side of the hearth in the hall, and began to read by the firelight. Presently Jasper came in from his ride, and began taking off his greatcoat, leggings, and boots, whistling as he did so, then, perceiving the tempting object of a black leg sticking out of the chair, he stole up across the soft carpet, and caught hold of the ankle. He received a vigorous kick in return (which perhaps he expected) but what he did not expect was the black figure that rose up in outraged dignity and indignation. 'For shame! I won't be insulted!'

'Whew! I thought 'twas Val! I beg your pardon.'

'I shall ask my aunt if I am to be insulted.'

'Well, if you choose to take it in that way—A man can't do more than beg pardon! I'm sure I would never have presumed to touch you if I had known it was your Dolorousness.'

And he turned to walk away, just as the babbling ripple of laughter began to flow downstairs, and a whole mass of little girls intertwined together was descending. 'I always hop,' said a voice new to him, 'except on the great staircase, and mother doesn't like it there. But this is such a jolly stair. Can't you hop?'

Hopping in a threefold embrace on a slippery stair was hardly a safe pastime, and before Jasper had time to utter more than' Holloa there! take care!' there descended suddenly on him an avalanche of little girls, 'knocking him off his feet, so that all promiscuously rolled down two or three steps together. Fergus and Primrose, who had somehow been holding on behind,' remained upright, but nevertheless screaming. The shrieks of the fallen were, however, laughter. There was a soft rug below, and by the time the gentlemen had rushed out of the dining-room, and the ladies from the curtained recess, giggling below and legs above were chiefly apparent.

'Any one hurt?' was of course Lady Merrifield's cry.

'Oh no, mamma. Only we are so mixed up we can't get up,' called out Mysie.

'Is this arm you or me?' exclaimed Phyllis, following up the joke.

'Come, sort yourselves, ladies and gentlemen,' said Lord Rotherwood. 'What's this, a Fly's wing?'

'No, it's mine,' cried Val, as his hand pulled her out, and the others extricated themselves, still laughing, go that they could hardly stand, and Fly declaring, 'Oh, daddy, daddy, it is such fun! I am so glad we came,' and taking a gratuitous leap into the air.

'Every one to her taste,' said Lady Merrifield, 'I congratulate those to whom a compound tumble-down-stairs is felicity.'

'She has found her congenial element, you see,' said her father, as the elders proceeded upstairs to their toilette.' 'Tis laughing-gas with her to be with other children, and the most laughingest of all are naturally yours, old Lily.'

Meanwhile Jasper, risen on his stocking soles, looked all over at the little figure, dressed old picture fashion, in the simplest white frock with blue sash, and short-cut hair tied back with blue.

'Well, you are a jolly little girl,' he said, 'and a cool customer, too! What do you mean by knocking a fellow over the first time you see him?'

'And what do you mean by coming like a great—huge—big elephant in our way to stop up the stairs?' demanded Fly, in return.

'Do you mean to insinivate that 'twas I that made you fall?' said Jasper— 'I, that was quietly walking up the stairs, when down there came on me a shower—not cats and dogs, but worserer, far worserer! Why, I'm kilt! my nose is flat as a pancake, I shan't recover my beauty all the evening for the great swells that are coming.'

'Jasper, Japs,' called his mother's warning voice, 'you must come up and dress, for tea is going in.'

He obeyed, rushing two steps at a time; but meeting, at the bottom of the attic flight, his sister Gillian, he demanded, 'Gill, what awfully jolly little girl have they got down there?'

'Why, Fly, of course, Lady Phyllis Devereux—'

'No, no, nothing swell, a comical little soul, with no nonsense about her, in a white thing.'

'Well, that's Phyllis. There's no one else there.'

'I say. Gill, 'tis like sunshine and clouds. She and the other, I mean. Why, I gave a little pull to a foot I saw in the armchair, thinking it belonged to Val, and out breaks my Lady of the Rueful Countenance, vowing she'll complain that I've insulted her; and as to the other, the whole lot of them tumbled over me together on the stairs, and she did nothing but laugh and chaff.'

'I hope she is not a romp,' said the staid Gillian, sagely, as she went downstairs.

But on that score she was soon satisfied. Phyllis Devereux was a thorough little lady, wild and merry as she was, and enchanted to be in the rare fairyland of child companionship. And that indeed she had, Mysie and Valetta, between whose ages she stood, hung to her inseparably, and Jasper was quite transformed from his grim superciliousness into her devoted knight. At tea-time there was a competition for the seats next to her, determined by Valetta's taking one side, in right of the birthday, and Jasper the other, because he secured it, and Mysie gave way to him because he was Japs, and she always did. While Dolores laid up a store of moralizings on the adulation paid to the little lady of title, and at the same time speculated what concatenation of circumstances could ever make her Lady Dolores Mohun. On the whole, it would be more likely that her father should gain a peerage by putting down a Fijian rebellion than that it should be discovered that his mother, Lady Emily, had been the true heiress of the marquessate, and even so, an uncomfortable number of people must be disposed of before it could come to him. She had one consolation, however, for Uncle Reginald, always kind to her, was particularly affectionate this evening, as if he would not have that little foolish Fly set up before her.

The tea and the tree both went off joyously. There is no need to describe the spectacle to folks who can count their Christmas-trees by the years of their life and the memorable part of this one was that much of the fruit that had been left hanging on it was now metamorphosed into something much more gorgeous—oranges had become eggs full of sugar-plums, gutta-percha monkeys grinned on the branches, golden flowers had sprung to life on the ends of the twigs, a lovely jewel-like lantern crowned the whole, and as to sweets, everybody—servants and all—had some delightful devices containing them, whether drum, bird, or bird's nest.

Before the distribution was over, it was observed that Aunt Jane and Uncle Reginald, also Harry, had vanished from the scene. There was a pause, during which such tapers as began to burn perilously low, were extinguished, an operation as delightful apparently as the fixing them. Presently a horn was heard, and a start or shudder of mysterious ecstasy pervaded the audience, as a tall figure came through the curtains, and announced:

'Ladies and gentlemen, I have the honour to inform you that a fresh discovery has been made in the secret chambers of the Pyramid of Chops, otherwise known as Te-Gun-Ter-ra. A mummy has been disinterred, which is about to be opened by the celebrated Egyptologist, Herr Professor Freudigfeldius, who has likewise discovered the means of making such a conjuration of the Sphinx that she will not only summon each of the present company by name, but will require of each of them to reply to a question. The penalty of a refusal is well known!'

Therewith the curtains were drawn back, and a scene was presented which made some of the spectators start. Behind was the semblance of a wall marked with the joints of large stones, and lighted (apparently) with two brass lamps. On the floor lay extended an enormous mummy, with the regulation canvas case, and huge flaps of ears, between which appeared a small, painted face, and below lay a long, gaily coloured scroll in hieroglyphics. Exalted stiffly in a seat placed on a seeming block of stone, was a figure, with elbows, as it were glued to its sides, and hands crossed, altogether stone-coloured and monumental, and with the true Sphinx head, surrounded with beetles, lizards, and other mystic creatures (very chocolate-coloured). And beside her stood the Herr Professor, in a red fez, long dark gown, and spectacles, a flowing beard concealing the rest of his face. How delightful to see such an Egyptologist! Even though one perfectly knew the family beard and fez; also that the gown was papa's old dressing-gown, captured for the theatrical wardrobe. And how grand to hear him speak, even though his broken English continually became more vernacular.

'Liebes Herrschaft,' he began, 'I would, nobles, gentry, and ladies say. You here see the embalmed rests of the celebrated monarch Nic-nac-ci-no. Lately up have I them graben, and likewise his tutelar Sphinx have found, and have even to give signs of animation compelled.'

Touching the effigy with his wand, she emitted certain growls and hisses, which made Primrose hide her face in alarm at anything so uncanny, and Lord Rotherwood observe—

'Nearly related to the cat-goddess Pasht; I thought so.'

'There was something of the lion or cat in the Sphynx,' said Gillian, gravely, while the three little girls clasped each other's hands with delightful thrills of awe and expectation.

'Observe,' continued the Professor, 'the outer case with the features of the deceased is painted. I should conclude that King Nic-nac, etcetera, had been of a peculiarly jolly—I mean frolich—nature, judging by the grin on his face. We proceed—'

As he laid his hand on the wrapper, the Sphynx gave utterance to sounds so like the bad language of a cat that some looked round for one. The Professor waved at her, and she subsided. He turned back the covering, and demanded, 'Will the amiable Fraulein there. Mademoiselle Valetta, come and see what treasures she can discover in the secrets of the tomb?'

Val, who in right of her birthday, had expected the first call, jumped up, but the Sphynx made awful noises as she advanced, and the Professor explained that she would have to answer the Sphynx's question first.

'But I don't know Egyptian,' she observed.

'Never mind, it will sound like English.'

It did so, for it was, 'How many months old art thou, maiden?'

Val's arithmetic was slightly scared. She clasped her hand nervously, and was indebted to the Professor for the sotto voce hint, 'twelve nines,' before she uttered 'a hundred and eight.'

The Sphynx relapsed into stoniness, and the Herr Professor guided the hands, which trembled a little, to the interior of the mummy, whence they drew out a basket, labelled (wonderful to relate) 'Val,' and containing—oh! such treasures, a blue egg full of needlework implements, a new book, an Indian ivory case, a skipping-rope, a shuttlecock, and other delights past description. The exhibition of them was only beginning when the Professor called for Primrose, who was too much frightened to come alone, and therefore was permitted to be brought by Mrs. Halfpenny. The Sphynx was particularly amiable on this occasion, and only asked 'When Primroses came?' and as the little one, in her shy fright did not reply, nurse did so, with, 'Come, missie, can't you find a word to tell that mamma's Primrose came in spring.' This was allowed to pass, and Mrs. Halfpenny bore off her child, clutching a doll's cradle, stuffed with pretty things, and for herself a bundle wrapped up in a shawl from Sir Jasper himself.

After Primrose was gone to bed, the Sphynx became much more ill-tempered and demonstrative, snarling considerably at the approach of some of the party, some of whom replied with convulsive laughter, some, such as Jasper, with demonstrations of 'poking up the Sphynx.' She had a question for everybody—Fly was asked, 'Which was best, a tree or a Butterfly's ball?' and answered, with truthful politeness, that where Mysie and Val were was best of all. She carried off a collection that had hastily been made of Indian curiosities, photographs of her two friends, and a book; and her father, after being asked, 'What was the best of insects?' and replying, 'On the whole, I think it is my housefly, even when she isn't a butterfly,' received a letter-weight of brass, fashioned like an enormous fly, which Lady Merrifield had snatched up from the table for the purpose. The maids giggled at the well-known conundrums proposed to them, and Dolores had a very easy question—' What was the weather this day week?'

'A horrid wet day,' she promptly answered, and found herself endowed with a parcel containing some of the best presents of all, bangles from the Indian box, a beautiful pair of stork-like scissors, a writing-case, etc.

'The Sphynx's invention is running low,' observed Jasper to Gillian, when the creature put the same question about last week's weather to Herbert, the page-boy, as a prelude to his discovering the treasures of the mummy, as a knife and an umbrella. His view of the weather was that it was 'A fine day ma'am! yes, a fine day.'

Macrae came last, and the Sphynx asked him which of the two contrary views was right.

'It was fine, ma'am, that I know. For I walked down with nurse, and little Miss Primrose into Silverton, to help to carry her in case she was tired, and we never had occasion to put up an umbrella.'

Wherewith Macrae received his combination of gifts and retired; the mummy being completely rifled, and the construction of the body, a frame of light, open wicker-work, revealed. Aunt Jane had had it made at the basketmaker's, while as to the head and covering, her own ingenious fingers had painted and fashioned them. Everybody had to look at everybody's presents, a lengthened operation, and then there was a splendid game at blindman's-buff in the hall, in which all the elders joined, except mamma, who had to go and sit in the nursery with the restless and excited Primrose while Mrs. Halfpenny and Lots went down to the servants' festivity.

When she came down again, it was to quiet the tempest of merriment, and send off the younger folks in succession to bed, till only the four elders and Hal remained on the scene, waiting till there was reason to think the household would be ready for prayers.

'It was Dolores that you saw at Darminster, Reginald,' said Miss Mohun, quietly.

'You Sphynx woman, how do you know?'

'You said it was raining at Darminster.'

'Yes, that it was, everywhere beyond the tunnel through the Darfield hills.'

'Exactly, I know they make a line in the rainfall. Well, here it was dry, but Dolores called it a wet day.'

'Now I call that too bad, Jane, to lay a trap for the poor child in the game,' cried Colonel Mohun, just as if they had still been boy and girl together.

'It was to satisfy my own mind,' she said, colouring a little. 'I didn't want any one to act on it. Indeed, I think there will be no occasion.'

'Besides,' he added, 'it is nothing to go upon! No doubt, if it wasn't raining, it was the next thing to it here, and bow was she to recollect at this distance of time? I won't have her caught out in that way!'

'I am glad she has a champion, Regie,' said Lady Merrifield. 'Here come the servants.'

CHAPTER XIV
A CYPHER AND A TY

Dolores was coming down to breakfast the next morning when Colonel Mohun's door opened. He exclaimed, 'My little Dolly, good morning!' stooped down and kissed her.

Then, standing still a moment, and holding her hand, he said—

'Dolly, it was not you I saw at Darminster station?'

It was a terrible shock. Some one, no doubt, was trying to set him against her. And should she betray Constance and her uncle? At any rate, almost before she knew what she was saying, 'No, Uncle Regie,' was out of her mouth, and her conscience was being answered with 'How do I know it was me that he saw? these fur capes are very common.'

'I thought not,' he answered, kindly. 'Look here, Dolly, I want one word with you. Did your father ever leave anything in charge with you for Mr. Flinders? Did he ever speak to you about him?'

'Never,' Dolores truly answered.

'Because, my dear, though it's a hard thing to say, and your poor mother felt bound to him, he is a slippery fellow—a scamp, in fact, and if ever he writes to you here, you had better send the letter straight off to me, and I'll see what's to be done. He never has, I suppose?'

'No,' said Dolores, answering the word here, and foolishly feeling the involvement too great, and Constance too much concerned in it for her to confess to her uncle what had really happened. Indeed, the first falsehood held her to the second; and there was no more time, for Lord Rotherwood was coming out of his room further down the passage. And after the greetings, as she went downstairs before the two gentlemen, she was sure she heard Uncle Regie say, 'She's all right.' What could it mean? Was a storm averted? or was it brewing? Could that spiteful Aunt Jane and her questions about the weather be at the bottom of it?

The fun that was going on at breakfast seemed a mere roar of folly to her, and she had an instinct of nothing but getting away to Constance. She soon found that there would be opportunity enough, for the tree was to be taken down in a barrow, and all the youthful world was to carry down the decorations in baskets, and help to put them on. She dashed off among the first to put on her things, and then was disappointed to find that first all the pets were to be fed and shown off to Fly, who appreciated them far more than she had done—knew how to lay hold of a rabbit, nursed the guinea-pigs and puppies in turn, and was rapturous in her acceptance of two young guinea-pigs and one puppy.

'I can keep them up in daddy's dressing-room while we are at High Court, and it will be such fun,' she said.

'Will he let you?' asked Gillian, in some doubt.

'Oh! daddy will always let me, and so will Griffin—his man, you know, only we left him in London because daddy said he would be in your butler's way, but I can't think why. Griffin would have helped about the tree and learnt to make a mummy when we have our party. Louise would not let me have them in the nursery, I know, but daddy and Griffin would, and I could go and feed them in the morning before breakfast. Griffin would get me bran! That is, if we do go to High Court; I wish we were to stay on here. There's nobody to play with at High Court, and grandpapa always keeps daddy talking politics, so that I can hardly ever get him! Mysie, whatever do you do with your father away in India?'

'Yes, it is horrid. But then, there's mamma,' said Mysie, whispering, however, as she saw Dolores near, and feared to hurt her feelings.

'Ah!' said Fly, with a tender little shake of her head; ''tis worse for her to have no mother at all! Is that why she looks so sad?'

'Cross' is the word,' said Wilfred. 'I can't think what she is come bothering down here for!'

'Oh! for shame, Wilfred!' said Fly. 'You should be sorry for her.' And she went up to Dolores, and by way of doing the kindest thing in the world, said—

'Here's my new puppy. Is not he a dear? I'll let you hold him,' and she attempted to deposit the fat, curly, satiny creature in Dolores's arms, which instantly hung down stiff, as she answered, half in fright, 'I hate dogs!' The puppy fell down with a flop, and began to squeak, while the girls, crying, 'Oh! Dolly, how could you!' and 'Poor little pup!' all crowded round in pity and indignation, and Wilfred observed, 'I told you so!'

'You'll get no change but that out of the Lady of the Rueful Countenance,' said Jasper.

Mysie had for once nothing to say in Dolores's defence, being equally hurt for Fly's sake and the puppy's. Dolores found herself virtually sent to Coventry, as she accompanied the party across the paddock, only just near enough to benefit by their protection from the herd of half-grown calves which were there disporting themselves; and, as if to make the contrast still more provoking, Fly, who had a natural affinity for all animals, insisted on trying to attract them, calling, 'Sukkey! sukkey!' and hold out bunches of grass, in vain, for they only galloped away, and she could only explain how tame those at home were, and how she went out farming with daddy whenever he had time, and mother and Fraulein would let her out.

The tree meantime came trundling down, a wonderful spectacle, with all its gilt balls and fir-cones nodding and dangling wildly, and its other embellishments turning upside down. There were greetings of delight at Casement Cottage, and Miss Hacket had kissed everybody all round before Gillian had time to present the new-comer, and then the good lady was shocked at her own presumption, and exclaimed —

'I beg your ladyship's pardon! Dear me! I had no notion who it was!'

'Then please kiss me again now you do know!' said Fly, holding up her funny little face to that very lovable kind one, and they were all soon absorbed in the difficulty of getting the tree in at the front door, and setting it up in the room that had been prepared for it.

Dolores had hoped to confide her alarms to Constance's sympathetic ear, but her friend, who had written and dreamt of many a magnificently titled scion of the peerage, but had never before seen one in her own house, had not a minute to spare for her, being far too much engrossed in observing the habits of the animal. These certainly were peculiar, since she insisted on a waltz round the room with the tabby cat, and ascended a step-ladder, merrily spurning Jasper's protection, to insert the circle of tapers on the crowning chandelier. There was nothing left for Dolores to do but to sit by in the window-seat, philosophizing on the remarkable effects of a handle to one's name, and feeling cruelly neglected.

Suddenly she saw a fly coming up to the gate. There was a general peeping and wondering. Then Uncle Reginald and a stranger got out and came up to the door. There was a ring—everybody paused and wondered for a moment; then the maid tapped at the door and said, 'Would Miss Mohun come and speak to Colonel Mohun a minute in the drawing-room?'

There was a hush of dread throughout the room. 'Ah!' sighed Miss Hacket, looking at Gillian, and all the elders thought without saying that some terrible news of her father had to be told to the poor child. They let her go, frightened at the summons, but that idea not occurring to her.

'There!' said Uncle Regie, 'she can set it straight. Don't be frightened, my dear; only tell this gentleman whether that is your writing.'

The stranger held a strip so that she could only just see 'Dolores M. Mohun,' and she unhesitatingly answered 'Yes'—very much surprised.

'You are sure?' said her uncle, in a tone of disappointment that made her falter, as she added, 'I think so.' At the same time the stranger turned the paper round, and she knew it for the cheque that had so long resided in her desk, but with dilated eyes, she exclaimed, 'But—but—that was for seven pounds!'

'That,' said the stranger, 'then, Miss Mohun, you know this draft?'

'Only it was for seven,' repeated Dolores.

'You mean, I conclude, that it was drawn for seven pounds, and that it was still for seven when it left your handy?'

'Yes,' muttered Dolores, who was beginning to get very much frightened, at she knew not what, and to feel on her guard at all points.

'There's nothing to be afraid of, my dear,' said Uncle Reginald, tenderly; 'nobody suspects you of anything. Only tell us. Did your father give you this paper?'

'Yes.'

'And when did you cash it?' asked the clerk.

Dolores hung her head. 'I didn't,' she said.

'But how did it get out of your possession?' said her uncle. 'You are sure this is your own writing at the back. It could surely not have been stolen from her?' he added to the stranger.

'That could hardly be,' said that person. 'Miss Mohun, you had better speak out. To whom did you give this cheque?'

There was a whirl of terror all round about Dolores, a horror of bringing herself first, then Uncle Alfred, Constance, and everybody else into trouble. She took refuge in uttering not a word.

'Dolores,' said her uncle, and his tone was now much more grave and less tender, thus increasing her terror; 'this silence is of no use. Did you give this cheque to Mr. Flinders?'

In the silence, the ticks of the clock on the mantel-piece seemed like a hammer beating on her ears. Dolores thought of the morning's flat denial of all intercourse with Flinders! Then the word give occurred to her as a loophole, and her mind did not embrace all the consequences of the denial, she only saw one thing at a time, 'I didn't give it,' she answered, almost inaudibly.

'You did not give it?' repeated her uncle, getting angry and speaking loud. 'Then how did it get into his hands? Is there no truth in you?' he added, after a pause, which only terrified her more and more. 'Whom did you give it to?'

'Constance!' The word came out she hardly knew how, as something which at least was true. Colonel Mohun knocked at the door of the room she had come from. It was instantly opened, and Miss Hacket began, 'The poor dear! Can I get anything for her, I am sure it is a terrible shock!' and as he stood, astonished, Gillian added, 'Oh! I see it isn't that. We were afraid it was something about Uncle Maurice.'

'No, my dear, no such thing. Only would Miss Constance Hacket be kind enough to come here a minute?'

'Oh! My apron! My fingers! Excuse me for being such a figure!' Constance ran on, as Colonel Mohun made her come across to the room opposite, where she looked about her in amazement. Was the stranger a publisher about to make her an offer for the 'Waif of the Moorland.' But Dolores's down-cast attitude and set, sullen face forbade the idea.

'Miss Constance Hacket,' said the colonel, 'here is an uncomfortable matter in which we want your assistance. Will you kindly answer a question or two from Mr. Ellis, the manager of the.... Bank?'

Then the manager politely asked her if she had seen the cheque before.

'Yes—why—what's wrong about it? Oh! It is for seventy! Why, Dolores, I thought it was only for seven?'

'It was for seven when you parted with it, then, Miss Hacket,' said the manager; 'let me ask whether you changed it yourself?'

'No,' she said, 'I sent it to—' and there she came to a dead pause, in alarm.

'Did you send it to Mr. Alfred Flinders?' said Mr. Ellis.

'Yes—oh!' another little scream, 'He can't have done it. He can't be such a villain! Your own uncle, Dolores.'

'He is no uncle of Dolores Mohun!' said the colonel. 'He is only the son of her mother's step-mother by her first marriage.'

'Oh, Dolores, then you deceived me!' exclaimed Constance; 'you told me he was your own uncle, or I would never—and oh! my fifteen pounds. Where is he?'

'That, madam,' said Mr. Ellis, gravely, 'I hope the police may discover. He has quitted Darminster after having cashed this cheque for seventy pounds. We have already telegraphed to the police to be on the look out for him, but I much fear that it will be too late.'

'Oh! my fifteen pounds! What shall I do? Oh, Dolores, how could you? I shall never trust any one again!'

Perhaps Uncle Reginald felt the same, but he only darted a look upon his niece, which she felt in every nerve, though to his eyes she only stood hard and stolid. The manager, who found Constance's torrent of words as hard to deal with as Dolores's silence, asked for pen and ink, and begged to take down Miss Hacket's statement to lay before a magistrate in case of Flinders's apprehension. It was not very easy to keep her to the point, especially as her chief interest was in her own fifteen pounds, of which Mr. Ellis only would say that she could prosecute the man for obtaining money on false pretences, and this she trusted meant getting it back again. As to the cheque in question, she told how Dolores had entrusted it to her to send to her supposed uncle, Mr. Flinders, to whom it had been promised the day they went to Darminster, and she was quite ready to depose that when it left her hands, it was only for seven pounds.

This was all that the bank manager wanted. He thanked her, told Colonel Mohun they should hear from him, and went off in a hurry, both to communicate with the police, and to leave the young ladies to be dealt with by their friends, who, he might well suppose, would rather that he removed himself.

'Put on your hat, Dolores,' said Colonel Mohun, gravely; 'you had better come home with me! Miss Hacket, excuse me, but I am afraid I must ask whether you have been assisting in a correspondence between my niece and this Flinders?'

'Oh! Colonel Mohun, you will believe me, I was quite deceived. Dolores represented that he was her uncle, to whom she was much attached, and that Lady Merrifield separated her from him out of mere family prejudice.'

'I am afraid you have paid dearly for your sympathy,' said the colonel. 'It certainly led you far when you assisted your friend to deceive the aunt who trusted you with her.'

The movement that was taking place seemed like licence to that roomful, burning with curiosity to break out. Mysie was running after Dolores to ask if she could do anything for her, but Colonel Mohun called her back with 'Not now, Mysie.' Miss Hacket came forward with agitated hopes that nothing was amiss, and, at sight of her, Constance collapsed quite. 'Oh, Mary,' she cried out, 'I have been so deceived! Oh! that man!' and she sunk upon a chair in a violent fit of crying, which alarmed Miss Hacket so dreadfully that she looked imploringly up to Colonel Mohun. He had meant to have left Miss Constance to explain, but he saw it was necessary to relieve the poor elder sister's mind from worse fears by saying, 'I am afraid it is my niece who deceived her, by leading her into forwarding letters and money to a person who calls himself a relation. He seems to have been guilty of a forgery, which may have unpleasant consequences. Children, I think you had better follow us home.'

Dolores had come down by this time, and Colonel Mohun walked home, at some paces from her, very much as if he had been guarding a criminal under arrest. Poor Uncle Reginald! He had put such absolute trust in the two answers she had made him in the morning; and had been so sure of her good faith, that when the manager brought word that the cheque had been traced to Flinders, who had absconded, he still held that it was a barefaced forgery, entirely due to Flinders himself, and that Dolores could show that she had no knowledge of it, and he had gone down in the fly expecting to come home triumphant, and confute his sister Jane, who persisted in being mournfully sagacious. And he was indignant in proportion to the confidence he had misplaced; grieved, too, for his brother's sake, and absolutely ashamed.

Once he asked, when they were within the paddock, out of the way of meeting any one, 'Have you nothing to say to me, Dolores?'

It was not said in a manner to draw out an answer, and she made none at all.

Again he spoke, as they came near the house:

'You had better go up to your room at once. I do not know how to think of the blow this will be to your father.'

It was so entirely what Dolores was thinking of, that it seemed to her barbarous to tell her of it In fact she was stunned, scarcely understanding what had happened, and too proud and miserable to ask for an explanation, for had not every one turned against her, even Uncle Reginald and Constance—and what had happened to that cheque?

She did not see Uncle Reginald turn into the drawing-room, and letting himself drop despairingly into an armchair, say, 'Well, Jane, you were right, more's the pity!'

'She really gave him the cheque!'

'Yes, but at least it was only for seven. The rascal himself must have altered it into seventy. She and the other girl both agree as to that. There's been a clandestine correspondence going on with that scamp ever since she has been here, under cover to that precious friend of hers—that Hacket girl.'

'Ah! you warned me, Jenny,' said Lady Merrifield 'But I'm quite sure Miss Hacket knew nothing of it.'

'I don't suppose she did. She seemed struck all of a heap. Any way they've quarrelled now; the other one has turned King's evidence—has lost some money too, and says Dolores deceived her. She's deceived every one all round, that's the fact. Why she told me two flat lies this very morning—lies—there's no other name for it. What will you do with her, Lily?'

'I don't know,' said Lady Merrifield, utterly shocked, and recollecting, but not mentioning, the falsehood told to her about the note. Lord Rotherwood said, 'Poor child,' and Colonel Mohun groaned, 'Poor Maurice.'

'Then she did go to Darminster?' said Miss Mohun.

'Yes; that came out from this Miss Constance, who seems to have been properly taken in about some publishing trash. Serve her right! But it seems Dolores beguiled her with stories about her dear uncle in distress. We left her nearly in hysterics, and I told the children to come away.'

'What does Dolores say?' asked Jane.

'Nothing! I could not get a word out of her after the first surprise at the alteration of the cheque. Not a word nor a tear. She is as hard—as hard as a bit of stone.'

'Really,' said Lady Merrifield, 'I can't help thinking there's a good deal of excuse for her.'

'What? That poor Maurice's wife was half a heathen, and afterwards the girl was left to chance?' said Colonel Mohun. 'I see no other. And you, Lily, are the last person I should expect to excuse untruth.'

'I did not mean to do that, Regie; but you all say that poor Mary was fond of this man and helped him.'

'That she did!' said Lord Rotherwood, 'and very much against the grain it went with Maurice.'

'Then don't you see that this poor child, who probably never had the matter explained to her, may have felt it a great hardship to be cut off from the man her mother taught her to care for; and that may have led her into concealments?'

'Well!' said Colonel Mohun, 'at that rate, at least one may be thankful never to have married.'

'One—or two, Regie?' said Jane, as they all laughed at his sally. 'I think I had better go up and see whether I can get anything out of the child. Do you mean to have her down to dinner, Lily,' she added, glancing at the clock.

'Oh yes, certainly. I don't want to put her to disgrace before all the children and servants—that is, if she is not crying herself out of condition to appear, poor child.'

'Not she,' said Uncle Reginald.

On opening the door, the children were all discovered in the hall, in anxious curiosity, not venturing in uncalled, but very much puzzled.

Gillian came forward and said, 'Mamma, may we know what is the matter?'

'I hardly understand it myself yet, my dear, only that Dolores and Constance Hacket have let themselves be taken in by a sort of relation of Dolores's mother, and Uncle Maurice has lost a good deal of money through it. It would not have happened if there had been fair and upright dealing towards me; but we do not know the rights of it, and you had better take no notice of it to her.'

'I thought,' said Valetta, sagaciously, 'no good could come of running after that stupid Miss Constance.'

'Who can't pull a cracker, and screams at a daddy long-legs,' added Fergus.

'But, mamma, what shall we do?' said Gillian. 'I came away because Uncle Regie told us, and Constance was crying so terribly; but what is poor Miss Hacket to do? There is the tree only half dressed, and all the girls coming to-night, unless she puts them off.'

'Yes, you had better go down alone as soon as dinner is over, and see what she would like,' said Lady Merrifield. 'We must not leave her in the lurch, as if we cast her off, though I am afraid Constance has been very foolish in this matter. Oh, Gillian, I wish we could have made Dolores happier amongst us, and then this would not have happened.'

'She would never let us, mamma,' said Gillian.

But Mysie, coming up close to her mother as they all went up the broad staircase to prepare for the midday meal, confessed in a grave little voice, 'Mamma, I think I have sometimes been cross to Dolly-more lately, because it has been so very tiresome.'

Lady Merrifield drew the little girl into her own room, stooped down, and kissed her, saying, 'My dear child, these things need a great deal of patience. You will have to be doubly kind and forbearing now, for she must be very unhappy, and perhaps not like to show it. You might say a little prayer for her, that God will help us to be kind to her, and soften her heart.'

'Oh yes, mamma; and, please, will you set it down for me?'

'Yes, my dear, and for myself too. You shall have it before bed-time.'

Aunt Jane had followed Dolores to her own room the girl, who was sitting on her bed, dazed, regretted that she had not bolted her door, as her aunt entered with the words, 'Oh, Dolores, I am very sorry I could not have thought you would so have abused the confidence that was placed in you.'

To this Dolores did not answer. To her mind she was the person ill-used by the prohibition of correspondence, but she could not say so. Every one was falling on her; but Aunt Jane's questions could not well help being answered.

'What will your father think of if?'

'He never forbade me to write to Uncle Alfred' said Dolores.

'Because he never thought of your doing such a thing. Did he give you this cheque?'

'Yes.'

'For yourself?'

'N-n-o. But it was the same.'

'What do you mean by that?'

'It was to pay a man—a man's that's dead.'

'That may be; but what right did that give you to spend the money otherwise? Who was the man?'

'Professor Muhlwasser, for some books of plates.'

'How do you know he is dead! Who told you so? Eh! Was it Flinders? Ah! you see what comes of trusting to an unprincipled man like that. If you had only been open and straightforward with Aunt Lily, or with any of us, you would have been saved from this tissue of falsehood; forfeiting your Uncle Reginald's good opinion, and enabling Flinders to do your father this great injury.' She paused, and, as Dolores made no answer, she went on again—'Indeed, there is no saying what you have not brought on yourself by your deceit and disobedience. If Flinders is apprehended, you will have to appear against him in court, and publicly avow that you gave away what your father trusted to you.'

Dolores gave a little moan and start, and her aunt, perceiving that she had touched an apparently vulnerable spot, proceeded—'The only thing left for you to do is to tell the whole story frankly and honestly. I don't say so only for the sake of showing Aunt Lily that you are sorry for having abused her confidence. I wish I could think that you are; but, unless we know all, we cannot shield you from any further consequences, and that of course we should wish to do, for your father's sake.'

Dolores did not feel drawn to confession, but she knew that when Aunt Jane once set herself to ask questions, there was no use in trying to conceal anything. So she made answers, chiefly 'Yes' or No,' and her aunt, by severe and diligent pumping, had extracted bit by bit what it was most essential should be known, before the gong summoned them. Dolores would rather have been a solitary prisoner, able to chafe against oppression, than have been obliged to come down and confront everybody; but she crept into the place left for her between Mysie and Wilfred. She had very little appetite, and never found out how Mysie was fulfilling her resolution of kindness by baulking Wilfred of sundry attempts to tease; by substituting her own kissing-crust for Dolly's more unpoetical piece of bread; and offering to exchange her delicious strawberry-jam tartlet for the black-currant one at which her cousin was looking with reluctant eyes.

Mysie and Valetta were grievously exercised about their chances of returning to the G.F.S. Tree. Indeed Gillian went the length of telling them that Fly was behaving far better in her disappointment as to the Butterfly's Ball than they were as to this 'old second-hand tree.' Fly laughed and observed, 'Dear me, things one would like are always being stopped. If one was to mind every time, how horrid it would be! And there's always something to make up!'

Then it occurred to Gillian, though not to her younger sisters, that Lady Phyllis Devereux lived in general a much less indulged, and more frequently disappointed, life than did herself and her sisters.

However, there was great delight at that dinner-table. Jasper had ridden to get the letters of the second post, and Lord Rotherwood had his hands and his head full of them when he came in to luncheon—there being what Lady Merrifield called a respectable dinner in view. In the first place. Lord Ivinghoe was getting on very well, and was up, sitting by the fire, playing patience. Nobody was catching the measles, and quarantine would be over on the 9th of January. Secondly, 'Fly, shall you be very broken-hearted if I tell you.'

'Oh, daddy, you wouldn't look like that if it was anything very bad! Lion isn't dead?'

'No; but I grieve to say your unnatural grand-parents don't want you! Grandmamma is nervous about having you without mamma. What did we do last time we were there, Fly?'

'Don't you remember, daddy? they said there was nothing for me to ride to the meet, and you and Griffin put the side-saddle on Crazy Kate, and we went out with the hounds, and I've got the brush up in my room!'

'I don't wonder grandmamma is nervous,' observed Lady Merrifield.

'Will you be nervous, Lily,' said Lord Rotherwood, 'if this same flyaway mortal is left on your hands till the 9th?'

Dinner, manners, silence before company, and all, could not repress a general scream of ecstacy, which called forth the reply. 'I should think you and her mother were the people to be nervous.

'Oh! my lady has been duly instructed in Merrifield perfections, and esteems you a model mother.'

The children's nods and smiles said 'Hear, hear!'

'Well, you've got it all in her own letter,' continued Lord Rotherwood. 'You see, they've got a caucus at High Court, and a dinner, and I must go up there on Monday; but if you'll keep this dangerous Fly—'

'I can answer for the pleasure it will give,'

'Well then, I'll come back for her by the 9th, and you've Victoria's letter, haven't you?'

'Yes, it is very kind of her.'

'Then I shall expect you to be ready to start with me for the Butterfly's Ball. Eh, young ladies, what will you come out as?'

'Oh daddy, daddy, is it? Has mamma asked them? Oh! it is more delicious than anything ever was. Mysie, Mysie, what will you be?'

'The sly little dormouse crept out of his hole,' quoted Mysie, in a very low, happy voice.

'And I will be a jolly old frog,' shouted Fergus, finding the ordinance of silence broken and making the most of it, on the presumption that the whole family were invited. However, the tone, rather than the uncomprehended words of his mother's answer, 'Nobody asked you, sir,' she said, reduced him to silence, and it became understood, through Fly's inquiries, that the invitation included Lady Merrifield must make her acceptance doubtful. And besides, the question which three were to go was the unspoken drawback to full bliss, and yet the delight was exceedingly great in the prospect, great enough to make the contrast of gloom in poor Dolores's spirit all the darker, as she sat, left out of everything, and she could not now say, with absolute injustice, though she still clung to the belief that there was more misfortune than fault in her disgrace.

She crept away, shivering with unhappiness, to the schoolroom, while the others frisked off discussing the wonderful Butterfly's Ball. Lady Merrifield looked in on her, and she hardened herself to endure either another probing or fresh reproaches, but all she heard was, 'My dear, I cannot talk over this sad affair now, as I have to go out. But, if you can, I think you had better write to your father about it, and let him understand exactly how it happened. Or, if you had rather write than speak in explaining it to me, you can do so, and we can consider tomorrow what is to be done about it.'

Then she went out with her brother and cousin to drive to some Industrial schools which Lord Rotherwood wanted to see.

CHAPTER XV
THE BUTTERFLY'S BALL

Miss Mohun went to the Casement Cottages with Gillian to see what the elder Miss Hacket might wish and whether they could be of use to her; the young people being left to exercise themselves within call in case the Tree was to be continued.

This proved to be an act of great kindness, for poor Mary Hacket was suffering all the distress of an upright and honourable woman at her sister's abuse of confidence; and had felt as if Colonel Mohun's summons to his nieces was the close of all intimacy with such an unworthy household. Moreover, the evenings entertainment could not be given up and Gillian was despatched to summon the eager assistants, while Aunt Jane repeated her assurances that Lady Merrifield perfectly understood Miss Hacket's ignorance of the doings in Constance's room—listening patiently even when the tender-hearted woman began to excuse her sister for having accepted Dolores's lamentations at being cut off from her so-called uncle. 'Dear Connie is so romantic, and so easily touched,' she said, 'though, of course, it was very wrong of her to suppose that Lady Merrifield could do anything harsh or unkind. She is in great grief now, poor darling, she feels so bitterly that her friend led her into it by deceiving her about the relationship and character.'

This, Aunt Jane did not think the worst part of the affair, and she said that the girl had been brought up to call the man Uncle Alfred, and very possibly did not understand that he was only so by courtesy, nor that he was so utterly untrustworthy.

'I thought so,' said Mary Hacket. 'I told Connie that such a child could not possibly have been a willing party to his fraud—for fraud, I fear, it was—Miss Mohun. Do you think there is any hope of her recovering the sum she advanced.'

'I am afraid there is not, even if the wretched man is apprehended.'

'Ah! if she had only told me what she wanted it for!'

'I hope it was all her own.'

'Oh, Miss Mohun, no doubt you know that two sisters living together must accommodate one another a little, and Connie's dress expenses, at her age, are necessarily more than mine. But here come the dear children, and we ought to dismiss all painful subjects, though I declare I am so nervous I hardly know what I am about.'

However, by Miss Mohun's help, the good lady rose to the occasion, and when once busy, the trouble was thrown off, so that no guests would have detected how unhappy she had been in the forenoon. Constance soon came down, and confided to Gillian a parcel directed to Miss D. Mohun, containing all the notes written to her, and all the books lent to her, by the false friend whom she had cast off, after which she threw herself into the interests of the present.

The London ornaments, and the residue of the gifts and bonbons, made the Christmas-tree a most memorable one to the G.F.S. mind.

As to Fly, she fraternized to a great extent with a very small maid, in a very long, brown dress, and very thick boots, who did not taste a single bonbon, and being asked whether she understood that they were good to eat, replied that she was keeping them for 'our Bertie and Minnie;' and, on encouragement, launched into such a description of her charges—the blacksmith's small children—that Lady Phyllis went back, not without regrets that she could not be a little nurse who had done with school at twelve years old, and spent her days at the back of a perambulator.

'Oh, daddy,' she said, 'I do wish you had come down; it was such lovely fun—the best tree I ever saw. Why wouldn't you come?'

'If thirty odd years should pass over that little head of yours, my Lady Fly, and you should then meet with Mysie and Val, maybe you will then learn the reason why.'

'We will recollect that in thirty years' time.'

'When our children go to a Christmas-tree.'

'And we sit over the fire instead.'

'Oh! but should we ever not care for a dear, delightful Christmas-tree?'

'If we had each other instead.'

'Then we would all go still together!'

'And tell our little boys and girls all about this one, and the Butterfly's Ball!'

'Perhaps our husbands would want us, and not let us go.'

'Oh! I don't want a husband. He'd be in the way. We'd send him off to India or somewhere, like Aunt Lily's.'

'Don't, Fly; it is not at all nice to have papa away.'

'Oh yes, it would be ten hundred times better if he were at home.'

Such were the mingled sentiments of the triad, as they went upstairs to bed, linked together in their curious fashion.

Some time later, a bedroom discussion of affairs was held by Lady Merrifield and Miss Mohun, who had not had a moment alone together all day, to converse upon the two versions of the disaster which the latter had extracted from Dolores and Constance, and which fairly agreed, though Constance had been by far the most voluble, and somewhat ungenerously violent against her former friend, at least so Lady Merrifield remarked.

'You should take into account the authoress's disappointed vanity.'

'Yes, poor thing! How he must have nattered her!'

'Besides, there is the loss of the money, which, I fear, falls as seriously on good Miss Hacket as on the goose herself.'

'Does it, indeed? That must not be. How much is it?'

'Fifteen pounds; and that foolish Constance fancies that poor Dolores assisted in duping her. I really had to defend the girl; though I am just as angry myself when I watch her adamantine sullenness.'

'I am the person to be angry with for having allowed the intimacy, in spite of your warnings, Jenny.'

'You were too innocent to know what girls are made of. Oh yes, you are very welcome to have six of your own, but you might have six dozen without knowing what a girl brought up at a second-rate boarding-school is capable of, or what it is to have had no development of conscience. What shall you do? send her to school?'

'After that recommendation of yours?'

'I didn't propose a second-rate boarding-school, ma'am. There's a High School starting after the holidays at Rockstone. Let me have her, and send her there.'

'Ada would not like it.'

'Never mind Ada, I'll settle her. I would keep Dolly well up to her lessons, and prevent these friendships.'

'I suppose you would manage her better than I have been able to do,' said Lady Merrifield, reluctantly. 'Yet I should like to try again; I don't want to let her go. Is it the old story of duty and love, Jane? Have I failed again through negligence and ignorance, and deceived myself by calling weakness and blindness love?'

'You don't fail with your own, Lily. Rotherwood runs about admiring them, and saying he never saw a better union of freedom and obedience. It was really a treat to see Gillian's ways tonight; she had so much consideration, and managed her sisters so well.'

'Ah, but there's their father! I do so dread spoiling them for him before he comes home; but then he is a present influence with us all the time.'

'They would all clap their hands if I carried Dolly off.'

'Yes, and that is one reason I don't want to give her up; it seems so sad to send Maurice's child away leaving such an impression. One thing I am thankful for, that it will be all over before grandmamma and Bessie Merrifield come.'

At that moment there was a knock at the door, and a small figure appeared in a scarlet robe, bare feet, and dishevelled hair.

'Mysie, dear child! What's the matter? who is ill?'

'Oh, please come, mamma, Dolly is choking and crying in such a dreadful way, and I can't stop her.'

'I give up, Lily. This is mother-work,' said Miss Mohun.

Hurrying upstairs, Lady Merrifield found very distressing sounds issuing from Dolores's room; sobs, not loud, but almost strangled into a perfect agony of choking down by the resolute instinct, for it was scarcely will.

'My dear, my dear, don't stop it!' she exclaimed, lifting up the girl in her arms. 'Let it out; cry freely; never mind. She will be better soon, Mysie dear. Only get me a glass of water, and find a fresh handkerchief. There, there, that's right!' as Dolores let herself lean on the kind breast, and conscious that the utmost effects of the disturbance had come, allowed her long-drawn sobs to come freely, and moaned as they shook her whole frame, though without screaming. Her aunt propped her up on her own bosom, parted back her hair, kissed her, and saying she was getting better, sent Mysie back to her bed. The first words that were gasped out between the rending sobs were, 'Oh! is my—he—to be tried?'

'Most likely not, my dear. He has had full time to get away, and I hope it is so.'

'But wasn't he there? Haven't they got him? Weren't they asking me about him, and saying I must be tried for stealing father's cheque?'

'You were dreaming, my poor child. They have not taken him, and I am quite sure you will not be tried anyway.'

'They said—Aunt Jane and Uncle Reginald and all, and 'that dreadful man that came—'

'Perhaps they said you might have to be examined, but only if he is apprehended, and I fully expect that he is out of reach, so that you need not frighten yourself about that, my dear.'

'Oh, don't go!' cried Dolores, as her aunt stirred.

'No, I'm not going. I was only reaching some water for you. Let me sponge your face.'

To this Dolores submitted gratefully, and then sighed, as if under heavy oppression, 'And did he really do it?'

'I am afraid he must have done so.'

'I never thought it. Mother always helped him.'

'Yes, my dear, that made it very hard for you to know what was right to do, and this is a most terrible shock for you,' said her aunt, feeling unable to utter another reproach just then to one who had been so loaded with blame, and she was touched the more when Dolores moaned, 'Mother would have cared so much.'

She answered with a kiss, was glad to find her hand still held, and forgot that it was past eleven o'clock.

'Please, will it quite ruin father?' asked Dolores, who had not outgrown childish confusion about large sums of money.

'Not exactly, my dear. It was more than he had in the bank, and Uncle Regie thinks the bankers will undertake part of the loss if he will let them. It is more inconvenient than ruinous.'

'Ah!' There was a faintness and oppression in the sound which made Lady Merrifield think the girl ought not to be left, and before long, sickness came on. Nurse Halfpenny had to be called up, and it was one o'clock before there was a quiet, comfortable sleep, which satisfied the aunt and nurse that it was safe to repair to their own beds again.

The dreary, undefined self-reproach and vague alarms, intensified by the sullen, reserved temper, and culminating in such a shock, alienating the only persons she cared for, and filling her with terror for the future, could not but have a physical effect, and Dolores was found on the morrow with a bad head-ache, and altogether in a state to be kept in bed, with a fire in her room.

Gillian and Mysie were much impressed by the intelligence of their cousin's illness when they came to their mother's room on the way to breakfast, and Mysie turned to her sister, saying, 'There Gill, you see she did care, though she didn't cry like us. Being ill is more than crying.'

'Well,' said Gillian, 'it is a good deal more than such things as you and Val cry for, Mysie.'

'It was a trial such as you don't understand, my dears,' said Lady Merrifield. 'I don't, of course, excuse much that she did, but she had been used to see her mother make every exertion to help the man.'

'That does make a difference,' said Gillian, 'but she shouldn't have taken her father's money. And wasn't it dreadful of Constance to smuggle her letters? I'm quite glad Constance gets part of the punishment.'

'Certainly, that might be just, Gillian, but unfortunately the loss falls infinitely more heavily upon Miss Hacket, who cannot afford the loss at all.'

'Oh dear!' cried Mysie.

'I'm very sorry,' said Gillian.

'And, my dear girls, in all honour and honesty, we must make it up to her.'

'Can't we save it out of our allowance?' said Mysie.

'Sixpence a month from you, a shilling perhaps from Gill, how long would that take? No, my dear girls, I am going to put you to a heavy trial.'

'Oh, mamma, don't!' cried Gillian, seeing what she was driving at. 'Don't give up the Butterfly's Ball.'

'Oh, don't!' implored Mysie, tears starting in her eyes. 'We never saw a costume ball, and Fly wishes it so.'

'And I thought you had promised,' said Gillian.

'Cousin Rotherwood assumes that I did; but I did not really accept. I told him I could not tell, for you know your Grandmamma Merrifield talked of coming here, and I cannot put her off. And now I see that it must be given up.'

'It need only be calico!' sighed Gillian, sticking pins in and out of the pincushion.

'Fancy dresses even in calico are very expensive. Besides, I could not go to a place like Rotherwood without at least two new dresses, and it is not right to put papa to more expense.'

'Oh, mamma! couldn't you? You always do look nicer than any one,' said Mysie.

'My dear, I am afraid nothing I have at present would be suitable for a General's wife at Lady Rotherwood's party, and we must think of what would be fitting both towards our hostess and papa. Don't you see?'

'Ah! your velvet dress!' sighed Gillian.

'My poor old faithful state apparel,' smiled Lady Merrifield. 'Poor Gill, you did not think again to have to mourn for it, but I don't know that even that could have been sufficiently revivified, though it was my cheval de bataille for so many years.

For Lady Merrifield's black velvet of many years' usefulness, had been put on for her p.p.c. party at Belfast, when Gillian, in abetting Jasper in roasting chestnuts over a paraffin-lamp, had set herself and the tablecloth on fire, and had been extinguished with such damages as singed hair, a scar on Jasper's hands, and the destruction of her mother's 'front breadth.' There had been such relief and thankfulness at its being no worse that the 'state apparel' had not been much mourned, especially as the remains made a charming pelisse for Primrose; and in the retirement of Silverton, it had not been missed till the present occasion.

'Do gowns cost so very much?' said Mysie.

'Indeed they do, my poor Mouse. The lamented cost more than twenty pounds. I had been thinking whether I could afford the requisite garments—not quite so costly—and thought I might get them for about sixteen, with contrivance; but you see I feel it my fault that I let Dolores go and lead Constance to get cheated, and I cannot take the money out of what papa gives for household expenses and your education, so it must come out of my own personal allowance. Don't you see?'

'Ye—es,' said Gillian, apparently intent on getting a big, black-headed pin repeatedly into the same hole, while Mysie was trying with all her might not to cry.

'You are thinking it is very hard that you should suffer for Dolly's faults. Perhaps it is, but such things may often happen to you, my dears. Christians bear them well for love's sake, you know.'

'And it is a little my fault,' said Gillian, thoughtfully; 'for it was I that let the chestnut fall into the lamp.'

'I—I don't think I should have minded so much,' said Mysie, almost crying, 'if we had done it our own selves—and Fly too—for some very poor woman in the snow.'

'I know that very well, Mysie, and this is a much harder trial, as you don't get the honour and glory of it; and, besides, you will have to take care to say not a word of this reason to Fly or Valetta, or any one else.'

'Val will be awfully disappointed,' said Gillian.

'Poor Val! But I should not have taken her anyway, so that matters the less. I should have taken Jasper, for that would have been more convenient than so many girls. In fact, I did not mean anybody to have heard of it till I had made up my mind, so that there would have been no disappointment; but that naughty Cousin Rotherwood could not keep it to himself; and so, my poor maidens, you have to bear it with a good grace, and to be treated as my confidential friends.'

Mysie smiled and kissed her mother—Gillian cleared somewhat, but observing, 'I only wish it wasn't clothes;' tried to dismiss the subject as the gong began to sound, but Mysie caught her mother's dress, and said, 'Mayn't I tell Fly, for a great secret?'

'No, my dear, certainly not. Fly is a dear little girl, but we don't know how she can keep secrets, and it would never do to let the Rotherwoods know; papa and Uncle William would be exceedingly annoyed. And only think of Miss Hacket's feelings if it came round. It will be hard enough to get her to take it now.'

'Perhaps she won't,' flashed into the minds of both girls; but Mysie said entreatingly, 'One moment more, mamma, please! What can I say to Fly that will be the truth?'

'Say that I find we cannot go, and that I had never promised,' said Lady Merrifield. 'I trust you, my dears.'

And as she opened the door to hurry down to prayers, the two sisters felt the words very precious and inspiriting. Mysie lingered on the step and bravely asked Gillian whether her eyes looked like crying—

'No, only a little twinkly,' answered the elder sister; 'they will be all right after prayers if you don't rub them.'

'No, I won't, said Mysie; "I'll try to mean 'Thy will be done.' For I suppose it is His will, though it is mamma's."

'I'm glad you thought of that, Mysie,' said Gillian; 'you see it is mamma's goodness.' And Gillian added to herself, "dear little Mysie too. If it had not been for her, I believe I should have 'grizzled' all prayer-time, and now I hope I shall attend instead."

When everybody rose up from their knees, Lady Merrifield was glad to see two fairly cheerful faces. She tried to lessen the responsibility of the confidants, and to get the matter settled by telling Lord Rotherwood at once and publicly that she had thought his kind invitation over, and that she found she must not accept it. Perhaps she warily took the moment after she had seen the postman coming up the drive, for he had only time to say, 'Now, that's too bad, Lily, you don't mean it,' and she to answer, 'Yes, in sad earnest, I do,' before the letters came in, and the attention of the elders was taken off by the distribution.

But Valetta whispered to Gillian, 'Not going; oh why?'

'No; never mind, you wouldn't have gone, anyway—hush—' said Gillian, beginning, it may be, a little sharply, but then becoming dismayed as Valetta, perhaps a little unhinged by the late pleasures, burst forth into such a fit of crying as made everybody look up, and her mother tell her to go away if she could not behave better. Gillian, understanding a sign of the head as permission, led her away, hearing Lord Rotherwood observe,—

'There, you cruel party!' before again becoming absorbed in his letter.

'Oh dear!' sighed Fly, turning to Mysie as they rose from table, 'I am so sorry! It would have been so nice; and I thought we were safe, as mamma had written herself!'

'Ah! but my mamma hadn't accepted,' said Mysie.

Phyllis seemed to take this as final, and sighed, but Mysie presently exclaimed, 'I say! can't we all play at Butterfly's Ball in the hall after lessons?'

'Lessons?' said Fly; 'but it's holiday-time?'

'Mamma always makes us do a sort of little lesson, even in the holidays, as she says we get naughty. But I suppose you need not; and perhaps she will not make us now you are here.'

Colonel Mohun and Lord Rotherwood were going to Darminster to see what was the state of the investigation about Mr. Flinders. They set out directly after breakfast, and after the feeding of the pets, where Valetta joined them, much consoled by the prospect of the extemporary Butterfly's Ball at home, Lady Phyllis, with her usual ready adaptability, repaired with the others to the schoolroom, where the Psalms and Lessons were read, and a small amount of French reading in turn from 'En Quarantaine' followed, with accompaniment of needlework or drawing, after which the children were free.

Aunt Jane was going home to her Sunday school and the Rockstone festivities. She came down for her final talk with her sister just in time to perceive the folding up of three five-pound notes.

'Lily,' she said, with instant perception, 'I could beat myself for what I told you yesterday.'

Lady Merrifield laughed. 'The girls are very good about it!' she said. 'Now you have found it out, see whether that note will make Miss Hacket swallow it.'

'Can't be better! But oh. Lily, it is disgusting! Could not I rig up something fanciful for the children?'

'That's not so much the point. 'The General's lady,' as Mrs. Halfpenny would say, is bound not to look like 'ane scrub,' as she would be unwelcome to Victoria, and what would be William's feelings? I could hardly have accomplished it even with this, and the catastrophe settles the matter.'

'You could not get into my black satin?'

'No, I thank you, my dear little Brownie,' said Lady Merrifield, elongating herself like a girl measuring heights.

'Ada has a larger assortment, as well as a taller person,' continued Miss Jane, 'but then they are rather 'henspeckle,' and they have all made their first appearance at Rotherwood.'

'No, no, thank you, my dear, Jasper would not like the notion—even if there was not more of me than of Ada. I have no doubt it is much better for us.'

'Should you have liked it, Lily?'

'For once in a way. For Rotherwood's sake, dear old fellow. Yes, I should.'

'Ah, well! You are a bit of a grande dame yourself. Ada enjoys it, too, or I don't think I ever should go there.'

'Surely Victoria behaves well to you?'

'Far be it from me to say she is not exemplary in her perfect civility to all her husband's relations. Ada thinks her charming; but oh. Lily, you've never found out what it is to be a little person in a great person's house, and to feel one's self scrupulously made one of the family, because her husband is so much attached to all of them. There's nothing spontaneous about it! I dare say you would get on better, though You are not a country-town old maid; you would have an air of the world and of distinction even if you went in your old grey poplin.'

'Well, I thought better of my lady.'

'You ought not! She makes great efforts, I am sure, and is a pattern of graciousness and cordiality—only that's just what riles one, when one knows one is just as well born, and all the rest of it. And then I'm provided with the clever men, and the philanthropical folk to talk to. I know it's a great compliment, and they are very nice, but I'd ten times rather take my chance among them. However, now I've made the grapes sour for you, what do you think about Dolores? Will you send her to us?'

'Not immediately, at any rate, dear Jane. It is very kind in you to wish to take her off our hands, but I do want to try her a little longer. I thought she seemed to be softening last night.'

'She was as hard as ever when I went in to wish her good-bye.'

'I thought she had too much headache for conversation when I went in last; I think this is a regular upset from unhappiness and reserve.'

'Alias temper and deceitfulness.'

'Something of both. You know the body often suffers when things are not thrown out in a wholesome explosion at once, but go simmering on; and I mean to let this poor child alone till she is well.'

'Ah! here comes the pony-carriage. Well, Lily, send her to me if you repent.'

The sisters came out to find the Butterfly's Ball in full action. Fly had become a Butterfly by the help of a battered pair of fairy wings, stretched on wire, which were part of the theatrical stock. 'The shy little Dormouse' was creeping about on all fours under a fur jacket, with a dilapidated boa for a long tail, but her 'blind brother the Mole' had escaped from her, and had been transformed into the Frog, by means of a spotted handkerchief over his back, and tremendous leap-frog jumps. Primrose, in another pair of fairy wings, was personating the Dragon-fly and all his relations, 'green, orange, and blue.' Valetta, in perfect content with the present, with a queer pair of ears, and a tail made of an old brush, sat up and nibbled as Squirrel. The Grasshopper was performing antics which made him not easily distinguishable from the Frog, and the Spider was actually descending by a rope from the balusters, while his mother, standing somewhat aghast, breathed a hope that 'poor Harlequin's' fall was not part of the programme. But she did not interfere, having trust in the gymnastics that were studied at school by Jasper, who had been beguiled into the game by Fly's fascinations.

'A far more realistic performance than the Rotherwood Butterfly's Ball is likely to be,' said Aunt Jane, aside, as the various guests came up for her departing kiss. 'And much more entertaining, if they could only think so. Where's Gillian?'

Gillian appeared on the stairs in her own person at the moment. She said Mrs. Halfpenny had called her, and told her that 'Miss Dollars' was crying, and that she did not think the child ought to be left alone long to fret herself, but Saturday morning needments called away nurse herself, so she had ordered in Miss Gillian as her substitute. Gillian was reading to her, and had only come away to make her farewells to Aunt Jane.

'That is right, my dear,' said her mother; 'I will come and sit with her after luncheon.'

For the whole youthful family were to turn out to superintend the replantation of the much-enduring fir, which, it was hoped, might survive for many another Christmas.

However, Lady Merrifield could not keep her promise, for a whole party of visitors arrived just after the children's dinner was over.

'And it's old Mrs. Norgood,' sighed Gillian, looking over the balusters, 'and she always slays for ages!'

'One of you young ladies must bide with Miss Dollars,' said Nurse Halfpenny, decidedly, 'or we shall have her fretting herself ill again.'

'Oh, nursie, can't you?' entreated Gillian.

'Me, Miss Gillian! How can I, when Miss Primrose is going out with the whole clamjamfrie, and all the laddies, into the wet plantations? Na—one of ye maun keep the lassie company. Ye've had your turn, Miss Gillian, so it should be Miss Mysie. It winna hurt ye, bairn, ye that hae been rampaging ower the house all the morning.'

Mysie knew it was her turn, but she also knew that nurse always favoured Gillian and snubbed her. She had a devouring longing to be with her dear Fly, and a certain sense that she was the preferred one. Must another pleasure be sacrificed to that very naughty Dolores, whose misdemeanours had deprived them of the visit to Rotherwood. She looked so dismal that Gillian said good-naturedly, 'Really, Mysie, I don't think mamma would mind Dolores's being left a little while; I must go down to see about the Tree, because mamma gave me a message to old Webb, but I'll come back directly. Or perhaps Dolly is going to sleep, and does not want any one. Go and see.'

Mysie on this crept quietly into the room, full of hope of escape, but Dolores was anything but asleep. 'Oh, are you come, Mysie? Now you'll go on with the story. I tried, but my eyes ache at the back of them, and I can't.'

Mysie's fate was sealed. She sat down by the fire and took up the book, 'A Story for the Schoolroom,' one of the new ones given from the Tree. It was the middle of the story, and she did not care about it at first, especially when she heard Fly's voice, and all the others laughing and chattering on the stairs.

'Didn't they care for her absence?' and her voice grew thick, and her eyes dim; but Dolores must not think her cross and unwilling, and she made a great effort, became interested in the girls there described, and wondered whether staying with Fly would have turned her head, after the example of the heroine of the book.

Dolores did not seem to want to talk. In fact, she was clinging to the reading, because she could not bear to speak or think of the state of affairs, and the story seemed, as it were, to drown her misery. She knew that her aunt and cousins were far less severe with her than she expected, but that could only be because she was ill. Had not Uncle Reginald turned against her, and Constance? It would all come upon her as soon as she came out of her room, and she was rather sorry to believe that she should be up and about to-morrow morning.

Mysie read on till the short, winter day showed the first symptoms of closing in. Then Lady Merrifield came up. 'You here, little nurse?' she said. 'Run out now and meet the others. I'll stay with Dolly.' Mysie knew by the kiss that her mother was pleased with her; but Dolores dreaded the talk with her aunt, and made herself sleepy.

CHAPTER XVI
THE INCONSTANCY OF CONSTANCE

The two gentlemen who had gone to Darminster brought home tidings that the police who had been put on the track of Flinders had telegraphed that it was thought that a person answering to his description had embarked at Liverpool in an American-bound steamer.

This idea, though very uncertain, was a relief, at least to all except the boys, who thought it a great shame that such a rascal should escape, and wanted to know whether the Americans could not be made to give him up. They did not at all understand their elders being glad, for the sake of Maurice Mohun and his dead wife, that the man should not be publicly convicted, and above all that Dolores should not have to bear testimony against him in court, and describe her own very doubtful proceedings. Besides, there would have been other things to try him for, since he had cheated the publishing house which employed him of all he had been able to get into his hands. There was reason to believe that he had heavy debts, especially gambling ones, and that he had become desperate since he no longer had his step-sister to fall back upon.

Looking into his room, among other papers, a half-burnt manuscript was found upon his grate among some exhausted cinders, as if he had been trying to use the unfortunate 'Waif of the Moorland' to eke out his last fire. Moreover, the proprietor of the Politician told Colonel Mohun of having remonstrated with him on the exceeding weakness and poorness of the 'Constantia' poetry, 'which,' as that indignant personage added, 'was evidently done merely as a lure to the unfortunate young lady.'

The fifteen pounds had been accepted in an honourable and ladylike manner by the elder sister—but without any overpowering expression of gratitude. No doubt it was a bitter pill to her, forced down by necessity, and without guessing that it cost the donors anything.

Dolores's mind was set at rest as to Flinders's evasion before night, and on the Sunday morning even Nurse Halfpenny could find out nothing the matter with her, so that she was obliged to make her appearance as usual. Uncle Reginald did not kiss her, he only gave a cold nod, and said 'Good

morning.' Otherwise all went on as usual, and it was pleasant to find that Fly was as entirely used as they were to learning Collect and hymn, and copying out texts illustrating Catechism, and that she was expected to have them ready to repeat them to her mother some time in the afternoon. There was something, too, that Mysie could not have described, but which she liked, in the manner in which, on this morning, Dolores accepted small acts of good nature, such as finding a book for her, getting a new pen and helping her to the whereabouts of a Scriptural reference. It seemed for the first time as if she liked to receive a kindness, and her 'thank you' really had a sound of thanks, instead of being much more like 'I wish you would not.' Mysie felt really encouraged to be kind, and when, on setting forth to church, everybody was crowding round trying to walk with Fly, and Dolores was going along lonely and deserted, Mysie resigned her chance of one side of the favourite Phyllis, and dropped back to give her company to the solitary one. To her surprise and gratification, Dolores took hold of her hand, and listened quite willingly to her chatter about the schemes for the fortnight that Fly was to be left with them. Presently Constance was seen going markedly by the other gate of the churchyard, quite out of her usual way, and not even looking towards them.

It was the last day of the old year, and, in the midst of the Christmas joy, there were allusions to it in the services and hymns. Something in the tune of 'Days and moments quickly flying,' touched some chord in Dolores's spirit, and set her off crying. She would have done anything to stop it, but there was no helping it, great round splashes came down, and the more she was afraid of being noticed, the worse the choking grew. At last, the very worst person—she thought—to take notice. Uncle Reginald, did so, and, under cover of a general rising, said sternly, 'Stop that, or go out.'

Stop that! Much did the colonel know about a girl's tears, or how she would have given anything to check them. But here was Aunt Lily edging down to her, taking her by the hand, leading her out, she did not know how, stopping all who would have come after them with help—then pausing a little in the open, frosty air.

'Oh, Aunt Lily! I am very sorry!'

'Never mind that, my dear. Do you feel poorly?'

'Oh no; I'm quite well—only—'

'Only overcome—I don't wonder—my dear—can you walk quietly home with me?'

'Yes, please.'

Nothing was said till they had passed the 'idle corner,' where men and half-grown lads smoked their pipes in anything but Sunday trim; and stared at the lady making her exit, till they were through the short street with shop windows closed, and a strong atmosphere of cooking, and had come into the quiet lane leading to the paddock. Then Lady Merrifield laid her hand on the girl's shoulder very gently, and said, 'It was too much for you, my dear, you are not quite strong yet.'

'Oh yes; I'm well. Only I am so very—very miserable,' and the gust of sobs and tears rushed on her again.

'Dear child, I should like to be able to help you!'

'You can't! I've done it! And—and they'll all be against me always—Uncle Regie and all!'

'Uncle Regie was very much hurt, but I'm sure he will forgive you when he sees how sorry you are. You know we all hope this is going to be a fresh start. I am sure you were deceived.'

'Yes,' said Dolores. 'I never could have thought he—Uncle Alfred—was such a dreadful man.'

'I expect that since he lost your mother's influence and help he may have sunk lower than when you had seen him before. Did your father give you any directions about him?'

'No. Father hated to hear of him' and never spoke about him if he could help it; and we thought it was all Mohun high notions because he wasn't quite a gentleman.'

'I see. Indeed, my dear, though you have done very wrong, I have already felt that there was great excuse for you in trying to keep up intercourse with a person who belonged to your mother. I wish you had told me, but I suppose you were afraid.'

'Yes' said Dolores. 'And I thought you were sure to be cross and harsh,' she muttered. And then suddenly looking up, 'Oh, Aunt Lily! everybody is angry but you—you and Mysie! Please go on being kind! I believe you've been good to me always.'

'My dear, I've tried,' said Lady Merrifield, with fears in her brown eyes and a choke in her voice caressing the hand that had been put into hers. 'I have wished very much to make you happy with us; but the ways of a large family must be a trial to a new-comer.'

Dolores raised her face for a kiss, and said, 'I see it now. But I did not like everything always, and I thought aunts were sure to be unkind.'

'That was very hard. And why?'

She was heard to mutter something about aunts in books always being cross.

'Ah! my dear! I suppose there are some unkind aunts, but I am sure there are a great many more who wish with all their hearts to make happy homes for their nieces. I hope now we may do so. I have more hope than ever I had, and so I shall write to your father.'

'And please—please,' cried Dolores, 'don't let Uncle Regie write him a very dreadful letter! I know he will.'

'I think you can prevent that best yourself, by telling Uncle Regie how sorry you are. He was specially grieved because he thinks you told him two direct falsehoods.'

'Oh! I didn't think they were that,' said Dolores, 'for it was true that father did not leave anything with me for Uncle Alfred. And I did not know whether it was me whom he saw at Darminster. I did tell you one once, Aunt Lily, when you asked if I gave Constance a note. At least, she gave it to me, and not I to her. Indeed, I don't tell falsehoods, Aunt Lily—I mean I never did at home, but Constance said everybody said those sort of things at school, and that one was driven to it when one was—'

'Was what, my dear?'

'Tyrannized over,' Dolores got out.

'Ah! Dolly, I am afraid Constance was no real friend. It was a great mistake to think her like Miss Hacket.'

'And now she has sent back all my notes, and won't look at me or speak to me,' and Dolores's tears began afresh.

'It is very ungenerous of her, but very likely she will be very sorry to have done so when her first anger is over, and she understands that you were quite as much deceived as she was.'

'But I shall never care for her again. It is not like Mysie, who never stopped being kind all the time—nor Gillian either. I shall cut her next time!'

'You should remember that she has something to forgive. I don't want you to be intimate with her but I think it would be better if, instead of quarrelling openly, you wrote a note to say that you were deceived and that you are very sorry for what you brought on her.'

'I should not have gone on with it but for her and Her stupid poems!'

'Can you bear to tell me how it all was, my dear? I do not half understand it.'

The Two Sides of the Shield | 185

And on the way home, and in Lady Merrifield's own room Dolores found it a relief to pour forth an explanation of the whole affair, beginning with that meeting with Mr. Flinders at Exeter, of which no one had heard, and going on to her indignation at the inspection of her letters; and how Constance had undertaken to conduct her correspondence, 'and that made it seem as if she must write to some one,'—so she wrote to Uncle Alfred. And then Constance, becoming excited at the prospect of a literary connection, all the rest followed. It was a great relief to have told it all, and Lady Merrifield was glad to see that the sense of deceit was what weighed most heavily upon her niece, and seemed to have depressed her all along. Indeed, the aunt came to the conclusion that though Dolores alone might still have been sullen, morose and disagreeable, perhaps very reserved, she never would have kept up the systematic deceit but for Constance. The errors, regarded as sin, weighed on Lady Merrifield's mind, but she judged it wiser not to press that thought on an unprepared spirit, trusting that just as Dolores had wakened to the sense of the human love that surrounded her, hitherto disbelieved and disregarded, so she might yet awake to the feeling of the Divine love and her offence against it.

The afternoon was tolerably free, for the gentlemen, including the elder boys, walked to evensong at a neighbouring church noted for its musical services, and Lady Merrifield, as she said, 'lashed herself up' to go with Gillian, carry back the remnant of the unhappy 'Waif,' and 'have it out' with Constance, who would, she feared, never otherwise understand the measure of her own delinquency, and from whom, perhaps, evidence might be extracted which would palliate the poor child's offence in the eyes of Colonel Mohun. Both the Hacket sisters looked terribly frightened when she appeared, and the elder one made an excuse for getting her outside the door to beseech her to be careful, dear Constance was so nervous and so dreadfully upset by all she had undergone. Lady Merrifield was not the least nervous of the two, and she felt additionally displeased with Constance for not having said one word of commiseration when her sister had inquired for Dolores. On returning to the drawing-room, Lady Merrifield found the young lady standing by the window, playing with the blind, and looking as if she wanted to make her escape.

'I do not know whether you will be sorry or glad to see this,' said Lady Merrifield, producing a half-burnt roll of paper. 'It was found in Mr. Flinders's grate, and my brother thought you would be glad that it should not get into strange hands.'

'Oh, it was cruel! it was base! What a wicked man he is!' cried Constance, with hot tears, as she beheld the mutilated condition of her poor 'Waif.'

'Yes, it was a most unfortunate thing that you should have run into intercourse with such an utterly untrustworthy person.'

'I was grossly deceived, Lady Merrifield!' said Constance, clasping her hands somewhat theatrically.

'I shall never believe in any one again!'

'Not without better grounds, I hope,' was the answer. 'Your poor little friend is terribly broken down by all this.'

'Don't call her my friend. Lady Merrifield. She has used me shamefully! What business had she to tell me he was her uncle when he was no such thing?'

'She had been always used to call him so.'

'Don't tell me, Lady Merrifield,' said Constance, who, after her first fright, was working herself into a passion. 'You don't know what a little viper you have been warming, nor what things she has been continually saying of you. She told me—'

Lady Merrifield held up her hand with authority.

'Stay, Constance. Do you think it is generous in you to tell me this?'

'I am sure you ought to know.'

'Then why did you encourage her?'

'I pitied her—I believed her—I never thought she would have led me into this!'

'How did she lead you?'

'Always talking about her precious, persecuted uncle. I believe she was in league with him all the time!'

'That is nonsense,' said Lady Merrifield, 'as you must see if you reflect a little. Dolores was too young to have been told this man's real character; she only knew that her mother, who had spent her childhood with him, treated him as a brother, and did all she could for him. Dolores did very wrongly and foolishly in keeping up a connection with him unknown to me; but I cannot help feeling there was great excuse for her, and she was quite as much deceived as you were.'

'Oh, of course, you stand by your own niece, Lady Merrifield. If you knew what horrid things she said about your pride and unkindness, as she called it, you would not think she deserved it.'

'Nay, that is exactly what does most excuse her in my eyes. Her fancying such things of me was what did prevent her from confiding in me.'

Constance had believed herself romantic, but the Christian chivalry of Lady Merrifield's nature was something quite beyond her. She muttered something about Dolores not deserving, which made her visitor really angry, and say, 'We had better not talk of deserts. Dolores is a mere child—a mother-less child, who had been a good deal left to herself for many months. I let her come to you because she seemed shy and unhappy with us, and I did not like to deny her the one pleasure she seemed to care for. I knew what an excellent person and thorough lady your sister is, and I thought I could perfectly trust her with you. I little thought you would have encouraged her in concealment, and—I must say—deceit, and thus made me fail in the trust her father reposed in me.'

'I would never have done it,' Constance sobbed, 'but for what she said about you. Lady Merrifield!'

'Well, and even if I am such a hard, severe person, does that make it honourable or right to help the child I trusted to you to carry on this underhand correspondence?'

Constance hung her head. Her sister had said the same to her, but she still felt herself the most injured party, and thought it very hard that she should be so severely blamed for what the girls at her school treated so lightly. She said, 'I am very sorry. Lady Merrifield,' but it was not exactly the tone of repentance, and it ended with: 'If it had not been for her, I should never have done it.'

'I suppose not, for there would have been no temptation. I was in hopes that you would have shown some kindlier and more generous feeling towards the younger girl, who could not have gone so far wrong without your assistance, and who feels your treatment of her very bitterly. But to find you incapable of understanding what you have done, makes me all the more glad that the friendship—if friendship it can be called—is broken off between you. Good-bye. I think when you are older and wiser, you will be very sorry to recollect the doings of the last few months.'

Lady Merrifield walked away, and found on her return that Dolores had succeeded in writing to her father, and was so utterly tired out by the feelings it had cost her that she was only fit to lie on the sofa and sleep.

Gillian was, of course, not seen till she came home from evening service.

'Oh, mamma,' she said, 'what did you do to Constance?'

'Why?'

'Well, I heard you shut the front door. And presently after there came such a noise through the wall that all the girls pricked up their ears, and Miss Hacket jumped up in a fright. If it had been Val, one would have called it a naughty child roaring.'

'What! did I send her into hysterics?'

'I suppose, as she is grown up, it must have the fine name, but it wasn't a bit like poor Dolly's choking. I am sure she did it to make her sister come! Well, of course, Miss Hacket went away, and I did the best I could, but what could one do with all these screeches and bellowings breaking out?'

'For shame. Gill!'

'I can't help it, mamma. If you had only seen their faces when the uproar came in a fresh gust! How they whispered, and some looked awestruck. I thought I had better get rid of them, and come home myself; but Miss Hacket met me, and implored me to stay, and I was weak-minded enough to do so. I wish I hadn't, for it was only to be provoked past bearing. That horrid girl has poisoned even Miss Hacket's mind, and she thinks you have been hard on her darling. You did not know how nervous and timid dear Connie is!'

'Well, Gill, I confess she made me very angry, and I told her what I thought of her.'

'And that she didn't choose to hear!'

'Did you see her again?'

'No, I am thankful to say, I did not. But Miss Hacket would go on all tea-time, explaining and explaining for me to tell you how dear Connie is so affectionate and so easily led, and how Dolores came over her with persuasions, and deceived her. I declare I never liked Dolly so well before. At any rate, she doesn't make professions, and not a bit more fuss than she can help. And there was Miss Hacket getting brandy cherries and strong coffee, and I don't know what all, because dear Connie was so overcome, and dear Lady Merrifield was quite under a mistake, and so deceived by Dolores. I told Miss Hacket you were never under a mistake nor deceived.'

'You didn't, Gillian!'

'Yes, I did, and the stupid woman only wanted to kiss me (but I wouldn't let her) and said I was very right to stand up for my dear mamma. As if that had anything to do with it! What are you laughing at, mamma? Why, Uncle Regie is laughing, and Cousin Rotherwood! What is it?'

'At the two partisans who never stand up for their own families,' said Uncle Regie.

'But it's true!' cried Gillian.

'What! that I am never mistaken nor deceived?' said Lady Merrifield.

'Except when you took Miss Constance for a sensible woman, eh?' said her brother.

'That I never did! But I did take her for a moderately honourable one.'

'Well, that was a mistake,' owned Gillian. 'And Miss Hacket is as bad! There's no gratitude—'

'Hush!' broke in her mother; and Gillian stopped abashed, while Lady Merrifield continued, 'I won't have Miss Hacket abused. She is only blinded by sisterly affection.'

'I don't think I can go there again,' said Gillian, 'after what she said about you.'

'Nonsense!' said her mother. 'Don't be as bad as Constance in trying to make me angry by telling me all poor Dolly's grumblings.'

'Follow your mother's example, Gillian,' said Lord Rotherwood, 'and, if possible, never hear, certainly never attend to, what any one says of you behind your back.'

'Is said to have said of you, you should add, Rotherwood,' put in the colonel. 'It is a decree worse than eavesdropping.'

'Oh, Regie!' exclaimed his sister.

'Well, not perhaps for your own honour and conscience, but the keyhole is a more trustworthy medium than the reporter.'

'That's a strong way of stating it, but, at any rate, the keyhole has no temper nor imagination, or prejudice of its own,' said Lady Merrifield.

'No, and as far as it goes, it enables you to judge of the frame in which the words, even if correctly reported, were spoken,' added Colonel Mohun.

'The moral of which is,' said Lord Rotherwood, drolly, 'that Gillian is not to take notice of anyone's observations upon her unless she has heard them through the keyhole.'

'And so one would never hear them at all.'

'Q. E. D.,' said Lord Rotherwood. 'And now, Lily, do you. ever sing the two evening-hymns. Ken and Keble, now, as the family used to do on Sundays at the Old Court, long ere the days of 'Hymns Ancient and Modern'?

'Don't we?' said Lady Merrifield. 'Only all our best voices will be singing it at Rawul Pindee!'

And, as she struck a note on the piano, all the younger people still up, Mysie, Phyllis, Wilfred and Valetta, gathered round from the outer room to join in their evening Sunday delight. Fly put her hand into her father's and whispered, 'You told me about it, daddy.' He began to sing, but his voice thickened as he missed the tones once associated with it. And Lady Merrifield, too, nearly broke down as with all her heart she sang, hopefully,

'Now Lord, the gracious work begin.'

CHAPTER XVII
THE STONE MELTING

It was with a strange feeling that Dolores woke on the New Year's morning, that something was very sad and strange, and yet that there was a sense of relief. For one thing, that terrible confession to her father was written, and was no longer a weight hanging over her. And though his answer was still to come, that was months away. There was Uncle Regie greatly displeased with her; there was Constance treating her as a traitor; there was the mischief done, and yet something hard and heavy was gone? Something sweet and precious had come in on her! Surely it was, that now she knew and felt that she could trust in Aunt Lilias—yes, and in Mysie. She got up, quite looking forward to meeting those gentle, brown eyes of her aunt's, that she seemed never before to have looked into, and to feeling the sweet, motherly kiss which had so mud, more meaning in it now, as almost to make up for Uncle Reginald's estrangement.

She even anticipated gladly those ten minutes alone with her aunt, which she used to dislike so much, hoping that the holiday-time would not hinder them. Really wishing to please her aunt, she had learnt her portion perfectly, and Lady Merrifield showed that she appreciated the effort, though still it was more a lesson than a reality.

'My dear!' she said, 'I am afraid this is another blow for you—it came this morning.'

It was the account from Professor Muhlwasser's German publisher, amounting to a few shillings more than six pounds. And an announcement that the books were on the way.

'Oh,' cried Dolores, 'I thought he was dead! He told me so! Uncle Alfred, I mean! And it was only to get the money! How could he be so wicked?'

'I am afraid that was all he cared for.'

'And what shall I do. Aunt Lily? Will you pay it, please, and take all my allowance till it is made up?'

'I think it will be more comfortable for you if I do something of that sort, though I don't think you should go entirely without money. You have a pound a quarter. I was going to give you yours at once.'

'When did you part with it?'

'On the Friday before Christmas Day.'

'Did you do anything to it first?'

'I wrote my name on the back.'

'What did you do with it.'

'I sent it to—' her voice became a little hoarse, but she brought out the words—'to Mr. Flinders.'

'Is this the same?'

'Yes—only some one has put 'ty' to the 'seven' in writing, and 0 to the figure 7.'

'Can you swear to the rest as your father's writing and your own?'

The evidence of the banker's clerk as to the cashing of the cheque had been already taken, and the magistrate said, 'Thank you. Miss Mohun, I think the case is complete, and we need not trouble you any more.'

But the prisoner's voice made Dolores start and shudder again, as he said,

'I beg your pardon, sir, but you have not asked the young lady'—there was a sort of sneer in his voice—'how she sent this draft.'

'Did not you send it direct by the post?' demanded the magistrate.

'No; I gave it to—' Again she paused, and the words 'Gave it to—?' were authoritatively repeated, so that she had no choice.

'I gave it to Miss Constance Hacket to send.'

'You will observe, sir,' said Flinders, in a somewhat insolent tone, 'that the evidence which the witness has been so ready to adduce is incomplete. There is another link between her hands and mine.'

'You may reserve that point for your defence on your trial,' rejoined the magistrate. 'There is quite sufficient evidence for your committal.'

There was already a movement to let Dolores be taken away by her uncle and aunt, so as to spare her from any reproach or impertinence that Flinders might launch at her. She was like some one moving in a dream, glad that her aunt should hold her hand as if she were a little child, saying, as they came out into the street, 'Very clearly and steadily done, Dolly! Wasn't it, Uncle Regie?'

'Yes,' he said, absently. 'We must look out, or we shan't catch the 4.50 train.'

He almost threw them into a cab, and made the driver go his quickest, so that, after all, they had full ten minutes to spare. It made Dolores sick at heart to go near the waiting and refreshment-rooms where she and Constance had spent all that time with Flinders; but she could not bear to say so before her uncle, and he was bent on getting some food for Lady Merrifield.

'Not soup, Regie; there might not be time to swallow it. A glass of milk for us each, please; we can drink that at once, and anything solid that we can take with us. I am sure your mouth must be dry, my dear.'

Very dry it was, and Dolores gladly swallowed the milk, and found, when seated in the train, that she was really hungry enough to eat her full share of the sandwiches and buns which the colonel had brought in with him; and then she sat resting against her aunt, closed her eyes, and half dozed in the rattle of the train, not moving in the pause at the stations, but quite conscious that Colonel Mohun said, 'Not a spark of feeling for anybody, not even for that man! As hard as a stone!'

'For shame, Regie!' said her aunt. 'How angry you would have been if she had made a scene.'

'I should have liked her better.'

'No, you wouldn't, when you come to understand. There's stuff in her, and depth too.'

'Aye, she's deep enough.'

'Poor child!' said Lady Merrifield, tenderly. And then the train went on, and the noise drowned the voices, so that Dolores only partly heard, 'You will see how she will rise,' and the answer, 'You may be right; I hope so. But I can't get over deliberate deceit.'

He settled himself in his corner, and Lady Merrifield durst not move nor raise her voice lest she should break what seemed such deep slumber, but which really was half torpor, half a dull dismay, holding fast eyes, lips, and limbs, and which really became sleep, so that Dolores did not hear the next bit of conversation during the ensuing halt.

'I say, Lily, I did not like the fellow's last question. He means to give trouble about it.'

'I was sorry the other name was brought in, but it must have come sooner or later.'

'That's true; but if she can't swear to the figures on the draft, ten to one that the fellow will get off.'

'You don't doubt—'

'No, no; but there's the chance for the defence, and he was sharp enough to see it.'

'There is nothing to be said or done about it, of course.'

'Of course not. There's nothing for it but to let it alone.'

They went on again, and when the train reached Silverton, Dolly was dreaming that her father had come, and that he said Uncle Alfred should be hanged unless she found the money for Professor Muhlwasser. She even looked about for him, and said, 'Where's father?' when she was wakened to get out.

Gillian came up to her mother's room to hear what had happened, and to give an account of the day, which had gone off prosperously by Harry's help. He had kept excellent order at dinner, and 'there's something about Fly which makes even Wilfred be mannerly before her.' And then they had gone out and had made Fly free of the Thorn Fortress.

'My dear, that must have been terribly damp and cold at this time of year.'

'I thought of that, mamma, and so we didn't sit down, and made it a guerrilla war; only Fergus couldn't understand the difference between guerrillas and gorillas, and would thump upon himself and roar when they were in ambush.'

'Rather awkward for the ambush!'

'Yes, Wilfred said he was a traitor, and tied him to a tree, and then Fly found him crying, and would have let him out; but she couldn't get the knots undone; and what do you think? She made Wilfred cut the string himself with his own knife! I never knew such a girl for making every one do as she pleases. Then, when it got dark, we came in, and had a sort of a kind of a rehearsal, only that nobody knew any of the parts, or what each was to be.'

'A sort of a kind, indeed, it must have been!'

'But we think the play will be lovely! You can't think how nice Fly was. You know we settled for her to be Annette, the dear, funny, naughty girl, but as soon as she saw that Val wanted the part, she said she didn't care, and gave it up directly, and I don't think we ought to let her, and Hal thinks so too; and all the boys are very angry, and say Val will make a horrid mess of it. Then Mysie wanted to give up the good girl to Fly, and only be one of the chorus, but Fly says she had rather be one of the chorus ones herself than that. So we settled that you should fix the parts, and we would abide by your choice.'

'I hope there was no quarrelling.'

'N—no; only a little falling upon Val by the boys, and Fly put a stop to that. Oh, mamma, if it were only possible to turn Dolly into Fly! I can't help saying it, we seemed to get on so much better just because we hadn't poor Dolly to make a deadweight, and tempt the boys to be tiresome: while Fly made everything go off well. I can't describe it, she didn't in the least mean to keep order or interfere, but somehow squabbles seem to die away before her, and nobody wants to be troublesome.'

'Dear little thing! It is a very sweet disposition. But, Gill, I do believe that we shall see poor Dolly take a turn now!'

'Well! having quarrelled with that Constance is in her favour!'

'Try and think kindly of her trouble. Gill, and then it will be easier to be kind to her.'

Gillian sighed. Falsehood and determined opposition to her mother were the greatest possible crimes in her eyes; and at her age it was not easy to separate the sin from the sinner.

New Year's night was always held to be one of especial merriment, but Lady Merrifield was so much tired out by her expedition that she hardly felt equal to presiding over any sports, and proposed that instead the young folk should dance. Gillian and Hal took turns to play for them, and Uncle Reginald and Fly were in equal request as partners. It was Mysie who came to draw Dolores out of her corner, and begged her to be her partner—'If you wouldn't very much rather not,' she said, in a pleading, wistful, voice.

Dolores would 'very much rather not;' but she saw that Mysie would be left out altogether if she did not consent, as Hal was playing and Uncle Regie was dancing with Primrose. She thought of resolutions to turn over a new leaf, and not to refuse everything so she said, 'Yes, this once,' and it was wonderful how much freshened she felt by the gay motion, and perhaps by Mysie's merry, good-natured eyes and caressing hand. After that she had another turn with Gillian and one with Hal, and even one with Fergus because, as he politely informed her, no one else would have him for a quadrille. But, just as this was in progress, and she could not help laughing at his ridiculous mistakes and contempt of rules she met Uncle Reginald's eye fixed on her in wonder 'He thinks I don't care,' thought she to herself. All her pleasure was gone, and she moved so dejectedly that her aunt, watching from the sofa, called her and told her she was over-tired, and sent her to bed.

'Oh, take it—pray—'

'Suppose I give you five shillings, instead of twenty. I do not think it well to leave you with nothing for a year and a half, and this is nearly what Mysie has.'

'A shilling a month—very well. I wish I could pay it all at once!'

'No doubt you do, my dear, but this will keep you in mind for a long time what a dangerous thing you did in giving away money you had no right to dispose of.'

'Yes,' said Dolores. 'Mother earned money for him. I know she never took father's without asking him; but I couldn't earn, and couldn't ask.'

Lady Merrifield kissed her, for very joy, to hear no sullenness in her tone; and then all went to church together on the New Year's day that was to be the beginning of better things. Lord Rotherwood had just time to go before meeting the train which was to take him to High Court, leaving his Fly too much used to his absences to be distressed about them, and, in fact, somewhat crazy about a notion which Gillian had started that morning, of getting up a little play to surprise him when he came back for Twelfth Day, as he promised to do.

Mamma declared that if it was in French, and the words were learnt every morning before half-past eleven, it should supersede all other lessons; but such was the hatred of the whole boy faction to French, that they declared they had rather do rational sensible lessons twice over than learn such rot, and this carried the day. The drama proposed was that one in an old number of 'Aunt Judy,' where the village mayor is persuaded by the drummer to fine the girls for wearing lace caps. The French original existed in the house, and Fly started the idea that the male performers should speak English and the female French; but this was laughed down.

In the midst Uncle Reginald came to the door and called, 'Lilias, can you speak to me a minute?'

Lady Merrifield went out into the hall to him.

'Here's a policeman come over, Lily. They have got the fellow!'
'Flinders?'

'Yes; arrested him on board a steamer at Bristol.'

'Oh, I wish they had let it alone!'

'So do I. They are bringing him back. The Darminster City bench sits to-day, and they want that unlucky child over there to make her deposition for his committal.'

'Can't they commit him without her?'

'Not for the forgery. The bank people are bent on prosecuting for that, and we can't stop them. I suppose she can be depended on?'

'Reginald, don't! I told you the deceit was an unnatural growth from Constance's pseudo sentiment.'

'Well, get her ready to come with me,' said the colonel, with a gesture of doubt; 'we must catch the 12.50. The superintendent brought a fly.'

'You will frighten her out of her senses. I can't let her go alone with you in this mood.'

'As you please, if you choose to knock yourself up. I'll tell the superintendent, and walk on to the station. You've not a moment to lose, so don't let her stand dawdling and crying.'

It was a hard task for Lady Merrifield. She called Dolores, whom Mysie was inviting to be one of the village maidens, and bade her put on her things quickly. She ordered cold meat and wine into the dining-room, called Gillian into her room, and explained while dressing, and bade her keep the others away. Then, meeting Dolores on the stairs took her into the dining-room and made her swallow some cold beef, and drink some sherry, before telling her that the magistrates at Darminster wanted to ask her some questions. Dolores looked pale and frightened, and exclaimed,

'Oh, but he has got away!'

'My dear, I am grieved to say that he has not.'

Dolores understood, and submitted more quietly and resignedly than her aunt had feared. She was a barrister's daughter, and once or twice her father had taken her and her mother part of the way on circuit with him, and she had been in court, so that she had known from the first that if her uncle were arrested there was no choice but that she must speak out. So she only trembled very much and said—

'Aunt Lily, are you going with me?'

'Indeed I am, my poor child. Uncle Regie is gone on.'

No more was spoken then, but Dolores put her cold hand into her aunt's muff.

Gillian kept all the flock prisoned in the schoolroom. Wilfred, Val, and Fergus rushed to the window, and were greatly disappointed not to see a policeman on the box, 'taking Dolores to be tried'—as Fergus declared, and Wilfred insisted, just because Gillian and Mysie contradicted it with all their might. He continued to repeat it with variations and exaggerations, until

'What does make you always go after Dolly instead of me, Mysie? Do you like her so much better?'

'Oh no! but you have them all, and she has nobody.'

'Well, but she has been so horridly naughty, hasn't she?'

'I don't think she meant it.'

'One never does. At least, I'm sure I don't—and mamma always says it is nonsense to say that.'

'I'm not sure whether it is always,' said Mysie, thoughtfully, 'for sometimes one does worse than one knows. Once I made a mouse-trap of a beautiful large sheet of bluey paper, and it turned out to be an order come down to papa. Mamma and Alethea gummed it up as well as ever they could again, but all the officers had to know what had happened to it.'

'And were you punished?'

'I was not allowed to go into papa's room without one of the elder ones till after my next birthday, but that wasn't so bad as papa's being so vexed, and everybody knowing it; and Major Denny would talk about mice and mouse-traps every time he saw me till I quite hated my name.'

'And I'm sure you didn't mean to cut up an important paper.'

'No; but I did do a little wrong, for we had no leave to take anything not quite in the waste basket, and this had been blown off the table, and was on the floor outside. They didn't punish me so much I think because of that. Papa said it was partly his own fault for not securing it when he was called off. You see little wrongs that one knows turn out great wrongs that one would never think of, and that is so very dreadful, and makes me so very sorry for Dolores.'

'I didn't think you would like a cross, naughty girl like that more than your own Fly.'

'No, no! Fly, don't say that. I don't really like her half so well, you know, only if you would help me to be kind to her.'

'I am sure my mother wouldn't wish me to have anything to do with her. I don't think she would have let me come here if she had known what sort of girl she is.'

'But your papa knew when he left you—'

'Oh, papa! yes; but he can never see anything amiss in a Mohun; I heard her say so. And he wants me to be friends with you; dear, darling friends like him and your Uncle Claude, Mysie, so you must be, and not be always after that Dolores.'

'I want to be friends with both. One can have two friends.'

'No! no! no! not two best friends. And you are my best friend, Mysie, ever so much better than Alberta Fitzhugh, if only you'll come always to me this little time when I'm here, and sit by me instead of that Dolly.'

'I do love you very much, Fly.'

'And you'll sit by me at the penny reading to-night?'

'I promised Dolly. But she may sit on the other side.'

'No,' said Phyllis, with jealous perverseness. 'I don't care if that Dolly is to be on the other side, you'll talk to nobody but her! Now, Mysie, I had been writing to ask daddy to let you come home with me, you yourself, to the Butterfly's Ball, but if you won't sit by me, you may stay with your dear Dolores.'

'Oh, Fly! When you know I promised, and there is the other side.'

But Fly had been courted enough by all the cousinhood to have become exacting and displeased at having any rival to the honour of her hand—so she pouted and said, 'I don't care about it, if you have her. I shall sit between Val and Jasper.'

One must be thirteen, with a dash of the sentiment of a budding friendship, to enter into all that 'sitting by' involves; and in Mysie's case, here was her compassionate promise standing not only between her and the avowed preference of one so charming as Fly, but possibly depriving her of the chances of the wonders of the Butterfly's Ball. No wonder that disconsolate tears came into her eyes as she uttered another pleading, 'Oh, Fly, how can you?'

'You must choose,' said the offended young lady; 'you can't have us both.'

To which argument she stuck, being offended as well as scandalized at being set aside for such a culprit as Dolores, whose misdemeanours and discourtesy were equally shocking to her imagination.

Mysie could confide her troubles to no one, for she was aware that caring about sitting together was treated by the elders as egregious folly; but a promise was a promise with her, and she held staunchly to her purpose, though between Dolores and Miss Vincent she lost all those delightful asides which enhanced the charms of the amusing parts of the penny reading and beguiled the duller ones—of which there were many, since it was more concert than penny reading, people being rather shy of committing themselves to reading—Hal, Mr. Pollock and the schoolmaster being the only volunteers in that line.

Gillian had, sorely against the grain, to play a duet with Constance Hacket. The two young ladies had met one another with freezing civility in the classroom, and to those who understood matters, the stiffness of their necks and shoulders, as they sat at the piano, spoke unutterable things. But there had never been any real liking between Constance and the younger Merrifields, and the mother did not trouble herself much about this, knowing that the vexation of the elder sister, about whom she did care, would pass off with friendly intercourse.

Fly's displeasure did not last long, for Mysie bad more attractions for her than any one else, and she was a good-humoured creature. There was a joyous Twelfth-Night, with home-made cake and home-characters, prepared by mamma and Gillian, and followed up by games, in which Dolores had a share, promoted by her aunt, who was very anxious to keep her from feeling set apart from every one; but this was difficult to manage, as she was so generally disliked, that even Gillian was only good-natured to her in accordance with her mother's desire that she should not be treated as 'out of the pale of humanity.' Mysie alone sought her out and brought her forward with any real earnestness, and good little Mysie had a somewhat difficult part to play between kindness to her and Fly's occasional little jealous tiffs and decided disapproval. Mysie never thought, however, about the situation or its difficulties, she simply followed the moment's call of kindness to Dolores, and, when it was possible, followed her own inclinations, and enjoyed Fly's lively society.

And Dolores was certainly softening and improving. A word to Mrs. Halfpenny had secured the two girls being permitted to say their prayers together in Dolores's room unmolested; and what was a reality to a contemporary became less and less to Dolores a mere lesson imposed by the authority of an elder. That link between religious instruction and daily life, which is all important, yet so difficult to find, was being gradually put into Dolores's hands by her little cousin-friend. Lady Merrifield hoped and guessed it might be thus, from the questions that Mysie asked her at times, and from the quickened attention Dolores showed to her religious lessons, and her less dull and indifferent air at church.

It could not be said that she was different with the others. She was depressed, and wanted spirits for enjoyment, nor would active romping diversions ever be pleasant to her. She had not the nature for them, and was not young enough to learn to like them. It could not but seem foolish to her to race about as a Croat or a savage, and she only beheld with wonder Gillian's genuine delight in games not merely entered into for the sake of the little ones. But there was a strong devotion growing up in her to her aunt and to Mysie, and what they asked of her she did—even when on a wet day her aunt condemned her to learn battledore and shuttle-cock of Gillian, who was equally to be pitied for the awkwardness of her pupil and the banter of her brothers, while Dolly picked up her shuttlecock and tossed it off with grim determination, as if doing penance for this dismal half hour. She managed better in the games where ready sharpness of intellect or memory was wanted, and she liked these, and would have liked them still better if Uncle Reginald had not always looked astonished if she laughed.

She did her part, too, in the little play, being one of the chorus of the maidens who 'make a vow to make a row.' Lady Merrifield had, according to the general request, saved disputes by casting the parts, Gillian being the sage old woman who brought the damsels to reason. Fly, the prime mover of the tumult, and Mysie, her confidante, while Val and Dolly made up the mob. A little manipulation of skirts, tennis-aprons, ribbons, and caps made very nice peasant costumes. Hal was the self-important Bailli, and Jasper the drummer, the part of gens-d'armes being all that Wilfred and Fergus could be trusted with.

Lord Rotherwood came back, and his little daughter's ecstacy was goodly to see, as she danced about her daddy, almost bursting with the secret of what he was to see after dinner, and showing herself so brilliantly well and happy that he congratulated himself upon her mother's satisfaction.

While the elders were at dinner, Gillian, with Miss Vincent's help, finished off the arrangements. There were no outsiders, except the Vicar and Mr. Pollock who had been asked to dinner, for Lady Merrifield said she never liked to make her children an exhibition.

'You are an old-fashioned Lily,' said her cousin, 'and happily not concerned with popularity. It is a fine thing to be able to consult one's children's absolute best.'

The performance went off beautifully—at least so thought both actors and spectators. The dignity of the Bailli and the meddling of the drummer were alike delightful; Fly was charmingly arch and mutinous; Mysie very straightforward; and the least successful personation was that of Gillian, who had a fit of stage-fright, forgot sentences, and whirred her spinning-wheel nervously, all the worse for being scolded by her brothers behind the scenes, and assured that she was making a mull of the whole affair. And she had been so spirited at the rehearsals, but she was at a self-conscious age, and could not forget the four spectators. Very little was required of Dolores, but that little she did simply and well, and Lord Rotherwood, after watching her all the evening, observed to Lady Merrifield, 'I should say

So Gillian was called to her mother's room to be told first of the arrangement, which certainly in some aspects was rather hard on her.

'I could not help it, my dear,' said Lady Merrifield, 'without absolutely asking for an invitation for you.'

'No, mamma; and it is Mysie who is Fly's friend, being the same age and all. It is quite right, and I understand it.'

'My dear, I am so glad I can do such a thing as this. If there were small jealousies among you, I could not venture on letting you be set aside, for I know the disappointment was quite as great to you as to Mysie, when we gave it up.'

'But she was better about it than I,' said Gillian; 'mamma, your trusting me in that way is better than a dozen balls. Besides, I know I should hate being there without you; I'm a great old thing, as Jasper says, neither fish nor fowl, you know, not come out, and not a little girl in the schoolroom, and it would be very horrid going to a grand place like that on one's own account.'

'That's right, Gillyflower. 'Tis very wholesome to discover the sourness of the grapes. And as I think grandmamma is really coming, I shall want you at home, and to look after Dolores.'

'That's the worst of it, mamma; I shall never get on with her as Mysie does.'

'We must do our best, for I do think really the poor child is improving.'

'Lessons will begin again! That's one comfort,' said Gillian, rather quaintly, thinking of the length of time that Dolores would thus be off her hands.

'And now call Mysie. I must speak to her.'

As for Mysie, she was in a state of rapture. She knew her bliss before her mother had communicated it, for Lord Rotherwood could not refrain from telling his daughter that consent was gained, and Fly darted headlong to embrace Mysie, dance round her and rejoice. The boys declared that Mysie at once sprang into the air like a chamois, and that her head touched the ceiling, but this is believed to be a figment of Jasper's.

It was only on the summons to her mother's room that Mysie discovered that Gillian was not going with her. It dimmed the lustre of her delight for a little while, 'Oh, Gill, aren't you very sorry? You ought to have had the first turn.'

'Never mind, Mysie, you are Fly's friend,'—and the two sisters' looks at one another at that moment were a real pleasure to their mother.

Mysie was of a less shy nature than Gillian, as well as at a less awkward age, so that the visiting without her mother was less formidable, and she rushed about wild with delight; but Dolores was very disconsolate.

'Every one I care for goes away and changes,' she said in her melancholy little sentiment.

'But it's only for a fortnight, Dolly, I don't think I could change so fast.'

'Oh yes, you will, among all those swells. You like Fly ever so much better than me.'

Mysie looked grieved and puzzled, but then exclaimed, in the tone of a discovery, 'There are different sorts of likings, Dolly, don't you see. I do love Fly very much, but you know you are like a sort of almost twin sister to me. I like her best, but I care about you most!'

With which curious distinction Dolores had to put up.

CHAPTER XIX
A SADDER AND A WISER AUTHORESS

Colonel Mohun took Wilfred to his school, which began its term earlier than did Jasper's, and Silver-ton was wonderfully quiet. The elder Mrs. Merrifield was not to come for nearly a week, so that it would have been possible for her daughter-in-law to go to the Rotherwood festivities without interfering with her visit, but this no one except Gillian and Mysie knew, and they kept the secret well.

The departure of the boys was a great relief to Dolores. Her aunt did not rank her with Valetta and Fergus, but let her consort with herself and Gillian, and this suited her much better. Even Gillian allowed that she was ever so much nicer when there was no one to tease her. It was true that Jasper certainly, and perhaps Wilfred, would not have molested her if she had not offended the latter, and offered herself as fair game; but Gillian, who had to forestall and prevent their pranks, could not feel their absence quite the privation her sisterly spirit usually did!

Valetta and Fergus were harmless without them, but they were forlorn, being so much used to having their sports led by their two seniors that they hardly knew what to do without them, and the entreaty, or rather the whine, 'I want something to do,' was heard unusually often. This led to Gillian's being often called off to attend to them during the course of wet days that ensued, and thus Dolores was a good deal alone with her aunt, who was superintending her knitting a pair of silk stockings to send out to her father, it was hoped in time for his next birthday.

At the first proposal, Dolores looked dull and unwilling, and at last she squeezed out, 'I don't think father will ever want me to do anything for him again.'

'My poor child, do you think a father does not forgive and love all the more one who is in deep sorrow for a fault?'

'I don't think my letter seemed sorry! I was not half so sorry then as I am now,' then at a kind word from her aunt her eyes overflowed, and she said, 'No, I wasn't; I didn't know how good you were, or how bad I was!'

And when Aunt Lily kissed her, she put her arms round the kind neck that bent down to her, and laid her head against it, as if it was quite a rest to feel that love. Her aunt encouraged her to write again to her father, and to try to express something of her grief and entreaty for forgiveness, and she was somewhat cheered after this; as though something of the load on her mind was removed. One day she brought down all the books in her room and said, 'Please, Aunt Lily, look at them, and let them be with the rest in the schoolroom, I want to be just like the others.'

Lady Merrifield was much pleased with this surrender. Some of the books were really well worth having and reading, indeed, the best of them she knew, but there were eight or ten which she suspected of being what Mysie called silly stories, and she kept them back to look over. She had been trying in this quiet interval to get Dolly to read something besides mere childish stories for recreation; and when she saw how well worn the story books were, and how untouched the 'easy history,' and the books about animals and foreign countries were, she saw why so clever a girl as Dolores seemed so stupid about everything she had not learnt as a lesson, and entirely ignorant of English poetry.

Lady Merrifield read to her and Gillian in the evenings, and how they did enjoy it, and bemoaned the coming of grandmamma, to spoil their snugness and occupy 'mamma.' For Dolores began so to call Lady Merrifield. She had never so termed her own mother, and it seemed to her that with the words 'Aunt Lily' she put away all sorts of foolish, sinister feelings.

'Mrs Merrifield was a wonderful old lady, brisk of mind and body, though of great age. She had been spending Christmas with her eldest son, the Admiral, at Stokesley, and was going to take on her way the daughter-in-law, of whom she knew but little in comparison; and with her she brought the granddaughter, Elizabeth Merrifield, who—since her own daughter had died—generally lived with her in London, to take care of her.

'It will be all company and horrid, and nobody will be allowed to make a noise!' sighed Valetta to Fergus, as the waggonette, well shut up, drove to the door.

'There's cousin Bessie,' said Fergus.

'Oh, cousin Bessie is thirty-four, and that is as bad as being as old as grandmamma!'

And they hung back while the old lady was helped out, and brought across the hall into the warm drawing-room before her fur cloak was taken off. There was a quiet little person with her, and Val whispered, 'She'll be just like Aunt Jane.'

But the eyes that Bessie turned on her cousins were not at an like Aunt Jane's little searching black ones. They were of a dark shade of grey, and had a wonderful softness and sweetness in them. Gillian knew her a little already, but very little, for there had always been the elder sisters at their former short meetings. Mamma lamented that there should be so few grandchildren at home to be shown, though, as she said, 'the full number might have been too noisy.'

Grandmamma shook her head. 'I like the house full,' she said, 'I'm all right, but it is a pity to see the nest emptied, like Stokesley, now. Nobody left at home but Susan and little Sally! Make the most of them while you have them about you!'

The old lady was quite delighted to find Primrose so nearly a baby, and to have one grandchild still quite as small or smaller than some of her great grandchildren whom she had never seen. Her great pleasure, however, soon proved to be in talking about her son Jasper, and hearing all his wife could tell her about his life in India; and as Lady Merrifield liked no other subject so well, they were very happy together, and quite absorbed.

Meanwhile Bessie made herself a companion to Gillian and Dolores, and though so much older, seemed to consider herself as a girl like them. Then, living for the most part in town, she could talk about London matters to Dolly, and this was a great treat, while yet she had country tastes enough to suit Gillian, and was not in the least afraid of a long walk to the fir plantations to pick up Weymouth pine cones, and the still more precious pinaster ones.

For the first time Gillian began to see Dolores as Uncle Reginald used to know her, free from that heavy mist of sullen dislike to everything and everybody. It seemed to bring them together, but, in spite of Bessie's charms, they both continually missed Mysie, out of doors and in, in schoolroom and drawing-room, and, above all, in Dolly's bedroom. She seemed to be, as Gillian told Bessie, 'a sort of family cement, holding the two ends, big and little, together;' and Bessie responded that her elder sister Susan was one of that sort.

The evenings now were quite unlike the usual ones. Dinner was late, and the two girls came down to it. Afterwards the young ones sat round the fire in the hall, where Bessie, who was a wonderful story-teller, kept Fergus and Valetta quiet and delighted, either with invented tales or histories of the feats of her own brothers and sisters, who were so much older than their Silverton first cousins as to be like an elder generation.

When the two young ones were gone to bed, the others came into the drawing-room, where mamma and grandmamma were to be found, either going over papa's letters, or else Mrs. Merrifield talking about her Stokesley grandchildren, the same whose pranks Bessie had just been telling, so that it was not easy to believe in Sam, a captain in the navy. Harry and John farming in Canada, David working as a clergy-man in the Black Country, George in a government office, Anne a clergyman's wife, and mother to the great grandchildren who were always being compared to Primrose, Susan keeping her father's house, and Sarah, though as old as Alethea, still treated as the youngest—the child of the family.

The bits of conversation came to the girls as they sat over their work, and Bessie would join in, and tell interesting things, till she saw that grandmamma was ready for her nap, and then one or other gave a little music, during which Dolly's bed-time generally came.

'You can't think how grateful I am to you for helping to brighten up that poor child in a wholesome way!' said Lady Merrifield to Bessie, under cover of Gillian's performance.

'One can't help being very sorry for her,' said Elizabeth, who knew what was hanging over Dolly.

'Yes, it is a terrible punishment, especially as she has a certain affection for her step-uncle, or whatever he should be called, for her mother's sake. It really was a perplexed situation.'

'But why did she not consult you?'

'Do you know, I think I have found out. She held aloof from us all, and treated us—especially me—as if we were her natural enemies, and I never could guess what was the reason till the other day; she voluntarily gave me up all her books to be looked over and put into the common stock, which you saw in the schoolroom.'

'You look over all the children's books?'

'Yes. While we were wandering, they did not get enough to make it a very arduous task, and now I find that they want weeding. If children read nothing but a multitude of stories rather beneath their capacity, they are likely never to exert themselves to anything beyond novel reading.'

'That is quite true, I believe.'

'Well, among this literature of Dolly's I found no less than four stories based on the cruelty and injustice suffered by orphans from their aunts. The wicked step-mothers are gone out, and the barbarous aunts are come in. It is the stock subject. I really think it is cruel, considering that there are your difficulties were diminishing, are they not? The thunder-cloud seems to be a little lightened.'

'I am so glad you think so, Rotherwood. I feel sure that all this distress has drawn her nearer to us, only Regie won't believe it.'

'Regie is prejudiced.'

'Is he? I thought him specially fond of Maurice's child, and that this was revulsion of feeling; but what I am afraid of is, that he will never believe in her or like her again, whatever she may be, and she is really fond of him.'

'Yes, Reginald is not over disposed to believe in any woman's truth— outside his own family and sisters. Poor fellow! I can't say he was well used.'

'What? I suppose he has had his romance like other people—his little episode, as my husband calls it.'

'Yes; and I am afraid we were accountable for it. You remember we were at Harthope Castle for the first two years after I was married, while Rotherwood was brought up to the requirements of the Victorian age.

The —th was quartered at Harfield, within easy distance, and a splendid looking fellow like Regie was invaluable to Victoria, whenever she wanted anything to go off well. Well, in those days I had a ward, my mother's great niece, Maude Conway. A pretty winsome creature it was, and an heiress in a moderate sort of way, and poor old Redge, after all his little affairs, and he had had his share of them, was evidently in for it at last. Victoria thought, as well as myself, it was the best thing for them both. He was the sound-hearted, good fellow to keep her matters straight, and she had enough for comfort without overweighting the balance. So they were engaged but unluckily they had to wait till she was of age, about eight months off, and they were both ridiculously shy, and would not have the thing known, though Victoria said it was unwise. I don't think even Jane suspected it.'

'No; I don't think she could have done so.'

'Well, there was the season, and Victoria was not in condition for going out, and Maude was all for staying quietly with her; but old Lady Conway came about—a regular schemer—a woman I never could abide. She had married off her own daughters, and wanted her niece to practise on, that was the fact. Victoria says she always knew that she, Maude I mean, was very impressionable and impulsive, and so she wanted to have her out of harm's way; but one could not prevent her aunt from getting hold of her and taking her out. Then people told us of her goings on with that scamp Clanmacklosky and that sister of his. Victoria talked to her by the yard, but she denied it, and we thought it all gossip. Regie came up for a couple of nights, and she was as sweet on him as ever, and sent him away thinking it all right; but the end of it was, she fought off going down to Rotherwood with us, but went to Brighton with Lady Conway, and the next thing we heard was that she wrote to throw Reginald over, and she married Clanmacklosky a month after she was twenty-one! I don't think I ever saw Victoria so cut up, for we had really liked the girl and thought well of her. To this hour I believe it was all that woman's doing, and that poor Maude has supped sorrow. She has lost all her good looks.'

'And Regie has never got over it?'

'Not so as to believe in a woman again.'

'He used to be rather a joke for susceptibility, and was still a regular boy when we went out to Gibraltar. I thought him much graver.'

'Exactly; since that affair his soul has gone into his regiment. It's a wife to him, and luckily he got his promotion in time, so as not to be shelved.'

'I suppose it was really an escape.'

'I don't know—she would have done very well in his hands. She is the sort of woman to be as you make her, and even now is a world too good for Clan. Victoria can never be quite cordial with her, but I can't see the poor harassed thing without thinking what a sweet creature she once was, and wishing I'd had the sense to look after her better. But what I came here for, Lily, was to say you must let me have that Mysie of yours, since you won't come yourself to this concern of ours. I'm afraid you won't think much good has come of us, but we couldn't do the Country Mouse much harm in a fortnight; and you know it is the wish of my heart that my lonely Fly should grow up on such terms with your flock as Florence and I did with you all.'

He pleaded quite piteously, and he was backed up by a letter from his wife, very grateful for her little Phyllis's happy visit, reiterating the invitation to Lady Merrifield, and begging that if she still could not come herself, she would at least send Jasper and Mysie for the Butterfly's Ball. Mysie's fancy dress would be ready for her, only waiting for the final touches after it was tried on. Lady Florence Devereux, too, was near at hand, and wrote to promise to look after Mysie.

There was no refusing after this. Lady Florence was not far from being like a sister to her cousins. She had tended her mother's old age, and had subsequently settled down into the lady of all work of Rotherwood parish. Lady Merrifield had much confidence in her, and indeed all she saw of Fly gave her a great respect for Lady Rotherwood's management of her child. Harry was going to his uncle's at Beechcroft for some shooting, and would bring Mysie home when Jasper went back to school.

CHAPTER XVIII
MYSIE AND DOLORES

Things were going on more quietly at Silverton. That is to say, there were no outward agitations, for the house was anything but quiet. Lady Merrifield had no great love for children's parties, where, as she said, they sat up too late, to eat and drink what was not good for them, and to get presents that they did not care about; and though at Dublin it had been necessary on her husband's account to give and take such civilities, she had kept out of the exchange at Silverton. But, on the other hand, there were festivals, and she promoted a full amount of special treats at home among themselves, or with only an outsider or two, and she endured any amount of noise, provided it was not quarrelsome, over-boisterous, or at unfit times.

There was the school tea, and magic-lantern, when Mr. Pollock acted as exhibitor, and Harry as spokesman, and worked them up gradually from grave and beautiful scenes like the cedars of Lebanon, the Parthenon and Colosseum, with full explanations, through dissolving views of cottage and bridge by day and night, summer and winter, of life-boat rescue, and the siege of Sevastopol, with shells flying, on to Jack and the Beanstalk and the New Tale of a Tub, the sea-serpent, and the nose-grinding! Lady Phyllis's ecstacy was surpassing, more especially as she found her beloved little maid-of-all-work, and was introduced to all that small person's younger brothers and sisters.

Here they met Miss Hacket, who was in charge of a class. She comported herself just as usual, and Gillian's dignity and displeasure gave way before her homely cordiality. Constance had not come, as indeed nothing but childhood, sympathy with responsibility for childhood, could make the darkness, stuffiness, and noise of the exhibition tolerable. Even Lady Merrifield trusted her flock to its two elders, and enjoyed a tete-a-tete evening with her brother, who profited by it to advise her strongly to send Dolores to their sister Jane before harm was done to her own children.

'I would not see that little Mysie of yours spoilt for all the world,' said he.

'Nor I; but I don't think it likely to happen.'

'Do you know that they are always after each other, chattering in their bedrooms at night. I hear them through the floor.'

'Only one night—Mysie told me all about it—I believe Mysie will do more for that poor child than any of us.'

Uncle Regie shrugged his shoulders a little.

'Yes, I know I was wrong before, when I wouldn't take Jane's warning; but that was not about one of my own, and, besides, poor Dolores is very much altered.'

'I'll tell you what, Lily, when any one, I don't care who, man, or woman, or child, once is given up to that sort of humbug and deceit, carrying it on a that girl, Dolores, had done, I would never trust again an inch beyond what I could see. It eats into the very marrow of the bones—everything is acting afterwards.'

'That would be saying no repentance was possible—that Jacob never could become Israel.'

'I only say I have never seen it.'

'Then I hope you will, nay, that you do. I believe your displeasure is the climax of all Dolly's troubles.'

But Colonel Reginald Mohun could not forgive the having been so entirely deceived where he had so fully trusted; and there was no shaking his opinion that Dolores was essentially deceitful and devoid of feeling and that the few demonstrations of emotion that were brought before him were only put on to excite the compassion of her weakly, good-natured aunt, so he only answered, 'You always were a soft one Lily.'

To which she only answered, 'We shall see knowing that in his present state of mind he would only set down the hopeful tokens that she perceived either to hypocrisy on the girl's side, or weakness on hers.

Dolores had indeed gone with the others rather because she could not bear remaining to see her uncle's altered looks than because she expected much pleasure. And she had the satisfaction of sitting by Mysie, and holding her hand, which had become a very great comfort in her forlorn state—so great that she forebore to hurt her cousin's feelings by discoursing of the dissolving views she had seen at a London party. Also she exacted a promise that this station should always be hers.

Mysie, on her side, was in some of the difficulties of a popular character, for Fly felt herself deserted, and attacked her on the first opportunity.

many children who have to be adopted into uncles' families, to add to their distress and terror, by raising this prejudice. Just look at this one'—taking up Dolly's favourite, 'Clare; or No Home'—'it is not at all badly written, which makes it all the worse.'

'Oh, Aunt Lilias,' cried Bessie, whose colour had been rising all this time. 'How shall I tell you? I wrote it!'

'You! I never guessed you did anything in that line.'

'We don't talk about it. My father knows, and so does grandmamma, in a way; but I never bring it before her if I can help it, for she does not half like the notion. But, indeed, they aren't all as bad as that! I know now there is a great deal of silly imitation in it; but I never thought of doing harm in this way. It is a punishment for thoughtlessness,' cried poor Bessie, reddening desperately, and with tears in her eyes.

'My dear, I am so sorry I said it! If I bad not one of these aunts, I should think it a very effective story.'

'I'm afraid that's so much the worse! Let me tell you about it, Aunt Lilias. At home, they always laughed at me for my turn for dismalities.'

'I believe one always has such a turn when one is young.'

'Well, when I went to live with grandmamma, it was very different from the houseful at home, I had so much time on my hands, and I took to dreaming and writing because I could not help it, and all my stories were fearfully doleful. I did not think of publishing them for ever so long, but at last when David terribly wanted some money for his mission church, I thought I would try, and this Clare was about the best. They took it, and gave me five pounds for it, and I was so pleased and never thought of its doing harm, and now I don't know how much more mischief it may have done!'

'You only thought of piling up the agony! But don't be unhappy about it. You don't know how many aunts it may have warned.'

'I'm afraid aunts are not so impressionable as nieces. And, indeed, among ourselves story-books seemed quite outside from life, we never thought of getting any ideas from them any more than from Bluebeard.'

'So it has been with some of mine, while, on the other hand, Dolores seemed to Mysie an interesting story-book heroine—which indeed she is, rather too much so. But you have not stood still with Clare.'

'No, I hope I have grown rather more sensible. David set me to do stories for his lads, and, as he is dreadfully critical, it was very improving.'

'Did you write 'Kate's Jewel'? That is delightful. Aunt Jane gave it to Val this Christmas, and all of us have enjoyed it! We shall be quite proud of it—that is—may I tell the children?'

'Oh, aunt, you are very good to try to make me forget that miserable Clare. I wonder whether it will do any good to tell Dolores all about it. Only I can't get at all the other girls I may have hurt.'

'Nay, Bessie, I think it most likely that Dolores would have been an uncomfortable damsel, even if Clare had remained in your brain. There were other causes, at any rate, here are three more persecuted nieces in her library. Besides, as you observed, everybody does not go to story-books for views of human nature, and happily, also, homeless children are commoner in books than out of them, so I don't think the damage can be very extensive.'

'One such case is quite enough! Indeed, it is a great lesson to think whether what one writes can give any wrong notion.'

'I believe one always does begin with imitation.'

'Yes, it is extraordinary how little originality there is in the world. In the literature of my time, everybody had small hands and high foreheads, the girls wanted to do great things, and did, or did not do, little ones, and the boys all took first classes, and the fashion was to have violet eyes, so dark you could not tell their colour, and golden hair.'

'Whereas now the hair is apt to be bronze, whatever that may be like.'

'And all the dresses, and all the complexions, and all the lace, and all the roses, are creamy. Bessie, I hope you don't deal in creaminess!'

'I'm afraid skim milk is more like me, and that you would say I had taken to the goody line. I never thought of the responsibility then, only when I wrote for David's classes.'

'It is a responsibility, I suppose, in the way in which every word one speaks and every letter one writes is so. And now—here is Gillian finishing her piece. How far is it a secret, my dear.'

'It need not be so here, Aunt Lilias. Only my people are rather old-fashioned, you know, and are inclined to think it rather shocking of me, so it ought not to go beyond the family, and especially don't 'let her,' indicating her grandmother, 'hear about it. She knows I do such things—it would not be honest not to tell her—but it goes against the grain, and she has never heard one word of it all.'

It appeared that Bessie daily read the psalms and lessons to grandmamma, followed up by a sermon. Then, with her wonderful eyes, Mrs. Merrifield read the newspaper from end to end, which lasted her till few childish words of confession, pleading and entreating for strength, and then the Lord's Prayer, and the sweet old verse:—

> 'I lay my body down to sleep,
> I give my soul to Christ to keep,
> Wake I at morn, as wake I never,
> I give my soul to Christ for ever.'

'Ah! but I am afraid of that. I don't like it,' said Dolores, as they lay down again.

'It won't make one never wake,' returned Mysie; 'and I do like to give my soul to Christ. It seems so to rest one, and make one not afraid.'

'I don't know,' said Dolores; 'and why did you say the Lord's Prayer? That hasn't anything to do with it!'

'Oh, Dolly, when He is our Father near, though our own dear fathers are far away, and there's deliver us from evil—all that hurts us, you know—and forgive us. It's all there.'

'I never thought that,' said Dolores. 'I think you have some different prayers from mine. Old nurse taught me long ago. I wish you would always say yours with me. You make them nicer.'

Mysie answered with a hug, and a murmured 'If I can,' and offered to say the 121st Psalm, her other step to comfort, and, as she said it, she resolved in her mind whether she could grant Dolores's request; for she was not sure whether she should be allowed to leave her room before saying her own, and she I knew enough of Dolores by this time to be aware that to say she would ask mamma's leave would put an end to all. 'I know,' was her final decision; 'I'll say my own first, and then come to Dolly's room.'

But by that time Dolores was asleep, even if Mysie had not been too sleepy to speak.

She meant to have rushed to the room she shared with Valetta before it was time to get up, but Lots found the black head and the brown together on Dolores's pillow, wrapped in slumber; and though Mysie flew home as soon as she was well awake, Mrs. Halfpenny descended on her while she was yet in her bath, and inflicted a sharp scolding for the malpractice of getting into her cousin's bed.

'But Dolly was so miserable, nurse, and mamma was too tired to call.'

'Then you should have called me, Miss Mysie, and I'd have sorted her well! You kenned well 'tis a thing not to be done and at your age; ye should have minded your duties better.'

And nurse even intercepted Mysie on her way to Dolores's room, and declared she would have no messing and gossiping in one another's rooms. Miss Mysie was getting spoilt among strangers.

Mysie went down with a strong sense of having been disobedient, as well as of grief for Dolores's disappointment. Happily mamma was late that morning, and nobody was in her room but Primrose. Poor Mysie had soon, with tears in her eyes, confessed her transgression. Her mother's tears, to her great surprise, were on her cheek together with a kiss. 'Dear child, I am not displeased. Indeed, I am not; I will tell nurse. It must not be a habit, but this was an exception, and I am only thankful you could comfort her.

'And, mamma, may I go now to her. She said I could help her to say her prayers, and I think she only has little baby ones that her nurse taught her and she doesn't see into the Lord's Prayer.'

'My dear, my dear, if you can help her to pray you will do the thing most sure to be a blessing to her of all.'

And when Mysie was gone, Lady Merrifield knelt down afresh in thankfulness.

luncheon, then came a drive in the brougham, followed by a rest in her own room, dinner, and then Bessie read her to sleep with a book of travels or biography, of the old book-club class of her youth. Her principles were against novels, and the tale she viewed as only fit for children.

Lady Merrifield could not help thinking what a dull life it must be for Bessie, a woman full of natural gifts and of great powers of enjoyment, accustomed to a country home and a large family, and she said something of the kind. 'I did not like it at first,' said Bessie, 'but I have plenty of occupations now, besides all these companions that I've made for myself, or that came to me, for I think they come of themselves.'

'But what time have you to yourself?'

'Grandmamma does not want me till half-past ten in the morning, except for a little visit. And she does not mind my writing letters while she is reading the paper, provided I am ready to answer anything remarkable. I am quite the family newsmonger! Then there's always from four to half-past six when I can go out if I like. There's a dear old governess of ours living not far off, and we have nice little expeditions together. And you know it is nice to be at the family headquarters in London, and have every one dropping in.'

'Oh dear! how good you are to like going on like that,' said Gillian, who had come up while this was passing; 'I should eat my heart out; you must be made up of contentment.'

Elizabeth held up her hand in warning lest her grandmother should be wakened, but she laughed and said, 'My brothers would tell you I used to be Pipy Bet. But that dear old governess. Miss Fosbrook, was the making of me, and taught me how to be jolly like Mark Tapley among the rattlesnakes,' she finished, looking drolly up to Gillian.

'And, Gill, you don't know what Bessie has made her companions instead of the rattlesnakes,' said Lady Merrifield. 'What do you think of "Kate's Jewel?"'

Gillian's astonishment and rapture actually woke grandmamma; not that she made much noise, but there was a disturbing force about her excitement; and the subject had to be abandoned.

As the great secret might be shared with Dolores, though not with the younger ones, whose discretion could not be depended upon, Gillian could enter upon it the more freely, though she was rather disappointed that an author was not such an extraordinary sight to Dolly as to herself. But it was charming to both that Bessie let them look at the proofs of the story she was publishing in a magazine; and allowed them as well as mamma, to read the manuscript of the tale, romance, or novel, whichever it was to be called, on which she wished for her aunt's opinion.

Bessie took care, when complying with the girls' entreaty, that she would tell them all she had written; to observe that, she thought 'Clare' a very foolish book indeed, and that she wished heartily she had never written it. Gillian asked why she had done it?

'Oh,' said Dolores, 'things aren't interesting unless something horrid happens, or some one is frightened, or very miserable.'

'I like things best just and exactly as they really are—or were,' said Gillian.

'The question between sensation and character,' said Bessie to her aunt. 'I suppose that, on the whole, it is the few who are palpably affected by the mass of fiction in the world; but that it is needful to take good care that those few gather at least no harm from one's work—to be faithful in it, in fact, like other things.'

And there was no doubt that Bessie had been faithful in her work ever since she had realized her vocation. Her lending library books, written with a purpose, were excellent, and were already so much valued by Miss Hacket, that Gillian thought how once she should have felt it a privation not to be allowed to tell her whence they came; but to her surprise on the Sunday, instead of the constraint with which of late she had been treated at tea-time, the eager inquiry was made whether this was really the authoress, Miss Merrifield?

Secrets are not kept as well as people think. The Hackets' married sister was a neighbour of Bessie's married sister, and through these ladies it had just come round, not only who was the author of 'Charlie's Whistle,' etc., but that she wrote in the — — Magazine, and was in the neighbourhood.

All offences seemed to be forgiven in the burning desire for an introduction to this marvel of success. Constance had made the most of her opportunities in gazing at church; but if she called, would she be introduced?

'Of course,' said Gillian, 'if my cousin is in the room.' She spoke rather coldly and gravely, and Miss Hacket exclaimed—

'I know we have been a little remiss, my dear, I hope Lady Merrifield was not offended.'

'Mamma is never offended,' said Gillian—'but, I do think, and so would she and all of us, that if Constance comes, she ought to treat Dolores Mohun—as—as usual.'

Dolores was tired, but not in the way which made it harder instead of easier to sleep, or, rather, she slept just enough to relax her full consciousness and hold over herself, and bring on her a misery of terror and loneliness, and feeling of being forsaken by the whole world. And when she woke fully enough to understand the reality, it was no better; she felt, then, the position she had put herself into, and almost saw in the dark, Flinders's malicious vindictive glance Constance's anger, Uncle Regie's cold, severe look and, worse than all, her father reading her letter'

She fell again into an agony of sobbing, not without a little hope that Aunt Lily would be again brought to her side. At last the door was softly pushed open in the dark, but it was not Aunt Lily, it was Mysie's little bare feet that patted up to the bed, her arms that embraced, her cheek that was squeezed against the tearful one—'Oh, Dolly, Dolly! please don't cry so sadly!'

'Oh! it is so dreadful, Mysie!'

'Are you ill—like the other night?'

'No—but—Mysie—I can't bear it!'

'I don't want to call mamma,' said Mysie, thoughtfully, 'for she is so much tired, and Uncle Regie and Gill said she would be quite knocked up, and got her to come up to bed when we went. Dolly, would it be better if I got into your bed and cuddled you up?'

'Oh yes! oh yes! please do, there's a dear good Mysie.'

There was not much room, but that mattered the less, and the hugging of the warm arms seemed to heal the terrible sense of being unloved and forsaken, the presence to drive away the visions of angry faces that had haunted her; but there was the longing for fellow-feeling on her, and she said, 'That's nice! Oh, Mysie! you can't think what it is like! Uncle Regie said I didn't care, and he could never forgive deliberate deceit—and I was so fond of Uncle Regie!'

'Oh! but he will, if you never tell a story again,' said Mysie—and, as she felt a gesture implying despair—'Yes, they do; I told a story once.'

'You, Mysie! I thought you never did?'

'Yes, once, when we were crossing to Ireland and nurse wouldn't let Wilfred tie our handkerchiefs together and fish over the side, and he was very angry, and threw her parasol into the sea when she wasn't looking; and I knew she would be so cross, that when she asked me if I knew what was become of it, I said 'No,' and thought I didn't, really. But then it came over me, again and again, that I had told a story, and, oh! I was so miserable whenever I thought of it—at church, and saying my prayers, you know; and mamma was poorly, and couldn't come to us at night for ever so long, but at last I could bear it no longer, I heard her say, 'Mysie is always truthful,' and then I did get it out, and told her. And, oh! she and papa were so kind, and they did quite and entirely forgive me!'

'Yes, you told of your own accord; and they were your own—not Uncle Regie. Ah! Mysie, everybody hates me. I saw them all looking at me.'

'No, no! Don't say such things. Dolly. None of us do anything so shocking.'

'Yes, Jasper does, and Wilfred and Val!'

'No! no! no! they don't hate; only they are tiresome sometimes; but if you wouldn't be cross they would be nice directly—at least Japs and Val. And 'tisn't hating with Willie, only he thinks teasing is fun.'

'And you and Gillian. You can only just bear me.

'No! no! no!' with a great hug, 'that's not true.'

'You like Fly ever so much better!'

'She is so dear, and so funny,' said Mysie, the truthful, 'but somehow, Dolly dear, do you know, I think if you and I got to love one another like real friends, it would be nicer still than even Fly—because you are here like one of us, you know; and besides, it would be more, because you are harder to get at. Will you be my own friend. Dolly?'

'Oh, Mysie, I must!' and there was a fresh kissing and hugging.

'And there's mamma,' added Mysie.

'Yes, I know Aunt Lily does now; but, oh! if you had seen Uncle Alfred's face, and heard Uncle Regie,' and Dolly began to sob again as they returned on her. 'I see them whenever I shut my eyes!'

'Darling,' whispered Mysie, 'when I feel bad at night, I always kneel up in bed and say my prayers again!'

'Do you ever feel bad?'

'Oh yes, when I'm frightened, or if I've been naughty, and haven't told mamma. Shall we do it, Dolly?'

'I don't know what that has to do with it, but we'll try.'

'Mamma told me something to say out of.'

The two little girls rose up, with clasped hands in their bed, and Mysie whispered very low, but so that her companion heard, and said with her a

Jasper heard him, and declared that he should have a thorough good licking if he said so again, administering a cuff by way of earnest. Wilfred howled, and was ordered not to be such an ape, and Fly looked on in wonder at the domestic discipline.

The superintendent had, in fact, walked on with Uncle Reginald, and Dolores saw nothing of him, but was put into an empty first-class carriage, into which her aunt followed her, but her uncle, observing, 'You know how to manage her, Lily,' betook himself to a smoking-carriage, and left them to themselves.

Dolores was never a very talking girl, and the habit of silence had grown upon her. She leant against her aunt and she put her arm round her, and did not attempt to say anything till she asked,

'Will he be there?'

'I don't know, I am afraid he will. It is very sad for you, my poor Dolly; but we must recollect that, after all, it may be much better for him to be stopped now than to go on and get worse and worse in some strange country.'

Dolores did not ask what she was to do, she knew enough already about trials to understand that she was only to answer questions, and she presently said,

'This can't be his trial. There are no assizes now.'

'No, this is only for the committal. It will very soon be over, if you will only answer quietly and steadily. If you do so, I think Uncle Regie will be pleased, and tell your father I am sure I shall!'

Dolores pressed up closer and laid her cheek against the soft sealskin. In the midst of her trouble there was a strange wonder in her. Could this be really the aunt whom she had thought so cruel, unjust, and tyrannical, and from whom she had so carefully hidden her feelings? Nobody got into the carriage, and just before reaching Darminster, Lady Merrifield made a great effort over her own shyness and said,

'Now, Dolly, we will pray a little prayer that you may be a faithful witness, and that God may turn it, all to good for your poor uncle.'

Dolores was very much surprised, and did not know whether she liked it or not, but she saw her aunt's closed eyes and uplifted hands, and she tried to follow the example.

The train stopped, and her uncle came to the door, looking inquiringly at her.

'She will be good and brave,' said her aunt; and quickly passing across the platform, Dolores found herself beside her aunt, with her uncle opposite in another fly.

Things had been arranged for them considerately, and after they came to the Guildhall, where the city magistrates were sitting, Colonel Mohun went at once into court; the others were taken to a little room, and waited there a few minutes before Colonel Mohun came to call for his niece. It was a long room, with a rail at one end, and Dolores knew, with a strange thrill which made her shudder, that Mr. Flinders was there, but she could not bear to look at him, and only squeezed hard at the hand of her aunt, who asked, in a somewhat shaky voice, if she might come with her niece.

'Certainly, certainly. Lady Merrifield,' said one of the magistrates, and chairs were set both for her and Colonel Mohun.

'You are Miss Mohun, I think—may I ask your Christian name in full?' And then she had to spell it, and likewise tell her exact age, after which she was put on oath—as she knew enough of trials to expect.

'Are you residing with Lady Merrifield?'

'Yes.'

'But your father is living?'

'Yes, but he is in the Fiji Islands.'

'Will you favour us with his exact name?'

'Maurice Devereux Mohun.'

'When did he leave England?'

'The fifth of last September.'

'Did he leave any money with you?'

'Yes.'

'In what form?'

'A cheque on W——'s Bank.

'To bearer or order?'

'To order.'

'What was the date?'

'I think it was the 31st of August, but I am not sure.'

'For how much?'

'For seven pounds.'

The two sisters were silent, perhaps from sheer amazement at this outbreak of Gillian's, who had never seemed particularly fond of her cousin. Gillian was quite as much surprised at herself, but something seemed to drive her on, with flaming cheeks. 'Dolores is half broken-hearted about it all. She did not thoroughly know how wrong it was; and it does make her miserable that the one who went along with her in it should turn against her, and cut her and all.'

'Connie never meant to keep it up, I'm sure,' said Miss Hacket; 'but she was very much hurt.'

'So was Dolly,' said Gillian.

'Is she so fond of me?' said Constance, in a softened tone.

'She was,' replied Gillian.

'I'm sure,' said Miss Hacket, 'our only wish is to forget and forgive as Christians. Lady Merrifield has behaved most handsomely, and it is our most earnest wish that this unfortunate transaction should be forgotten.'

'And I'm sure I'm willing to overlook it all,' said Constance. 'One must have scrapes, you know; but friendship will triumph over all.'

Gillian did not exactly wish to unravel this fine sentiment, and was glad that the little G.F.S. maid came in with the tea.

Lady Merrifield was a good deal diverted with Gillian's report, and invited the two sisters to luncheon on the plea of their slight acquaintance with Anne—otherwise Mrs. Daventry—with a hint in the note not to compliment Mrs. Merrifield on Elizabeth's production.

Then Dolores had to be prepared to receive any advance from Constance. She looked disgusted at first, and then, when she heard that Gillian had spoken her mind, said, 'I can't think why you should care.'

'Of course I care, to have Constance behaving so ill to one of us.'

'Do you think me one of you, Gillian?'

'Who, what else are you?'

And Dolores held up her face for a kiss, a heartier one than had ever passed between the cousins. There was no kiss between the quondam friends, but they shook hands with perfect civility, and no stranger would have guessed their former or their present terms from their manner. In fact, Constance was perfectly absorbed in the contemplation of the successful authoress, the object of her envy and veneration, and only wanted to forget all the unpleasantness connected with the dark head on the opposite side of the table.

'Oh Miss Merrifield,' she asked, in an interval afterwards, when hats were being put on, 'bow do you make them take your things?'

'I don't know,' said Bessie, smiling. 'I take all the pains I can, and try to make them useful.'

'Useful, but that's so dull—and the critics always laugh at things with a purpose.'

'But I don't think that is a reason for not trying to do good, even in this very small and uncertain way. Indeed,' she added, earnestly. 'I have no right to speak, for I have made great mistakes; but I wanted to tell you that the one thing I did get published, which was not written conscientiously—as I may say—but only to work out a silly, sentimental fancy, has brought me pain and punishment by the harm I know I did.'

This was a very new idea to Constance, and she actually carried it away with her. The visit had restored the usual terms of intercourse with the Hackets, though there was no resumption of intimacy such as there had been, between Constance and Dolores. It had, however, done much to make the latter feel that the others considered themselves one with them, and there was something that drew them together in the universal missing of Mysie, and eagerness for her letters.

These were, however, rather disappointing. Mysie had not a genius for correspondence, and dealt in very bare facts. There was an enclosure which made Lady Merrifield somewhat anxious:

'My Dear Mamma, 'This is for you all by yourself. I have been in sad mischief, for I broke the conservatory and a palm-tree with my umbrella; and I did still worse, for I broke my promise and told all about what you told me never to. I will tell you all when I come home, and I hope you will forgive me. I wish I was at home. It is very horrid when they say one is good and one knows one is not; but I am very happy, and Lord Rotherwood is nicer than ever, and so is Fly. 'I am your affectionate and penitent and dutiful little daughter,

'MARIA MILLICENT MERRIFIELD.'

With all mamma's intuitive knowledge of her little daughter's mind and forms of expression, she was puzzled by this note and the various fractures it described. She obeyed its injunctions of secrecy, even with regard to Gillian and Bessie, though she could not help wishing that the latter could have seen and judged of her Mysie.

Grandmamma was somewhat disappointed to have missed her eldest grandson, but she was obliged to leave Silverton two days before his return with his little sister. She had certainly escaped the full tumult of the entire household, but Bessie observed that she suspected that it might have been preferred to the general quiescence.

In spite of all the regrets that Bessie's more coeval cousins, Alethea and Phyllis were not at home, she and her aunt each felt that a new friendship had been made, and that they understood each other, and Bessie had uttered her resolution henceforth always to think of the impression for good or evil produced on the readers, as well as of the effectiveness of her story. 'Little did I suppose that 'Clare' would add to any one's difficulties,' she said, 'still less to yours, Aunt Lilias.'

CHAPTER XX
CONFESSIONS OF A COUNTRY MOUSE

Here were the travellers at home again, and Mysie clinging to her mother, with, 'Oh, Mamma!' and a look of perfect rest. They arrived at the same time as Dolores had come, so late that Mysie was tired out, and only half awake. She was consigned to Mrs. Halfpenny after her first kiss, but as she passed along the corridor, a door was thrown back, and a white figure sprang upon her. 'Oh, Mysie! Mysie!' and in spite of the nurse's chidings, held her fast in an embrace of delight. Dolores had been lying awake watching for her, and implored permission at least to look on while she was going to bed!

Harry meanwhile related his experiences to his mother and Gillian over the supper-table. The Butterfly's Ball had been a great success. He had never seen anything prettier in his life. Plants and lights had been judiciously disposed so as to make the hall a continuation of the conservatory, almost a fairy land, and the children in their costumes had been more like fairies than flesh and blood, pinafore and bread-and-butter beings. There was a most perfect tableau at the opening of the scenery constructed with moss and plants, so as to form a bower, where the Butterfly and Grasshopper, with their immediate attendants, welcomed their company, and afterwards formed the first quadrille, Lady Phyllis, with Mysie and two other little girls staying in the house, being the butterflies, and Lord Ivinghoe and three more boys of the same ages, the grasshoppers, in pages' dresses of suitable colours.

'I never thought,' said Harry, 'that our little brown mouse would come out so pretty or so swell.'

'She wanted to be the dormouse,' said Gillian.

'That was impracticable. They were all heath butterflies of different sorts, wings very correctly coloured and dresses to correspond. Phyllis the ringlet with the blue lining, Mysie, the blue one, little Lady Alberta, the orange-tip, and the other child the burnet moth.'

'How did Mysie dance?'

'Very fairly, if she had not looked so awfully serious. The dancing-mistress, French, of course, had trained them, it was more ballet than quadrille, and they looked uncommonly pretty. Uncle William granted that, though he grumbled at the whole concern as nonsense, and wondered you should send your nice little girl into it to have her head turned.'

'Do you think she was happy?'

'Oh, yes, of course. She always is, but she was in prodigious spirits when we started to come home. Lady Rotherwood said I was to tell you that no child could be more truthful and conscientious. Still somehow she did not look like the swells. Except that once, when she was got up regardless of expense for the ball, she always had the country mouse look about her. She hadn't—'

'The 'Jenny Say Caw,' as Macrae calls it?' said his mother. 'Well, I can endure that! You need not look so disgusted, Gill. You didn't hear of her getting into any scrape, did you?'

'No,' said Hal. 'Stay, I believe she did break some glass or other, and blurted out her confession in full assembly, but I was over at Beechcroft, and I am happy to say I didn't see her.'

Mysie's tap came early to her mother's door the next morning, and it was in the midst of her toilette that Lady Merrifield was called on to hear the confession that had been weighing on the little girl's mind.

'I was too sleepy to tell you last night, mamma, but I did want to do so.'

'Well, then, my dear, begin at the beginning, for I could not understand your letter.'

'The beginning was, mamma, that we had just come in from our walk, and we went out into the schoolroom balcony, because we could see round the corner who was coming up the drive. And we began playing at camps, with umbrellas up as tents. Ivinghoe, and Alberta, and I. Ivy was general, and I was the sentry, with my umbrella shut up, and over my shoulder. I was the only one who knew how to present arms. I heard something coming, and called out, 'Who goes there?' and Alberta jumped up in such a hurry that the points other tent—her umbrella, I mean—scratched my face, and before I could recover arms, over went my umbrella, perpendicular, straight smash through the glass of the conservatory, and we heard it.'

'And what did you do? Of course you told!'

"Oh yes! I jumped up and said, 'I'll go and tell Lady Rotherwood.' I knew I must before I got into a fright, and Ivinghoe said I couldn't then, and he would speak to his mother and make it easy for me, and Ply says he really meant it; but I thought then that's the way the bad ones always get the others into concealments and lies. So I wouldn't listen a moment, and I ran down, with him after me, saying, 'Hear reason, Mysie.' And I ran full butt up against some-body—Lord Ormersfield it was, I found—but I didn't know then. I only said something about begging pardon, and dashed on, and opened the door. I saw a whole lot of fine people all at five-o'clock tea, but I couldn't stop to get more frightened, and I went up straight to Lady Rotherwood and said, 'Please, I did it.' Mamma do you think I ought not?"

'There are such things as fit places and times, my dear. What did she say?'

"At first she just said, 'My dear, I cannot attend to you now, run away;' but then in the midst, a thought seemed to strike her, and she said, rather frightened, 'Is any one hurt?' and I said, Oh no; only my umbrella has gone right through the roof of the conservatory, and I thought I ought to come and tell her directly. 'That was the noise,' said some of the people, and everybody got up and went to look. And there were Fly and Ivy, who had got in some other way, and the umbrella was sticking right upright in the top of one of those palm-trees with leaves like screens, and somebody said it was a new development of fruit. Lady Rotherwood asked them what they were doing there, and Ivy said they had come to see what harm was done. Dear Fly ran up to her and said, 'We were all at play together, mother; it was not one more than another;' but Lady Rotherwood only said, 'That's enough, Phyllis, I will come to you by-and-by in the schoolroom,' and she would have sent us away if Cousin Rotherwood himself had not come in just then, and asked what was the matter. I heard some of the answers; they were very odd, mamma. One was, 'A storm of umbrellas and of untimely confessions;' and another was, 'Truth in undress.'"

'Oh, my dear? I hope you were fit to be seen?'

'I forgot about that, mamma, I had taken off my ulster, and had my little scarlet flannel underbody, so as to make a better soldier.'

'Oh!' groaned Lady Merrifield.

'And then that dear, good Fly gave a jump and flew at him, and said, 'Oh, daddy, daddy, it's Mysie, and she has been telling the truth like—like Frank, or Sir Thomas More, or George Washington, or anybody.' She really did say so, mamma.'

'I can quite believe it of her, Mysie! And how did Cousin Rotherwood respond?'

'He sat down upon one of the seats, and took Fly on one knee and me on the other, though we were big for it—just like papa, you know—and made us tell him all about it. Lady Rotherwood got the others out of the way somehow—I don't know how, for my back was that way, and I think Ivinghoe went after them, but there was some use in talking to Cousin Rotherwood; he has got some sense, and knows what one means, as if he was at the dear, nice playing age, and Ivinghoe was his stupid old father in a book.'

'Exactly,' said Lady Merrifield, delighted, and longing to laugh.

'But that was the worst of it,' said Mysie, sadly; 'he was so nice that I said all sorts of things I didn't mean or ought to have said. I told him I would pay for the glass if he would only wait till we had helped Dolores pay for those books that the cheque was for, because the man came alive again, after her wicked uncle said he was dead, and so somehow it all came out; how you made up to Miss Constance and couldn't come to the Butterfly's Ball for want of new dresses.'

'Oh, Mysie, you should not have said that! I thought you were to be trusted!'

'Yes, mamma, I know,' said Mysie, meekly. 'I recollected as soon as I had said it; and told him, and he kissed me and promised he would never tell anyone, and made Fly promise that she never would. But I have been so miserable about it ever since, mamma; I tried to write it in a letter, but I am afraid you didn't half understand.'

'I only saw that something was on your mind, my dear. Now that is all over, I do not so much mind Cousin Rotherwood's knowing, he has always been so like a brother; but I do hope both he and Fly will keep their word. I am more sorry for my little girl's telling than about his knowing.'

'And Ivinghoe said my running in that way on all the company was worse than breaking the glass or the palm-tree. Was it, mamma?'

'Well, you know, Mysie, there is a time for all things, and very likely it vexed Lady Rotherwood more to be invaded by such a little wild colt.'

'But not Cousin Rotherwood himself, mamma,' said Mysie, 'for he said I was quite right, and an honourable little fellow, just like old times. And so I told Ivy. And he said in such a way, 'Every one knew what his father was.' So I told him his father was ten thousand times nicer than ever he would be if he lived a hundred years, and I could not bear him if he talked in that wicked, disrespectful way, and Fly kissed me for it, mamma, and said her daddy was worth a hundred of such a prig as he was.'

'My dear, I am afraid neither you nor Fly showed your good manners.'

'It was only Ivinghoe, mamma, and I'm sure I don't care what he thinks, if he could talk of his father in that way. Isn't it what you call metallical— no—ironical?'

'Indeed, Mysie, I don't wonder it made you very angry, and I can't be sorry you showed your indignation.'

'But please, mamma, what ought I to have done about the glass?'

'I don't quite know; I think a very wise little girl might have gone to Cousin Florence's room and consulted her. It would have been better than making an explosion before so many people. Florence was kind to you, I hope.'

'Oh yes, mamma, it was almost like being at home in her room; and she has such a dear little house at the end of the park.'

A good deal more oozed out from Mysie to different auditors at different times. By her account everything was delightful, and yet mamma concluded that all had not absolutely fulfilled the paradisiacal expectation with which her country mouse had viewed Rotherwood from afar. Lady Rotherwood was very kind, and so was the governess, and Cousin Florence especially. Cousin Florence's house felt just like a bit of home. It really was the dearest little house—and fluffy cat and kittens, and the sweetest love birds. It was perfectly delicious when they drank tea there, but unluckily she was not allowed to go thither without the governess or Louise, as it was all across the park, and a bit of village.

And Fly? Oh, Fly was always dear and good and funny; but there was Alberta to be attended to, and other little girls sometimes, and it was not like having her here at home; nor was there any making a row in the galleries, nor playing at anything really jolly, though the great pillars in the hall seemed made for tying cords to make a spider's web. It was always company, except when Cousin Rotherwood called them into his den for a little fun. But he had gentlemen to entertain most of the time, and the only day that he could have taken them to see the farm and the pheasants, Lady Rotherwood said that Phyllis was a little hoarse and must not get a cold before the ball.

And as to the Butterfly's Ball itself? Imagination had depicted a splendid realization of the verses, and it was flat to find it merely a children's fancy ball, no acting at all, only dancing, and most of the children not attempting any characteristic dress, only with some insect attached to head or shoulder; nothing approaching to the fun of the rehearsal at Silverton, as indeed Fly had predicted. The only attempt at representation had cost Mysie more trouble than pleasure, for the training to dance together had been a difficult and wearisome business. Two of the grass-hoppers had been greatly displeased about it, and called it a beastly shame, words much shocking gentle Mysie from aristocratic lips. One of them had been as sulky, angry, and impracticable as possible, just like a log, and the other had consoled himself with all manner of tricks, especially upon the teacher and on Ivinghoe. He would skip like a real grasshopper, he made faces that set all laughing, he tripped Ivinghoe up, he uttered saucy speeches that Mysie considered too shocking to repeat, but which convulsed every one with laughter, Fly most especially, and her governess had punished her for it. 'She would not punish me,' said Mysie, 'though I know I was just as bad, and I think that was a shame!' At last the practising had to be carried on without the boys, and yet, when it came to the point, both the recusants behaved as well and danced as suitably as if they had submitted to the training like their sisters! And oh! the dressing, that was worse.

'I did not think I was so stupid,' said Mysie, 'but I heard Louise tell mademoiselle that I was trop bourgeoise, and mademoiselle answered that I was plutot petite paysanne, and would never have l'air de distinction.

'Abominable impertinence!' cried Gillian.

"They thought I did not understand,' said Mysie, 'and I knew it was fair to tell them, so I said, 'Mais non, car je suis la petite souris de compagne.'"

'Well done, Mysie!' cried her sister.

'They did jump, and Louise began apologizing in a perfect gabble, and mademoiselle said I had de l'esprit, but I am sure I did not mean it.'

'But how could they?' exclaimed Gillian. 'I'm sure Mysie looks like a lady, a gentleman's child—I mean as much as Fly or any one else.'

'I trust you all look like gentlewomen, and are such in refinement and manners, but there is an air, which comes partly of birth, partly of breeding, and that none of you, except, perhaps, Alethea, can boast of, and about which papa and I don't care one rush.'

'Has Fly got it, mamma?' said Valetta. 'She seemed like one of ourselves.'

'Oh, yes,' put in Dolores. 'It was what made me think her stuck up. I should have known her for a swell anywhere.'

'I'm sure Fly has no airs!' exclaimed Val, hotly, and Gillian was ready to second her; but Lady Merrifield explained. 'The absence of airs is one ingredient, Val, both in being ladylike, and in the distinction in which the maid justly perceived our Mouse to be deficient. Come, you foolish girls, don't look concerned. Nobody but the maid would have ever let Mysie perceive the difference.'

Mysie coloured and answered, 'I don't know; I saw the Fitzhughs look at me at first as if they did not think I belonged, and Ivinghoe was always so awfully polite that I thought he was laughing at me.'

'Ivinghoe must be horrid,' broke out Valetta.

'The Fitzhughs said they would knock it out of him at Eton,' returned Mysie. 'They got very nice after the first day, and said Fly and I were twice as jolly fellows as he was.'

It further appeared that Mysie had had plenty of partners at the ball, and on all occasions her full share of notice, the country neighbours welcoming her as her mother's daughter, but most of them saying she was far more like her Aunt Phyllis than her own mother. The dancing and excitement so late at night had, however, tired her overmuch, she had cramp all the remainder of the night, could eat no breakfast the next day, and was quite miserable.

'I should like to have cried for you, mamma' she said, 'but they were all quite used to it, and not a bit tired. However, Cousin Florence came in, and she was so kind. She took me to the little west room, and made me lie on the sofa, and read to me till I went to sleep, and I was all right after dinner and had a ride on Fly's old pony, Dormouse. She has the loveliest new one, all bay, with a black mane and tail, called Fairy, but Alberta had that. Oh it was so nice.'

Altogether Lady Merrifield was satisfied that her little girl had not been spoilt for home by her taste of dissipation, though she did not hear the further confidence to Dolores in the twilight by the schoolroom fire.

'Do you know, Dolly, though Fly is such a darling, and they all wanted to be kind as well as they knew how, I came to understand how horrid you must have felt when you came among the whole lot of us.'

'But you knew Fly already?'

'That made it better, but I don't like it. To feel one does not belong, and to be afraid to open a door for fear it should be somebody's room, and not quite to know who every one is. Oh, dear! it is enough to make anybody cross and stupid. Oh, I am so glad to be back again.'

'I'm sure I am glad you are,' and there was a little kissing match. 'You'll always come to my room, won't you? Do you know, when Constance came to luncheon, I only shook hands, I wouldn't try to kiss her. Was that unforgiving?'

'I am sure I couldn't,' said Mysie; 'did she try?'

'I don't think so; I don't think I ever could kiss her; for I never should have said what was not true without her, and that is what makes Uncle Reginald so angry still. He would not kiss me even when he went away. Oh, Mysie! that's worse than anything,' and Dolores's face contracted with tears very near at hand. 'I did always so love Uncle Regie, and he won't forgive me, and father will be just the same.'

'Poor dear, dear Dolly,' said Mysie, hugging her.

'But you know fathers always forgive, and we will try and make a little prayer about it, like the Prodigal Son's, you know.'

'I don't blow properly,' said Dolores.

'I think I can say him,' said Mysie, and the little girls sat with enfolded arms, while Mysie reverently went through the parable.

'But he had been very wicked indeed,' objected Dolores, 'what one calls dissipated. Isn't that making too much of such things as girls like us can do.'

'I don't know,' said Mysie, knitting her young brows; 'you see if we are as bad as ever we can be while we are at home, it is really and truly as bad in us ourselves as in shocking people that run away, because it shows we might have done anything if we had not been taken care of. And the poor son felt as if he could not be pardoned, which is just what you do feel.'

'Aunt Lily forgives me,' said Dolores, wistfully.

'And your father will, I'm sure,' said Mysie, 'though he is yet a great way off. And as to Uncle Regie, I do wish something would happen that you could tell the truth about. If you had only broken the palm-tree instead of me, and I didn't do right even about that! But if any mischief does happen, or accident, I promise you, Dolly, you shall have the telling of it, if you have had ever so little to do with it, and then mamma will write to Uncle Regie that you have proved yourself truthful.'

Dolores did not seem much consoled by this curious promise, and Mysie's childishness suddenly gave way to something deeper. 'I suppose,' she said, 'if one is true, people find it out and trust one.'

'People can't see into one,' said Dolly.

'Mamma says there is a bright side and a dark side from which to look at everybody and everything,' said Mysie.

'I know that,' said Dolores; 'I looked at the dark side of you all when I came here.'

'Some day,' said Mysie, 'your bright side will come round to Uncle Regie, as it has to us, you dear, dear old Dolly.'

'But do you know, Mysie,' whispered Dolores, in her embrace, 'there's something more dreadful that I'm very much afraid of. Do you know there hasn't been a letter from father since he was staying with Aunt Phyllis—not to me, nor Aunt Jane, nor anybody!'

'Well, he couldn't write when he was at sea, I mean there wasn't any post.'

'It would not take so long as this to get to Fiji; and besides. Uncle Regie telegraphed to ask about that dreadful cheque, and there hasn't been any answer at all.'

'Perhaps he is gone about sailing somewhere in the Pacific Ocean; I heard Uncle William saying so to Cousin Rotherwood.' He said, 'Maurice is not a fellow to resist a cruise.'

'Then they are thinking about it. They are anxious.'

'Not very,' said Mysie, 'for they think he is sure to be gone on a cruise. They said something about his going down like a carpenter into the deep sea.'

'Making deep-sea soundings, like Dr. Carpenter! A carpenter, indeed!' said Dolores, laughing for a moment. 'Oh! if it is that, I don't mind.'

The weight was lifted, but by-and-by, when the two girls said their prayers together, poor Dolores broke forth again, 'Oh, Mysie, Mysie, your papa has all—all of you, besides mamma, to pray that he may be kept safe, and my father has only me, only horrid me, to pray for him, and even I have never cared to do it really till just lately! Oh, poor, poor father! And suppose he should be drowned, and never, never have forgiven me!'

It was a trouble and misery that recurred night after night, though apparently it weighed much less during the day—and nobody but Mysie knew how much Dolores was suffering from it. Lady Merrifield was increasingly anxious as time went on, and still no mail brought letters from Mr. Mohun, but confidence based on his erratic habits, and the uncertainty of communication began to fail. And as she grieved more for the possible loss, she became more and more tender to her niece, and strange to say, in spite of the terror that gnawed so achingly every night, and of the ordeal that the Lent Assizes would bring, Dolores was happier and more peaceful than ever before at Silverton, and developed more of her bright side.

'I really think,' wrote Lady Merrifield to Miss Mohun, 'that she is growing more simple and child-like, poor little maid. She is apparently free from all our apprehensions about dear Maurice, and I would not inspire her with them for the world. Neither does she seem to dread the trial, as I do for her, nor to guess what cross-examination may be. Constance Hacket has been subpoenaed, and her sister expatiates on her nervousness. It is one comfort that Reginald must be there as a witness, so that it is not in the power of Irish disturbances to keep him from us! May we only be at ease about Maurice by that time!'

CHAPTER XXI
IN COURT AND OUT

How Dolores's heart beat when Colonel Mohun drove up to the door! She durst not run out to greet him among her cousins; but stood by her aunt, feeling hot and cold and trembling, in the doubt whether he would kiss her.

Yes, she did feel his kiss, and Mysie looked at her in congratulation. But what did it mean? Was it only that it came as a matter of course, and he forgot to withhold it, or was it that he had given up hopes of her father, and was sorry for her? She could not make up her mind, for he came so late in the evening that she scarcely saw him before bedtime, and he did not take any special notice of her the next morning. He had done his best to save her from being long detained at Darminster, by ascertaining as nearly as possible when Flinders's case would come on, and securing a room at the nearest inn, where she might await a summons into court. Lady Merrifield was going with them, but would not take either of her daughters, thinking that every home eye would be an additional distress, and that it was better that no one should see or remember Dolores as a witness.

Miss Mohun met the party at the station, going off, however, with her brother into court, after having established Lady Merrifield and her niece in an inn parlour, where they kept as quiet as they could, by the help of knitting, and reading aloud. Lady Merrifield found that Dolores had been into court before, and knew enough about it to need no explanation or preparation, and being much afraid of causing agitation, she thought it best only to try to interest her in such tales as 'Neale's Triumphs of the Cross,' instead of letting her dwell on what she most dreaded, the sight of the prisoner, and the punishment her words might bring upon him.

The morning ended, and Uncle Reginald brought word that his case would come on immediately after luncheon. This he shared with his sister and niece, saying that Jane had gone to a pastrycook's with—with Rotherwood—thinking this best for Dolly. He seemed to be in strangely excited spirits, and was quite his old self to Dolores, tempting her to eat, and showing himself so entirely the kind uncle that she would have been quite cheered up if she had not been afraid that it was all out of pity, and that he knew something dreadful.

Lord Rotherwood met them at the hotel entrance, and took his cousin on his arm; Dolores following with her uncle, was sure that she gave a great start at something that he said; but she had to turn in a different direction to wait under the charge of her uncle, who treated her as if she were far more childish and inexperienced in the ways of courts than she really was, and instructed her in much that she knew perfectly well; but it was too comfortable to have him kind to her for her to take the least offence, and she only said 'Yes' and 'Thank you' at the proper places.

The sheriff, meantime, had given Lord Rotherwood and Lady Merrifield seats near the judge, where Miss Mohun was already installed. Alfred Flinders was already at the bar, and for the first time Lady Merrifield saw his somewhat handsome but shifty-looking face and red beard, as the counsel for the prosecution was giving a detailed account of his embarrassed finances, and of his having obtained from the inexperienced kindness of a young lady, a mere child in age, who called him uncle, though without blood relationship, a draft of her father's for seven pounds, which, when presented at the bank, had become one for seventy.

As before, the presenting and cashing of the seventy pounds was sworn to by the banker's clerk, and then Dolores Mary Mohun was called.

There she stood, looking smaller than usual in her black, close-fitting dress and hat, in a place meant for grown people, her dark face pale and set, keeping her eyes as much as she could from the prisoner. When the counsel spoke she gave a little start, for she knew him, as one who had often spent an evening with her parents, in the cheerful times while her mother lived. There was something in the familiar glance of his eyes that encouraged her, though he looked so much altered by his wig and gown, and it seemed strange that he should question her, as a stranger, on her exact name and age, her father's absence, the connection with the prisoner, and present residence. Then came:

'Did your father leave any money with you?'

'Yes.'

'What was the amount?'

'Five pounds for myself; seven besides.'

'In what form was the seven pounds?'

'A cheque from W.'s bank.'

'Did you part with it?'

'Yes.'

'To whom?'

'I sent it to him.'

'To whom if you please?'

'To Mr. Alfred Flinders.' And her voice trembled.

'Can you tell me when you sent it away?'

'It was on the 22nd of December.'

'Is this the cheque?'

'It has been altered.'

'Explain in what manner?'

'There has 'ty' been put at the end of the written 'seven,' and a cipher after the figure 7 making it 70.'

'You are sure that it was not so when it went out of your possession?'

'Perfectly sure.'

Mr. Calderwood seemed to have done with her, and said, 'Thank you;' but then there stood up a barrister, whom she suspected of being a man her mother had disliked, and she knew that the worst was coming when he said, in a specially polite voice too, 'Allow me to ask whether the cheque in question had been intended by Mr. Mohun for the prisoner?'

'No.'

'Or was it given to you as pocket-money?'

'No, it was to pay a bill.'

'Then did you divert it from that purpose?'

'I thought the man was dead.'

'What man?'

'Professor Muhlwasser.'

'The creditor?'

'Yes.'

Mr. Calderwood objected to these questions as irrelevant; but the prisoner's counsel declared them to be essential, and the judge let him go on to extract from Dolores that the payment was intended for an expensive illustrated work on natural history, which was to be published in Germany. Her father had promised to take two copies of it if it were completed; but being doubtful whether this would ever be the case, he had preferred leaving a draft with her to letting the account be discharged by his brother, and he had reckoned that seven pounds would cover the expense.

'You say you supposed the author was dead. What reason had you for thinking so?'

'He told me; Mr. Flinders did.'

'Had Mr. Mohun sanctioned your applying this sum to any other purpose than that specified?'

'No, he had not. I did wrong,' said Dolores, firmly.

He wrinkled up his forehead, so that the point of his wig went upwards, and proceeded to inquire whether she had herself given the cheque to the prisoner.

'I sent it.'

'Did you post it?'

'Not myself. I gave it to Miss Constance Hacket to send it for me.'

'Can you swear to the sum for which it was drawn when you parted with it?'

'Yes. I looked at it to see whether it was pounds or guineas.'

'Did you give it loose or in an envelope?'

'In an envelope.'

'Was any other person aware of your doing so?'

'Nobody.'

'What led you to make this advance to the prisoner?'

'Because he told me that he was in great distress.'

'He told you. By letter or in person?'

'In person.'

'When did he tell you so?'

'On the 22nd of December.'

'And where?'

'At Darminster.'

'Let me ask whether this interview at Darminster took place with the knowledge of the lady with whom you reside?'

'No, it did not,' said Dolores, colouring deeply.

'Was it a chance meeting?'

'No—by appointment.'

'How was the appointment made?'

'We wrote to say we would come that day.'

'We—who was the other party?'

'Miss Constance Hacket.'

'You were then in correspondence with the prisoner. Was it with the sanction of Lady Merrifield?'

'No.'

'A secret correspondence, then, romantically carried on—by what means?'

'Constance Hacket sent the letters and received them for me.'

'What was the motive for this arrangement?'

'I knew my aunt would prevent my having anything to do with him.'

'And you—excuse me—what interest had you in doing so?'

'My mother had been like his sister, and always helped him.'

All these answers were made with a grave, resolute straightforwardness, generally with something of Dolores's peculiar stony look, and only twice was there any involuntary token of feeling, when she blushed at confessing the concealment from her aunt, and at the last question, when her voice trembled as she spoke of her mother. She kept her eyes on her interrogators all the time, never once glancing towards the prisoner, though all the time she had a sensation as if his reproachful looks were piercing her through.

She was dismissed, and Constance Hacket was brought in, looking about in every direction, carrying a handkerchief and scent bottle, and not attempting to conceal her flutter of agitation.

Mr. Calderwood had nothing to ask her but about her having received the cheque from Miss Mohun and forwarded it to Flinders, though she could not answer for the date without a public computation back from Christmas Day, and forward from St. Thomas's. As to the amount—

'Oh, yes, certainly, seven pounds.'

Moreover she had posted it herself.

Then came the cross-examination,

'Had she seen the draft before posting it?'

'Well—she really did not remember exactly.'

'How did she know the amount then?'

'Well, I think—yes—I think Dolores told me so.'

'You think,' he said, in a sort of sneer. 'On your oath. Do you know?'

'Yes, yes, yes. She assured me! I know something was said about seven.'

'Then you cannot swear to the contents of the envelope you forwarded?'

'I don't know. It was all such a confusion and hurry.'

'Why so?'

'Oh! because it was a secret.'

The counsel of course availed himself of this handle to elicit that the witness had conducted a secret correspondence between the prisoner and her young friend without the knowledge of the child's natural protectors. 'A perfect romance,' he said, 'I believe the prisoner is unmarried.'

Perhaps this insinuation would have been checked, but before any one had time to interfere, Constance, blushing crimson, exclaimed, 'Oh! Oh! I assure you it was not that. It was because she said he was her uncle and that they ill-used him.'

This brought upon her the searching question whether the last witness had stated the prisoner to be really her uncle, and Constance replied, rather hotly, that she had always understood that he was.

'In fact, she gave you to understand that the prisoner was actually related to her by blood. Did you say that she also told you that he was persecuted or ill-used by her other relations?'

'I thought so. Yes, I am sure she said so.'

'And it was wholly and solely on these grounds that you assisted in this clandestine correspondence?'

'Why—yes—partly,' faltered Constance, thinking of her literary efforts, 'so it began.'

There was a manifest inclination to laugh in the audience, who naturally thought her hesitation implied something very different; and the judge, thinking that there was no need to push her further, when Mr. Calderwood represented that all this did not bear on the matter, and was no evidence, silenced Mr. Yokes, and the witness was dismissed.

The next point was that Colonel Reginald Mohun was called upon to attest that the handwriting was his brother's. He answered for the main body of the draft, and the signature, but the additions, in which the forgery lay, were so slight that it was impossible to swear that they did not come from the hand of Maurice Mohun.

'Had application been made to Mr. Mohun on the subject?'

'Yes, Colonel Mohun had immediately telegraphed to him at the address in the Fiji Islands.'

'Has any answer been received?'

'No!' but Colonel Mohun had a curious expression in his eyes, and Mr. Calderwood electrified the court by begging to call upon Mr. Maurice Mohun.

There he was in the witness-box, looking sunburnt but vigorous. He replied immediately to the question that the cheque was his own, and that it had been left under his daughter's charge, also that it had been for seven pounds, and the 'ty' and the cypher had never been written by him. The prisoner winced for a moment, and then looked at him defiantly.

The connection with Alfred Flinders was inquired into and explained, and being asked as to the term 'Uncle,' he replied, 'My daughter was allowed to get into the habit of so terming him.'

The sisters saw his look of pain, and Jane remembered his strong objection to the title, and his wife's indignant defence of it.

Dolores stood trembling outside in the waiting-room, by her Uncle Reginald, from whom she heard that her father had come that morning from London with Lord Rotherwood, but that it had been thought better not to agitate her by letting her know of it before she gave her evidence.

'Has he had my letter?' she asked.

'No; he knew nothing till he saw Rotherwood last night.'

All the misery of writing the confession came back upon poor Dolores, and she turned quite white and sick, but her uncle said kindly, 'Never mind, my dear, he was very much pleased with your manner of giving evidence. Such a contrast to your friend's. Faugh!'

In a few more seconds Mr. Mohun had come out. He took the cold, trembling hands in his own, pressed them close, met the anxious eyes with his own, full of moisture, and said, 'My poor little girl,' in a tone that somehow lightened Dolly's heart of its worst dread.

'Will you go back into court?' asked the colonel.

'You don't wish it, Dolly?' said her father.

'Oh no! please not.'

'Then,' said the colonel, 'take your father back to the room at the hotel, and we will come to you. I suppose this will not last much longer.'

'Probably not half an hour. I don't want to see that fellow either convicted or acquitted.'

Then Dolores found herself steered out of the passages and from among the people waiting or gazing, into the clearer space in the street, her father holding her hand as if she had been a little child. Neither of them spoke till they had reached the sitting-room, and there, the first thing he did when the door was shut, was to sit down, take her between his knees, put an arm round her, and kiss her, saying again, 'My poor child!'

'You never got my letter!' she said, leaning against him, feeling the peace and rest his embrace gave.

'No; but I have heard all. I should have warned you, Dolly; but I never imagined that he could get at you there; and I was unwilling to accuse one for whom your mother had a certain affection.'

'That was why I helped him,' whispered Dolores.

'I knew it,' he said kindly. 'But how did he find you out, and how had he the impertinence to write to you at your Aunt Lily's—'

'I wrote to him first,' she said, hanging down her head.

'How was that? You surely had not been in the habit of doing so whilst I was at home.'

'No; but he came and spoke to me at Exeter, the day you went away. Uncle William was not there, he had gone into the town. And he—Mr. Flinders, said he was going down to see you, and was very much disappointed to hear that you were gone.'

'Did he ask you to write to him?'

'I don't think he did. Father, it seems too silly now, but I was very angry because Aunt Lilias said she must see all my letters except yours and Maude Sefton's, and I told Constance Hacket. She said she would send anything for me, and I could not think of any one I wanted to write to, so I wrote to—to him.'

'Ah! I saw you did not get on with your aunt,' was the answer, 'that was partly what brought me home.' And either not hearing or not heeding her exclamation, 'Oh, but now I do,' he went on to explain that on his arrival at Fiji he had found that circumstances had altered there, and that the person with whom he was to have been associated had died, so that the whole scheme had been broken up. A still better appointment had, however, been offered to him in New Zealand, on the resignation of the present holder after a half-year's notice, and he had at once written to accept it. A proposal had been made to him to spend the intermediate time in a scientific cruise among the Polynesian Islands; but the letters he had found awaiting him at Vanua Levu had convinced him that the arrangements he had made in England had been a mistake, and he had therefore hurried home via San Francisco, as fast as any letter could have gone, to wind up his English affairs, and fetch his daughter to the permanent home in Auckland, which her Aunt Phyllis would prepare for her.

Her countenance betrayed a sudden dismay, which made him recollect that she was a strangely undemonstrative girl; but before she had recovered the shock so as to utter more than a long 'Oh!' they were interrupted by the cup of tea that had been ordered for Dolores, and in a minute more, steps were heard, and the two aunts were in the room. 'Seven years,' were Jane's first words, and 'My dear Maurice,' Lady Merrifield's, 'Oh! I wish I could have spared you this,' and then among greetings came again, 'Seven years,' from the brother and cousin who had seen the traveller before.

'I'm glad you were not there, Maurice,' said Lady Merrifield. 'It was dreadful.'

'I never saw a more insolent fellow!' said Lord Rotherwood.

'That Yokes, you mean,' said Miss Mohun. 'I declare I think he is worse than Flinders!'

'That's like you women, Jenny,' returned the colonel; 'you can't understand that a man's business is to get off his client!'

'When he gave him up as an honest man altogether!' cried Lady Merrifield.

'And cast such imputations!' exclaimed Aunt Jane. 'I saw what the wretch was driving at all the time of the cross-examination; and if I'd been the judge, would not I have stopped him?'

'There you go. Lily and Jenny!' said the colonel, 'and Rotherwood just as bad! Why, Maurice would have had to take just the same line if he had been for the defence.'

'He would not have done it in such a blackguard fashion though,' said Lord Rotherwood.

'I saw what his defence would be,' said Mr. Mohun, briefly.

'There!' said Colonel Mohun, with a boyish pleasure in confuting his sisters; but they were not subdued.

'Now Maurice,' cried Jane, 'when that man was known to be utterly dishonourable and good for nothing, was it fair—was it not contrary to all common sense—to try to cast the imputation between those two poor girls? So the judge and jury felt it, I am happy to say! but I call it abominable to have thrown out the mere suggestion—'

'Nay now, Jane,' said the colonel, 'if the man was to be defended at all, how else was it to be done?'

'I wouldn't have had him defended at all! but, unfortunately, that's his right as an Englishman.'

'That's another thing! But as the cheque did not alter itself, one of the three must have done it, and nothing was left but to show that there had been an amount of shuffling, and—in short, nonsense—that might cast enough doubt on their evidence to make it insufficient for a conviction.'

'Reginald! I can't think how you can stand up for such a wretch, a vulgar wretch,' cried Miss Mohun. 'You put it delicately, as a gentleman who had the misfortune to be counsel in such a case might do, but he was infinitely worse than that, though that was bad enough.'

'It was Yokes,' put in Mr. Mohun; 'but what did he say?' looking anxiously at his daughter.

'It was not so bad about her,' said her uncle, 'he only made her out a foolish child, easily played upon by everybody, and possibly ignorant and frightened, or led away by her regard for her supposed relation. It was the other poor girl—

'The amiable susceptibilities of romantic young ladies!' broke out Lady Merrifield. 'Oh, the creature!' To think of that poor foolish Constance sitting by to hear it represented that the expedition to Darminster, and all the rest of it, was because she was actually touched by that fellow. I really felt ready to take her part.'

'She had certainly brought it on herself,' said Aunt Jane; 'but it was atrocious of him and if the other counsel had only known it, he stopped the cross examination just at the wrong time, or it would have come out that it was literary vanity that was the lure. No doubt he would have made a laughing-stock of that, but it would not have been as bad as the other.'

'Poor thing,' said Lady Merrifield; 'it was a trying retribution for schoolgirl folly and want of conscientiousness. I should think she was a sadder and a wiser woman.'

'He must have overdone it,' said Mr. Mohun, 'he is a vulgar fellow, and always does so; but, as Reginald says, the only available defence was to enhance the folly and sentiment of the girls; but of course the judge charged the other way—

'Entirely,' said Lord Rotherwood, 'he brought Dolly rather well out of it, saying that as he understood it, a young girl who had seen a needy connection assisted from her home might think herself justified in corresponding with him, and even in diverting to his use money left in her charge, when it was probable that it would not be required for the original object. He did not say it was right, but it was an error of judgment by no means implying swindling—in fact. He disposed of Miss Hacket in the same way—foolish, sentimental, unscrupulous, but not to that degree. Girls might be silly enough in all conscience, but not so as to commit forgery or perjury. That was the gist of it, and happily the jury were of the same opinion.'

'Happily? Well, I suppose so,' said Mr. Mohun, with a certain sorrowfulness of tone, into which his little daughter entered.

'I say, Rotherwood,' exclaimed the colonel, as the town clock's two strokes for the half-hour echoed loudly, 'if you mean to catch the 4.50, you must fly.'

'Fly!' he coolly repeated. 'Tell Mysie, Lily, that Fly has never ceased talking of her. That child has been saving her money to fit out one of Florence's orphan's. She—'

'Rotherwood,' broke in Mr. Mohun, 'your wife charged me to see that you were in time for that dinner. A ministerial one.'

'Don't encourage him, Lily,' chimed in the colonel. 'I'll call a cab. See him safe off, Maurice.'

And off he was hunted amid the laughter of the ladies; the manner of all to one another was so exactly what it had been in the old times.

'I could hardly help telling him to take care, or Victoria would never let him out again,' said Miss Mohun. 'Poor old fellow, it would have been a fine chance for him with four of us together.'

'You can come back with us, Jenny!'

'I brought my bag in case of accidents.'

'And we'll telegraph to Adeline to join us tomorrow,' said Mr. Mohun, who seemed to have been seized with a hunger for the sight of his kindred.

'Telegraph! My dear Maurice, Ada's nerves would be torn to smithereens by a telegram without me to open it for her. I've a card here to post to her; but I expect that I must go down tomorrow and fetch her, which will be the best way, for I have a meeting.'

'Jenny, I declare you are a caution even to Miss Hacket,' said Colonel Reginald, re-entering.

'Well, Ada always was the family pet. Besides, I told you I had a G.F.S. meeting. Did you get a cab for us; Lily has had quite walking enough.'

The ladies went in a cab, while the gentlemen walked. There was not much time to spare, and in the compartment into which the first comers threw themselves, they found both the Hacket sisters installed, and the gentlemen coming up in haste, nodded and got into a smoking-carriage, on seeing how theirs was occupied.

'Oh, we could have made room,' said Constance, to whom a gentleman was a gentleman under whatever circumstances.

'Dear Miss Dolores's papa! Is it indeed?' said Miss Hacket.

'So wonderfully interesting,' chimed in Constance. And they both made a dart at Dolores to kiss her in congratulation, much against her will.

The train clattered on, and Lady Merrifield hoped it would hush all other voices, but neither of the Hackets could refrain from discussing the trial, and heaping such unmitigated censure on the counsel for the prisoner, that Miss Mohun felt herself constrained to fly in the face of all she had said at the hotel, and to maintain the right of even such an Englishman to be defended, and of his advocate to prevent his conviction if possible. On which the regular sentiment against becoming lawyers was produced, and the subject might have been dropped if Constance had not broken out again, as if she could not leave it. 'So atrocious, so abominably insolent, asking if he was unmarried.'

'Evidently flattered!' muttered Aunt Jane, between her teeth, and unheard; but the speed slackened, and Constance's voice went on,

'I really thought I should have died of it on the spot. The bare idea of thinking I could endure such a being.'

'Well,' said Dolores, just as the clatter ceased at a little station. 'You know you did walk up and down with him ever so long, and I am sure you liked him very much.'

An indignant 'You don't understand' was absolutely cut off by an imperative grasp and hush from Miss Hacket the elder; Aunt Jane was suffocating with laughter, Lady Merrifield, between that and a certain shame for womanhood, which made her begin to talk at random about anything or everything else.

CHAPTER XXII
NAY

'What a mull they have made of it!' were Mr. Maurice Mohun's first words when he found the compartment free for a tete-a-tete with his brother.

'All's well that ends well,' was the brief reply.

'Well, indeed! Mary would not have thought so.' To which the colonel had nothing to say.

'It serves me out,' his brother went on presently. 'I ought to have done something for that wretched fellow before I went, or, at any rate, have put Dolly on her guard; but I always shirked the very thought of him.'

'Nothing would have kept him out of harm's way.'

'It might have kept the child; but she must have been thicker with him than I ever knew. However I shall have her with me for the future, and in better hands.'

'You really mean to take her out?'

'That's what brought me home. She isn't happy; that is plain from her letters; and Jane does not know what to make of her, nor Lilias either.'

'When were your last letters dated?'

'The last week in September.'

'Early days,' muttered the colonel.

'I thought it an experiment, you know; but you said so much about Lily's girls being patterns, that I thought Jasper Merrifield might have made her more rational and less flighty, and all that sort of thing; but of course it was a very different tone from what the child was used to, and you couldn't tell what the young barbarians were out of sight.'

'So I began to think last winter; but I fancy you will find that she and Lily understand one another a good deal better than they did at first.'

'I thought she did not receive my intelligence as a deliverance. I am glad if she can carry away an affectionate remembrance, but I want to have her under my own eye.'

'I suppose that's all right,' was the half reluctant reply.

'There's Phyllis. She is full of good sense, with no nonsense about her or May, and her girls are downright charming.'

'Very likely; but I say, Maurice, you must not underrate Lilias. She has gone through a good deal with Dolores, and I believe she has been the making of her. You've had to leave the poor child a good deal to herself and Fraulein, and, as you see by this affair, she had some ways that made it hard for Lily to deal with her at first.'

Her father plainly did not like this. 'There was no harm in the poor child, but as I should have foreseen, there's always an atmosphere of sentiment and ritual and flummery about Lilias, totally different from what she was used to.'

Colonel Mohun had nearly said, 'So much the better,' but turned it into, 'I think you will change your opinion.'

Brothers and sisters, and cousins, whatever they may be to the external world, always remain relatively to each other pretty much as they knew one another when a single home held them all. The familiar Christian names seemed to revive the old ways, and it was amusing to see the somewhat grave and silent colonel treated by his elder brother as the dashing, heedless boy, needing to be looked after, while his sister Jane remained the ready helper and counsellor, and Lady Merrifield was still in his eyes the unpractical, fanciful Lily with an unfortunately suggestive rhyme to her name.

Perhaps it maintained him in this opinion, that when he had answered all questions about Captain and Mrs. Harry May, and had dilated on their pretty house in the suburbs of Auckland, his sisters expected him to tell of the work of the Church among the Maoris and Fijians. He laughed at them for thinking colonists troubled their heads about natives.

'I know Phyllis does. One of Harry May's brothers went out as a missionary.'

'Disenchanted and came home again when his wife came into a fortune.'

'Not a bit of it,' said Aunt Jane. 'I know him and all about him. He stayed till his health broke, and now he is one of the most useful men in the country. He is coming to speak for the S.P.G. at Rockquay, Lily; and you must come and meet him and his charming wife. They will tell you a very different story about Harry's doings.'

'Well,' allowed Mr. Mohun, 'there are apparitions of brown niggers done up as smart as twopence prancing about the house. Perfectly uninteresting, you know, the savage sophisticated out of his picturesqueness. I made a point of asking no questions, not knowing what I might be let in for.'

'Then you heard nothing of Mr. Ward, the Melanesian missionary, whom Phyllis keeps a room for when he comes to New Zealand to recruit.'

'The man who was convicted of murder on circumstantial evidence! Oh yes. I heard of him. I believe the labour-traffic agents heartily wish him at Portland still, he makes the natives so much too sharp.'

'Aye,' said the colonel, 'as long as Britons aren't slaves they have no objection to anything but the name for other people.'

'Wait till you get out there, Regie, and see what they all say about those lazy fellows—except, of course, ladies and parsons, and a few whom they've bitten, like May.'

'The few are on the Christian side, of course,' said Lady Merrifield, with irony in her tone.

Indeed, she was not at all sure that half this colonial prejudice was not assumed in order to tease her, just as in former times her brother would make game of her enthusiasms about school children; for he was altogether returned to his old self, his sister Jane, who had seen the most of him, testifying that the original Maurice had revived, as never in the course of his married life.

Dolores tried to forget or disbelieve the words she had heard about his having come to fetch her away, and said no word about them until they had been unmistakably repeated. Then she felt a sort of despair at the idea of being separated from her aunt and Mysie, for indeed they had penetrated to affections deeper than had ever been consciously stirred in her before. Yet she was old enough to shrink from allowing to her father that she preferred staying with them to going with him, and it was to her Aunt Jane that she had recourse. That lady, after returning from her expedition to bring her sister Adeline to Silverton, was surprised by a timid knock at the door, and Dolores's entrance.

'Oh, if you please, Aunt Jane, may I come in? I do so want to speak to you alone. Don't you think it is a sad pity that I should go away from the Cambridge examination? Could not you tell my father so?'

'You want to stay for the Cambridge examination,' said Aunt Jane, a little amused at the manner of touching on the subject, though sorry for the girl.

'I have been taking great pains under Miss Vincent, and it does seem a pity to miss it.'

'I don't think it will make much difference to you.'

'Oh, but I do want to be thoroughly well educated. I meant to go through them all, like Gillian and Mysie, and I am sure father must wish it too. I know he meant it when he went out last year.'

'Yes, he did,' said Miss Mohun. 'It was very unlucky that he did not get any of our later letters.'

'I have tried to tell him that it is all different now, but he does not seem to care,' said Dolores.

'He has quite made up his mind,' said her aunt.

'Has he quite?' said Dolores. 'I thought perhaps if you talked to him about the examination and the confirmation too—'

'But, Dolly, you are not going to a heathen country. Your confirmation will be as much attended to in New Zealand as here.'

'Oh, but I should be confirmed with Mysie, and Aunt Lily would read with me, and help me!'

'Yes, I see.'

'Do please tell him. Aunt Jane. He heeds what you say more than any one. Do tell him that the only hope of my being good is if I stay with Aunt Lily just these few years!'

'Ah, Dolly, that is what you really mean and care about—not the Cambridge business.'

'Of course it is. Please tell him, Aunt Jane—somehow I can't—that I was bad and foolish when I wrote all the letters he had; but now I know better, and—and—I don't want to vex him, but I shall be ever so much better a daughter to him if he will leave me with Aunt Lily, to learn some of her goodness'—and there were tears in her eyes, for these months had softened her greatly.

'My poor Dolly!' said Aunt Jane, much more tenderly than she generally spoke. 'I am very sorry for you. I do think Aunt Lily has been the making of you, and that it is very hard that you should have to be uprooted from her, just as you had learnt to value her, I will tell your father so; but honestly, I do not think it is likely to make him change his mind.'

Miss Mohun sought her brother out the next day, and told him that they had all been waiting in patience when thinking that his daughter's residence at Silverton was an unsuccessful experiment. The explosion she had predicted had come, and Dolores had been a different creature ever since, owing to Lady Merrifield's management of her in the crisis; and she added that the girl was most unwilling to leave her aunt, and that she herself thought it would be much better to leave her for a few years to the advantages of her present training, where her affections had been gained. Mr. Mohun could not see it in the same light. The intimacy with Constance Hacket was in his eyes a folly, consequent on his sister's passion for Sunday schools and charities; and Jane, being infected with the like ardour, he disregarded her explanations. The underhand correspondence could not have been carried on without great blindness and carelessness, or, at least, injudiciousness, on Lady Merrifield's part, and there was no denying that she had trusted to a sense of honour that was nonexistent. Nor did he appreciate Jane's argument that the conquest of the heart and will had thus been far more thoroughly gained than it would have been by constant thwarting and watching. It was hard to forgive such an exposure as had taken place, or to believe that it had not been brought about by unjustifiable errors, more especially as Lady Merrifield was the first to accuse herself of them. Moreover, he had become sensible of a strong natural yearning for the presence of his only child, and he had been so much struck with his sister Phyllis's family that he sincerely believed himself consulting the girl's best interests. He was by no means an irreligious or ungodly man, but he had always thought his sister Lilias more or less of an enthusiast, and he did not wish to see Dolores the same. Perhaps, indeed, the poor child's manifest clinging to her aunt and cousins made him all the more resolute to remove her before her affection should be entirely weaned from himself.

He made his headquarters at Silverton, and during the next two months modified his opinions so far as to confess to his sister Jane that Lilias was a much more sensible woman than he had believed her, and had her children well in hand. He even allowed that Dolores was improved, and owed much to her kindness; and when the first sting of the exposure was over, he could see that the treatment had been far from injudicious as regarded the girl's own character. He was even glad that warm love and friendship had grown up towards her aunt and cousins; but all this left his purpose unchanged; although, after the first, nothing was said about it, Dolores tried to forget it, and hoped that the sight of her going on well and peaceably would convince him of the inexpediency of disturbing her. She could not even mention it to Mysie, lest the dread should become a reality by being uttered. So no more passed on the subject till it became necessary to take her outfit in hand, and he also wished to take her to Beechcroft, that the old family home which he regarded with fresh tenderness might be impressed on her memory.

Then, though she never durst directly oppose the fate which he destined for her, she surprised him by a violent burst of tears and sobbing, and an entreaty that he would not take her away from Aunt Lily and Mysie a moment sooner than could be helped.

She clung to everything, even to the guinea-pigs, and she was the first in the Easter holidays to beg for the 'Thorn Fortress.' Indeed, Mysie was a little shocked at her grief, as disloyal and unfilial. 'One ought not to mind going anywhere with one's father,' she said; 'we all thought it a great honour for Phyllis and Alethea.'

'They are grown up!' said Dolores, 'and Aunt Lily does get into one so! Oh, don't say there's Aunt Phyllis. I hate the very name of her.'

'She must be nice,' said Mysie, 'Whenever the 'grown-ups' are pleased with me they say I am getting like her, as if it was the best thing one could be.'

'But I don't want Mysie old and grown up, I want my Mysie now, as you are!—And you'll forget and leave off writing, like Maude Sefton.'

'Never!' cried Mysie. 'Eight across the world you will always be my own twin cousin.'

The wishes of the girl were so far fulfilled that Lady Merrifield took her to London to provide her outfit, and Mysie accompanied them. A room and its dressing-room received the three at old Mrs. Merrifield's, and the two cousins thought their close quarters ineffably precious.

Mysie was introduced to Maude Sefton, who seemed entirely unconscious of her treachery to friendship. 'One had so little time, and couldn't always be writing,' she said, when Dolores reproached her; 'exercises were enough to tire out one's hand!'

They also drank tea with Lady Phyllis Devereux and her governess. Fly could not pour forth questions and reminiscences fast enough about all the beloved animals at Silverton, not forgetting the little G.F.S. nursemaid, for whom she had actually made an apron in her plain-work lessons. Moreover, she deemed Dolores's fate most enviable, to be going off with her father to strange countries, away from lessons, and masters, and towns. It would be almost as good as Leila on the island.

As to the Beechcroft visit, Mr. and Mrs. Mohun collected all the brothers and sisters in England there for a week, and still Mysie and Dolores were allowed to be together, squeezed into a corner of Lady Merrifield's room. It was high summer, bright and glowing, and so dry, and even the invalidish sisters, Lady Henry Gray and Miss Adeline Mohun could not object to the sitting out on the lawn, among the dragonflies, as in days of yore.

Much of old thought and feeling was then and there taken up again, and it was on one of the last evenings of the visit that Mr. Mohun, walking up and down the alley with Lady Merrifield, said—

'Well, Lily, I think my determination to take Dolly away was hasty. I cannot leave her now, but if I had understood all that I see at present, I should have been both content and grateful to have her among your children. I am afraid I have been ungracious.'

'I never thought so, Maurice. It is quite right that she should be with you, and Phyllis will do every-thing for her much better than I.'

'Poor child! I believe she is very sorry to go,' said Mr. Mohun; 'but, at any rate, she will remember Silverton as, I hope, a lasting influence on her life.'

Dolores truly believed that so it would be, and that her aunt's guidance would be always looked back upon as the turning-point of her life.

'It is my own fault,' she said, as on the last night she clung tearfully to Lady Merrifield; 'if I had behaved better I might have gone on just like one of your own.'

'You will still be in my heart like one of my own, dear child,' said Lady Merrifield. 'We know the way in which we all can hold together as one; keep to that, and the distance apart will matter the less.'

And as they watched Dolores and her father driven away to the station the next morning, Jane Mohun laid her hand on her sister's arm and said, 'You thought you had made a great failure. Lily, but is not the other side of a failure often a success?'

By-and-by came letters from Dolores. She seemed after the first to have enjoyed her journey, for, as she wrote to Lady Merrifield, in a letter, very private, and all to her own self, 'Father was so very good and kind to me, I don't know how to tell you. It was as if a little bit of mother had got into him, and now I am here I think I shall like the Mays. Indeed, I am trying to remember your advice, and not beginning by hating everybody and thinking who they are not. Aunt Phyllis is very nice indeed, and sometimes her eyes and mouth get like Mysie's, and her voice is just exactly yours. Only she is plump and roundabout, not a dear, tall, graceful figure like my White Lily Aunt. Please don't call it nonsense, for indeed I mean it, and Aunt Phyllis does like your photograph so much. I have the whole group hung up in my room, and you over it, and I wish you all good morning every day, for I never, never, as long as I live, shall love anybody like you and Mysie.'